D1100668

laim for
MAIL-ORDER

JILLIAN

'A lovely Americana romance, this book's intense
emotions reach out to touch readers. Betsy's
unwavering belief in Duncan and willingness to fight to
save him from himself is so moving you'll want to cry
with happiness as Hart plays on your heartstrings.'
—*RT Book Reviews* on
ROCKY MOUNTAIN MAN

'Ms Hart creates a world of tantalizing warmth
and tenderness, a toasty haven in which
the reader will find pure enjoyment.'
—*RT Book Reviews* on MONTANA MAN

CAROLYN DAVIDSON

'For romance centring on the joys and sorrows of
married life, readers can't do much better
than Davidson.'
—*RT Book Reviews*

'Her novels go beyond romance to the
depths of the ultimate healing power of love.'
—*RT Book Reviews*

KATE BRIDGES

WANTED IN ALASKA
'Bridges brings strong, admirable heroes
and independent-minded women to life.
There's nothing better in these cold locales than
her stories laced with humour, passion and danger.'
—*RT Book Reviews*

KLONDIKE FEVER

'Hum̲o̲   ̲ure…'

DORSET COUNTY LIBRARY

205135426 S

Jillian Hart grew up on her family's homestead, where she raised cattle, rode horses and scribbled stories in her spare time. After earning an English degree from Whitman College, she worked in advertising before selling her first novel to Mills & Boon® Historical. When she's not hard at work on her next story, Jillian can be found chatting over lunch with a friend, stopping for a café mocha with a book in hand, and spending quiet evenings at home with her family. Visit her website at www.jillianhart.net

Reading, writing and research—**Carolyn Davidson**'s life in three simple words. At least that area of her life having to do with her career as a historical romance author. The rest of her time is divided among husband, family and travel—her husband, of course, holding top priority in her busy schedule. Then there is their church, and the church choir in which they participate. Their sons and daughters, along with assorted spouses, are spread across the eastern half of America, together with numerous grandchildren. Carolyn welcomes mail at her post office box, PO Box 2757, Goose Creek, SC 29445, USA.

Kate Bridges was raised in rural Canada, and her stories reflect her love for wide-open spaces, country sunshine and the Rocky Mountains. She loves writing about the adventurous tales of men and women who tamed the West. Prior to becoming a full-time writer, Kate worked as a paediatric intensive care nurse. She often includes compelling medical situations in her books. Kate's novels have been translated into nine languages, studied in over a dozen colleges on their commercial fiction courses, and are sold worldwide. She lives in the beautiful cosmopolitan city of Toronto with her family. To find out more about Kate's books and to sign up for her free online newsletter, please visit www.katebridges.com

MAIL-ORDER MARRIAGES

BY

JILLIAN HART,
CAROLYN DAVIDSON,
KATE BRIDGES

Dorset Libraries
Withdrawn Stock

Dorset Libraries
Withdrawn Stock

MILLS
BOON®

All the characters in this book have no existence outside the imagination of the author, and have no relation whatsoever to anyone bearing the same name or names. They are not even distantly inspired by any individual known or unknown to the author, and all the incidents are pure invention.

All Rights Reserved including the right of reproduction in whole or in part in any form. This edition is published by arrangement with Harlequin Enterprises II BV/S.à.r.l. The text of this publication or any part thereof may not be reproduced or transmitted in any form or by any means, electronic or mechanical, including photocopying, recording, storage in an information retrieval system, or otherwise, without the written permission of the publisher.

® and TM are trademarks owned and used by the trademark owner and/or its licensee. Trademarks marked with ® are registered with the United Kingdom Patent Office and/or the Office for Harmonisation in the Internal Market and in other countries.

First published in Great Britain 2011
by Mills & Boon, an imprint of Harlequin (UK) Limited.
Large Print edition 2012
Harlequin (UK) Limited, Eton House,
18-24 Paradise Road, Richmond, Surrey TW9 1SR

© Harlequin Books S.A. 2010

ISBN: 978 0 263 22413 9

The publisher acknowledges the copyright holders of the individual works as follows:

ROCKY MOUNTAIN WEDDING © Jill Strickler 2010
MARRIED IN MISSOURI © Carolyn Davidson 2010
HER ALASKAN GROOM © Katherine Haupt 2010

Harlequin (UK) policy is to use papers that are natural, renewable and recyclable products and made from wood grown in sustainable forests. The logging and manufacturing process conform to the legal environmental regulations of the country of origin.

Printed and bound in Great Britain
by CPI Antony Rowe, Chippenham, Wiltshire

CONTENTS

ROCKY MOUNTAIN WEDDING

Jillian Hart

Dear Reader

You may remember the Brooks brothers, of Moose, Montana Territory, from my last two anthology stories, ROCKY MOUNTAIN BRIDE in the *Western Weddings* collection and ROCKY MOUNTAIN COURTSHIP in *Stetsons, Spring & Wedding Rings*. In this story Melody Pennington, who came from Boston to marry the youngest Brooks brother only to find him desperately in love with Clara, finds herself falling for oldest brother, Gabe. Gabe, stone-cold and determined to retain control of his heart, agrees to a marriage of convenience to protect the young Boston beauty, but is he strong enough to keep from falling in love with Melody? Or will this tough, brave mountain lawman fall hard and fall fast? I hope you enjoy this final instalment of the Brooks brothers' trilogy.

Thank you so much for choosing ROCKY MOUNTAIN WEDDING.

Happy reading!

Jillian

Chapter One

Montana Territory, 1882

"Miss, I don't want to have to put you out of the hotel." The kindly clerk gripped the bill in both hands, keeping his voice low in the hallway so it would not carry to the other guests in nearby rooms. "I can take it up with the Brooks family, if you'd rather. I know you came to marry one of their sons."

"No, please don't trouble them." Humiliation. Mortification. Defeat. All those emotions and more tangled up in tight painful knots, making it hard to think. Melody Pennington took a deep breath, straightened her spine and set her chin. She had been foolish to run away from her comfortable Boston home to escape a difficult problem. She had landed in another one the moment her foot touched down on Montana soil. The man she had come to marry had fallen in love with someone else—no, she didn't fault him for that. The heart had a mind of its own, and she wanted Joseph Brooks to be happy. But being stranded in this small mountain town with what little was left of her money *was* a serious concern.

"I will pay the bill, Mr. Owens." She snatched her reticule off the edge of the bureau, tugged open the strings and eyed the paltry sum within. "If I give you half…?"

"Sorry, miss. I need the payment in full. If you can't pay, then you will have to leave. It is hotel policy."

"But I have nowhere to go." She knew no one in town, save for the family she had been corresponding with, and their help was no longer an option. It would not be right to expect it to be.

Nor was it right to shortchange the hotel or put this kindly man's job in jeopardy. What were her options? She had fretted about nothing else the past few nights and days, worrying about what she should do, where she should go and how she was going to pay for all of it. She firmed her chin, determined to stay positive. This would work out for the best, surely. "Please, if you let me stay, I will find a way to pay you. I can give you my grandmother's pearls as collateral."

"Now, that don't seem right. I do not want to take a remembrance like that." Troubled now, the clerk's face was wreathed with concern. "I know you are in a pickle. Truth is, times are tough all over. But the hotel's owner does not make exceptions. I'm sorry for it."

"You have nothing to apologize for." Goodness, folks tended to be awfully nice in this part of the country. Back home she could not imagine a businessman apologizing for wanting his rightful compensation. She counted out the last of her bills and handed him the thick fold. "That is all I have. It's *almost* the entire sum. I will pay you the rest, I swear to it."

"I believe you, miss. I can see you mean well. I don't want to have to put you out on the street. It's raining like a cow—er—well, best I not say that in mixed company. Beggin' your pardon, miss." He slipped the cash into his vest pocket, blushing. "Sometimes I forget myself. My wife is always telling me I'm a bit coarse."

"I find you very charming, Mr. Owens. As for me, I don't mind a little rain." It was hard not to like the kindly man, who was about the age her father had been before he passed away. She ignored the streak of pain deep in her heart, the one she always felt when she thought of his loss. She liked to think Papa was watching over her. What would his opinion be of the dilemma she found herself in? Well, there was a boardinghouse in town. Perhaps she could find accommodation there. "Let me put my things together and I will be on my way. Thank you for your hospitality, and truly, do not worry. I will make good on the rest of my debt."

"That won't be necessary." A deep baritone—not the clerk's friendly tenor—boomed from the shadows in the hallway. Gabriel Brooks strode into sight—a big hulking man, brawny and intimidating, dressed all in black.

Every time she saw the Montana Range Rider, a territorial lawman, air caught sideways in her throat. Her palms went damp. She thought of her favorite heroes in her most beloved books—why, this man was a Mr. Darcy, Mr. Rochester and Heathcliff all rolled up into one muscled, black-eyed mystery. Gabriel was Joseph's older brother, an affirmed bachelor and the last man she wanted to know of her financial problems.

"My family will pay for her stay." Gabriel tugged a few large greenbacks from his billfold. "It is the least we can do. I do not approve of my mother finding mail-order brides for us *without our knowledge*."

His emphasis rang with bitterness, and she feared by the harsh look he tossed at her that he did not have a favorable view of young women seeking the shelter of marriage. A trickle of shame dug deep, and she stared hard at the floor. She could easily slip into despair, but where would that land her? She had to stay strong and positive; it was the only way to face her uncertain future. Finding her happiness was the only option that mattered. She had to forget the nightmare her life had become in Boston and the disappointment of lost opportunities here. The last thing she could afford to do was to let one disagreeable man's speculated opinion of her steal any of her strength.

"I would not have come all this way if I had known your brother knew nothing of me." She wanted to reassure the rugged, proud man as he handed over money to the clerk. She grabbed the bills out of Mr. Owens's hand. The poor clerk certainly appeared surprised at her actions. "Thank you, Mr. Brooks, but please take your money back. I will settle my own debts."

"Oh, you will? With what?" He stared with disdain at the money she held out. He might not realize how his deep voice thundered, echoing in the hall and in the pleasant room behind her. He might not know how intimidating he was, towering over her, all six feet plus of hard, chiseled, darkly scowling male.

"I heard you admit that you cannot pay for your stay here. You wanted to depend on my family's generosity. That's why you came on last week's train."

"You could not be more wrong, Mr. Brooks." She boldly tucked the bills into his coat pocket. "I do not want your family's money. In particular, I do not want *your* money."

"What kind of game is this, Miss Pennington?" His hand curled around hers, trapping her fingers against his at his pocket.

"What game?" she asked. Maybe he didn't realize how powerful he was, or that his hold on her hand felt bruising. "I am not that type of lady, I assure you."

"I take no stock in a woman's assurances."

"Then you have not met a lady like me." She tried to pull away, but he was strong, his touch too hot. There was simply too much of him, making her pulse speed and her breath catch in her throat. "Let go of me, Mr. Brooks."

"A woman takes money from a man. She doesn't return it. At least, that is something I have never seen. Not once in my life as a lawman."

"Then this is an exceptional day for you, isn't it?"

"I do not like your tone, Miss Pennington." He released her, and she stumbled back across the threshold. "Any woman who would marry a stranger is suspect. What is wrong with you that you could not find a worthy husband in Boston?"

His question boomed in her ears, echoed in the hallway surrounding them and tugged at her buried secrets. Heat scorched her face and horrible images swam in front of her eyes. Derrick in a red-faced rage, smashing his fist into the wall an inch from her left ear, throwing a chair at her head.

"I have returned your money, so I owe you no explanations. Since I am not marrying your brother, I no longer have any connections to your family."

"Then you would be wrong. My mother has invited you to supper." He swept off his hat, revealing his face to her. The lamplight adored him, glinting boldly in his thick black locks, a little too long for decency, and caressing his strong features that were too rough to be conventionally handsome. His eyes were midnight-blue, his nose straight and unbroken, his high cheekbones like carved granite. His mouth was lean but generous enough that on a man with a gentler personality it would be a wickedly intriguing mouth that with a single smile could dazzle every female for miles around.

It was his jawline she liked best. The square strong cut of it proved that he was a man of integrity. He radiated honor and strength. His unfriendly nature did nothing to detract from the way his black duster, black muslin shirt and trousers clung to the muscled contours and lines of his body to perfection. She had never seen such an attractive man, nor one who disliked her more.

"I am here to escort you to our ranch house." He frowned and deep lines bracketed his mouth—lines that would have been dimples if the man were capable of smiling.

"I am sure that's not appropriate." Mary Brooks had

visited her days ago with an apology. It seemed the woman felt responsible for the misunderstanding, and yet she had not shown any signs of remorse. Melody had fallen in love with the motherly woman immediately; the mother-in-law she would never have. She did not want to let anyone know how disappointed she was about that. She squared her shoulders, determined to face the intimidating Gabriel Brooks and somehow make him understand. No meant no. "Your mother is a dear, but as I'm sure you'll agree, it's not right that I accept her offer."

"I did not say I approved of the invitation." A muscle tightened in his jaw, perhaps a show of his displeasure. "I am only the messenger."

"So you think I should decline, too?"

"What I think doesn't matter. My mother's heart is set on having you as our dinner guest." He dismissed her darkly and yanked the folded bills from his coat pocket. "Mr. Owens, the matter of the bill is settled. Come along, Miss Pennington. I have no time to waste waiting for you, fine Boston lady or not."

"I am not going anywhere with you, Mr. Brooks." She planted her feet and glared at him. "Nor will I allow you to pay my bill. I will not be beholden to you."

"Truly? That would displease you?" He arched his brow darkly and dropped his hat back on his head.

"Yes, it would."

"Then, Owens, keep my money. Come on, fancy lady. My horse is waiting in this cold weather without a blanket."

"I do not understand you." She studied him with her

wide blue eyes, the exact color of lapis. Her lush, rosebud lips puckered into a puzzled frown.

Perhaps she was unaware of the effect that would have on most men. With her porcelain skin, delicate heart-shaped face and those golden wisps of hair spilling down from her braided topknot, she was the most beautiful female he had ever seen. Something so out of the ordinary and beyond what was real in this rural mountain town that she might as well be a tropical bird landed here by mistake. Anyone with eyes could see she did not belong here. No doubt she would be leaving as soon as she batted those curly lashes and got someone to pay for her ticket home. Women like her were princesses, used to getting what they wanted.

"I am not going anywhere with you, Mr. Brooks." She looked frail and lonely standing in the doorway. As a lawman, he had learned to read small details for the truth. Now he saw the strain around her eyes and the tense line of her exquisite jaw. The shadows of hurt that she tried to blink away in her eyes. She looked lost, as if she had no one at all to count on. Not at all the demanding princess he hoped she would be.

The last thing he wanted to feel was sympathy for her. It would be impossible to dislike her then. He bristled. "I don't have all day. Grab your coat and come with me."

"No. I would rather not. I have my reputation to think of. We would be alone. Without a chaperone. Please give your mother my apologies."

"I do not intend to disappoint Ma. Do you want me to carry you down the stairs, through the door and out into the rain? Or would you rather walk under your own power?" He gave her his best look, the bad one that startled most outlaws into complying and sent decent women running for safety.

Melody Pennington did not run. She wordlessly fetched her coat from the wall peg. "Just so we are clear, I do not like you. In fact, I was prepared to be civil to you, but you have changed my mind. Not another word to me, you understand? You are not to touch me."

"Excellent." Mission accomplished. Gabe wasn't proud of it, but what choice did he have? He knew his mother, and she wasn't going to stop in her quest to marry off all her sons. His two brothers were attached, thanks to her, and that meant he was next.

Marriage? Not on his life. He growled at Owens, "What are you standing there for? Why are you grinning like that?"

"Because that's how it started with me and my wife. The sparks flew for us, too." The older man backed toward the stairs. "Good luck to you, Gabe. Looks like there will be another Brooks wedding in the offing before long."

"Like hell there will be." He tore the coat from Melody's hands and held the garment for her, fighting the powerful surge of anger strumming through his veins. He was not falling victim to his mother's schemes. If it took every bit of strength he owned, he was going to make sure Miss Melody Pennington hated him and would continue to hate him. He was not marrying some fancy city princess.

"I will reimburse you." The lady's soft alto voice was like music, lovely and sweet. She smelled like budding roses and impossible dreams. She was all honesty—he could see that clearly as she turned to him, her graceful hands buttoning her expensive coat. "Gabriel, I know you are only trying to protect your family. But I didn't come here to hurt them. I came to love them. Since that is not possible, I don't want to cause any harm."

Disliking the woman was going to be harder than he thought.

"Follow me," he barked, and headed for the stairs.

Melody had never seen such lovely country, and if it hadn't been for Mr. Gabriel Brooks seething dislike on the buggy seat beside her, she would have described the journey through the mountain forest as divine. Surely heaven could not be as glorious as the riot of sun-blessed green mantling the world surrounding her. Evergreens held up their limbs proudly toward a cloud-filled sky rimmed by craggy granite peaks. Deciduous trees lifted newly opening leaves for every kind of bird to land on and sing from. A golden eagle soared overhead with his mate, wings spread wide to soar side by side on unseen currents. No ballet had ever been as beautiful or romantic.

Sadness threatened to creep in, because she would have been happy in this strange, rough country. The view alone could make her forget the cruelty she'd left behind. Not even the dour oldest Brooks brother could diminish the beauty of it and the hope rising through her like lark song through the trees. It would not be such a bad turn of events to spend time in this mountain paradise. She would find a job, earn her own living and look for another prospect.

She had placed one advertisement successfully—and the young Joseph Brooks would have been the perfect groom had he actually known she was coming. Why shouldn't she have just as much luck with a second advertisement?

"Great." Gabe's mutter rang with deep sarcasm. "The woman doesn't have a trace of remorse."

Melody jerked her attention from the stunning mountainsides to the clearing ahead. A two-story ranch house complete with dormers and a wraparound veranda crowned a lush green rise of lawn, gardens and orchard. Spring's touch had brushed budding leaves with bright new green and painted the world in wonder. Larks sang as a pleasantly plump woman with apple cheeks and sparkling blue eyes dashed down a walkway lined with daffodils.

"So happy to see you, dear!" Mary Brooks ignored her eldest son completely as she seized Melody's hands and held on tightly. "I worried Gabe would be so unpleasant that you would refuse to let him accompany you."

"It did cross my mind." She shot him a glowering look, not at all surprised to see the dark scowl etched into his handsome features. "But I wanted to see you again. I hadn't realized how much I relied on your letters. Corresponding with you had become the best part of my days."

"No doubt because you miss your own mother terribly." Mary gave her fingers a maternal squeeze, radiating a concern only the best of mothers with the most loving of hearts could give. "You must be freezing. There's a chill in the air made colder because of Gabe's mood, no doubt.

Come inside. I have tea steeping. We'll have a chance to chat before supper is on the table."

"That sounds lovely." Before Melody could blink, Gabriel removed her hand from his mother's, his big, impressive frame standing in front of her to block the wind.

"Allow me." The deep notes of his baritone rumbled through her, a strangely intimate sensation. The heat of his grip, iron strength sheathed in a battered driving glove, seared through layers of leather and wool like a brand.

A shiver coursed through her. Numb with surprise and confusion, she hardly remembered climbing out of the buggy, only that she stood before him with cheerful flowers at her feet and Gabe towering over her stealing the very breath from her lungs.

What was happening? Surely this couldn't be fear she felt, for the formidable man did not frighten her in the least. She, who'd known fear from another man's touch, felt safe standing in his shadow. That could not be the reason her heart hammered against her ribs with almost enough force to break bone. Gabe's dark blue gaze fastened on hers, penetrating her as if he could see deep inside to her secrets and her fears. Exposed, she took a startled step back, her pulse skipping through her veins, but again it was not fear that trembled in her hands or turned her knees to jelly. Never had she felt so vulnerable before a man, exposed, as if there could never be a secret between them.

"You ought to look sorry for what you've done, Ma." Disapproval knelled like thunder in his deep voice.

"Dragging this young woman all the way out here with false promises."

"Are you accusing me of being a liar?" Mary Brooks gave a light trill of a laugh, like a couplet of lark song, before she reached up to pat her son's shoulder. "I told Melody nothing but the truth, didn't I, dear?"

"The whole truth," Melody agreed. "Didn't you try to pretend to be one of your sons when you were searching for a bride for him?"

"That would be for my middle son, Nate, and yes, I did mislead poor Savannah just a tad in those letters we exchanged, and while I still argue the ends justify the means in that case, my sons have never let me live it down. All's well that ends well—my Nate is happily married and I have a beautiful granddaughter. I was right in matchmaking. Now that my youngest son has lost his heart to our dear Clara, that can only mean one thing—"

"Keep me out of your schemes." The big man glowered, jerking away and storming off to secure the horse by the bridle bits. Something dark passed across the rugged contours of his face.

Melody's hand felt cold where he'd held it, which made no sense. Because of their gloves, their skin had not touched. The bite of the wind pummeled her, needle sharp because Gabe no longer stood before her to block it. The sunshine dimmed and the temperature plummeted as he stalked away.

"If I want a wife, I can find her myself," he shot over his shoulder, and although he spoke to his mother, his midnight-blue gaze fastened on Melody. "Not some castoff who couldn't find a decent man to marry her back home."

"Gabriel Adam Brooks!" Mary burst out, as if shocked to the core. "You come back here and apologize at once. I did not raise you to speak like that in front of a lady."

"If I ever meet one, I'll keep that in mind." The wind carried his words, and the intonation of disgust and judgment, with it. He strode away, the buggy faintly rattling and the rigging jingling pleasantly through the beautiful fall of sunshine. The vivid fresh greens on the trees and bushes blurred and Melody took a slow, painful breath.

So that's what he thought of her.

"He was the sweetest little boy." Mary's hand gripped hers, tugging her gently up the walk. "Then he grew up and turned into a man, and you know what men are like."

"I do." Rough and unpredictable, capable of great cruelty. And yet she remembered how safe she'd felt in Gabriel's presence. The tingling sensation remained where he'd touched her. Gabriel Brooks was more than an ordinary man. In spite of his capacity to cause harm, an honest core of tenderness lived within him, too.

Intrigued by the combination of rough and tender, harsh and magnetic, she longed to glance over her shoulder and steal just one more glimpse of the man striding like a shadow through the thinning daylight.

Her good sense kicked in and she did not.

Chapter Two

The fact that he'd said those things to Melody Pennington gnawed at his gut. Gabe swiped the currycomb over Bucky's flank, shaking his head. He'd spoken out of self-defense. It was no different than taking a shot at an outlaw gunning for him, except for the fact that no outlaw had ever been nearly as innocent as the golden-haired fragile miss.

"If I hadn't taken a hard stand, then you know what would have happened next." He gave the old gelding a final swipe of the comb. "Ma would have started trying to match me up with the woman. I had to put a stop to it before she started hatching up a plan."

Bucky, gentleman that he was, gave a polite nicker as if to say he was in perfect agreement. Females were a wily bunch, and a male had to protect himself.

"I'm not saying marriage doesn't have its benefits." He couldn't argue that. A man had needs, life got lonely and he had to admit there was something pretty nice about the things a woman did to a house to make it a home, how she cooked hot meals and gave comfort to a man's life.

But the second you started adding love to the equation, he'd noticed that the man came up short every time. "I'm not about to fall head over heels for a gal no matter how much Ma wants it."

Bucky nickered, as if he wasn't fooled one bit.

Gabe sighed, deciding he might as well be honest with the horse. He set the comb on the nearby shelf. "Fine, so she's pretty. But that won't change my mind. A man has to keep the upper hand."

Bucky stomped his right front hoof, as if he was in agreement with that.

Melody Pennington was a darn beautiful female, no doubt about it. Good thing he was immune to a woman's charms and beauty. His head hadn't been swayed yet and he intended to keep it that way. Of course, if he ever found a sensible woman, he just might marry her—but he'd never tell his ma that. Women of the type he was looking for were dang scarce—a lady who understood that marriage was a bargain, one of give and take and duty and, if you were lucky, a respectful companionship.

Scarce? He shook his head as he led Bucky into his stall. *Scarce* wasn't the right word. *Nonexistent* was more accurate. Hell, he'd ridden nearly every square mile of the western half of the territory and he had yet to run into a gal like that. Didn't figure he ever would at this point.

Melody Pennington, with her dainty citified looks, expensive tailored clothes and seven trunks she had arrived with, was about as far from that kind of gal as a woman could get.

The setting sun sank low against the nearby peaks,

thinning the light and tossing deep shadows across the protected hillside as he hiked from the barn to the house. Greening limbs waved in the wind, as if showing off their fine new curling leaves. A robin tore old twigs from a shrub by the garden gate, his only company as he stood outside the kitchen door gathering his courage. As a territorial lawman, he'd seen his share of dangers and always rode into trouble without a lick of fear. So why did his palms break into a sweat knowing what waited for him in the parlor?

"There you are, son." His father stepped out of the shadows, smoke drifting from his newly lit pipe. "Your ma's looking for you."

"No surprise there." He could picture his mother settled down with Melody in the parlor, telling tales of his youth meant to capture the young woman's interest. "Miss Pennington is all wrong for me. She's not what I'm looking for."

"Well, sure, seeing as your ma and I picked her out for your brother." Not much troubled Jake Brooks, who had carved not just a living out of these rugged, unforgiving mountains, but an admirable success.

Gabe respected his father, and so he held his tongue when he had plenty to say about his parents writing away for brides for their sons. Just because there were little to no marriageable females in all of Mountain County didn't mean they had the right to take matters into their own hands.

"Miss Pennington is mighty easy on the eye." Pa puffed on his pipe, sending a cloud of tobacco smoke into the crisp air. "I figure a young buck like yourself might think she's more than a bit pretty."

"A man doesn't need beauty in a wife." He needed loyalty, fidelity and the ability to shoulder hard work without complaint, since he didn't make a salary that could pay a household staff. "Besides, she is too young for me."

"She's twenty-one. That's old enough." Pa opened the kitchen door to the delicious scents of pot roast and baking corn bread. "The problem isn't in the decade between your ages, but the fact that *you're* too old for your age."

"What does *that* mean?"

"You're a fuddy-duddy, son. Older than your years, and that ain't a compliment."

Great. Gabe stormed into the kitchen, his boots striking the floorboards like gunfire. "If you are trying to put me in a more agreeable mood for supper, you just failed."

"I'm trying to get you to see reason." Unaffected by his son's angry outburst, Jake took another puff on his pipe. Around him the cook, the cook's assistant and the new maid scurried from worktable to counter to stove, pots clanging and steam billowing, but he walked on, oblivious. "If you don't change your ways, you're going to wind up alone. You will have no wife to grow old with. No sons to take pride in. No daughters to dote on."

"Who says I want those things?" Gabe put enough *grr* in his growl to make sure his words sounded menacing, as if there was no hint of the truth beneath.

"Every man wants those things down deep."

"Not me." If he held the walls firm around his heart, then he wouldn't have to feel the impact of his father's words or the old yearning for home and hearth, a kindly wife's gentle touch and the laughter of their children—all of which could not be. He didn't trust a woman that much. He grimaced fiercely, so his father could not guess. "I'm immune to that brand of foolishness."

"Fine, if that's what you think." Pa didn't seem too troubled. "You doth protest too much."

Gabe would have argued that his protesting wasn't any more vigorous than usual except that the sweetest sound stopped him, drained every thought from his head and his convenient anger with it. A woman's voice, modulated and unguarded, lilted from down the hallway. Of course he knew the speaker had to be Melody Pennington— there was no other woman in the house save for Ma and the hired help. But away from sight, and safely protected from her by several thick walls, he didn't listen to her with fear for his bachelorhood. He could hear her true voice for the first time. Unclouded by his own prejudice and his desire not to like her, her gentle laughter touched him like lark song; the alto tones of her words were arresting as a poignant hymn.

"The poor dear has come all this way hoping to join our family and escape her problems," Pa sympathized.

"Problems?" He gritted his teeth, building a solid, stoic perimeter around his heart. He refused to feel sorry for Melody, for sympathy would weaken his defenses against her. "Who doesn't have problems? She ought to be more concerned with finding a job and earning her own living instead of finding some fool to marry and provide for her."

"You know how unkind this world is to a woman alone."

Pa grew serious, his tone solemn, disappointment cutting into the deep wrinkles at the corners of his eyes. "How did a son of mine become so unforgiving?"

"Experience," he said simply, waving his discomfort and his father's disappointment of him away, as if they didn't trouble him, but it did not work. The emotions lingered as if stuck to his soul. He followed his father into the parlor, where kerosene lamps glowed brightly and steadily against the encroaching twilight, and his mother clasped her hands in glee. "Finally! I swear men can waste more time in a barn than we women can in a fabric shop. Gabriel, put some wood on the fire, will you? I fear Melody might catch a chill. She's not used to our Montana evenings."

"Massachusetts gets its share of inclement weather," the beauty assured everyone, keeping her gaze carefully focused on his mother, and only his mother.

So she wasn't any more pleased with this gathering than he was. Had she figured out his mother's intention yet? He cut through the room, and when he crossed in front of her, he did his best to ignore the tug of awareness that came to life and spilled into his bloodstream. Settling one knee before the hearth, he grabbed a split quarter of cedar from the wood box and settled it in the red-hot flames. The moss and bark crackled when it caught. Not unlike the heat burning within him.

I'm not attracted to her, he reminded himself as he lifted the iron poker from its hook and prodded the log into a better position for burning. What he felt was a natural consequence of a man's hungers, which an affirmed bachelor like him could expect to flare up from time to time. Nothing to be troubled by.

"Melody was telling us she loves to read, too." Ma positively beamed as she sat in her favorite chair, her basket of embroidery at her feet. Ma loved her needlework, and that she avoided it now was a sure sign she wanted to put all her concentration on the beautiful blonde seated demurely on the sofa. "Guess what she confessed to be reading?"

"Not interested." He drew himself up to his full height, gazing down at Melody with his most piercing gaze. She didn't like him, which was the only bright spot to the evening, and he sure as hell intended to keep it that way.

"Journey to the Center of the Earth." Ma didn't seem to mind that he didn't care. She looked ready to burst with excitement. "Can you imagine? The same exact book you've had your nose in all week."

"You read Jules Verne?" Melody turned toward him, surprise making her blue eyes a truer blue—such a stunning color the sight of it knocked every bit of air from his lungs.

Not that he wanted her to know that. Was it his imagination, or was something missing? Some of the chairs in the room had vanished, and there was no other place to sit except to share the sofa with Melody. No doubt Ma's handiwork, too. He strode carefully to the far edge and chose the outer cushion, as far away from her as he could get.

"You looked surprised, Miss Pennington. You didn't think a rural mountain man like me would be literate?"

"No, that's not what I meant at all."

"I might be nothing like the men you're used to in your fancy social circles back home, but I assure you I'm not as dumb as you think."

"And exactly how do you know what I think, Mr. Brooks?" She didn't know what she'd done to arouse this man's dislike or to earn his derision, but she was starting to think it was a malady of men who couldn't easily find themselves a wife. There seemed to be a proliferation of them in the world, self-important and easily callous and quick to put a woman down. What a relief she wasn't naive enough to imagine all sorts of romantic and empathetic reasons behind his behavior. At least her experience with Derrick's attempts to court her had taught her something about life.

"I'm not sure women think at all, as a matter of fact." He didn't seem embarrassed by his outrageous statement. "In fact, I reckon most women are rather like cattle, content to be cared for and herded by much wiser men."

"Gabriel!" Across the well-appointed room, Mary appeared shocked and horrified as the full weight of his words sank in. "I cannot believe you would say such a thing. Jake, did you hear what your son just said?"

"I heard," returned the older man, who was looking longingly at the folded newspaper on the small table beside him, as if desperate to escape behind its pages. "I'll give him a talking-to later."

"You'll talk with him right now!"

How easy it would be to have been horrified right along with the parents, Melody reasoned—except for the quick flash of amusement in Gabe's midnight-blue eyes, a flash that was there and gone so fast she almost thought she'd imagined it. She gaped at the man doing his best imitation of a stoic, unyielding statue of carved granite, which could not be real. Maybe she had imagined that glimpse of humor. It did not look as if the briefest spark of life could survive inside such a man.

"A talking-to won't change my mind, Ma." His deep voice rumbled like the most terrible thunder, and when he unfolded his big muscular frame from the cushion beside her and drew himself up to his full height he looked formidable indeed. As he towered over her, she could well imagine the most vicious of outlaws quaking at the thought of Gabe Brooks on his trail. He set his iron shoulders and thrust out his carved jaw. "I'm over thirty and set in my ways."

This time there was no flash of humor, no inkling that he was anything aside from the hardest of men. Except for a sensation she could not explain—it was as if she could feel his unspoken jest even when he trained his dark unflinching gaze on her. She would have believed he harbored a great dislike for her except for this feeling, and suddenly she knew. He was asking for her help.

"I pity any woman who becomes smitten with you, Gabriel Brooks." Not that she could imagine it, and she could imagine a great deal. "For you would break the poor girl's heart with such attitudes."

"It's a shame, but the last time I looked this was a free country, and a man can believe what he likes."

There it was, that flicker again, brief and quick and straight to her heart. She felt the punch of it behind her breastbone. What was it? And why, when she didn't like Gabe at all?

"I'm afraid he's a lost cause, Mr. and Mrs. Brooks." It was only the truth. Oh, she knew the type of man Gabe was—commitment shy, too tough to be vulnerable, an embittered type who refused to believe in love. "I hope you have not written away for a bride for him."

"No, we have been afraid to," Mary admitted, shaking her head sadly, disappointed in her oldest son. "Can you imagine bringing a lovely young lady out all this way only to have him behave like this?"

"It's no use, Mary," Mr. Brooks muttered as he unfolded a newspaper. "It's not going to work."

"I know." Mary sighed heavily and blinked a tear from her eye. "Come, Melody, I'll show you the piano I wrote you about. We might as well have a pleasant evening and not waste your visit here."

Not waste her visit here? Whatever could that mean? She stood, her knees surprisingly trembly as the answer came to her. Since her commitment with the younger brother had not worked out, had the Brookses meant to match her up with Gabe instead? Had he figured it out and was that the reason for his disagreeable behavior?

"You ought to be a stage actor," she tossed to him in a low whisper. "I almost believed you."

His warm chuckle followed her out of the room, and the sound lingered in her memory long after he was out of her sight.

* * *

"You must excuse my son," Gabe could hear his ma explaining as he reined the carriage horse, Bucky, to a stop near the front door. Over the clatter the wheels made on the frozen ground, the jingle of the rigging and the *clink-clop* of the horse's steel shoes, he could pick out only pieces of the rest of what his mother was saying. Something like "complete embarrassment" and "why I didn't dare write away."

Good. What a relief. Satisfaction punched through him at a job well done. His disreputable act had worked. Looked as if he didn't need to worry about winding up with a leftover mail-order bride.

"Thank you so much for an enjoyable evening." Melody's musical voice could warm the chill from the high mountain air. "I can't tell you how much this meant to me, and how sorry I am our arrangement didn't work out. I would have loved having you for a mother-in-law."

"Poor dear, orphaned and all alone."

His ma was a sympathetic sort, but when he saw her wrap Melody in a warm embrace and hold her tight as if she didn't want to let go, he knew the feeling was mutual. Good thing he'd had the sense to nip any matchmaking in the bud.

He drew the horse to a stop and was halfway out of the seat before he stopped himself. If he got down to help Melody into the buggy, he might look more gentlemanly than was wise, at least in front of his ma, the woman who had a hard time taking no for an answer.

Choosing self-preservation, he sank back into the cushioned seat, rescued the buffalo rope that had fallen to the floorboards and cleared his throat for good measure. Too bad it was so dark, or he could use his worst scowl to his advantage.

He didn't hurry the women along, especially since a prickle snaked down his spine, the way it did on an assignment right before it went bad—a deep-set intuition that signaled danger. He gulped, glancing around in the darkness, glad for the revolver always at his hip. He might be off duty, but the truth was he'd hunted down dangerous men for a living and now and then those men escaped prison and wanted revenge. Hadn't it happened to him before?

The memory burned like an inferno in his stomach lining as he searched the dark shadows bordering the garden fence and the edges of the grazing land where the forests stretched ink-black for miles. Was there someone there? Or was this gut feeling due to something else?

"Gabe, where are your manners?" His mother's admonishment came from far away as he snapped his attention back to the buggy. His mother glared up at him as she had when he'd been a boy being threatened with a switching.

He chuckled. He wasn't worried. His ma was all bark and no bite, no matter how unhappy she was with him.

"It's cold out," he explained, staying firmly on the seat. "Miss Pennington can climb up by herself."

"If you were any younger, young man, I'd take a strap to you."

"Empty threats." Never once had she come close to

such a thing. "Which is probably why I turned out the way I did."

"The parents aren't always to blame when their child turns out poorly." A hint of mischief shaped the rosebud-pink of Melody Pennington's soft lips. "Sometimes there's no one to blame but the man himself."

"You're not the first female to tell me that." He reached across the length of the seat and offered her his hand.

"I'm not at all surprised. I can imagine women right and left of you constantly taking offense." Her china-blue eyes twinkled up at him, as if he wasn't fooling her one bit.

Her palm melted against his and her slender fingers twined around his much larger ones. Like a flame to kerosene, light and heat blazed up his arm. Shocked, he could only stare at her, gasping as if for breath, as she landed on the seat next to him. Time froze. The bite of the bitter wind, his worry of danger in the dark and his plan to convince his mother that he would never be interested in Melody Pennington faded from his mind. All that remained was the rustling sound of her movements as she settled her skirts, her rose fragrance and the ghostly fall of her hair, shades of platinum in the night.

"This is for you, dear." His ma broke the silence, unaware that anything had changed. She cast him a deeply disappointed look, tugged something out of her cloak pocket and pressed it into Melody's gloved hands. "Train passage for wherever love takes you next."

"Oh, I couldn't." She stared at the envelope, and then her chin came up. "It's not your fault this didn't work out,

Mrs. Brooks. I took too long deciding if I should come or not, and so this is squarely on my shoulders."

She was turning down the train ticket? It had to be worth more than several hundred dollars. His hand still burned where Melody had touched him. He flexed his fingers, but the fire did not fade.

"Nonsense," his ma argued. "I made you promises I intend to keep. We will cover your expenses at the hotel until you are ready to leave."

"No." Spine straight, shoulders set, she pressed the ticket into the older woman's hands gently. "I have to pay my own way. You know what I've been through. I can't be beholden to anyone ever again, even when the motive is kindness."

"I do." His ma's face fell, and Gabe knew she had been counting on helping Melody to make things right. He knew she felt a strong responsibility for the young lady. It was easy to do.

What had happened in Boston? He knew darn well she couldn't pay her hotel bill, so how exactly was she going to survive? The heat in his arm continued to creep along, aching in his biceps and inching into his shoulder, as if trying to worm its way into his heart.

This was the danger he'd sensed. He gave the reins a snap, Bucky leaped to life, the buggy rocked forward. He vowed never to say another word to Miss Melody Pennington again.

Chapter Three

Melody watched dawn come to the high mountain country from the window seat of her hotel room. She'd never
seen anything quite as beautiful. The golden crest of the
sun broke above the craggy, snow-capped peaks, bringing light to a dark world and painting the first strokes
of color—the palest blue to the sky, deep lavender to
the mountains, the darkest green to the forest. Soft rose
gilded the underbellies of shadowed clouds, and birdsong,
which had been as loud as any symphony, silenced as if in
reverence. Awed, she felt a world away—no, two worlds
away—from the life and the problems she'd left behind.

What must it be like to spend one's life in such a place?
She sipped her sweetened tea, her mind taking her back to
last night at the Brooks home. Dinner had been a casual
affair with the most delicious pot roast beef and buttermilk biscuits she'd ever tasted. Mary and Gabe's father
chatted and bantered with good humor, making the atmosphere merry and covering Gabe's stubborn silence
well. She'd hardly noticed him glowering over his plate,
his brawny shoulders set with great determination. Gabe's

father had a sense of humor that kept them laughing until the last drop of tea was drained and the last crumb of apple crisp consumed.

Quite a different experience from her own family. Although Mother had been gone five years, she still winced from the pain of her loss. And as for her father—Papa's more recent loss had been enough to break her heart. He'd shielded her from his illness the best he could for as long as he could, but he had no notion that what he'd done to try to save her had not only destroyed him but left her at the mercy of vultures. The bruises had faded, but the terror of the past remained. The old school friend she'd turned to for help, Derrick, had wanted a great deal more in return and didn't like taking no for an answer.

In traveling here, she'd hoped for safety from that danger with the warm and loving Brooks family. That was a closed door now, but watching the stunning paradise surrounding her, she hoped she would find a safe harbor in this peaceful mountain town.

A knock rattled her door, startling her from her thoughts. Cold tea sloshed over the rim of the cup she held and she realized the sun had climbed into the sky while she'd been ruminating. On the main street below, businesses had opened for the day and she ought to be out there trying to bargain a fair price at the jeweler's for her grandmother's pearls.

"Just a moment," she called, climbing to her feet. She hoped it wasn't Mr. Owens come to give her more grief about the bill. Gabe had tossed a wad of money at him yesterday, but there was no telling if it had been enough. Either way, she intended to find less expensive lodgings today.

She set the teacup on the bureau and opened the door. Instead of kindly, gray-haired Mr. Owens in his overalls standing at the threshold, a tall, dark-haired man with piercing blue eyes and a fierce scowl glared down at her.

Gabe.

"What are you doing here?" The words were out of her mouth before she could think to stop them. Whatever reason could he have for darkening her door two days in a row? Her fingers curled tight around the door handle. "Come to insult me some more?"

"No, I think the impact of my insults so far has been enough." A wry quirk lifted one corner of his severe mouth, reminding her of her revelation last night in the Brookses' parlor.

"Your mother is not here to fool, and since I've figured out you were acting, there is nothing to be gained by insulting me further. I certainly don't want to marry you."

"Lucky me." He swept off his black Stetson, revealing tousled dark hair and dimples that flirted with a hint of a grin. "I've got my mother convinced. I'd be grateful if you didn't tip her off."

"I wouldn't dream of it."

"Great. The last thing I need is for her to try finding me a wife. You know that's why she invited you to supper?"

"I realized that in the parlor about the same time I saw through your act." She left the door wide open and retreated into the room. "Did you want to come in?"

"Uh…" He hesitated, glancing past her into the small space. His gaze focused on the bed, which she'd neatly made after she'd arisen, and a deep flush spread across his sun-browned face. "This won't take more than a minute."

"Good." It wasn't exactly proper to invite the man in, but she didn't want him standing there in the doorway for any passersby to see or to overhear. She settled on the window seat, smoothing her skirts while he closed the door and crossed to the only available chair.

The deep red remained on his face, and it surprised her. Gabe might be gruff, rough and harsh, but he was also a gentleman. After what she'd endured before fleeing Boston, she appreciated that trait in the mountain lawman very much.

"My ma has sent me to talk you into taking the train ticket." From his jacket pocket he withdrew the same envelope she'd refused last night. "Something tells me you aren't any more interested in it this morning."

"I'm not."

"You're having financial problems. You can't deny it." His dark blue eyes softened—a man of might but of feeling, too.

"No, but I didn't come here to take advantage of your family. I knew in coming there was a risk my marriage to Joseph might not happen." She set her delicately cut chin—powerful determination in spite of her diminutive size. "My life is my responsibility. I love your mother for caring about me so much. She was the reason I chose Joseph out of all the letters I received from my advertisement."

"You *liked* her interfering with his life?" That was a

shock, he thought as he slid the train ticket back into his pocket. He couldn't think of one woman who would want a sometimes intrusive and meddlesome mother-in-law.

"I didn't see it that way. What I saw was her love for her sons. Her devotion came across on the page and made her letters shine with an affection missing from my life." She stared as if with all her concentration at her slender hands, worrying at a stray thread in her expensive skirt.

"My mother has been gone many years and I've missed her," she continued. "Mary's letters felt like finding what I'd lost. To have a caring mother in my life again seemed priceless and worth the risk of traveling so far."

"You came because you fell in love with my mother?"

"Don't be angry. I only meant that I came with hope of finding a little of what I had lost."

"I'm not angry." He swallowed hard against a hot, tight knot of emotion at his Adam's apple.

He wasn't moved by her honest confession. He'd been a Rider long enough to spot a liar. Everything about her—from the emotion raw in her voice to her relaxed body language to her open heart—told him she spoke the truth. Somehow he could feel the pain of her grief, a wound that had taken a piece out of her. He thought of what it would be like to lose his ma—his meddling, caring, dear mother. "I'm sorry for your loss. Are you alone, then?"

"My father passed away a year ago." She drew herself up straight as if gathering her strength and fighting to rein in her emotions.

Did she have any notion how vulnerable she looked? The effect she had on a man? He doubted it. He fumbled with his hat, worrying it with his fingers to give his hand something to do and a place for his gaze to go instead of noticing her. "And you've no other family?"

"Yes, but none I want to acknowledge as such." Strength laced with sadness made her ever more beautiful, and the tug of it on his heart unbearable. "Father's estate was quite sizable and his brother and my cousins swooped down like vultures, with lawyers and so-called good intentions."

"I've seen that before." There was in fact very little of human baseness he had not witnessed or had to see the consequence of in his line of work. "So you had no choice but to find a husband to support you?"

"Are you aware how offensive you are?" Her blue eyes challenged him with an uncommon might for so small a woman.

"I can't be offending you too much, because you're fighting to keep that perfect mouth of yours from smiling."

"You think my mouth is perfect?"

"Any man would." Perfect for smiling, for kissing, for whispering endearments in the darkest hours of the night. Heat spilled into his veins, burning like fire through every part of him. He swallowed hard, fighting an unwanted desire. Love could control a man, and so could lust. Those weaknesses weren't going to have power over him. Best to get right to his reason for coming and stop letting Melody's considerable charm get to him. "What are your plans?"

"Plans?" She blinked at him. "I'm still trying to figure that out."

"You need money and a place to stay."

"You mean a job and a less expensive room, perhaps at a boardinghouse." Doe-eyed, she focused her gaze on him.

She was an odd sort of female—as fragile as any, but the set of her lovely, perfectly kissable mouth and the proud set of her spine spoke of a strength he had to admire. She wanted to earn her own way. Hard not to like her for that.

"I could help you there." He ought to kick himself for volunteering. He knew better than to get involved in any way with a woman looking for marriage, but she wasn't interested in him—there was a big relief—and her honest goodness lured him. No sense in lying to himself about that.

"I know everyone in these parts. Trudy over at the boardinghouse ought to have room for you. There aren't a whole lot of jobs needing to be filled in a town this size, but I reckon we can find you something."

"You're serious, aren't you?" Her gaze searched his, and the tension carved into her delicate features began to ease. He'd seen nothing or no one more captivating than golden-haired Melody Pennington as she lit up with happiness in the soft glow of the morning light. Dimples bracketed the widest smile he'd ever seen. Joy sparkled within her with a brightness she did not hold back. She hopped off the cushion. "Gabe, I can't wait to get started. I've never worked for a living, but I loved spending time in the kitchen with our staff."

Hell, what in blazes was wrong with him? He was touched in the head not to have thought this through. She was a siren enchanting him, her and her alone, because his reaction to her wasn't his fault. He *refused* to let it be. He shook off the daze he must be in, struggled to clear his mind and launched himself out of the chair. Once his back was to her, his common sense kicked in. "Is there any sort of work you can do?"

"Lots of things." She grabbed her fancy wool coat with the pearl buttons and silk trim. "I'm good with a needle, so I could do seamstress work. I'm well-read, so I could be a private tutor. I have a knack for baking—"

"Baking?" Now, there was a possibility. He took her coat, the fine fabric soft against his calloused hands, and helped her into it. Her rose scent filled his nose, and his skin prickled as if every inch of him were about to burst into flame. As he settled the garment around her shoulders a wave of longing crashed through him. He squeezed his eyes shut, determined to gain self-control, but heat continued to pound through his bloodstream, a desire he did not want. He gritted his teeth, but it did not abate.

"Is there a bakery in town?" Her question came as if from far away. His pulse thundered so hard in his ears that he could barely hear her.

His eyes snapped open to find her gazing up at him. He'd seen everything in his line of work—horrors and violence, desperation and dishonor—so the hope radiating from her moved him. That had to be why he found his fingers against the luxuriously soft silk of her face, her cheek cradled against the palm of his hand. His tired soul was hungry for her hope, and *not* because he was drawn to the woman.

"We'll start there. The place is always open for business this time of morning." He withdrew his hand, cleared his throat and turned crisply away. "Folks drive for miles just to buy Mrs. McKaslin's cinnamon rolls."

"Maybe I should get my other bonnet. I want to make a good impression."

"You look fine." He sounded impatient and abrupt.

"No need to growl like a grizzly." She grabbed her reticule from the top of the bureau, feeling it to make sure her grandmother's pearls were still safely tucked inside. The side of her face tingled where his touch had been. "After this morning, I will be completely out of your way."

"I doubt it." He yanked open the door.

"You don't think I can get a job?"

"I think I won't be that lucky. You'll keep turning up like an old penny."

"If only to torture you," she agreed, and walked through the door he held open for her.

"I'm helping you on one condition." He took the key from her and locked her door. "You don't mention a word of this to my mother."

"I won't lie if she asks me outright. But I will assure her that I'm not interested in you whatsoever."

"Then come with me, Melody." Her name on his tongue rumbled low and deep as if from a dream.

His big hand covered hers, pressing warmly against her palm, skin to skin. Lightning jolted up her arm, blinding and sudden. Time stood still, and the lamplit hallway and stairwell faded from sight, leaving only Gabe Brooks. Dressed as usual all in black, he towered in front of her as dark as any shadow. Not even the light dared touch him as he strode through it, his boot heels sounding like a knell on the floorboards, taking all the air with him. She could not breathe. She could not think, only stare and blink blindly after him as he hesitated on the stairs.

"I suppose a fine lady like you would rather not be seen in public with a rough like me." His voice boomed, as if he were the hardest of men and nothing could injure him.

She did not believe it. Gabe had developed a way of coping with an often harsh job where he made his living with a gun, that was all. Somehow she managed to get her feet to carry her forward, bringing her close enough to see the faint, hard-to-read pinch of hurt in the pleasant crinkles at the corners of his eyes.

"I'm not so fine," she assured him. "And you are not so rough."

"That's what you think now, but wait until you know me better." He offered his arm to help her down the stairs.

"I thought you wanted nothing more to do with me after this morning." She slipped her arm through his, this time not startled by the bolt of sensation that hit the moment they touched. "Have you changed your mind about that?"

"No, but I took your threat of torturing me with your presence seriously."

"A big strong man like you isn't afraid of a woman half his size, is he?"

"It's not fear, sweetheart. It's experience."

Someone had broken Gabe's heart? No, she couldn't see a hint of it in the stony set of his profile or in the unyielding angle of his jaw. He was a man who would never let anyone that close.

They reached the bottom stair and he released her. Her arm felt odd without his touch. When his strides lengthened to put more distance between them, she ached with a strange loneliness.

"Good mornin', Gabe," Mr. Owens called from behind the front desk.

"Mornin'." Gabe nodded once as he pulled open the heavy door for her. Sunshine stung her eyes as she stumbled onto the boardwalk. Her breath rose in a misty fog. It might be early, but already the street teemed with horse and wagon traffic.

"Good morning, Marshal." A man with a mop of brown hair and kind brown eyes tipped his hat on the boardwalk. "Miss Pennington, hope you have a good day."

"You as well, Mr. Dermot." She remembered the livery stable owner, who had generously hauled her trunks from the depot to the hotel when she'd arrived. He had been friendly and endearingly respectful, and she'd considered him good-looking. But compared to Gabe, who stalked protectively at her side, Austin Dermot now seemed wanting.

I suppose that's not the best sign, she thought to herself. Men were everywhere in this town—dismounting from their horses at the hitching post, sweeping their bit of boardwalk in front of their shops, halting wagons in the street to allow her and Gabe to cross to the other side. Several bachelors tipped their hats to her and offered friendly smiles.

"If you're looking for a husband, you don't need to worry about taking out another advertisement." Gabe leaned closer, and the low notes of his voice seemed to ring inside her.

"Your mother explained in her letters there were few marriageable women in this remote county. I suppose that makes me something of a curiosity."

"More like a commodity."

"Don't tell me you're going to say something about how women are like cattle again. I understood you were trying to keep your mother from marrying us off, but if you truly believe such a thing, I intend to smack you with my reticule."

"Didn't you notice I'm carrying a gun?"

"Oh, I saw perfectly well. You would be mistaken if you think such a weapon would stop me."

His laughter joined hers, harmony to her melody. She hadn't noticed climbing up the steps to the boardwalk or that they'd come to the end of the block. Gabe captivated her. She hardly noticed the shop window directly in front of her, where a tray of pastries and iced rolls enticed passersby to come inside.

"The couple who own this place are my parents' age. Their older sons belonged to the same cavalry brigade as my brother Nate and I did during the war."

"You were a soldier?" That shouldn't have surprised her. She could see it now, especially with the soft morning light falling on him and emphasizing his muscled discipline and his mighty spirit. Easy to imagine him in a blue uniform astride his horse, riding fearlessly into the fray. Fine, so she had a soft spot for men in uniform. Maybe that's why her face felt suddenly warm.

"I enlisted as soon as I was of age. I spent two years in and another two after the war riding special missions for the army." He seemed remote again, his features as lifeless as granite.

Perhaps that was why he kept everyone at a distance. "My father fought, and he came home a different man."

"War will change you, that's for sure." Gabe cleared his throat, broke away from her as if ending the subject and opened the door. "Mrs. McKaslin?"

"Gabriel!" A cheerful women with a cap of silver-threaded hair peered up from her work at a long front counter. "How nice to see you. Is this the young woman I've been hearing about? The one your mother brought out for you?"

"Not for me," he denied affably. "With your daughter-in-law busy with her new baby, I figured you might need help around here."

"Do I!" The matronly woman circled the end of the counter, her smile welcoming.

"Melody is looking for work," he explained, stepping out of the way at the last moment as the bakery owner took her by the hands, her grip warm and comforting.

"Come have a hot cup of tea. You're freezing, child. I'll get you one of my cinnamon rolls and you and I shall have a good talk."

How nice that sounded. The potbellied stove in the center of the front room coughed out a puff of smoke when the wind gusted against the front windows. A few small tables and chairs, empty for now, ringed the stove. Curtains framed the wide windows, giving the shop a homey feel.

"I'll talk to Trudy at the boardinghouse for you." Gabe tipped his hat to her, a gesture of farewell. When the cowbell above the door jangled and cold blew in on a cruel wind, she felt twenty degrees colder within. Gabe walked away, closing the door behind him, taking all the warmth from her.

I don't even like him, she told herself. But did her heart listen?

Not a chance.

Chapter Four

Gabe rubbed at the pain hammering behind his fore-head, signed the warrant in front of him and squinted through the sun-glazed glass. The front windows gave a good view of town, and his pulse lurched at the sight of a dove-gray wool coat and the flash of bright blue skirts amid the weathered storefronts and the plainer clothes of the townsfolk.

Melody Pennington. What in blazes was he going to do about that woman? Ever since he'd strolled away from the bakery and from her, it had felt as if something was missing, as if he'd left something important behind.

"Is that the gal?" Mac McKaslin, one of his fellow Range Riders, ambled over to see what had grabbed Gabe's attention. He crossed his arms over his chest, his wedding ring glinting in the sun. As a married man, he thought himself wise in the mysteries of women and matrimony. "No wonder she's caught your eye."

"My eye isn't caught." So far, anyhow, and it would stay that way if he had anything to say about it. "And judging by the look of things, she'll be accepting some poor fool's marriage proposal by the end of the week."

"Some lucky man, you mean." Mac was the toughest of the tough, and how he'd succumbed to the wiles of romance was nothing short of a puzzle to Gabe. "I know what you're gonna say. That marriage is a trap men fall into, but the truth is, men don't fall into it alone. Women have it worse than we do."

"Says the man who is wrapped around his wife's little finger. She so much as whispers and you jump to do her bidding."

"I want to make her happy." Mac chuckled, convinced he was the wiser one. "Marriage comes with a lot of comforts."

"Only one, you mean." Desire fired in his blood again and he imagined Melody in his bed, with her hair strewn across his pillow and the buttons marching primly down her dress half undone...

Whoa, there, man. He pulled the reins on that thought, but nothing short of sudden death was going to put a halt to the fire for her licking through his veins. Watching her through the window wasn't helping, because the wind snatched at the curls tumbling from her topknot and tousled them, just as he would do if she were his to claim.

His palms broke into a sweat as she waltzed closer. Traffic stopped in the street for her and bachelors tipped their hats as she stepped onto the boardwalk. Her smile was shy and her manner cordial but reserved, and that impressed him. He could think of any number of women who would use their wiles to find a quick resolution to their financial problems. And if a small voice at the back of his head warned him that he'd become too cynical, then he pushed it away.

"It's awful nice to come home at the end of the day to a tasty supper on the table and a loving wife to share it with." Mac sounded as if he were already looking forward to that, now the workday's end was near.

"Having someone to cook and serve your meals wouldn't be bad." That was why he lived with his folks. He was gone more often than not, and when he'd lived in his little house in town he'd hated coming back to an empty place and frying up something to eat, the silence echoing around him like heartache. "She could clean, too. Earn her keep."

"You can't be serious." Mac shook his head, casting him a look of mild disappointment. "A wife shouldn't be convenient. She should be the pinnacle."

"The what?"

"The pinnacle. The reason for it all."

Jeesh. He shook his head. Look what love did to a man. Good thing he didn't have to worry about that happening to him. Normally he had iron control, so he couldn't explain why his gaze remained glued to Melody as she swept along the front windows. Bathed in the afternoon sun, her golden hair absorbed the light and reflected it in different dazzling hues—flax, amber, honey, pure gold. Her creamy skin held a blush of rose from the wind, and why hadn't he noticed her round breasts and her small waist? Quite appealing.

"Looks like you're in trouble now," Mac commented, retreating to his desk.

Gabe gulped, the last physical act he had control of as his stomach swooped downward. He could see her slender hand reach and grasp the doorknob. She was coming in! His pulse reared like a panicked horse and took off galloping.

"Gabe Brooks." Melody blew in on a ray of sunshine. "I don't believe it. You're sitting at a desk working like any other man. You're mortal, after all."

Behind him, Mac choked on a hoot of laughter as he closed the back door. The hinges creaked, and Gabe was alone in the room with Melody.

"Of course I'm human," he argued, pushing out of his chair.

"That's a point to argue." Merriment deepened the dimples bracketing her amazing mouth. She reached into her reticule and withdrew a fold of greenbacks. "I checked with Mr. Owens to see what you paid him yesterday. This is the same amount to the dollar."

"What?" For some reason his mind had gone dim again. He stared at the money she laid on the corner of his desk. Why wouldn't his brain work? He breathed her soft rose fragrance into every part of him. The drum of his pulse thundered in his ears and yearning he didn't understand seized him by the gut. He wanted to taste the pearled pink softness of her mouth and kiss each deep-set dimple. He wanted to—

Whoa, man. What had happened to self-control? To his vow not to let this female affect him?

"I'm paying you back for my hotel stay." Her chin went up. "I meant what I said, and you will take this money. Trust me, you don't want to make me angry."

"Sure." She couldn't hurt a fly. In fact, he'd wager she was the type of lady who carefully carried spiders and ladybugs from her home and set them safely free outside. "I'm an armed man, but I'm quaking in my boots."

"Are you making fun of me?" She squinted at him, and with the furrows at her brow and the way her nose crinkled slightly, he'd never seen anyone more adorable.

What was wrong with him? The barriers he put between him and all women seemed to have tumbled down.

She's just a nice lady, he thought to himself. And it was his own fault that a nice lady was the one weakness he had.

"No, ma'am," he said seriously. "I can see you are dead serious. Where did you get the money?"

"Not your business." She blew out a puff of breath, stirring a curl that had fallen into her eyes. She looked relieved, glad there wouldn't be an argument. "Did I thank you for helping me this morning?"

"I can't rightly say." Mostly because his brain had turned to quicksand, sucking down his every thought. Nothing could escape it.

She didn't seem to notice. She went right on, her wispy curls bouncing, her tempting mouth moving, her fine bosom rising and falling with every breath.

"I am grateful, Gabe. I had a wonderful talk with Mrs. McKaslin, and tomorrow will be my first day. I've secured a room at the boardinghouse, and Mr. Owens has agreed to haul my trunks for me."

"Looks like you are squared away." He pushed away from his desk, drawing himself to his full height. "It must be a relief. You must have been real worried. I can see the difference in you."

"I've never been on my own before." She worried her bottom lip. "I'm determined to do it well."

"I'm sure you will." His hand was moving before he could stop it. His fingers touched the impossibly soft silk of her hair and he could not halt a rising tide of need that crashed through him. It pounded like a storm on the sea as he stroked the errant gold curl across her cheek and tucked it behind the perfect shell of her ear. He thought he felt her shiver, but then he realized it was him. A second shudder rocked through him and he drew his hand away.

The door shot open, and Mr. Owens from the hotel filled the doorway. "Pardon me, miss, but I saw you through the window. I was just finishing my shift when a fellow came in looking for you."

"A fellow?" Anxiety flashed across her face as she spun away from him, but he could feel her emotion thrumming in the air between them.

"Reckon he'll catch up with you, but you might want to head over to the hotel and see." He tipped his hat, backing through the door. "I'll see to your trunks, don't you worry. You all have a fine evenin', now."

"Thanks, Owens." Gabe circled the desk. A chill settled in his gut, a tingle at the back of his neck. A warning sign. Something was wrong. He didn't need to see the worry crinkling her creamy complexion or the tension at her jaw. Everyone had a secret to protect, and it stood to reason a woman looking for a new start might have more than one.

"Seems I've got me a wad of money to burn." He picked up the thick fold she'd left on his desk and pocketed it. "Want to help me out?"

"No." A tiny piece of humor glimmered, in spite of the tightness around her eyes.

"You owe me, pretty lady." It was a few minutes before closing, but in the morning he would make up for leaving early. He laid a hand on Melody's back and ignored the twist of tenderness he did not want to feel. "It's your fault I can't go home for supper."

"My fault? How do you figure that?" She couldn't fully hide the hint of her dimples as she let him guide her through the door.

"Everyone saw us walking around town this morning. Ma has heard about it by now. How can I go home to that?"

"Oh, I'm sure you of all men will have no difficulty explaining the truth to her."

"Sure, but over supper?" He closed the office door and locked it. "I've worked hard all day. I want to eat without agitation. So, are you coming?"

"Will you take no for an answer?"

"Not a chance." He offered her his arm. To hell with what everyone was going to think. Pretty Melody Pennington was in a bushel of trouble. He could feel it in his gut, and his instincts were never wrong.

Maybe it was the lawman in him, or maybe it was something intensely personal, but he felt protective of the woman. With her dainty arm resting in his, he escorted her down the boardwalk, laying his claim.

As the hotel came into sight, Melody went weak. The westbound train had arrived less than an hour ago. She recalled hearing the whistle that had blasted through town when she was standing in the sunny corner room discussing the rent with Trudy Ludwig. A fellow had been looking for her, Mr. Owens had said. She'd been too stunned to ask who it had been. Was it someone from here in town, or had the unthinkable happened? Had Derrick been able to figure out where she'd gone and tracked her down?

Fear slammed through her. The strength slid from her knees. Thank goodness for Gabe's strong arm. She clutched him more tightly and hoped he didn't notice her stumbling gait. What if Derrick was watching her right now? What if he were waiting for her at the hotel?

"You're shivering." Gabe held the ornate glass door for her, concern shaping the harsh planes of his face. "We'll get you a hot cup of tea."

She didn't trust her voice. She nodded, her shoes tapping on the wood floor as she swept into the hotel. It wasn't easy, but she wriggled out of Gabe's grip, standing alone in the foyer. The entrance was busy—a guest was checking in. His back was to her. She didn't recognize the old wool coat, but the sloping shoulders and blond hair were close enough that he *could* be Derrick. Her throat went dry.

No, she decided. It wasn't him. This man was taller than Derrick.

"Come, Melody." Gabe caught her wrist, his touch as hot as flame. The concern enriching the low tones of his voice lured her. "Let me take care of you."

A lot of men since her father's death had said those same words to her. She thought of her uncle, greedy to get his hands on the Pennington fortune; of her cousin trying to trick her into signing over her inheritance; and of Derrick, who thought he deserved to marry her for help with answering a few legal questions. Not one of those men had meant those words.

Gabe did. He did not want anything from her. Her feet carried her toward him, and suddenly the pleasant weight of his arm curved around her shoulders. Not since she'd buried her father had she felt so protected. The roof could cave in, the sky could fall and the world end and she knew this man of steel and kindness would keep her safe. It was hard not to like him for that.

Like him? Be honest, Melody. This is not like, but something far more. She settled into the chair he held for her in the cozy dining room. His nearness affected her like opium. He smelled pleasantly of leather and soap and salty male skin. His fingers grazed her neck as he helped her out of her coat. She shivered again, dizzy, and realized it was because she had forgotten to breathe.

"Bring some tea, please," he murmured to a waiter.

She drew in air and her light-headedness faded. So did her shivers when Gabe moved away and settled across the small round table. Nearby, a roaring fire crackled in a big stone hearth, radiating a heat she could not feel.

"Want to tell me about your problem?" Gabe asked without a hint of gruffness, no longer the defensive, harsh man she'd first met.

This was the type of man a girl could depend on. One who stood firm when he should, fought when he had to and hid a softer side. Exactly the kind of man she had a soft spot for. She straightened in her chair.

Don't start wanting to lean on him, she told herself. His granite shoulder could never be her soft, sheltering place. Hadn't he been clear about that?

She drew in a breath, debating. He sat across from her like a hero straight out of a dime novel—piercing blue eyes, dimpled chin, a dark five-o'clock shadow rough on his jaw and radiating a mix of integrity and ruggedness. Definitely a man who could be trusted.

"Are you sure you want to know the truth?" she asked. "It isn't pretty."

"Trouble rarely is. Maybe I can help you with it. I do that for a living. I'm pretty good at it." His wry grin only made him more dashing.

Thump went her heart. She was falling hard for him. He would withdraw his offer and get away from her as fast as he could if he knew what she was feeling. "Perhaps it's something I should manage on my own."

"Seems to me you've been doing a lot of that lately." The teapot arrived and he thanked the waiter before filling two steaming cups. "The fellow you're hiding from—"

"Who said I was hiding from anyone?"

"I saw your reaction in my office." He slid a full cup across the table for her, his gaze pinning hers. "I can take this up with my mother, because I think you told her. She mentioned you had been through something back in Boston. I would rather you trusted me."

"A man I trusted, someone I'd known all my life. We had grown up together. We'd always been friends. Our parents had been friends. Derrick and I went to the same school, and studied piano under the same instructor—"

"You play piano?" He nudged the sugar bowl in her direction.

"Since I was young. Derrick and I used to play duets and sing in the church choir. He was a part of a group of friends. When we were older we would go caroling and sleigh riding and to symphonies and the theater together." Worry furrowed her forehead and crept like sorrow into her gentle voice. "When my father died this last winter, Derrick felt protective of me. But it wasn't me exactly. I was my father's sole heir, and when Derrick proposed and I refused, he became distraught."

"You mean violent?" Fury snapped through him and he had to fist his hands and clench his jaw to hold it in.

"Yes." Her hand shook as she added two lumps of sugar to her tea, the only outward sign of trauma. "He'd gotten the idea into his head that I would marry him and he could take over my father's estate."

"And get his hands on your inheritance?"

"Yes." Her chin went up. "I had no notion he'd been assuming this. I don't think he is well. I think something inside him snapped. He became someone I didn't know, and I was afraid. I was already corresponding with your mother before this happened. After Father passed, I decided to start looking for a new family and someplace to belong."

"Boston held too many sad memories for you."

"Yes. That's true. How did you know?"

"You mean a rugged, unfeeling man like me?" Sadness sliced into him. He was not the man he wanted to be; not the man he'd started out being. "Going through a war teaches you a lot of things."

"I see. So you know that sometimes the pain is too much. You have to leave it behind you and hope that the road ahead of you will take you to someplace better."

"I do." That's how he felt gazing upon her, the woman who without complaint had sold her grandmother's pearls to reimburse him for her hotel room. The woman who'd expected nothing from the family who had falsely promised her a wedding, a home and security. The woman of such sweetness and good heart that she made even a disillusioned curmudgeon like him want to believe in her.

"So I got on the train and came here. I didn't take the time to write and let your mother know when I was coming. I packed and climbed aboard and prayed I would never have to look back."

"Did he hit you?" She didn't need to answer. She trembled just once, barely noticeable, but his guts twisted.

He closed his mind to all the sadness he'd seen—the carnage of war, the devastation caused by criminals on the run, the faces of victims, the crosses above fresh graves of innocent folks he hadn't been able to save. His throat wedged tight, and feeling flooded him.

How could anyone treat a woman like that and still consider himself a man? Red stained his vision. He wanted to hunt this Derrick down. He wanted to make him hurt.

Take a deep breath, Gabe. Count to ten. He willed the rage down and forced his white-knuckled fists to relax. Across the table Melody had gone stark pale, wrestling memories of her own.

How could anyone hurt her? She was enchanting. The lamplight danced over her as if happy to burnish her golden curls and to stroke her soft cheeks. She looked like a fairy tale come true, everything good and honest in the world, a woman even he could trust.

"If this man knew where you were, would he come for you?" he asked, his voice harder than he meant it to be. Vestiges of his rage remained, strengthening him, making his decision crystal clear.

"Yes."

"Would he hurt you?"

"Yes. Your mother already knows this." She gave up trying to lift her cup. Tea sloshed over the rim, and she set it delicately into its saucer. "I told her about my worries. I don't want you to think I would deceive her."

"No, not you." There was nothing else to do but to say it and do the right thing for them both. "Then there's only one solution. Marry me."

Chapter Five

"*Marry* you?" Melody couldn't believe her ears. Had he really just proposed to her? Or had she lost her mind?

"Yes. It would keep you safe."

"Safe?" She *had* absolutely lost her mind, because why else would Gabe Brooks, who had been very vocal against the subject, offer marriage?

"Take a look at me. If this Derrick you're afraid of comes to town, do you think he would dare to threaten me?" A muscle ticked in his rock-hard jaw.

"Not if he were smart." She let her gaze roam over Gabe's brawny shoulders and powerful arms. Fearless, he watched her with a quiet confidence. There was no loud posturing or grandiose bragging. Just the thought of him as her protector made the fear drain away. "I don't think Derrick would dare to cross you. Would anyone?"

"If they do, they will regret it." The corner of his mouth flickered. "Then we have a deal?"

"What? Marriage isn't a deal."

"Then what is it?" His gaze narrowed. He hadn't moved, not even a blink of an eyelash, but she felt skewered in her chair like a criminal under interrogation. The waiter approached to take their orders, and he relaxed.

She rubbed at the tension gathering behind her forehead, trying to focus on the waiter, who was reciting something she had to fight to hear—the supper specials. She chose the chicken dish, hardly caring what she ate. She doubted she would be able to taste any of it. Gabe Brooks expected her to marry him.

What would that be like? she wondered as she watched him. He'd leaned back in his chair, crossing his muscled arms over his impressive chest, and was listening to the rest of the waiter's list. With whisker stubble dark against his jaw, he looked like an outlaw riding the wild Montana rangelands and certainly not the kindly book-loving gentleman she'd hoped to marry one day—the type of man she'd always been drawn to.

But Gabe? He wasn't at all what she would choose. He could be domineering, intimidating, and just because he'd confessed to reading Jules Verne did not mean they had anything else in common. Shouldn't she marry someone compatible? Or at least someone who shared some of her interests in life? And what about love? Could she come to love the man perched across the table from her ordering the steak-and-potato dish?

Yes, her heart answered. Wasn't she already partway there? Yearning filled her. What would it be like to lay her cheek against the unyielding plane of his chest? To have the privilege of calling him her own?

"Marriage is about two people working together for

their common good." The waiter had gone and Gabe's intensity returned. He leaned his forearms against the table, his suntan dark compared to the snowy cloth. "Let's face it, a lot of couples I can think of fall out of love along the way. That leaves them together, earning a living, making ends meet, raising their kids."

Children. She curled her hands around her warm teacup, considering. Gabe's babies? She shuddered deep inside at the thought. What would it be like lying in his arms? To have him honor her with his lovemaking in the dark of night? A languid heat curled around her insides, and she blushed. The last thing she wanted was for Gabe to know about her reaction to him. She took a sip of tea, gathering her dignity. "I thought you were opposed to marriage."

"I always told myself that if I found a sensible woman, someone I could trust, I would marry her." His voice dipped so low, the notes rumbled through her as if they were a part of her.

"You trust me?"

"God help me, but I do." The corner of his mouth quirked. "Think about what I'm offering you. Protection, shelter, security. You would never have to worry about providing for yourself or how to pay your way in this world."

"And your mother could be my mother-in-law." Happiness lit her up.

"See? It's not such a bad suggestion after all." He studied her over his cup rim. "You would have a family again."

"Yes, but what would you get out of this?"

"Me?" He liked that she considered him. He was right

about her. Melody had a caring heart, generous instead of self-absorbed. A rare female indeed. A fair amount of tenderness swooped into his chest, and he didn't bother to deny it. "I would get the comforts a woman brings to a man's life. Three meals a day, a nice home, clean clothes."

"You could hire someone to do the same."

"Yes, but I want you." The words were out before he could stop them. Shocked, he watched her rosebud-soft mouth round into a surprised O. He cleared his throat, forcing a gruff tone. "I meant to say, I wouldn't mind you doing those things. As long as you aren't a bad cook."

"How do you know that I can cook at all?"

"I hadn't thought of that, but I know you can bake." He felt like a fool. Why would a fancy Boston lady want to be his wife? She had probably grown up with servants and staff who'd taken care of all household duties. Disappointment ripped through him, but he set his face, refusing to let it show. "Then I'll agree to keep you safe anyway. You have my word of honor."

"Gabe." She said his name like music, and she reached across the small table.

Her warm fingertips landed on the back of his hand and sent a fierce bolt of heat into him. Desire rose, teasing him with what he was sure he could never have—sweet and lovely Melody in his life and in his bed.

"No man aside from my father has ever been as kind to me." Her touch remained. She did not withdraw or move away. "I've had men order me around, pretend to care for me while they tried to manipulate what they wanted from me, and try to terrify me to do their will. But you, you're making a sacrifice for me."

"Well, I will get something out of the deal." *You,* he wanted to say. *I would get you.*

"I know you don't love me, but that's part of what love is. Sacrifice for one another." Her fingers threaded through his, the contact the most magical thing he'd ever known. "I can't tell you what your offer means to me, so yes."

"Yes?" Her answer surprised him. She wasn't letting him down gently.

"I'll marry you." She worried her bottom lip, a sure sign she was nervous.

She wasn't alone there. Panic kicked him in the ribs. Marriage. That was an awfully big step, but in return he wouldn't be alone. His heart would be safe in Melody's hands. She wouldn't cheat on him when he was gone on a case, she wouldn't spend his hard-earned money carelessly or be prone to fits of drama or complaining. She would be like spring coming into his life, bringing sunshine and serenity and the warmth he hungered for.

"Then it's settled." Imagine what his mother was going to say. And his brothers. And his friends. He grimaced.

"You don't look very happy about it."

"That's because I'm imagining what everyone is going to say. I'm going to take a lot of ribbing. Everything I've ever said about marriage is going to come back to haunt me."

"Rightfully so. That's what you get for being so sour. I hope you know I won't put up with any sourness." She winked, playful and enchanting. "I hope you aren't expecting a meek, submissive kind of wife."

"No, but I am worried about your cooking."

"You'll have to wait and see. It will be something for you to look forward to."

No doubt about it. He was hooked, line and sinker. Not that he was fool enough to fall in love with the woman, but he cared for her. That was as far as he intended to go.

"Miss Pennington?" A man's voice broke into his thoughts.

"Austin." Gabe frowned at the livery stable owner staring with outright abhorrence at the sight of their linked hands. Remembering how interested the other man was in his new fiancée, Gabe managed his fiercest of scowls. "Can I help you?"

"Uh, no. I've been looking for Miss Pennington." Austin's shoulders sank. Disappointment hung on his face. "I heard you were moving to the boardinghouse."

"You were the one looking for me?" She untwined her hand from Gabe's. "It was you."

"Guilty. I wanted to offer to haul your trunks." He gulped, looking vulnerable. "I'd still like to do that for you?"

She knew he wasn't asking about the trunks. He was asking about her and Gabe. She didn't know what to tell him. Derrick hadn't been the one looking for her, so that meant she didn't need Gabe's protection as much as she'd first thought. Why was she so disappointed? Shouldn't she be relieved?

"That's good of you," Gabe boomed out. "But Melody is my responsibility now."

"So it's true, what I overheard?" Austin asked.

"We're to be married." Her fiancé hadn't appeared to change his mind.

Austin muttered his congratulations and slunk away, and Melody remembered how Mary had written of so many bachelors in town with no one to marry. She felt sorry for him and for Gabe. He was the type of man who didn't go back on his word. The waiter returned with their meals, so she waited until the plates were set before them and they were alone again.

"Are you sure?" she asked, hands trembling. "I understand if you want to change your mind."

"Is there a chance that Derrick fellow will come after you?" He set his shoulders, ignoring his steak, intent only on her.

"Not a big one, or at least I hope not. But I can't be sure. He was terribly mad at me." She had to be truthful with Gabe. "He might not think to check the train station. He would probably be looking for me at my friends' houses. When he can't find me, I'm hoping he will give up."

"But we can't be sure, so we'll be safe rather than sorry." His smile was rare, warming the shadows from his eyes and every trace of stoniness from his features. "I'll move your trunks after we eat. I'll get you settled in before I head for home. Is that all right?"

"Yes." How could it not be? He made her feel secure and cared for. She stuck her fork into the fluffy dumplings on the plate in front of her, delighted to discover she had an appetite after all.

"This is the last one." Gabe shouldered the trunk into the corner, biting his lip to keep from commenting. Seven trunks. That was a lot of dresses, shoes and frippery. *Fashionable* dresses, shoes and frippery, he reminded himself. All it took was one look at Melody to know she was used to being pampered. She was probably used to ordering a new wardrobe with every change of season. He straightened, ignoring the pop of his spine when he straightened his back.

"You're mad at me, aren't you?" With a flip of her wrist, she removed two enormous and deadly-looking pins from her hair. Her carefully coiled locks tumbled past her shoulders and over the rise of her bosom.

Gabe gulped, forcing his attention away from her perfect curves. He was walking a dangerous line and he intended to hold his position. Desire was one thing, but he refused to let it rule him.

"Not mad," he barked. Well, maybe a little. "It would have been easier to keep the room at the hotel."

"But this is a wiser use of money."

She must have no notion how captivating she was, perched on the edge of the bed with her hair caressing the curves of her face and body. Even more alluring was her common sense with his cash. He wrestled down the urge to kiss her right then and there, married or not.

"Thank you for moving my things." She looked uncertain. "I know some of those trunks are heavy."

"Heavy? I've known horses who weigh less." He liked that his joke made her laugh, a silvery lilting sound that stirred him. "You are aware that I'm a lawman, right? And I make a lawman's salary?"

"That's obvious, Gabe. I helped my father handle his finances during his illness. I know how to budget and purchase wisely."

The problem with Melody was that she was too perfect. His perfect gal, and she didn't seem to know it. Everything she said made him want her more. The blood pounding through him was proof of that.

"I don't want you to be disappointed with the life I can give you." Might as well be honest about that.

"Are you having second thoughts?"

"Looking at those trunks, any smart man would."

That made her laugh again. "I never would have left my family home if I cared about material possessions. I could have made different choices that would have assured me a very fine and comfortable life."

"But you didn't?"

"No. What truly matters in life are the things you cannot buy. Surely you know that, Gabe?"

"I do." He brushed a tangle of hair out of her eyes. He couldn't resist. Nothing was silkier than her hair or softer than her skin. In his opinion, a good woman was beyond price. Damn if he could stop the caring rushing into him until he felt filled up with it and brimming over.

Being a bachelor was hard on a man. He lived with his parents because he'd tried living alone and he'd hated it. It had been an empty life, and it was easier to pretend he'd moved back home out of convenience, since he was gone more days of the month than he was home. But in truth, living alone he'd been unable to hide from the loneliness. He, like any man, had needs both in the bedroom and out. Needs for companionship and a family. He'd always wanted a son, and now, because of Melody, he would have the chance for one.

Heat thrummed through him and he closed his mind, refusing to imagine Melody in his bed. Hard not to picture it, though, since she was sitting on the edge of the mattress with her hair down, her face tipped upward and his hand cradling her jaw. Her flawless mouth tempted him. He ached to slant his lips over hers and kiss her until she moaned his name.

Maybe marrying her wasn't such a good idea. He swallowed hard, on the edge of control. He lowered his hand and moved away.

"Is there anything else you need for tonight?" His words were brusque, his boot heels striking the floor like bullets.

"No. I'm fine, Gabe." Her voice was thick, not at all her own. "Thank you."

"I'll talk to the pastor tomorrow." He hesitated at the door, impassive, impossible to read. "See when he's free to do the ceremony."

"Fine." Her lips still tingled from a kiss that had never happened. She licked her bottom lip, but the sensation remained, a brand that would not leave. A reminder that he'd had the chance to kiss her and had declined. She'd been the one wanting him, not the other way around.

"I'll let you know what I find out." He didn't move, a formidable statue as dark as the gathering shadows.

"Fine," she said again. Watching him was agony; pretending she wasn't breaking apart inside, torture. Why wasn't he leaving? He stood frozen in the doorway and she couldn't tell if he was unhappy with her or himself. The milder side of Gabriel Brooks had vanished, replaced by a cold granite man who was a stranger to her.

"See you tomorrow, then." He tipped his hat. "Good night."

"Night," she called, hating that her voice trembled. The door swung shut and closed with a click. She waited until the sound of his boots had faded before she buried her face in her hands.

What had she been thinking? Gabe hadn't wanted to kiss her. How much of his attitude toward marriage was real, regardless of his reassurance? He couldn't stomach kissing her. The thought of pressing his lips to hers had put a severe, unfeeling look on him that chilled her to the bone.

If he didn't want her, then what kind of marriage would they have? What kind of sanctuary? Cool air crept through the floorboards as night temperatures set in. Not even the fire roaring in the small potbellied stove in the corner could drive the chill from the room or from her soul.

Cold rain chased him home. By the time he'd closed the kitchen door behind him and peeled off his wet riding coat, he was soaked through and frozen to the bone. The kitchen was dark, the counters spotless, the cook and her assistant gone for the night. The water in the kettle was still warm, so he poured a cup of tea and rummaged in the pantry until he found a molasses cookie.

Melody had said she was a good baker. At least that was something. His sweet tooth would be satisfied in this marriage, if nothing else. He wouldn't need to worry about losing his dignity or his self-control over baked goods.

Voices carried down the hallway—his ma's and pa's. They were locked in a good-natured argument from the sound of things. Something about his little brother Joseph's upcoming nuptials. Funny how he'd always figured he would be the last of the three Brooks brothers to marry, but if things went the way he planned, he'd be a husband before he went out of town at the end of the week—and before Joseph and Clara's wedding.

Since he wanted to avoid his mother, he padded quietly down the hallway, stepping over the few boards that squeaked. The library sat in the far back of the house in a separate wing, but the vast room was not dark when he opened the door. Lamps blazed and a fire crackled on the hearth.

"Hey, big brother." Joseph peered around the edge of a wingback chair. "Surprised to see you here when you have much prettier company in town."

"How do you know about me and Melody?"

"*Everyone* knows about you and Melody."

Great. Gabe took his usual chair by the fire. "I suppose we were hard to miss walking through town together."

"According to Nate—"

"Nate?" What did their other brother have to do with

it? Gabe set his cup on the nearby side table and bit into his cookie so hard, pain shot through his jaw.

"He owns the feed store, remember? He's got a clear view of the street from his front windows. As I heard it, he got an eyeful watching you parade Miss Melody past his window this morning and again arm in arm this evening. Took her to supper at the hotel, did you?"

"None of your business." If his brothers knew, then that meant that his mother did, too. Good thing she hadn't heard him come in.

"I thought so." Joe looked pleased. A book sat open on his lap and he ignored it. "Couldn't resist a damsel in distress, could you? And not to be disrespectful, but admit it, Gabe. You want her."

"I'm taking the Fifth." As far as he knew, a man didn't have to incriminate himself. His family would eventually have to be told he was engaged, but he could hold off for a few days at most.

"Melody would make you a fine wife," Joe persisted. "Nate also caught a glimpse of you hauling a trunk or two out of the hotel. After dining with the lady in question."

"Nate ought to mind his own business." He ground out the words, brushing cookie crumbs off his shirt. What did a man have to do to get a little privacy?

"Over supper tonight I asked Ma a few questions about Melody." Joe turned serious. "Seems she received some sort of threat and she decided to leave Boston. To get as far away as she could to start a new life."

"She mentioned something like that." Curious, he took a sip of tea. He didn't want to tip his hand and let Joe know exactly how much he wanted more information. "Melody said there had been an incident over money."

"I don't know what it's about, only that Ma thought Melody had been hurt worse than she'd let on. That this fellow who wanted her pa's estate was desperate. Owed money to gamblers or some such. Now, Ma had promised that she would be safe here. That we would all stand up and make sure of it."

"That sounds like Ma." He could see her glibly making those promises, sure that all would work out well. His mother was an optimist.

He was not.

"Hello, Gabe." A woman's dulcet voice broke the silence. It was Joe's fiancée, Miss Clara Woodrow, standing uncertainly in the doorway, a book tucked in the crook of her arm. "I didn't mean to interrupt. I can come back later—"

"No." Gabe launched himself out of the chair and grabbed his book on the table, eager to leave. He could see how things were. Joe had been waiting for Clara so they could spend their evening together. They ought to be alone, so he hoofed it out of the room. By the time he'd reached the hallway, he could hear his brother's voice drop low, and Clara's gentle answer.

They sounded like a young couple in love. It couldn't be envy that curled around his insides, squeezing tight. Not only wasn't he the jealous sort, but he didn't want to be in love. He didn't believe in it, he didn't trust it and he wasn't foolish enough to give it power over him.

With his book by Jules Verne in one hand and his teacup

in the other, he headed upstairs. Ma's and Pa's contented voices murmured after him. He'd never felt more alone. It was Melody's fault. Spending time with her had driven away his loneliness, and now that it was back, it felt larger than before. He closed the door to his room, aching for a woman he refused to need.

Chapter Six

"I remember being young and in love."

Startled to realize she'd been staring off into space again, Melody shook her head to clear it and went back to work wiping down the table in front of the wide bay window. Thank goodness she had an understanding employer. She didn't want to be reprimanded on her third day of work. "I promise I won't drift off again."

"Daydreaming is part of being in love." Mrs. McKaslin knelt before the stove to add a scoop of coal from the hod. "Missing him when you're apart, savoring all the things you love about him, longing for the sound of his voice and his arms to wrap around you."

"I was only staring off down the street." And certainly not imagining being in his arms. Heat scorched her face, and she gave the table a final swipe. The task was done, but she discovered she wasn't moving away from the window. She'd been waiting for word from Gabe yesterday and had heard nothing. All day long she'd expected to look up from the front counter or hear a knock at her door, but nothing. He hadn't come.

He'd changed his mind. Her hands clenched and squeezed soapy droplets from the cloth she held. When he'd been unable to kiss her—when the thought of kissing her had repelled him—and he'd stormed away, had he known then he couldn't marry her? And why would he marry a woman he did not want?

Shame crawled through her. His rejection hadn't stopped her longing for him. Her mouth still tingled with anticipation; her lips craved his kiss. Every part of her ached for something she'd never wanted before—Gabe.

She felt him before she spotted him striding purposefully down the boardwalk. Dressed in black, his collar-length hair wind tousled, he could have been a Western legend come to life. The surrounding world faded away. The other men on the boardwalk and in the street vanished until there was only him.

Behind her, the stove door clanked shut, and Mrs. McKaslin's skirts rustled as she climbed to her feet. "There you go again. Yep, it's definitely love."

"No, not love." She couldn't let it be. Wouldn't falling in love with Gabe be a catastrophe waiting to happen?

"I was the same way after I met my Fred. Our hearts beat in synchrony. Am I wrong, or did Gabe just come out of the jewelry store?"

"I hadn't noticed." All she could see was him, his Stetson shading his face, the glisten of raindrops on his coat, the proud, athletic way he moved as he crossed the street. Her eyes worshipped him, tracing every hard line and muscled curve, her pulse speeding like a runaway train.

Don't fall any further for him, she ordered, but it was

like standing on the edge of a crumbling cliff, the earth giving way beneath her shoes and gravity pulling her inexorably down.

The bell above the door chimed and Gabe walked in, bringing with him the feel of damp wind and gray skies. Melody gripped the back of a nearby chair, leaning on it for support. Had he come to break their engagement?

"Gabriel!" Mrs. McKaslin, who had grown sons Gabe's age, welcomed him with a motherly smile. "Come sit by the stove and dry off. Spring is coming in like a lion! I'll get you a nice hot cup of coffee."

"Thank you, ma'am." Gabe swept off his hat, droplets pinging to the floor.

He's not looking at me. She watched him turn his back to her and hang his hat on a wall peg. He took his time unbuttoning his coat. Tension hardened the angle of his jaw and the straight proud line of his back. Her fingertips wanted to smooth away the tenseness of his muscles. If only she could kiss away the tightness in his jaw. She didn't remember crossing the bakery floor. She only knew she was beside him, staying her hand from reaching out to him. The fierce need to reassure him made her break the silence. "Gabe? Tell me what's troubling you."

"Nothing. I talked to the pastor. He's free this afternoon." He faced her as grim as a man arranging a funeral, not a wedding. "Will that be all right?"

"Yes." She squeezed her eyes shut. So he was sticking to his word. Relief warred with gratitude and a touch of fear. A mail-order marriage had sounded like a grand solution back home, but now faced with the reality of it, her hands turned cold. Nerves prickled in the pit of her stomach.

"I figure these next few hours will be the toughest part." He looked as cold as the revolver he wore. "Once we get past the vows, it ought to get better. It'll be like jumping off a cliff into a cold lake. After you get up the gumption to take the leap, it's out of your hands."

"In other words, a terrifying fall into water cold enough to kill you?" He had to be joking, right?

"It doesn't matter if it's the fall that gets you *or* the water. You're doomed either way." The impossibly hard line of his mouth softened in the corners.

A joke, then. "Very funny. I'm not sure I like that you look at me and see doom."

"Sweetheart, any man who can look at you and not see doom is a darn fool." He strolled past her and yanked out a chair at the closest table, which he held for her. "The moment I saw you, I knew you were going to be trouble. Now, sit down."

"I'm still working. I have fifteen minutes left to go."

"Mrs. McKaslin won't mind. Sit down. I have something for you." He waited for her to settle her skirts before drawing out the facing chair. He hauled it around so the small table wouldn't be between them. This might not be a love match, but he intended to do this right. Melody was to be his wife and he intended to honor her. He reached into his pocket. "My pa bought my ma a necklace to wear at her wedding. She still has the ruby pendant, and every time she wears it my pa reminds her how lucky he was to find her."

Melody bit her lip and bowed her head as if in pain, as if he'd said something wrong or done the wrong thing. He sighed, searched his mind, but he had no notion what it could be. Maybe it was proof this venture of theirs was a bad idea, and he hesitated.

He very nearly changed his mind, but she looked fragile and so very vulnerable. He'd never noticed before how little she was compared to him—just a bit of a thing, dear and delicate and so fine. An honest woman, one he could trust—that didn't come along often. He liked the idea that he was the one she'd chosen to keep her safe and provide for her. So he withdrew the strand of gleaming pearls from his pocket.

"These are for you." He'd never seen such a fine strand, each polished pearl fat and lustrous and perfectly formed. He heard Melody gasp. She straightened, her face contoured with some emotion he couldn't guess at. She didn't look happy.

"My grandmother's pearls." Tears stood in her eyes, shivering, but did not fall.

Then he understood. The tightness eased from his chest and he unclasped the gold catch with his too-big fingers. "I bought them back from the jeweler. You didn't think I would keep your money, did you?"

"No. But I never thought—" She leaned forward so he could fasten the strand around her neck. "I can't thank you enough."

"No need." Gossamer wisps falling from her hair knot caressed his cheek, catching on his jaw. The scent of roses, soap and sweet woman filled his senses as he leaned kissing close.

His knuckles grazed her neck as he fastened the necklace. An inferno roared through him. There was no single flame of desire, not this time. Need engulfed him, threatening to overtake him completely. He was a man and only so strong. He tore away from her and out of the chair, ashamed at his lack of control.

Twice he'd been close to her and twice he'd almost lost his senses. Well, he wouldn't let down his guard. He wouldn't lose his discipline. He'd kept a wall up between himself and everyone else, even family. What was it about Melody that could disarm him so completely?

"Gabe, this is so wonderful of you." Gratitude deepened her baby blues, drawing him like a tornado's updraft, and he felt on the verge of falling.

Hell. He was in serious trouble. He had to figure out a way to resist the lure of her emotions or she would suck him in, shatter his defenses and leave him vulnerable. Vulnerable was one thing that he, Gabriel Adam Brooks, did not allow.

"I talked to Candace at the dress shop. She will help you find something new for the wedding." He might not know much about women, but he knew their affinity for new dresses. He tried to ignore the fact that she had all those trunks stuffed with fancy clothes. "Get something nice. I've sent a message out to my folks. I figure we should meet at the church around five o'clock when I get off work. Will that give you enough time?"

"Yes." Her hand rested on the pearls at her collar. The tears stood in her eyes.

Those tears were killing him. At least he knew he'd done the right thing. "Is there anything else I can get you?"

"No." Hard to believe it, but she smiled. "I have everything I need."

The way she looked at him made him feel ten feet tall. He gritted his teeth, seeing the mistake he was about to make. He'd thought he was a smart enough man not to fall into love's trap. It took all his might to keep from drawing her into his arms, all his will to keep his guard up. She felt way too close—physically and emotionally—so he pushed his chair back until the table was safely between them again.

In the church's vestibule, Melody felt for her grandmother's pearls clasped at her neck. Gabe had placed them there. She shivered, remembering his closeness. The graze of his knuckles against her nape, the fan of his breath against her neck made her long for him. It was hard to reconcile the man who'd given her the necklace with the one standing like a soldier in front of the altar. Rigid, shoulders back, legs braced, stony look, he could have been a warrior preparing for a battle to the death. He did not look like a man who could love.

His touch had been gentle, she remembered. She'd glimpsed true tenderness hidden beneath his well-defended exterior. The moment she'd seen the pearls in his hand she'd known she'd been wrong about the kiss.

He might not love her now, but maybe love would come in time. Her heart was certainly falling and her resolve weakening. A smart woman wouldn't confuse necessity with romance and duty with desire, but as she shrugged off her coat she wanted romance. She wanted desire. She wanted Gabe's love.

"Every bride is lovely." Mary Brooks raced down the aisle to wrap her in a warm hug. "But you are more stunning than any bride I've yet to see. Look at Gabe. He's standing there with his mouth hanging open."

"You're exaggerating. He hasn't noticed me."

"He's enchanted." Mary dabbed at a tear in her eye.

"He looks like he's about to be tortured." Not that she blamed him. Nerves were quaking through her. She wasn't sure her knees would hold up long enough for her to get down the aisle—and it was a very short aisle, as it was a very small church.

"All bridegrooms look that way. You should have seen Jake on our wedding day. He stood in front of the altar with his knees knocking. The reverend had to ask him if he was all right before he began."

Across the sanctuary Gabe turned toward her, hazarding a look. No reaction rippled across him. He looked as stony as ever. Maybe he'd been watching her since she'd breezed in with the rain, keeping check on her out of the corner of his eye. Did he have hopes for this marriage, too? Surely he did. The pearls, the consideration, the new dress he'd arranged for her all spoke more loudly than his silence.

"Come." Mary took her hand. "Let's get you and Gabe married. Oh, this is working out just as I'd hoped it would!"

The warm pressure of Mary's palm against hers felt like a gift. She'd come here without family and now she had a mother's affection. With every step she took, she no longer felt alone in the world. She had two new brothers in one row, a sister-in-law and baby niece in another. A kindly father standing beside the most handsome man she'd ever seen—her husband-to-be. Mary released her, steering her into place before a simple wooden pulpit and a kind-faced minister.

Gabe held out his hand, palm up. He wore a black suit, his Sunday finest. The reverence of his gaze told her that he did not take their marriage lightly. The instant their flesh touched, a connection telegraphed from his skin to hers, from his heart to hers and deeper, a bond she could not explain. His irises had gone black. Had he felt it, too? His gaze raked her from head to toe, slowly taking in her carefully styled hair, the ivory-colored lawn dress with simple lace edgings that she had thought was both affordable and complemented her eyes.

He leaned close, his cheek scorching hers.

"I've never seen any woman so beautiful." His whisper shivered through her, as if his words were a part of her.

Love blazed within her. Not the first flickering of it or the dread of it pulling her helplessly along, but true and strong, the real thing. All it took was the appreciation for her in his eyes and she tumbled, her heart falling endlessly. "Who knew you would clean up so nice? You look handsome in a suit."

She loved that a smile cracked the stone and let the real Gabe through. How had she gotten so lucky? She had the very best man—a man of integrity and tenderness she would honor all the days of her life. Her worries melted away as the minister broke the silence.

"Are we ready to begin?" he asked, opening the pages of his Bible.

"Yes," she breathed and bit her bottom lip, waiting for her groom's answer.

"Guess so," he bit out too gruffly, and it echoed through the church like the rain beating on the roof above. He shifted uncomfortably and ran a finger beneath his buttoned-up collar.

"Dearly beloved…" the minister began, and it was as if everyone in the church took a breath at once, perhaps amazed that this was really going to happen. Gabe could feel the shock in the air, not that he could blame his family. He'd always been vocal about his opinion of marriage.

But it hadn't turned out badly for his folks or for his brother Nate. A man just had to find the right woman, one who was compatible. In his case, he'd found Melody. Pride filled him simply from looking at her. She was a vision in that dress, as lustrous as the pearls at her throat, and she would be his. Only his. If emotion lumped in his throat, then he denied it. He wasn't a weak man given to sappiness and softer feelings, but he supposed it wasn't a weakness to admire Melody for what she was—genuine, captivating and true.

"We are gathered here to join this man and this woman in holy matrimony," the minister continued.

Nerves threatened, but he drew himself taller, battling them down. Melody's hand in his began to quake, and tenderness burst within him, spreading outward until he was engulfed with it, until all he could feel was the sweet bliss of his caring for her. Surely it was not weak to care about one's bride—caring wasn't love, it wasn't weakness, it wouldn't be a threat to the walls around his heart. He smiled, so she would know that he was with her. From this moment on, however difficult or uncertain life became, she wouldn't face it alone. She had him.

"Gabriel Adam Brooks." The pastor's voice boomed through the sanctuary. "Do you take Melody Joy Pennington to be your lawfully wedded wife?"

Emotions, sugary and fierce, warred within him. He wasn't a man given to tenderness, but it struck like a flash flood engulfing him, drowning him, washing him away. Helpless to resist, he could only answer, "I do."

He wasn't marrying Melody out of a sense of duty, he realized, or to help her or to keep her safe. He could do that without placing a ring on her finger. No, he stood here repeating sacred vows to love her and honor her for himself. She was spring come into his life; she was hope on a wind-driven rain.

"We never thought this day would come." Gabe's middle brother, Nate, shook his head as he passed the sugar bowl to his wife and sipped his black coffee. The hotel's dining room was the perfect place to celebrate. "Never in all my days would I have thought my tough-as-nails big brother would meet his match."

"You make it sound like I've been bested," Gabe protested at her side.

"Only matched," Melody assured him.

He didn't look comfortable with that thought either. The poor man was used to being tough, closed off and solitary. She supposed it was because he'd spent years as a soldier, where softer feelings could destroy a warrior from the inside out, and also because of his time spent in the most respected law agency in the territory. He'd had to be hard all those years to do his job well and to keep tragedy and hardship from hurting him. Her poor husband, looking lost as his family teased him lovingly.

My husband, she thought, pride and joy making her buoyant.

"I remember when I first met Gabe." Her sister-in-law, Savannah, married to Nate, shifted their baby daughter in her arms and took a sip of coffee. "He'd just come in off the trail, covered with snow and looking like something out of a dime novel. He asked me out to supper, since Nate had decided to have nothing to do with me."

"I was only being courteous." Gabe spoke up. "Do you think I couldn't tell my brother was in love with you?"

"It did make him jealous, so your plan worked." Savannah laughed, a warm and friendly sound. It was easy to love her new sister-in-law. They had already made plans to get together and sew and talk.

"The first time I met Gabriel, I was serving supper," Clara, soon to be Joseph's wife, chimed in. She'd been working as a maid in the Brooks household at the time. "He was so gruff and big and dark, just the sight of him made me spill the gravy. The housekeeper was furious with me."

"I'm not scary," Gabe protested.

"Yes, you are," half the table argued.

Poor Gabe. High color stained his cheekbones and he drained his coffee cup. He really had no idea how he came across. *Intimidating* was one word, but *amazing* was another. She'd never met a bigger man—in all possible ways. Fine, so she was more than a little biased. She'd heard that love could make a woman blind, but not in her case. She saw Gabe clearly—he stood out to her when the rest of the world remained in the background. She slipped her hand under the table and covered his, which rested on his knee. His skin was warm and rough, and she curled her fingers around his, willing comforting into her touch.

He must have felt it, because he held on tight. His gaze felt like a caress to her lips. Remembering the kiss that had never happened, the one she'd wanted so badly, she felt the wish pound through her veins and into every inch of her. She wanted to know her husband's kiss and the comfort of being loved by him. She adored that he wanted her, too. She knew by the way he held on to her, by the way his eyes turned black. He didn't look stony or remote—the harsh contours of his face softened. He really was the most handsome man.

"By this time next week, all of my sons will be married." Mary, rosy cheeked and beaming, clasped her hands together, looking happy beyond measure. "I can't tell you what it means to know my boys will be loved and happy."

"Not to mention the grandbabies we get to welcome into the world," Jake added with the look of a doting patriarch proud of his family.

"And I finally have daughters." Mary sniffled. "Three of the finest young women a mother could hope for. Hand over your handkerchief, Jake. I put an extra one in your jacket because I knew I would get all worked up."

Family. Melody closed her eyes, so full of gratitude it felt as if she would burst. The sadness she'd left behind, the hurt and fear she'd run from faded. The pain in life, regardless of how severe at the time, did not have the power that love did, she discovered. Love made the hard times fade. All that mattered—that could ever matter— was right here at this table.

As if Gabe felt the same, his grip on her hand tightened in unspoken understanding.

Chapter Seven

Gabe checked the last buckle on the harness, the rigging jangled pleasantly and Bucky stomped his right front hoof as if to say he was ready to go. Rain beat angrily against the livery stable roof as he grabbed the gelding by the bit and glanced over his shoulder. His brothers were busy—Nate was unrolling the rain curtains and Joseph was securing them in place. The long ride home for his family would be cool but not wet.

He couldn't explain why he felt a warning tingle at the back of his neck, or that instinctive punch to his gut when there was something he ought to be noticing, something that was amiss.

"Need any advice for the wedding night?" Nate hopped down from the buggy with a two-footed thump. Judging by the grin on his face, he was getting a kick out of this.

"I don't need help from you." Maybe the upcoming night was troubling him some. He waited until Joseph was done before he led the gelding, buggy rattling, through the double doors and into the storm. He caught sight of Austin Dermot looking depressed as he tossed back a shot of what looked like whiskey in his front office, poor fellow. He felt bad for the livery owner, but he was glad of the gold ring on his left hand.

He'd won the best gal, and it took all his strength not to let his mind leap ahead of him, but it kept whispering at him and it was hard keeping those whisperings silent. Tonight he would be staying with Melody. They would share a bed and more. He swallowed hard, trying to block images from his mind. Of how desirous she looked with her hair down, of her round full breasts and long legs hidden beneath layers of clothes he would get to peel away one by one.

"Yep, looks like he's sure thinking pretty hard," Joe was saying, his hoot of laughter breaking into Gabe's thoughts. "He must be thinking about the wedding night. I know how taxing that can be on a man, since it's about all I've been thinking about lately."

"Good luck, big brother." Nate clapped him on the shoulder.

"Not to be disrespectful, but have a great night." Joseph winked and shoved something into his hands.

His saddlebag. He'd packed for tonight's stay. Rain cuffed him in cold, wet punches as he watched his brothers leave with the horse and buggy, heading to the hotel three doors down. The feeling of unease intensified. He searched the boardwalks and streets, but nothing odd stood out to him. A man he didn't recognize was turning into a saloon at the end of the street, but that was all.

A crowd gathered beneath the covered boardwalk; his ma and pa were arm in arm. He couldn't remember the last time they'd looked as happy. A dove-gray coat and baby-blue bonnet drew him with a force that made the rain disappear. Her back was to him as she chatted with Savannah and Clara. She stood out, regal as a princess, as gracefully poised as a ballet dancer, and never had he figured such a fine woman would agree to be his. But she was.

And tonight he would make her his completely. He would have the privilege of loosening the button at the base of her throat, of slanting his mouth to hers, of drawing her against him flesh to flesh—

Whoa, there. He clenched his jaw, fisted his hands and still his desire for her inflamed him. His blood thrummed hard enough to echo in his skull, each *thump-thump* a shameful reminder that he was losing control. His emotions were on the edge and ready to fall. He hiked up the boardwalk, glad of the cold rain bathing his face, glad for the company of his family to keep his mind where it belonged.

"Gabe." Melody twirled toward him. She sparkled, reaching out one hand, happy to see him.

His feelings sharpened. Intense. Overwhelming. Never had he expected this, not from a straightforward, simple marriage. He was no prize, but she gazed upon him as if he were the best of men. His throat tightened. He couldn't force his brain to conjure up even one intelligent word. For fear of stuttering and spitting out something unrecognizable, he kept quiet and let Melody's fingers fit between his. Need telegraphed through her touch, need for what he did not think he had to give.

Maybe for her, he should try.

"I'm so proud of you." Ma went up on tiptoe to kiss his cheek, tears threatening again. "And you, Melody. I can't wait to be a proper mother to you. I'm going to bring by a basket of meals to help you out as soon as the renters are out of Gabe's house."

"What house?" She shook her head, stumped. "He said nothing about owning a house."

"Oh, he's had it for years." Mary gave her hand to her husband and allowed him to help her into the front seat of the family buggy. "Gabe used to live there. He said he didn't like doing his own cooking, but I know he's a softy at heart. He needs people around him. He needs love."

"Ma, that's enough." He scowled, and no one looking at him would ever dare to describe him as a softy.

Everyone was laughing as they climbed into the buggy and shouted out merry goodbyes as they drove away. With Gabe at her side, she felt enlivened. Hopeful.

"Why didn't you mention the house before?" She wanted to know.

"It was supposed to be a surprise." He shook his head, scattering his long hair, probably thinking he looked disreputable when in fact he was like a legend standing in the falling twilight, as if part of the night, larger than life.

"I found another house for my renters to live in and they were kind enough to agree to move quickly," he explained as they ambled down the boardwalk together, walking in the rain.

She didn't doubt his renters were friends of his and admired him. She was beginning to see that was how everyone viewed her husband.

"Evenin', Gabe." A solid, pleasant-looking man approaching them on the boardwalk tipped his cap. "Mrs. Brooks."

Mrs. Brooks. That was the first time anyone had called her that. Joy flooded her. She couldn't remember ever feeling as happy. Her shoes didn't seem to touch the boardwalk or to make so much as a ripple in the puddles at her feet. Maybe she *was* floating.

"Good evening to you, Langley," Gabe answered in his rumbling, gruff way.

"I hear congratulations are in order." Mr. Langley did not stop to chat, but turned so he walked backward for a few paces.

"They are. Thanks." Gabe led her around the corner, protecting her from the wind and rain, his closeness the most wonderful thing she'd ever known.

The boardinghouse loomed ahead on Second Street, windows glowing cheerfully. Her stomach fluttered at the thought of him joining her in her room—no, their room. Sure, she was a little nervous, but she would be one with Gabe. She would finally get to discover the bliss of his touch and the heat of his bare skin against hers. She longed to hear her name whispered in the dark. What would loving him be like?

Tender. That was without a doubt. Thrilling. What she wanted more than anything was to be as close to him as she could—and for him to be close to her, to surrender everything.

Her room was at the top of the stairs. He took the key from her and unlocked the door. The hinges squeaked, loud in the silence that had fallen between them. Was he anxious, too? she wondered as she stepped into the room. Her shoes rang in the stillness, her skirts rustling. The lock rattled as Gabe withdrew the key, the hinges squeaked, the door clicked shut and they were alone in the darkness. Anticipation buzzed inside her like a hive of agitated bees. Was he feeling self-conscious, too? Worrying because he wanted everything to be right and wonderful between them?

"I'm leaving tomorrow morning." When he spoke, the confident tones of his voice boomed like thunder, unmistakable and sure. His boots echoed on the hardwood, and as he strode around her, the tiny hairs on her arms stood. His nearness was like a force drawing her to him body and soul.

"And you shall be gone for two weeks?" He had explained to her that his office was the only one in the northwestern section of the territory. He had rounds to make to towns in his jurisdiction. Any problems that arose might keep him out of town longer. At any time he could get a dispatch from the territorial prisons or the governor and leave for an undetermined time.

"The renters have promised to be out by early morning," he continued. There was a scrape of a match tin being drawn across a wooden shelf and the rasp of a match striking. Flame burst to life, light flickering across the contours of Gabe's chin and mouth. The glass chimney gave a muted clink as he lifted it to light the wick. "I hired a cleaning lady to go through the house, so by afternoon you ought to be able to move in."

"Alone?" The word escaped before she could stop it. Of course he would want her to move right away. It wouldn't be financially responsible to pay for a fortnight at the boardinghouse when a home was waiting for her.

"My brothers will bring a horse and wagon with my furniture that had been stored in one of the outsheds on the ranch, load up those trunks of yours and haul it all into the house." He shook out the match. "Keep in mind this is a little place. Two rooms and a couple of bedrooms. It's nothing fancy."

"But it will be our home." He had to know by now she didn't care about grand mansions. She'd lost her family members one by one, those she loved most, and she'd learned one great lesson the hard way—love was the true treasure in life.

"I'll make sure the mercantile and grocery owners know to put any purchases you make on my account." He closed the space between them to help her out of her coat. "I'm sure Ma will be happy to help you unpack and settle in."

"Savannah and Clara, too." She slipped her arms from the garment. The heat from his body and the fan of his breath against the back of her neck made her melt. She ached to lay her cheek against his chest, to have his arms hold her tight.

Soon, she thought. Tonight she would know the tenderness of Gabe's love.

"It's good you have them." Gabe marched to hang up her coat on the wall peg and to slip out of his jacket.

What was he talking about? She'd been so wrapped up in him she'd forgotten everything else. "Oh, Savannah and Clara. I think we are going to be the best of friends."

"So I figured." He knelt in front of the stove. "All that

talk over dinner about sewing together and stitching or some such."

"We were talking about embroidering."

"You are a good match with my family. No wonder my mother picked you." He stirred the embers until they glowed. "I'm glad she did."

That was quite an admission coming from the man of stone, and the warmth of his tone felt delicious. Like the most perfect wedding gift. He might be too tough to say it, but he loved her. She had to believe that was proof. This marriage would not be one-sided after all. She wanted to dance with joy.

"There looks like plenty of light from the lamp for both of us to read by." He closed the stove door and grabbed up his saddlebag. "Does it sound like a good plan to you?"

"The best of plans." The nerves were gone, she realized as she settled onto the cushioned window seat and reached for her book.

They were so alike in ways she'd never imagined. Gabe did not whittle or retreat out to the stables to spend an evening. She didn't know how it was possible that she could fall in love with him more as he drew a volume out of his leather pack. *Journey to the Center of the Earth*, the same title she held in her hand.

Perhaps their match was not one of convenience but of destiny. Smiling, Melody opened her book to the marked page and began to read.

He'd kept an eye on the small clock on the wall, its black hands marking the passage of the evening. Time had slowed down, giving him plenty of chance to worry. He'd been staring at the same page for ten minutes and he still didn't know what it said. Professor Lidenbrock was in great peril, but for the life of him, Gabe couldn't fall into the adventure on the page. Maybe because he had a perfect view of his wife across the top of his book.

She was his wife, his to claim, his to bed. He tore his gaze away from her, hiding a grimace. Not that he wasn't looking forward to that. Laying Melody down on that soft-looking bed and drawing her close was something he was more than happy to get started on. Except for one thing—the way she looked at him. As if she could feel his attention on her, she glanced up from her book. He'd have to be a blind man not to see the affection glimmering in her blue irises.

It will be all right, he told himself. He needed to believe that he hadn't made the worst mistake of his life by marrying her. She ducked back to her book, intent on the story in front of her, and he did the same.

Hell, he tried to. But her beauty lured him from the written word. That, and the need knocking through him. That bed was right in the middle of the room and his field of vision. Want for her strummed through him no matter how hard he fought to control it.

The clock struck nine. To his surprise she closed her book. A delicate flush stole across her cheeks.

"I have an early morning," she explained. "I promised Selma I would continue to work for her."

"I expected that you would quit."

"She needs the help, and I want to contribute. I don't

want to be a burden to you." She set the book aside and stood with a swish of skirts and grace. "You will be out of town half of any given month, and this will fill my time."

"What if I ordered you to quit?" He closed his book and stood, curious what his bride would say.

"Then I would fear something had happened to your mind, perhaps an apoplexy or a blow to the head, because no man I'd marry would be that foolish." Dimples framed her mouth, her amazing mouth. "Isn't that right?"

"I suppose so." He didn't want to admire her. He sure as hell didn't think he would ever be the one without the power in the relationship. He'd best be careful, or he'd be standing on his head just to make Melody happy. No way could he let her mean so much. No way would he ever give her that brand of control over him. "I'll allow you to work, at least for the time being."

"Allow?" She raised one brow, holding back laughter. "Gabe, you've watched your parents over the years. You can't tell me you're unaware of how a marriage works?"

"I know how this marriage is going to work." He set his jaw, determined not to be swayed by her playful humor. "The man is the head of the household."

"Poor, poor Gabe. You are about to be terribly disillusioned." She swirled by him with a whisper of petticoats and sass. "I hope you didn't think I would be one of those submissive wives unable to speak up for myself."

"No, I didn't. But a man can hold out hope, can't he?"

"Hope? You never had a chance of that." She let down

her hair, and it tumbled in a riot of honeyed silk over her slender shoulders and bounced against her lean back.

The bureau's round beveled mirror tossed her reflection to him. There was a secret smile shaping her mouth—that mouth he could not wait to claim—and if the faintest trace of tenderness shot to life in his chest, he did his best to fight it down. He intended to keep his desire for his wife free of emotional entanglements. The one thing she didn't get was authority over his heart.

"If I can't have a submissive wife, then I suppose I'm glad to have you." He crossed to her, put his hands on her shoulders.

"You *suppose?*"

"Fine. I know. You're everything I've ever wanted in a wife."

"Wanted?"

"Hell. *Dreamed* of. Are you happy now?"

"Blissfully." She turned, the weight of his hands light as he pulled her into his arms, against the comfort of his chest. She relaxed against him, savoring the moment. He felt as invincible as he looked, but his touch to her chin was gentle. He tipped her face to his. His eyes went dark, and she could feel his heartbeat racing beneath the flat of her palm, as crazy as her own fluttering pulse. The line of his mouth eased and closer he came, inch by inch until his lips slanted over hers in the lightest kiss.

Sensation washed through her like a slam of an intense ocean wave. Startled, she gasped and he kissed her again, one mesmerizing brush of his lips after another. His mouth was hot velvet. His kiss was like being swept out on a dizzying, exhilarating sea. A thousand lapping waves of pleasure coursed through her as she curled her fingers into his shirt and held on, wanting more.

He obliged with a groan and twined his fingers into her hair, cradling her neck as he deepened the kiss. At the first sweep of his tongue against the seam of her lips, she opened for him. Her eyes drifted shut, and she was lost. Did he know how much she loved him? Could he feel it in the tenderness of her kiss?

"You're trembling." He broke away, one hand at her nape, the other tenderly cradling her jaw and cheek.

"You overwhelm me."

"I'm not done yet, so I'd better get you sitting down." He didn't want to admit he felt a little shaky himself. She was like fine whiskey a man wanted to savor, but it packed a punch. Sweat popped out on his brow as he led her around the corner of the bed and waited while she sat on the edge.

"Better?" he asked.

"That was quite a kiss." She nodded, blushing.

"Glad you liked it," he quipped, settling onto the mattress beside her.

"Very much." Her confession was accompanied by another shy blush.

He hardly recognized her. Starry-eyed and dreamy, she looked untouched and untroubled, a bride awaiting her beloved. She was lustrous, her gaze gentle with the most amazing affection he'd ever seen. He wanted nothing more than to unbutton her pearl by pearl, to peel back the layers of cotton and silk and kiss the treasures hidden there, to touch every part of her, to hear her call his name with her release.

But her touch stopped him. The brush of her hand to his jaw should have been pleasurable, just simple physical attraction between a man and his wife. But it went deeper, as if she were trying to touch a more intimate place within him, a place he could not go.

"I love you, Gabe." Her bashful confession confirmed his worst fears.

"Love?" He pulled away from her, hating the hurt that pinched instantly across her beautiful face. Panic overwhelmed him. He leaped to his feet and paced the length of the room, his steps ringing with fury. His emotions felt too powerful, ready to rise up and take him over. The lure of her love tightened around him like a noose and he had to throw it off, stay in control, keep his defenses strong.

"I thought you understood." He ground out the words, doing his best to soften his tone, but they came out like blows. "I don't love you. I don't want to love you. Love has no place in this marriage."

"But I can't help what I feel." Tears silvered her eyes, hovering, but did not fall. "I thought you felt the same. I thought I sensed it from you—"

"This isn't a fairy tale." He raked his hands through his hair. Furious, coming apart at the seams. "We had an agreement, Melody."

"I know." Miserable, she blinked back her tears, spine straight, chin up, refusing to let them fall.

She sat there fighting so hard. She was a good woman— she would be a good wife. That's all he'd ever wanted.

Something guaranteed, something predictable, something that wouldn't twist him all up in knots, turn him upside down and leave him raw and bleeding from the inside out.

Looked as if it was too late for that.

"I need to take a walk," he said and, tempering his anger the best he could, he grabbed his coat from the peg and walked out of the room.

Chapter Eight

Melody squeezed her eyes shut, the click of the door echoing in the shadowed corners and in the chambers of her heart. Gabe's anger bounced around in her skull, obliterating the pure, sweet love that had infiltrated every part of her. She went cold, unable to forget what he'd said. *I don't love you. I don't want to love you. Love has no place in this marriage.*

He's decided not to love me, she realized, opening her eyes and dashing the tears from them. *He means to never love me.*

She swallowed hard, willing back her shattered hopes and dreams and all the love her heart could hold. The ring of pearls and sapphires winked on her left hand, taunting her with the truth. From the first, she'd known how Gabe felt. He had told her exactly what he wanted from their marriage. He'd been quite clear. *The comforts a woman brings to a man's life,* he'd said. *Three meals a day, a nice home, clean clothes.*

She'd been the foolish one. She had confused necessity with romance and duty with desire, but she'd wanted

Gabe's love. She'd wanted too much. She sniffed, blinking hard enough to drive the tears back where they'd come from.

This wasn't Gabe's fault. It was hers. She had done this to herself. The blame was hers alone. He was out there in the cold rainy night, angry and alone and disappointed in her. Did he think she had betrayed him? What if he'd lost his respect for her?

Anguish tore a cry from her throat, and she covered her mouth with her left hand, her gold wedding band warm against her skin. She had meant to love him. What if she'd destroyed her chance for happiness? The image of Gabe storming from the room haunted her. If only she could call him back, turn back time and relive the past few moments. What if she'd never been so naive as to blurt out her love for him? Then he would be with her right now, spoiling her with his amazing kisses and showing her all the ways a man could cherish his wife.

Instead she was alone with the truth, one that she could never have kept hidden, not in the end. Eventually they would have come to this place—torn apart irrevocably because she wanted a real marriage.

He did not.

Gabe wasn't in the best of moods. He'd walked around town last night until the high mountain temperatures had driven him back to Melody's room. He'd found her asleep, slipped beneath the warm covers without waking her and had lain there, staring up at the ceiling wishing he had made a different choice. But if he'd slept in the office, his coworkers would have known. If he'd chosen the livery stable, then Austin Dermot would have known. He already had a crush on Melody. No way did he want any man thinking the marriage was rocky and she was up for grabs. But he couldn't be what she wanted.

He took one last glance at Melody asleep, her riot of golden hair fanning across the snowy pillow slip, her delicate features relaxed, looking so small and vulnerable his emotions flared. Tenderness, caring, something more—something he was reluctant to name—and he battled every emotion down. He hiked his saddlebag onto his shoulder and pulled the door closed quietly, carefully releasing the handle. As he took the stairs, his step the only sound in the sleeping boardinghouse, he shored up his defenses.

He'd done the right thing walking away last night. It was better than leading her on. He stalked out into the crisp morning. The rain had stopped, but water was puddled everywhere, muddying the roads and making the boardwalk slick. Tobacco smoke carried on the brisk wind. He glanced over his shoulder and saw a stranger turn the corner toward Main. His instincts didn't stand up and take note, but he was heading that way anyhow, so he picked up his pace. He knew everyone in this town and most folks for fifty miles in any direction. The stranger might be passing through—there was a cheap hotel not far from the boardinghouse. That might explain his presence, Gabe thought, but with what he knew about Melody's past, he wanted to make sure.

The instant he rounded the corner, his suspicions eased.

Maybe after last night his instincts were off-kilter—or maybe the newcomer meant no trouble. He wasn't hurrying along looking nervous or furtive but taking his time. The stranger nodded to Mac as the lawman came in sight, then ducked into Letty's diner.

"Surprised to see you this time of morning." Mac called out from the middle of the street. Not a horse was in sight, so he stood there, smirking. "More than that, I'm surprised you have enough starch to be out and about. Shouldn't you be with your bride?"

"I'm leaving town, remember? My turn for rounds." He jammed his hands into his pockets—the wind still had a nip to it—and took one final glance into the diner. The stranger—blond hair, medium build, buffalo coat—was dressed like any rancher in these parts. Nothing seemed amiss, so he joined his buddy in the street. "I don't like leaving today—"

"I'm sure Jeremiah will trade with you. He's still a bachelor."

"That's not fair to him, and besides, I'll have to go eventually." He was torn up inside and felt turned upside down, so the time away would do him good.

"I can't think your wife would want you to leave her."

"Melody is a practical woman." Most times. "She understands the nature of my work."

"All right. I'll get coffee perking at the office if you want to saddle up."

"Do me a favor, will you?" Gabe broke off, heading toward the livery. "My brothers will be keeping an eye on Melody. Can I ask you to do the same?"

"Count on it, buddy." Mac waved from the far side of the street. A family man himself—he was married with a little one on the way—he understood.

At least Melody would be safe. Grateful, Gabe shoved open the barn's heavy door. His back was to the board-walk, so he didn't see the stranger in the buffalo coat poke his head out the diner door or get a glimpse of the .45 at his hip.

I've faced harder days, she thought as she brushed her hair. *No one has died. I've lost nothing that I didn't have in the first place.* She set down the brush and picked up the comb, studying the pale woman in the mirror. Dark circles bruised the fragile skin beneath her eyes. She'd slept poorly and it showed. Worse, she feared her broken heart did, too. She'd wanted Gabe's love so much.

When she'd awoken, he was gone. His things were gone. Except for the slight indentation on her second pillow and the barely mussed covers on his side of the bed, it was as if he'd never been there at all.

She parted her hair down the middle and divided it into sections. If only she could figure out how best to handle this loveless marriage she'd gotten herself into.

With dignity, she decided as she began to braid. She would go on in the same way she'd started, intent on building a life with Gabe. She would set up their house, do her best to make a home for him as he'd asked, and work on her cooking skills. She knew she could rely on the women in the family for help.

At the thought of Mary, Savannah and Clara, a minuscule warmth edged into her, easing a small part of her misery. At least she wasn't completely alone. She had family, a place to belong and people to love. But it was a tiny comfort. She'd ruined everything with Gabe. He had meant what he said. He wanted a convenient marriage—not just for now, but forever.

The ring on her finger glinted mockingly. Well, she might never have Gabe's love, but she had known it from the start. Gabe had been honest, and a loveless relationship was what she'd agreed to. Now it was time to keep her word. Maybe one day Gabe would trust her and consent to touch her again, and she could look forward to children, their babies to love.

She tied a bit of ribbon at the end of her plait just as a man's heavy boot steps sounded outside her door. Gabe? Was there any chance he was feeling remorse, too? Or worse, what if he wanted to annul the marriage?

The glass knob turned. Had she forgotten to lock it when she'd fetched wash water? The door swung open with a bang and a man launched himself through the doorway. Before she could open her mouth to scream, he wrapped his hand around her throat, pulling her roughly against him with the nose of a revolver cold at her temple.

"You're about to become a widow," Derrick, real and not a nightmare, hissed against her ear.

A widow? Panic scrambled her brain. She couldn't pull her thoughts together. If she were a widow, then that would mean Gabe was dead.

"No way would I let that two-bit lawman get what belongs to me." His hatred beat with each word, his breathing ragged, his entire body quaking. A man on the edge.

Think, Melody. She gasped, fighting to draw in breath, willing down the icy fear threatening to take over. At least Gabe wasn't here. With any luck, he was already out of town. He would be safe. That's all that mattered.

"You can h-have the money," she stammered. "Gabe doesn't know about it."

"It doesn't work that way, Melody. Control of your inheritance goes to the man who marries you, and it's a fortune. Do you know how bad I need that money?" His fingers at her throat became bruising and cut off her air.

"Let. Me. Go." She rasped the words, the pressure on her throat becoming a tearing pain. She couldn't breathe.

"Believe me, I earned your inheritance. Courting you was torture. All the tedious pretending. Do you think I enjoyed it? You were to get so much money, when I don't stand to inherit a penny. I couldn't stomach looking at you, and you didn't even know." Wrath blasted her with each word, and the gun dug into her temple painfully. "Now it doesn't matter. I want my money."

"Der-rick." She forced his name out with the last of her breath. Terror. Last time she'd seen his temper, he'd knocked her around and thrown objects at her. This time she knew she wouldn't be as fortunate to escape.

"All the time I wasted with you. Those endless trips to the bookstore, sitting hours on the damn porch listening to you go on about this charity and that." His face contorted with selfish jealousy and rage.

Her throat burned and her lungs were ready to burst.

Her consciousness narrowed to that one need, her body straining to breathe, her eyes watering at the pressure. She grasped his hand with hers, fighting to break his hold.

"You're coming with me," he said, as if from far away. "With him gone, no one back home will know. There will be no one to claim your money but me. We'll marry and…"

Gone? The thought of Gabe gunned down horrified her. She had to stop it, do whatever it took to save him. She tore at Derrick's grip, but her hands weren't strong enough—she couldn't win. Spots danced in front of her eyes and she fought it. She had to stay conscious. She had to figure out a way to save Gabe.

"Now, you're going to cooperate, aren't you? If you don't, I swear I will—"

A board creaked outside the open door, the sound louder to her than the rush of blood in her ears. Derrick must have heard it, too, because he fell silent. As he spun around to face the threshold, his grip on her throat eased. Something else grabbed his attention. She drew in a lungful of wonderful air, the ringing in her head quieted and she could see a dark figure poised in the doorway, his hands at his sides as if ready to draw, a man of stone.

Gabe.

Chapter Nine

Gabe stared disbelieving at the man using Melody as a shield, his white-knuckled hand at her throat, the other holding a .45 against her head. He read the terror on her face, the concern for him in her eyes and his mind leaped ahead, racing along on a future chain of events that hadn't happened yet—the gun firing, Melody falling, her life gone.

Agony ripped through him with more force than a bullet and he drew. Time slowed down, seconds stretched as if each were a lifetime. Siting, exhaling, squeezing the trigger; Gabe didn't think, he simply acted. The flash as the Colt fired, the bang and recoil that jerked through his arm, his aim true. Surprise warred with the fury on Derrick's face and he reacted a second too late. The bullet tore into him, the gun tumbled from his hand and Gabe caught Melody in his arms before she hit the floor.

Never in his life had he been so scared. Blood speckled her, so he caressed the curve of her head with one hand, making sure she was not hurt. The thought drained the life out of him. But his hand came away fine and relief cannoned through him. She was safe. She was unharmed. Gratitude dropped him to his knees and he held her tight and for all he was worth.

"Oh, G-Gabe." She choked out his name, burying her face in the hollow of his throat. Her arms wound around his neck tightly; no one had ever held on to him like that.

No one—*ever*—had mattered so much. Unbearable tenderness crashed through him, battering the walls around his heart until they fell to pieces and he was helpless. He kissed her forehead, vulnerable as she lifted her face to his.

"I could have lost you." He'd been prideful, too sure that being a tough, invincible man was more admirable than a besotted one. "What do you think you were doing, trying to get yourself shot like that?"

"You're scolding me?" She sniffled, half laughing, half crying. "He wanted to gun you down. When I saw you standing in the doorway, all I could think was that you were going to be k-killed and I would never see you again."

"That's what I thought, too." Every instinct he had shouted at him to move away, get some distance between them, get rid of the emotions running rampant like a flash flood and pretend his defenses had never fallen.

But he'd never thought about what his life would be without Melody. He could see it now. Cold and dull, like a world without color to brighten it, like winter without spring to thaw it. That wasn't the life he wanted. "All I could think about was how I left things last night. The things I said to you."

"You were being honest, that's all." She sat up, deftly pushing away from him as if she were the one with the greater strength. "You were right. I need to stick to our agreement. You'll have the marriage you want, I give you my word. As long as you're okay. You're here. You're alive. I can't believe you drew so fast. I've never seen anything like that."

"I'm rumored to be one of the fastest draws in the territory. Guess it came in handy today." He eased down onto the floor facing her, reaching out to take her left hand in his.

The ring he'd placed there was a token of his solemn vows and reminded him of how he'd failed her. Melody didn't deserve a man who couldn't love her. She deserved a man with the courage to give her everything he had inside him. Sure, that was a scary thought, but he tamped down the panic, left the walls around his heart down and gently kissed her hand.

"I'm sorry for the things I said." He'd never meant anything more. "Marriage shouldn't be a convenient arrangement of duty and obligation, and it's not what I want, not anymore."

"It isn't?" Hope brightened within her, the woman he treasured beyond imagining.

"I love you, Melody." When she smiled, he smiled. When joy filled her, it filled him. Maybe it wasn't so bad being this vulnerable to the right woman, one he could trust, one he needed with every fiber of his being. "Be my wife, my life, my everything. That's what I want from this moment forward."

"I do, too."

Maybe it was his imagination, but she looked even more desirable, her lush soft mouth even more tempting. How could a loving husband resist kissing his precious wife? Gabe cupped her chin in the palm of his hand and kissed her gently.

Epilogue

Two years later

Spring chased the shiver from the wind and Gabe was glad for it as he hiked along the garden path. Lamplight glowed through the windows as if to welcome him home. After a long fortnight on the trail hunting a fugitive, he wanted nothing more than to haul his wife into his arms and hold her until the ache of missing her was gone.

He stepped onto the porch. Hungry for the first sight of his wife, his gaze searched the windows until he found her in the rocking chair, her hair captured in twin braids. She was wearing a light green calico dress and looking sweet as a May day. The loving smile on her face added luster to her new mother's radiance as she gazed at the tiny bundle asleep in her arms.

Love filled him. They had gotten off to a rocky start, but that was his fault alone. From the day the walls around his heart had come down, they had stayed down. After shipping Derrick Spade's body back to Boston, he'd discovered he'd married not only the most beautiful woman in the world but an heiress, too. If anything would have made him revert to his old self, that would have done it, fearing she would leave him when he turned over control of her trust to her. But it didn't. Good thing, too, because she didn't leave him. She donated her vast inheritance to several charities without regret. She'd explained to him that she already had the greater treasure.

She was wrong about that. He was the lucky one. *She* was the greatest treasure of all.

He opened the door. Warmth from the stove washed over him, the scent of a pot roast in the oven made his mouth water, but Melody's smile welcoming him was the best part of coming home. He shucked off his coat, laid his saddlebag on the floor and kept his step quiet as he crossed the room.

"Welcome home," Melody whispered so as not to wake the baby. "I missed you so much."

"Not as much as I've missed you." He went down on his knees beside her, awash with devotion. "Nothing beats being with you. You made pot roast."

"I hear it's your favorite."

"You heard right. Deciding to snap you up when I did was the best decision I've made to date. Look what I've gained." Trouble twinkled in his eyes.

"What you've *gained?*" She arched an eyebrow.

"A wife to cook and clean for me. I left my dirty laundry by the door."

"Are you sure you don't want to rephrase that statement?" Happiness bubbled up inside her and it was hard to keep a straight face.

"Hold on, let me finish." Wicked, that's what he was, and he knew it. "I was also going to say that I'm lucky enough to have you for my wife. You are my heart."

"And you are mine. I love you, Gabe."

"I love you more." His baritone rang low, layered with adoration and commitment.

"Lucky me." She couldn't get enough of looking at him, of drinking in every detail. She'd longed for him day and night while he'd been gone, aching for the gentleness of his touch and the bliss of his love.

"Has our boy been giving you any trouble?"

"Only the best kind." It ought to have been impossible to be any happier, but more joy rose through her as they gazed down at their son, little Adam Gabriel, his button face scrunched up, his dark tousled hair the same shade as his pa's. He was a wonder, perfect and dear. The proof of their love, the most precious gift of all.

"I bet Ma stopped by every day I was gone to see this little guy."

"Every day." Not that she minded. Mary wasn't just a mother-in-law, but a true mother. She'd been by to help out in every way she could, not only to dote on her new grandson. "I'm afraid that she's doing too much, what with helping out with Savannah's new son and Clara's baby daughter."

"We're keeping her busy, that's for sure, but trust me. This is what she wanted. Ma is living her best dream, and so am I." The way Gabe lit up, she knew it was true.

"Did I mention how much I love my husband?" she asked, blinking hard to keep the happy tears at bay.

"No, why don't you show me?" His eyes darkened, both loving and desiring at once.

She intended to do just that. She tingled with anticipation as his lips claimed hers, promising a lifetime of love to come.

* * * * *

MARRIED
IN MISSOURI

Carolyn Davidson

Dear Reader

Once more I've met and married off two delightful characters. They were born and lived in my imagination for several weeks as I wrote their story for this anthology. Lucas and Elizabeth had a tough row to hoe, making a marriage work in a situation that was not conducive to happy-ever-after. Just my sort of story, and I enjoyed solving their problems and watching them fall in love.

I write old-fashioned love stories for you, my readers. My mail tells me that many of you involve yourselves in the lives and loves I create on my computer. And those of you who have shared my work with me, and even written me lovely notes of appreciation for the stories I've created, I thank you from the bottom of my heart.

Brides are always a marvellous subject, allowing a writer to take off in many directions. And marriages of convenience were much the norm in days gone by. Unlike many unions today, marriage in the nineteenth century was a 'for ever' business, and not entered into lightly. It is of those long-ago times that I write, for I sometimes think I should have been born a hundred years or so before my time. I yearn for an old-fashioned lifestyle, the values cherished by so many in those days, and the simple pleasures of hearth and home that made up towns and villages and the families they sheltered.

But we live in the here and now, and it is only in our imaginations that we can travel through time to the olden days. I hope my stories continue to please those of you who have become my friends throughout the past years. Sit back and read about Lucas and Elizabeth, share their lives for a short while and know that they were created with loving care from this author.

Carolyn Davidson

Dedication:

This story was written with my daughter-in-law, Rebecca,
peeking over my shoulder. Perhaps not literally,
but certainly in spirit, for she was enthusiastic
over the finished product and has been a cheering section
of one for this writer. To you, Rebecca,
I offer this novella with my love and appreciation.

Prologue

Boston, Massachusetts
May, 1869

The piece of newsprint was folded and creased, the result of having been opened and read many times over. Now it was drawn from Elizabeth Collins's pocket for the first time today, then offered to her friend Laura. The ad appeared to be forthright enough. It asked for a woman of mature age, experienced with children and able to travel to Missouri with the purpose of marriage in mind.

The gentleman described in the ad was Lucas Harrison, a man in his mid-thirties, who farmed over two hundred acres outside the town of Thomasville, southwest of St. Louis. A widower with two children, he was seeking a woman willing to become his wife and tend to his home and family.

"I've decided I can do that," Elizabeth said stoutly. "I've been tending children most of my life, and I can cook and sew and keep house with the best of them. And I'm definitely of mature age."

"I'd say so, being as your thirtieth birthday is right around the corner, so to speak," her friend Laura said, laughing at the face Elizabeth made in response to her blunt language.

"I sent off a letter to the man over three weeks ago," Elizabeth said quietly, and Laura made the expected response.

"You what?"

"You heard me. I sent him my acceptance, should he be willing to consider me for the job of tending his children and his home. And according to the mail I picked up at the post office this morning, I'll soon be in Missouri."

"He's not asking for a cook or child tender, Lizzie, but a *wife*."

"I'm willing to be a wife. In fact, I was more than willing before Amos Rogers jilted me for my sister." A fact Elizabeth admitted with reluctance, for she'd thought herself in love with Amos, and heartbroken at his perfidy. If she'd experienced a sense of relief over the past years that Amos had jilted her so unexpectedly, it was kept to herself. For after watching his seeming inability to accept the responsibilities of his position as husband and father to two children, Elizabeth recognized her own disdain for the man. Watching her sister's unhappiness with Amos, Elizabeth knew she was the more fortunate of the two women, and she was ready and willing to seek her fortune elsewhere. As wife to Lucas Harrison.

Laura sniffed disdainfully as she spoke her mind on the matter of Amos and his wife. "I always knew Sissy was a troublemaker. She proved it the day she walked down the aisle to Amos."

Elizabeth nodded and shrugged her acceptance of the fact. "Well, she's the one married, and I'm the one left to answer an ad in the newspaper for a mail-order bride, it seems."

"Are you sure you're not just looking for a chance to leave your beloved sister and her husband behind and get as far from Boston as you can go?" Laura asked.

"I'm sure that's part of my reason. I hate watching Amos playing my sister for a fool, leaving her to tend two babies while he waltzes around flirting with other women. It seems that he only wanted Sissy until after they were well married and she began having babies. Then he was ready for new game, and she's the one picking up the pieces.

"Another part of my reason for answering the ad is I've always yearned to see the western half of the country, and this might be my only chance. Even if it means I'll be married and tied to a man and his sons. If I stay here, what future do I have?" she asked her friend, but then answered her own query. "I'll be keeping house for the rest of my days for the local minister. Or running the quilting society."

"You've done all that and more," Laura said.

"And where has it got me? Without a husband or a home of my own. Now I have a chance for both in my future. It seems that Lucas Harrison has accepted my offer, and I'll be a married lady with two children right off the bat. A house to run and a family to tend. That's exactly what I've always wanted, Laura. A home of my own. It's for certain I won't live with my sister and Amos, even though Sissy has made it plain she'd gladly give over the care of her children if I wanted to move in with them. I'd never leave my parents for such a reason. But leaving home with a marriage and a family in my future is a different matter altogether."

"That's true enough. And heaven knows you have experience enough with tending children. You've put in six years at the orphanage looking after the children there—what the church board would call your Christian duty, for lack of better words."

"Well, whatever you call it, it's certainly prepared me for the job in question, Laura. I can be a proper mama to two dear little boys. And I've already made arrangements to leave on Monday morning. I'll take a train to St. Louis and then a stagecoach to Thomasville, where I'll be met by Lucas Harrison. He's sent me the fare and asked that I wire him my expected time of arrival."

Laura sat back on the sofa, stunned by the rapid turn of events. "I didn't realize you were this serious about it, Lizzie. It's a big move to make."

"I'm going home to pack, and come Monday, I'll be gone. You can tell my sister goodbye for me when you see her next."

Laura's face lit with surprise. "Your family isn't to know where you've gone, are they?"

"I'll not tell any of them ahead of time, for once I've gone, it'll be too late to try to talk me out of it. And my mind is made up. I'm going to Thomasville, Missouri."

Laura sighed and shook her head. "To get married to a stranger."

"Exactly."

Chapter One

Thomasville, Missouri
June, 1869

Lucas Harrison read the wire he held in his hand. Just received from Otto, the gentleman in the railway office, it was no surprise to him, yet he knew it signaled a turning point in his life. One he would not be able to reverse, even if he so chose. "Will arrive Wednesday on morning stage."

"That says it all," he muttered, stuffing the paper into his pocket and meeting the puzzled gaze of the station-master as he did so. "I'm gonna get married, Otto," he said with a smile.

"Kinda sudden, ain't it?" Otto asked. He was new to the job. The tracks from St. Louis were only just being laid, and the first task was to ready the station in Thomasville for the eventual appearance of a daily train from the city. But in the meantime, Otto had been hired to oversee the work in preparation for the big event. And to man the telegraph line from the city.

Lucas laughed as he thought of the *sudden* decision

he'd made. "Naw. Been a widower for three years, and my young'uns need a new mama and my house could use some help." His brow furrowed as he considered his decision. He was tired of being mother and father both to his sons, and it was more than true that the house was suffering the loss of a woman's hand. Even with his willingness to tackle the job, he'd found that farming his two hundred acres and tending to the boys was more of a job than he could handle alone.

Otto's voice cut into his meandering thoughts. "Your house needs a woman who knows how to clean. Is that what you mean?" Otto Cunningham had visited the farm more than once over the past months and knew the state of the Harrison home.

Lucas grinned. "I'll be the first to admit I'm not much of a hand with scrubbin' my duds out on a washboard, and my cooking leaves a bit to be desired, you might say." And wasn't that the understatement of the year? Burned eggs and tough beefsteaks were getting mighty hard to tolerate.

Otto leaned over the counter, speaking in a low voice, as though he offered a secret into Lucas's hearing. "There's plenty of women hereabouts who'd jump at the chance to marry Lucas Harrison, in case you didn't know it."

"Maybe so, but none of them is what I've got in mind. I had a wife who was just about perfect. In fact, the only thing Doris did that upset me was to die and leave me with the two children." *That, and the fact that she was not cut out to be a farmer's wife, what with her dainty ways and tendency to sicken and go to bed at the drop of a hat.*

Otto nodded sagely. "Yup, I'd say that was enough to upset any man."

"Well, I looked over the whole town, and the only women who were available were either too full of themselves to be a farmer's wife or looked to be dragging their feet when it came to takin' on another woman's children. I looked high and low for a decent candidate and there wasn't one hereabouts that fit the bill when it came to my children. And that's one thing I won't back down from. This gal says she's looked after young'uns aplenty and she can cook and sew and keep house. What more can a man ask?"

"Maybe a pretty face and a shape that wouldn't scare off a suitor?"

Lucas shrugged. "I'll settle for a kind disposition and a willingness to work. I'm willing to overlook a few faults in a woman if she can measure up to what I've got in mind. Large or skinny, homely or easy to look at, it doesn't make a whole lot of difference to me."

Otto looked at his pocket watch and offered a view of it to his friend. "We'll soon know what she looks like, anyway. That stage is due to roll down the road in about an hour. Good luck, Lucas. I have a notion you're gonna need it."

With a wave of his hand at Otto, Lucas took his leave of the stationmaster and walked back to the general store where his rig was parked, his team tied to the hitching rail before the emporium. He went inside and approached the counter. "You got my order of hardware all ready for me, Harvey? I'll be headin' home in about an hour."

"I'll have my boy load it up in the back of your wagon, Lucas." He glanced behind his customer. "Where's your young'uns?"

"Left them over at the barbershop. Thought it was a good idea to get their ears lowered a bit this morning. And I'm glad I did. My bride is going to arrive on the morning stage from St. Louis in about an hour."

"Otto said you were looking for a lady to show up. She's finally gonna make it, huh?"

"I put an ad in the newspaper—several papers, in fact—all over the East Coast. Got a few answers, and this one seemed to be the best of the bunch."

"Does the lady have a name?" Harvey asked.

"She's Elizabeth Collins. Formerly of Boston."

"Soon to be Elizabeth Harrison, of Thomasville, Missouri."

"That's the plan," Lucas felt a surge of elation that his plan was coming to pass.

Harvey held up a hand. "Listen. Ain't that the stage now? It's early."

"Sure is." Lucas drew his pocket watch from his trousers and checked the time. "Almost forty minutes early, as a matter of fact. Must have harnessed up some fast horses at the last way station."

He turned with a wave of his hand and walked to the front of the store. Through the door he watched as the stagecoach pulled up with a flourish before the hotel, directly across the street. The driver jumped down and tossed three bags from the top of the coach, a cloud of dust billowing as they hit the ground.

He opened the door and as Lucas watched, he handed a lady from the interior, a dark-garbed woman of perhaps thirty years of age, dark-haired beneath the bonnet she wore. She spoke to the driver and he waved at the hotel, apparently designating it as the place for her to wait. Then he deposited her luggage on the porch beside her before he climbed atop his coach and snapped the reins over his team of horses.

"There's my bride," Lucas said quietly, taking note of the lady's height, for she was a tall one. Not particularly pretty, but presentable, he decided. Definitely with a hefty shape, and healthy looking to boot.

He left the general store and strode across to the hotel, lifting a hand in greeting. "Ma'am? I'm Lucas Harrison. I take it you're the lady who wrote me in answer to my ad?"

"I'm Elizabeth Collins, sir," she replied, meeting his gaze with a forthright look from blue eyes.

He stepped up onto the sidewalk beside her and nodded at her bags. "I'll take these over to my rig. I'm in front of the dry goods store across the road. You want to wait here till I load them up?"

"I'll wait." Her stance was unchanging, her posture erect, her hands clasped before her. Purely a lady, through and through, Lucas thought with a smile. Staunch and sturdy, a true New Englander.

Lucas picked up the bags, stowing one beneath his arm, his grip on the other two firm as he lifted them and toted them to the wagon, where they fit nicely next to his supplies from the emporium. Untying the team from the hitching rail, he grasped the bridle and turned the horses, then crossed the road to where Elizabeth, his bride, waited.

He stepped onto the sidewalk and led her to the rig. His hands fit against her waist neatly and he lifted her onto the seat, unable to help noting the feel of her in his grasp. She was no lightweight, that was for certain, but her body was that of a woman, not a girl. She had hips enough to spare and her bosom was worthy of the name. He could not help but feel a surge of desire as he looked up at blue eyes and dark hair, and a face that was strong and lips that pressed together with determination.

His seat beside her was easily gained and he turned his team to the barbershop, where his children awaited his return. Josh was at the doorway, Toby already on the sidewalk, both of them sporting fresh haircuts, their tan line far below the edge of their shorn locks.

"Pa, we wondered where you was," Josh said, climbing up onto the back of the wagon. His brother squirmed to a seat beside him, both of them settling behind the wooden seat.

"I went to pick up Miss Collins from the stage stop," Lucas said briefly. He introduced the boys, then turned to the woman who had come here to be his bride.

"We can do this one of two ways, ma'am—either go to the minister's home now and have a ceremony, or you might want to take a look at what you're getting into, first. I'll be happy to take you to my farm for a look-see and let you make up your own mind."

"I made up my mind when I sent you an acceptance

letter, sir," she said quietly. "I have nothing to return to Boston for. I've cut all ties there. So unless you've changed your mind over the past few minutes, I'm ready to marry you now."

"That will put you smack-dab in my bedroom come nightfall, ma'am," he said quietly, lest his sons hear his words. "If you want to wait, you can take your time about it, but it will happen one time or another, so far as I'm concerned."

She looked up at him and her gaze was direct. "I have no need to consider the matter, Lucas. I said I'd marry you and it might as well be today as tomorrow. I'm well aware that being married generally includes sharing a bed. It's not called a marriage bed without good reason."

"That's what I was hoping you'd say, ma'am," he said with a grin and turned his buggy toward the community church, sitting back from the road at the end of the town proper. Next to it was a small dwelling—the parsonage where the minister, Reverend Blake, and his family lived.

The wagon pulled in front of the parsonage and Lucas jumped down, motioning to his sons to follow his lead. He assisted Elizabeth from her seat and took her arm, placing her hand on his forearm and walking with her through the open gate and up to the porch.

This was the final moment in which to change her mind, Elizabeth realized. But one long look at the man by her side gave her the reassurance she sought, for he was tall and well built, a man fit to run a farm and tend to a wife and children. His eyes were direct as they met hers and his raised brow asked a silent question of her.

Is this what you want, Elizabeth? The message was clear to her, almost as if he'd asked it aloud, and she tilted her chin and tossed him a look of her own. She hadn't traveled more miserable miles than she wanted to count to back out now. She'd marry him and take her chances, for he certainly looked to be a finer figure of a man than Amos.

Lucas nodded as he rapped at the door, and in mere moments they were ushered into the parlor, where the minister awaited them.

"I was at the bank when the stage came in and I hurried back home. I had a suspicion you'd be here right quick, Lucas," he said with a wide grin. "When I saw the lady arrive I assumed it was your bride. The whole town is atwitter at the news that you'd sent for a lady from back East to marry. This is the bride, I believe?"

"Sure enough," Lucas said, his high cheekbones ruddy as he performed the introductions. "This is Elizabeth Collins, sir. We'd like you to perform the ceremony for us today."

Elizabeth offered her hand to the minister, and it was taken in a gentlemanly manner and held for just a moment before he turned to his wife, who was standing next to him, and introduced Elizabeth to her.

"I have my book of prayers in my pocket, and if you two are ready, we'll go ahead with the ceremony, Lucas. I think it is prudent to have it done today rather than take the lady to your farm for any length of time without a marriage taking place. Gossip is too ready to begin when the ladies of the town are given food for their mill."

"I agree totally, Reverend," Elizabeth said, meeting his gaze and smiling. She took her place by Lucas's side and waited for the man to begin the ceremony.

It lasted but four or five minutes, and when he pronounced them husband and wife, Lucas turned to her and bent to drop a quick caress on her cheek. She was relived that he hadn't claimed a proper kiss, for she would have been most embarrassed by such a gesture. The warmth of his lips against her face seemed more the proper thing to do, and she smiled up at him. And then she realized Lucas was much taller than she. She'd been accustomed to looking down at most gentlemen of her acquaintance and surely her new husband was at least six inches taller than Amos. A fact that pleased her for some silly reason.

Elizabeth was within two inches of being six feet tall, the bane of her existence at home in Boston, where the accepted height for a woman topped out at three or four inches over the five-foot mark.

She'd been an anomaly all her life, from the time she was but a girl, for her father's height had been hers to inherit, instead of the petite blond looks and stature of her mother. Her sister, Sissy, had inherited those attributes, and had used them to her own gain, with young men thronging about her for several years—before she'd married Elizabeth's beau, the duplicitous Amos Rogers. At that thought, Elizabeth breathed a sigh of relief that she'd escaped the marriage Sissy was now a part of. Any man who would so easily go from one lady to another was surely the lowest of the low. And Amos fit the bill.

Even though Sissy was small and blond and pretty,

Elizabeth knew she herself was a handsome woman, with the blue eyes and dark hair of her Irish father. All her life she'd dealt with the height she'd been gifted from him, and she was relieved beyond measure to find that her new husband was more than she could have dreamed of.

"Shall we go home, Mrs. Harrison?" Lucas asked her in an undertone, his eyes scanning her face as if to gauge her mood.

"Yes, of course. I'll be able to prepare supper for all of us. We can have a celebration." She included the two boys in her reply, eager to know them by name, and more than ready to put into practice her experience with children. She would finally have a family of her own, with two ready-made sons to care for.

Lucas spoke in an undertone. "Perhaps we should stop at the emporium and choose items that are in short supply in my pantry. I've been there already to pick up my own supplies, but I'll leave it to you to select the foodstuffs we might need. There's always a need for sugar and flour and coffee and such. And the lard bucket is about empty, too." Lucas seemed willing to allow her a free hand at shopping, and she nodded, agreeing to his notion.

They rode to the general store—a short distance, but one fraught with confusion for the bride sitting atop the wagon seat. All about them folks waved and called greetings, until Elizabeth was almost overwhelmed by Lucas calling out to friends and neighbors who sang loudly with congratulations on his marriage. It seemed that all of Thomasville knew of his mail-order bride and the wedding that had taken place in the parsonage just minutes ago.

How such news traveled so rapidly was a conundrum, but one Elizabeth understood, for even in Boston there was a network of folks who passed along any small tidbit that came their way. And it was obvious that Lucas getting married was at the top of the list today. She was scanned and gaped at and in general given a complete dissection by the ladies who watched as the wagon traveled the short distance to the emporium. Elizabeth was ready to forgo the shopping expedition by the time they arrived there and Lucas was assisting her from the high seat.

He opened the door and ushered her inside the store, where several older gentlemen sat in one corner, playing checkers and discussing the state of the world, if she were any judge. The store owner was a gentleman named Harvey Klein, according to Lucas, and in mere moments Elizabeth was put at her ease by the man's smile and offer of help.

She named all the items Lucas had mentioned as lacking in his pantry, and then added a few of her own. Tea was one, for she was given to a cup in the middle of the day, when she'd completed her morning's work and was ready to begin on the afternoon's chores. A pound of crackers was added to Lucas's list, along with a ring of pickled bologna and a large chunk of cheese from the round on the counter. Harvey Klein wrapped it in a length of cheesecloth, to keep it fresh until it should be used up, and then seemed to think of something else, for he snapped his fingers and spoke up quickly.

"We've got in a fresh supply of beef today, Lucas. Mason Ridgeway butchered yesterday and brought me several sides of beef and a couple of hogs. Will you be needing anything like that, ma'am?"

She looked up at Lucas inquiringly. "Have you fresh meat at the farm?"

Lucas faced Harvey, his query surprising Elizabeth with its promise of hard work to come. "How much is a whole side of beef? I'll cut it up for Elizabeth and maybe she could can some up for the winter. I've got a pork barrel, lots of chops and roasts still in it, but the supply of beef is short right now. I don't have any steers ready for butchering till next year."

"Sold them all for a dandy price, I'll bet you," Harvey surmised with a grin.

"Couldn't turn down the fella who came lookin' for some hefty steers. Made me a bundle on them. But it cut the house short on beef for a while."

This was a different scene from what she was accustomed to back East, Elizabeth decided. For the local butcher shop in Boston had meat all cut up in tidy roasts and a tray of ground-up beef should a housewife want it ready for a meat loaf. It seemed now that she would be working in a kitchen doing the job of a butcher. She straightened her shoulders and tilted her chin as she determined she could do as well at the job as any man.

Harvey looked to be mentally counting the contents of Lucas's wallet. "I'll take care of it, for I can spare half a side for you. I'll get it wrapped up good and my boy will carry it out to the farm for you, on my wagon. He's got a couple other deliveries to make for me later on today. I see your wagon is pretty well loaded already, so you'll not be wanting to add to the load."

Lucas seemed to be satisfied with the arrangements. "That sounds fine. Just wrap up a piece of beef for my wife and we'll be on our way. She wants to get supper in the oven before too long."

He looked down at Elizabeth with a raised eyebrow as if asking a silent question. *Have I forgotten anything?*

Elizabeth nodded and smiled at the proprietor. "That's fine, Mr. Klein. Thank you."

She folded her hands at her waist again, and her gaze returned to the floor as Lucas finalized their purchases in the grocer's credit book. It was the way of things, that men and women shopped and then paid at the end of the month, or whenever the arrangements they'd made with the store decreed it was due.

Harvey wrapped up a piece of beef, looking to be about four pounds or so from the size of the package, and Lucas took it from him, then offered his arm to Elizabeth. The two boys were each holding a licorice whip, given them by Harvey as a form of appreciation for Lucas's willingness to part with a good sum of money today.

He handed the package up to Elizabeth when she was settled on the seat, and then climbed in beside her, waiting till his sons were in place before he turned his team and left town, traveling to the west, where his farm lay.

"It's a good-sized piece of land, well over two hundred acres, with a house and barn and assorted buildings. We've got a good flock of laying hens and a pigsty with two sows and their litters, all waiting for butchering in the fall. I put up a good-sized corncrib a couple of years back, and there's a dozen apple trees out back, a couple of varieties of them. They've kinda gone to waste the past couple of years, for no one was here to put them up or make good use of them. The boys and I just ate them out of hand and I fed a good share of them to the hogs."

"I'm a good hand at baking pies, and apple puddings are a favorite of mine. It's easy enough to make applesauce and can it up for later on," Elizabeth told him.

"That's what I wanted to hear from you," Lucas said with satisfaction. "We've been in need of a woman's touch for a long time. I fear you'll want to turn around and leave when you see the mess the three of us have managed to make in the house. It needs a good cleaning and the kitchen especially could use some work." And if this woman wasn't as eager for marriage as he, she might very well turn around and head back East once she saw the job she was expected to tackle. Lucas could only hope and pray she was all she seemed to be.

Elizabeth listened to his listing of the chores awaiting her. It sounded about the same as what had been going through her mind, recognizing that a man alone with two small boys wouldn't find a clean house to be his first priority. She was silent, thinking of the battle before her, the cleaning she faced and the supper she was committed to making within the next few hours.

The buggy turned into a lane leading to a farmhouse and assorted outbuildings about a hundred yards farther from the road. The house needed a good coat of paint, but the barn glistened with what looked to be a recently applied coat of shiny red enamel. That anyone would put such expensive stuff on a barn, and leave a house to look like a deserted shack was beyond her, but nevertheless, it was a picture she viewed and shuddered at as she awaited Lucas's help from the wagon. That she could slide down on her own hook was a given, but if the man wanted to play the part of a gentleman, she'd not deny him the privilege. And it seemed Lucas was indeed a man of good manners, for she was given a dose of courtesy as he lifted her down.

She carried her package of beef into the house, past the porch where boots stood beneath the roof and dirt was present in the form of sand and scrapings from shoes and boots. It all needed a good sweeping, she decided. Surely the man owned a broom.

Once inside the kitchen, she revised her opinion, for if he owned a broom, it hadn't been used here in some time. The sink was full of dirty dishes, the stove littered with foodstuffs that had been spilled on it, and the table had its own share of dishes and bowls, coffee cups and glasses with dried milk settled in the bottoms.

It was enough to frighten off a lesser woman, but Elizabeth Collins Harrison was up to any challenge and a dirty kitchen was not on her list of things to be avoided at any cost. After depositing the package of beef on the table she rolled up her sleeves and went to the stove, lifting a lid, checking to see the state of the fire within.

The reservoir at one end of the range held enough water to fill the basin, so she dug it out from the littered sink and, using a pan from the back of the stove, filled it with hot water. Carrying it back to the sink, she glanced beneath it to where there should be a container of soap of some sort. A quart Mason jar held the slimy stuff she required and she dumped a good bit of it into the basin, then added the dishes that looked to have been rinsed off, not wanting to get moldy foodstuff into the clean water.

The rest of the dishes were transferred to the drain board, leaving her an empty sink for her work. A trip to the pantry earned her two towels and a rag that appeared to have been washed and folded. She carried them back with her and, using the rag, washed the contents of her basin and then rinsed them beneath the pitcher pump and dried them before she found the shelves where they could be stored between meals.

Lucas went out the door with his boys, apparently deciding not to interfere with her cleaning activities, and she was left alone with the daunting task of preparing a meal in her new home. A roaster from the pantry held the meat and she found a sack of onions hanging from a nail, along with a burlap bag of potatoes beneath it on the floor. She cut up an onion and put it into the roasting pan, along with salt and pepper and a few bay leaves, found in a jar, probably left over from the days when Lucas had a wife here.

She slid the roast into the oven. splashing it with water and covering it tightly first. It could cook while she cleaned, she decided, and she set forth to make a decent kitchen out of the mess she'd inherited.

Then she walked down the back steps, seeking out a

plot of land where Lucas might have planted a garden of sorts. A weed-infested patch caught her eye, perhaps two hundred square feet of plants of one sort or another, beans being the most familiar to her. Reaching between the weeds, she found, to her surprise, a good crop of green beans, ripe and ready to be cooked on the black kitchen range.

She filled her skirt with a good peck of them, holding them up, exposing her legs to anyone who cared to look. But not mindful of an audience, she went back to the porch and into the kitchen. The basin she'd washed dishes in was clean, thanks to a thorough scrubbing, and she dumped her beans into it and pumped water over the lot. Rinsed and drained, her crop represented a good dish of vegetables to go with the roast, and given the presence of potatoes in the pantry, she was well on her way to preparing a meal.

Another cut-up onion and a hunk of fatback from a piece in the pantry sizzled in a saucepan as she snapped the beans and readied them for cooking. The onion was transparent in the grease from the fatback, and she dumped in her beans, then added water to the mix, slapping a cover on the pan and shoving it to the back of the stove, to simmer and cook till the roast was finished.

She scrubbed the table using a brush from beneath the sink, for the table showed signs of several meals being served there. Her hands had known harder work than this at the orphanage, scrubbing tables after fifty or so children had eaten, and this was no hardship, she thought, since the kitchen was her own and she could keep it to suit herself.

Finally a house of her own, even if the kitchen did show signs of neglect. She looked around, already plotting. Curtains for the window, an oilcloth for the table, some sort of order for the pantry shelves and a clean floor. She smiled to herself. Rather than hard work, it sounded like heaven to her, a woman married and with a home of her own. This was just what she'd always wanted. She couldn't ask for more as a new beginning, here in the West, where everyone was a pioneer of sorts.

The back door banged open and Lucas stood behind her as she scrubbed at the seat of one of the chairs. "Supper on its way yet?" he asked briskly.

"The roast is in the oven. I picked beans from what you might call a garden and they are cooking even now. I haven't begun peeling potatoes yet, but your dishes are all clean and the floors are swept. I don't work miracles, Mr. Harrison. I'm only a woman, not a magician. Supper will be ready in about an hour or so, when the roast is done."

She looked up at him and his quick smile surprised her. "Sure looks like a magician has been at work in here, ma'am. Haven't seen this kitchen look so good in several years, since before my wife took sick and died. I recognize that you're a woman, Elizabeth. As my father would have said, you're a fine figure of a woman. He spoke of my mama thataway, and I'd say you fit the bill. You're a good-lookin' woman, sure enough, and your eyes sparkle when you're hot under the collar. Makes you look right pretty."

She caught only one phrase he'd spoken. "Your mama? You had a mother?" Her sarcasm was evident as she stood before him, hands on her hips. She looked him in the eye, only a bit shorter than he.

"You betcha, lady. She was a mother to be proud of. She kept house and took care of a whole houseful of young'uns and kept my pa happy till the day he died."

"Well, I don't have a houseful of young'uns to tend, but I know how to cook and clean."

"You've proved that already. As to the houseful of young'uns, I think I could help you out with that." His look was enough to make her blush. "I warned you about sleeping in my bed, Elizabeth. I wasn't making a threat, but a promise. I hope you intend to be a stickler when it comes to your wedding vows. I've put your bags in my room. You can unpack them at your leisure—there's room in my dresser for your things. You may want to rearrange the drawers a bit to accommodate your belongings, but there's nails on the wall for you to hang stuff and a place behind the curtain for shoes and such."

"I'll take a look when I finish in here, Mr. Harrison. Sometime before supper."

It was a dismissal, pure and simple, and Lucas heeded it promptly. He waved a hand as he clapped his hat back on his head and took his leave. "Be back in an hour or so—give the boys a chance to wash up and help with setting the table."

She watched him go, noting the lean figure of a man

who worked hard and had formed the muscular build of a farmer. His hands were big, his feet the same, and he was broad shouldered and slim in the hips. All of that was noted in one sweeping glance up and down his form. He was several inches over six feet in height, and his sons promised to be similarly formed, for they were both tall and sturdy, and good-looking boys to boot.

Elizabeth left the kitchen to take a look at the bedroom she'd been directed to. It was up the stairs, and since the doors all stood open, it wasn't hard to find, for the first two rooms she passed were obviously those of his sons. Books and clothing were strewn over the floors, the beds were unmade and the usual collection of dirt and sand was mingled on the wooden floors.

The third room, across the hall from the other two, was larger, the bed wider, the windows more numerous; there were three of them open to the breeze—uncurtained, but screened.

There was indeed a dresser, a mammoth piece of furniture, hand hewn from what appeared to be walnut under the dust that weighed it down. Six drawers opened readily, three of them full of stockings and drawers and undershirts. One of them held neatly folded shirts and another contained three pair of trousers—two denim, one of wool.

She opened the three empty drawers, apparently left for her use, and turned to her baggage. She had but a small number of items to store, for she counted herself fortunate to have four changes of clothing to her name. Homemade underwear went into one drawer, along with two pairs of stockings. Her nightgown lay on the bed, a voluminous bit of apparel, made from heavy cotton. Her two dresses were hung on nails on the wall, where hopefully the wrinkles from being stuffed in a valise would hang out and she'd be spared the task of ironing them before she wore them again.

Her heavy boots she put behind the curtain he'd mentioned and her house slippers she put beneath the edge of the bed. The sheets looked to be fairly clean, but she doubted if they'd seen a washtub in pretty near a week. Tomorrow would be time enough to strip the bedding from all the beds in the house and find a length of clothesline to stretch across the yard.

She opened the box of books she'd brought with her, the heaviest of her pieces of luggage, and looked at them. No shelf offered a home for them, no drawer was available, so she closed the box, resolving to carry it to the parlor and perhaps find a shelf for them to be displayed.

She owned three aprons, and she donned one now, aware that it was too late for her dress to be saved from the dirt of the kitchen she'd cleaned, but at least it was a bit of tidiness she could hide behind. Her bosom was too large for a fashionable woman to possess and her body was shaped somewhat like an apple, with hips that demanded a gathered skirt to allow for their width.

It was all right. The man had married her, had made the decision sight unseen, and now she was a wife—well, a bride, anyway. The wife part would come later. Marriage to Amos Rogers would have meant climbing into bed with a man she'd known for years, a friend since childhood. But he'd taken one look at her sister, fresh from a three-year stay with her grandparents, and turned his back on Elizabeth.

Remembering Sissy's remarks about the marriage bed, Elizabeth shuddered. For *painful* and *messy* were but two of the words she'd heard from Sissy's lips when she'd spoken of her marriage and the demands Amos made on her. But surely not all men were so uncaring. Certainly her own mother had not experienced such things. Or else marriage and the acts that occurred between husband and wife were simply not spoken of by decent women.

But Sissy had chosen her route to travel in life when she'd betrayed Elizabeth and fallen for Amos and his glib promises. Now *she* was his wife and the mother of his children, instead of the woman he'd courted for the better part of a year. But Elizabeth found she no longer felt a twinge of envy for her smaller, prettier sister.

Amos and Elizabeth had grown up together and she knew there were no surprises to be found in a marriage with a woman who was tall, heavy and a good friend.

Her father had treated her almost as a son, teaching her how to ride a horse, milk a cow and clean stalls like a hired hand. She could help with almost anything that took place on a farm, and when they'd moved to Boston—her father choosing a banking job that perhaps appealed to a man who'd been a farmer all his life and was weary of the backbreaking work—Elizabeth was totally out of place.

A city was not her first choice as a place to live, yet she'd soon found the school she attended to be challenging to her intelligence, for the teachers loved a student who questioned everything and learned all they had to offer.

Elizabeth Collins was such a student, and she thrived in the atmosphere of learning.

She found friends there. Laura was her sole support some days, when the teasing of other girls became more than Elizabeth could stand. For she was not only taller and heavier than the slim, pretty little girls in her classes, she was smarter. And it galled her classmates enough to allow them to tease her about all her inadequacies.

And then there was the boy who had shared her love of learning, Amos Rogers, who studied with her at the kitchen table, who learned the finer points of math from her tutoring. He admired her, apparently more her mind than her body, she'd decided after he turned his back on her to marry her sister.

But she'd gotten the best of the bargain, she decided with a smile, for Lucas Harrison was all that Amos Rogers was not. A big, brawny man with property and a house, and apparently a good reputation in the town, where he knew and was known. And for that she was thankful, only wishing for a greedy moment that Sissy could see her now. See her with her handsome new husband.

The man she would be welcoming into her arms in just a few hours.

Chapter Two

Supper was a rousing success, the two boys eating as if they hadn't seen such a meal in years. And perhaps they hadn't, for their father was as pleased as his sons at the food Elizabeth had prepared for them. The potatoes were mashed and creamy, the gravy hot and fragrant with the scent of bay leaf and onion, and the meat tender and brown, as a roast should be. They exclaimed over the green beans, cooked to a frazzle on the back of the stove, and wanted to know, all three of them, what she planned for breakfast. If she had any doubts about their acceptance of her, she put them to the back of her mind, for both boys were open and friendly, as if they welcomed all she'd done to enhance their lives thus far.

Elizabeth was flushed with pleasure at their adulation. Never had she been so pleased with a piece of work, for Lucas drank the coffee she made and proclaimed it the best cup he'd had in years. She offered them a rice pudding for dessert, having found the bag of rice in the pantry and a crock of eggs on the kitchen dresser. Milk from this morning's milking had easily been carried into the house, and she'd taken off the cream to churn another day.

In all she did she found pleasure, for these male occupants of her new home seemed to have accepted her, and even enjoyed her company. Never had she thought it would be so simple to win over her new husband and sons.

After the boys left the table Lucas pushed his chair back and shot her a glance of admiration. "You're a better cook than I expected, Elizabeth. You weren't spinning me a story when you wrote and said you could cook and clean with the best of them. I'm a believer already, just from sitting in this tidy kitchen and eating the food you've prepared."

"Thank you, sir. I try to live up to my promises."

He cut her a glance that sought out her opinion. "Did you mind the love, honor and obey bit this afternoon, Elizabeth?"

"I don't love you, Lucas, but it may come in time. I'll honor you for being a good father to your sons and thus far a man to be respected by your wife. The obey part will probably be a sticking point with us, for I'm used to doing things my own way, and obligating myself to a man will be a tough row to hoe for a woman like me."

He laughed and leaned back in his chair. "I figured as much. But you might as well just relax and pick your battles. For I'm sure there will be times you want to take the shotgun to me, and times I'll be ready to throttle you. But we'll make it so long as we both do our share of getting along and making a go of it."

"Are you planning on telling me how to run the house?" she asked.

He shook his head. "Naw, the house is yours to do with as you like. If you want things to fancy it up a bit, curtains or oilcloth for the table or whatever, make a list of things you need and we'll pick them up at Harvey's store when we go to town. I don't go for ruffles and such, but I know the bedrooms need curtains. Just haven't cared enough to do something about it. The last few years have been rough on the boys, and not too easy on me, for that matter. I've let things go pretty badly, but I'm willing to go along with what you want to do in here."

He looked at the kitchen window, glistening from the vinegar she'd used to wash the panes before dinner. It hadn't shone so brightly in months. Hell, it had been a couple of years since he'd washed a window in the house. And then only because he knew that Doris would have wanted her kitchen window relieved of the sheen of dead flies and grease that covered it.

But Doris was relegated to the background now, he found. She'd been his wife, but the past couple of years had proved to him that his sorrow at her death was not because she'd been the love of his life, but more a sadness for his sons. No longer having a mother had been difficult for them to handle. Now, with Elizabeth here, a fresh breeze seemed to have blown through the house, wiping out all memory of the past. She was all that a woman should be, Lucas decided. Sturdy and capable, willing to win over his boys, and perhaps even himself. He'd find that out later.

It seemed Elizabeth was ready to tackle the matter of the house, for she pondered but a moment and then her clear voice gave chapter and verse of changes she was hoping to make. "You're right about one thing, Lucas. I'll want an oilcloth for the table. It'll save the surface of the wood, for scrubbing it makes it age fast. An oilcloth will look cheerful in here, and curtains on the window will help a lot. I like a cheerful place, not to mention a clean kitchen, to work in."

He nodded thoughtfully. All of that seemed reasonable to him. But he suspected there was more. She was willing to negotiate.

"I'll gather eggs for you if you like, work in the garden and try to salvage some of the stuff you planted. I don't milk cows, not with three men on the place, but I know how to churn butter and bake bread. I suppose what I'm saying is that I'll pull my share of the load."

That suited him just fine. "I suspect you will, Elizabeth. Is that the name they called you back home? Or did they shorten it?"

"My friend Laura called me Lizzie. The man I was pledged to marry, Amos Rogers, said that Lizzie sounded like a tramp and he refused to shorten my name. Of course, he didn't ever give me his, so I don't think his opinion really matters to me. It seemed he was partial to dainty women with golden hair, and I certainly didn't qualify in that department. But I'm better off without him, I've decided, for my lot is more to my liking here than what Sissy is putting up with back in Boston."

Lucas laughed aloud. "I think I kinda like Lizzie, no

matter what your suitor in Boston thought. It suits you, for it's forthright and honest, and believe me, it doesn't make you sound like a tramp, whatever he meant by that. It sounds like a woman, a name that's kinda comfortable and one that might not be spoke out in public, but saved for private times inside the home."

"And do your friends call you Lucas all the time? Or have any of them shortened it to Luc?"

"My wife used to call me Lucas. She said it was a solid name and she didn't go for nicknames or such."

Elizabeth moved her hands on the table, gripping them together as if she disliked opening a can of worms, which was where she was heading. "How long has she been dead, Lucas?"

"Three years, since Toby was a little tad. He's seven now and Josh is nine. They're fine boys, but they need a woman's hand. I'm hoping you'll take to them, Elizabeth. They've been a long time without a mother."

"I won't try to smother them with a load of *mothering* right off, Lucas. They won't take to that. I know children enough to recognize that there are barriers up between us. Give me some time to win them over. I've known a pile of young'uns in my days back home. We'll get along just fine. And if we don't, if there are problems to be faced, we'll work them out. I've dealt with young boys back at the orphanage, and I found that they respond well to honesty and plain speaking. And a kind word now and then. Not to mention cookies and such."

"I suspect you could charm the birds out of the trees, given good reason, ma'am. You've got a good way about you, a kind heart, I think, and one that'll hold two boys in its depths. They've looked forward to you being here. I don't see them giving you a hassle about anything."

She looked at him in surprise. Never had she heard a man express himself in such a way. "I'm honored by your words, Lucas. I only hope I can live up to your expectations."

He looked at her with a smile. "Well, what's the order of business for tomorrow, ma'am? I'm sure you must have a whole list of things you're planning on doing."

"Washing, for one thing. The sheets need to be stripped off the beds early on so I can get them scrubbed and hung out to dry. It looks to be a nice day tomorrow, so that shouldn't be a problem. I'll tackle as much of your wash as I can. There's not much of mine to do, but I'm certain the boys can find a bushel of clothes on their bedroom floors, should they be so inclined. And if there's a goodly amount of cream on the milking tonight and in the morning, I'll churn tomorrow afternoon. I think you're about out of butter."

"I don't suppose you'll find time to do any baking tomorrow, will you?"

She pursed her lips at his broad hint. "What did you have in mind?"

"Oh, maybe a pie. There's dried apples in the cellar. They're not much for eating, but they bake up pretty good. Or maybe cookies. The boys are real fond of sugar cookies. So am I, for that matter. We'll eat most anything sweet, in fact."

"Where's that pork barrel you spoke of in town, Lucas?"

"In the back of the pantry, with a cover on it and a stone holding it down. My pa set one up for my mother when I was a boy and we always had fresh pork all winter long. I've got a side of pork in that one." He pointed to the pantry. "It's all cut up into chops and roasts. You'll have to dig for what you want, but the lard keeps it fresh for months."

"I'm familiar with a pork barrel. We had one when I was just a little girl, before we moved to Boston and away from the farm. My father was offered a job in the city and it looked better to him than slaving away on a farm for the rest of his life."

Lucas shook his head. "You couldn't drag me to the city for the best job in the world. I think I've got an ideal spot right here, Elizabeth. All I needed to make it complete was a wife, and now I've got her and good reason to work hard and make a living for her to share. I know we're still strangers, so to speak, but getting comfortable with each other will come with time."

She felt a flush climb her cheeks as she heard his words. Apparently the man wasn't concerned about her size or shape or the fact that she wasn't a raving beauty. He was more concerned with her ability to do her job as a wife and mother. And that she could handle.

Well, maybe the wife part was somewhat beyond her, but she'd thrive on the mother bit, given a chance.

She rose from the table and cleared off the bowls they'd eaten their pudding in. Lucas sat and watched her and she felt as though she were on display, for his gaze did not leave her as she worked.

"Don't you have something you need to be doing out of doors?" she asked after fifteen minutes or so, when she'd washed and dried the dishes and cleaned up the table and sink thoroughly.

"I'm enjoying watching my wife," he said, astonishing her with the soft tone of his words as he all but named her as Mrs. Harrison.

"Surely you've seen a woman working in a kitchen before," she said sharply.

"Not in three years or so, I haven't. Not since Doris died. I'm enjoying watching you and the neat way you have of accomplishing so much with so little to do it with."

"I've got all I need to do things with, Lucas. You're a bit short on vinegar, for I used a good bit of it on the kitchen window, and there are several others that could use a good washing. I'll go to the cellar to see what's down there in the morning. And yes, I can bake pies or cookies or whatever you think the boys will enjoy eating. I'll plan on baked pork chops for dinner tomorrow at noontime when I suspect you'll be hungriest, and then something like soup for supper. Tonight I cooked a larger meal because we were in town for so long."

He grinned at her, his eyes crinkling as if he was enjoying their banter. "Elizabeth, could you stop fluttering around and sit down here and talk to me for a minute?"

She hung her dish towel over the front of the sink board and went to where he sat at the table, pulling out her chair and depositing herself on the seat. "Will this do?"

"I keep thinking you're worried about going to bed with me tonight. Am I right?"

"Absolutely right. I've never done such a thing in my life before. It opens up brand-new territory for me. I'm not at all sure I'll be a success at the bed part of marriage. I haven't heard a whole lot of good things about it, to tell the truth. I want to please you, Lucas, but I fear I'll not be what you want or need."

"Now, I'm not worried about you failing as a wife in the bedroom, Elizabeth. I'm not sure what I have to convince you of, but surely you had feelings for a man before. Good feelings, I mean."

And at that, she sighed, shaking her head. "Not likely."

"Not even when you planned on marrying the other fella—what was his name? Amos something or other, wasn't it?"

"It's not something a well-brought-up lady does, Lucas. My mother would pitch a fit to hear you speak so. And my daddy would be after Amos with a shotgun had he thought such a thing had come to pass."

He laughed, and to her mind, relief rode his countenance. "I'm just wondering how to go about this whole wedding-night thing with you. I don't want to scare you off, but it seems that someone should have spoken to you about it when you were growing up."

"My mother didn't think such things were fit topics of conversation, even between women, certainly not between mother and daughter. I suspect she thought I'd find out all I needed to know on my wedding night. Which didn't come to pass, as matters went."

"Ah, but it will tonight, Elizabeth. And I need to know that you aren't frightened of me. I'm rather relieved, to tell you the truth, that you're a tall woman, not likely to feel overpowered by a man of my size. I also want to let you know that I will never in any way cause you harm. I have nothing but disdain for men who misuse their wives and children. You won't ever see me beating on my boys, for although a good swat on the seat may sometimes be of good use, harming a child with a belt or fists or anything else is beneath a decent man's dignity."

"I feel the same way about children, Lucas. I don't think you realize that I worked with fifty children or so at the orphanage in Boston. It was less than a mile from our home and I offered to lend a hand there when I was but a young woman. They were thrilled to get a volunteer so easily, and accepted my offer."

He laughed, picking out one phrase of her explanation and commenting on it. "You're still a young woman, Elizabeth. You're hardly ready for a rocking chair and slippers yet."

"Well, I found my niche there anyway. I cooked and showed the girls how to clean and keep house and the boys were happy to eat everything I put on the table. I donated three full days a week to the orphanage, and enjoyed every minute of it. It was so rewarding and I grew to appreciate the life I'd been given as a child. My father wanted a son and so taught me the things he would have taught a boy when we lived on the farm in my early years. I've ridden a horse for almost twenty-five years."

"Well, that'll come in handy when we have to round up the steers for market, won't it?"

"Are you laughing at me?" she asked, cutting him a sharp look.

"Heavens, no—just pleased not to have to hire another cowhand for roundup."

"My, I'll be saving you all sorts of money, won't I? Will I be able to keep what I earn from selling butter and eggs to Harvey Klein if he's willing to buy them from me?"

"Oh, he'll be willing. Eggs are in short supply in town. The ladies there don't soil their hands with chickens and such, and butter is always a good item. They don't own churns in town either, it seems. Doris used to sell her butter and eggs weekly."

Elizabeth sobered, not able to judge if her query would be unanswered by the man across the table. "Was she pretty? Your wife, I mean?"

He looked at Elizabeth, took in her measure slowly, his gaze traveling over her tall form and resting for a moment on her dark hair, twisted up in a thick bun atop her head. She'd secured it with bone hairpins before dinner, for it had a tendency to slip from place and look untidy most days. She used to braid it in the mornings, but traveling had meant she must look a lady in all ways, and her bonnet kept her hair in place pretty well.

And then he shrugged. "I suppose you could call her pretty. She was short and delicate, looked like a good stiff wind would blow her away. Light haired and small boned she was. Probably that's what killed her eventually. She hadn't been well since Toby was born, for she labored long and hard to deliver him. The doctor said it was a miracle she survived it. And eventually she managed to let it take her from us. Almost like she was weary of the life she led here. She just closed her eyes and gave up."

"I doubt it was her choice," Elizabeth said, thinking of the woman who had left two little boys to be raised by their father.

"I don't know. She felt bad one day and stayed in bed. Then the next day she got up and made breakfast and told me she thought she was sickening, and by noontime she was back in bed. She'd bled something fierce, and I got the doctor out and he said she had a problem with her female organs, and it didn't look good for her. He was right, for she lived less than a month after that. Just kinda faded away, like she was too tired to breathe."

"A mother would not have left her children by choice, Lucas. She couldn't help dying."

He looked up, his eyes weary. "I know that. But at the end there, she just didn't care anymore. Said she was tired of working and not seeing an end to the work. I don't think she was cut out for this life. But she wanted to marry me real bad. Even proposed to me at a dance in town one night. Said I was the best prospect around, and I had a good piece of property and a house all built."

"Did you love her?" It was a daring question, but for some reason Elizabeth needed to know the answer.

He shook his head, then denied the gesture. "Hell, yes. I loved her. All men love their wives, don't they? And I'm a man." And then he dropped his head. "I don't know if I loved her or not. I wanted her, sure enough. She was pretty and all. But she didn't have any...call it depth, maybe, to her. She only thought about herself and what she wore and said that she was the envy of the women in town because she'd caught the most eligible bachelor around." He looked up at Elizabeth again and his words were harsh. "Hell, I don't know if I loved her or not. But like I said, most men love their wives or they wouldn't have married them, would they?"

"No, they don't, Lucas. There are a lot of unhappy women in this world who'd give their right arm to have a man around who truly loved them."

"And how would you know that, Miss Spinster?"

She was silent, her heart aching from his words. She shook her head and rose from the table, then stepped into the hallway and toward the stairs. Her hand on the newel post, she turned to where he stood in the kitchen doorway.

"I'm going up to bed, Lucas. I'm weary, it seems. Perhaps you'll excuse me from being a wife tonight. I feel the need of sleep. And I don't feel brave enough to tackle a husband tonight."

She lifted her skirts and walked slowly up the stairs, and the man behind her watched, noting her feet as they touched the risers, paying special mind to the slim ankles that were on display beneath the hem of her skirts. She might be a bit hefty, but doggone if she didn't have pretty ankles, he thought.

Then he remembered her dismissal of him, her words of sleeping and not being a wife tonight. His mind latched on to that phrase and anger was set alive in his chest, but so was a grudging respect. He watched her reach the second floor and walk from him, and his mouth uttered words she could not hear. "We'll see, lady. We'll see."

* * *

It was well past dark when Lucas entered his bedroom, carrying a candle, for he knew there were none on the table beside his bed. The boys were settled, their doors closed. He'd blown out the lantern in the kitchen, latched the door and then had trodden the stairs alone. And if he had things straight, his *loving wife* did not plan on welcoming him to the bed tonight.

That was too bad, he thought, tugging his boots from his feet and tucking his stockings inside for tomorrow. He slid the suspenders from his shoulders and lowered his trousers. His drawers were shed next and he walked to the bed, naked as the day he was born thirty-six years ago.

And that was another thing. Elizabeth hadn't told him her age. He'd guess her past her mid-twenties, but who knew? She'd already spent a number of years working at an orphanage, but he doubted she was over thirty yet.

He lifted the top sheet and lay down on the pillow, left on his side of the bed. He wasn't used to having any specific side to call his own—usually he spread out over the whole expanse since he'd been sleeping alone. Elizabeth was facing the window, her back covered with a white fabric of some sort. A nightgown, he suspected, and then his mind wandered to the soft skin that lay beneath.

The thought was enough to harden his manhood to a point of pain. It had been a long time since Lucas had held a woman in his arms, and the one sharing his bed tonight was surely woman enough for any man.

He'd make a subtle approach, he decided, tapping her shoulder and feeling her stiffen beneath his hand.

"Go to sleep, Lucas," she said quietly. No anger, no fear, just a woman intent on denying him his rights.

"Not a chance, Lizzie. Not a chance."

She turned over and faced him, holding the sheet before her like a shield. "And what do you mean by that? Do you plan on attacking me like a—"

"You're my wife and I'll be damned if I'll look at your back all night on my wedding night. At least let me hold you in my arms and allow me to enjoy the scent of a woman before I go to sleep."

"I didn't know that a woman had a particular scent," she said, looking puzzled in the dark. "And I don't want your arms around me while I sleep. I'm used to sleeping alone."

"Well, you won't sleep alone here, ma'am. You'll sleep with me, and since you asked so nicely downstairs, I'm willing to forgo my wedding night, so long as you don't give me any hassle about having my arms around you."

She sat up beside him, her hair long and flowing, released from the prim bun she'd concocted atop her head earlier. It lay against her gown, looking as dark as the night, even though he knew it was not black but a dark brown—a pretty dark brown, now that he considered it. He touched it, there at the small of her back, where the last wave curled. He twined it around his finger and she turned, taking it from him.

"What are you doing?"

"Just touching your hair. It's beautiful, Lizzie. You should leave it down all the time."

"A lady doesn't let her hair hang loose. It's slovenly. I sometimes braid it up and let the braid fall down my back, but otherwise I put it up."

"I can handle the braid, I think. But I'm not real fond of the bun thing. If you had any idea how pretty it looks right now, you'd never wind it up on top of your head again."

"Sometimes I put a braid in at night. Otherwise it's all tangled in the morning."

He smiled, reaching to touch a wave at the side of her face. "I can't wait to see you in the morning, all tangled and blushing."

She looked puzzled, pulling her hair from his hand. "Why would I be blushing?"

"You'll find out, sweetheart."

"I'm not your sweetheart. You don't even know me, Lucas. I'm barely your wife."

"That's where you're wrong, love. You're not my wife yet. But, trust me, you will be, maybe sooner than you think."

She cast him a dubious look, her face in shadow. "I don't know about you, but I'm going to sleep. I've had a dreadfully long day. And tomorrow doesn't look to be any better."

She turned away and his hands were quick, reaching for her and turning her in the bed. He then lay back down, with Elizabeth tucked neatly in his arms. Her head was on his shoulder, her body pressed against his and he knew she had to be feeling his arousal pressed against her.

She was silent, almost appearing frozen in his embrace, and he rued his quick action. This was almost guaranteed to give her a case of newlywed fright. But it seemed his fear was unfounded, for she slowly relaxed beside him, though both of her arms were against her chest, as if she would protect the soft curves of her breasts.

"I'm not going to hurt you, Lizzie. I've already told you that. You can let go. I won't deny I'm mighty tempted to touch those pretty breasts of yours, but I'm not a man to be grabbing at a woman."

Her breath was warm against his chest, her skin pebbled in the chilled air, and he took pity. Reaching down, he pulled the sheet up to cover them both and tucked it around her shoulder, protecting her from any stray draft from the windows.

"Thank you, Lucas," she murmured, the words almost lost against his chest, the movement of her lips bringing him to an even higher state of arousal.

"You'd *better* thank me, sweetheart, for I'm about to burst. I can't think of any other way to describe how I feel, but you've got me all tied up in trying to be nice and still have my way about some small thing tonight."

"Lucas." She wriggled against him. "Lucas, let me sit up. I want to say something."

He relaxed his hold and she leaned on the bed, sitting up beside him gingerly.

"What is it, Lizzie? Are you moving out of my bedroom?"

She turned to look down at him, a ghostly vision in white, outlined against the window appearing almost as a spirit. "Where would I go? The parlor? The sofa there looks awfully uncomfortable for anyone more than five feet tall, and I surely don't qualify in that department." She lifted her hands from her lap and her fingers worked at the buttons of her gown.

"What are you doing, Lizzie?" He sat up beside her and took careful note of the bodice of her nightgown opening downward, farther than he'd thought it would go, for the buttons apparently ended well below her waist.

"I'm undoing my gown. You won't be happy unless you claim your rights tonight, Lucas. And I don't want to argue with you over the consummation of our marriage. It has to happen sometime, so it might as well be tonight. I'm not planning on enjoying this, you might as well know. Sissy told me all about wedding nights, and if she was on target, this promises to be more than painful and messy."

She scooted her gown upward, lifting her hips from the mattress to facilitate its removal. In seconds she had pulled it over her head and dropped it to the floor. "All right, Lucas. Do what you like with me," she said in a whisper that sounded as if it carried a hint of tears.

Lucas watched, awestruck by her actions. Never had he thought to see such a thing happen. He'd planned on coaxing her, playing on her good nature, perhaps eventually opening the bodice, the better to see her breasts. And here she was, tossing the damn thing on the floor and lying down beside him again.

"I don't want any fooling around first, Lucas. I don't know how long I can hold my nerve, to tell you the truth.

I want you to go ahead and claim my body, as is your right. I won't fight you or cause a fuss of any kind. Just get it over with, and then let me sleep."

He pulled the sheet from her, for she'd pulled it up over her breasts, and he wasn't planning on missing one inch of her ample curves when he took this chance to look her over. She lay on her back, her face pale in the glow from the windows, and her gaze touched his.

He leaned over her and pressed his lips to hers, the kiss soft and seeking, with no trace of impatience, for he wanted to taste her, to know the womanly scent she exuded, the soft, plump curves of her breasts tempting him to touch them.

She would have spoken then, but his kiss silenced her and he pressed a bit, his tongue touching her tightly sealed lips. "Open for me, Elizabeth. Please."

She allowed the penetration of his tongue and he gloried in it, careful of his possession as he explored the ridges of her teeth, the length of her tongue, the heat of the woman. She whimpered a bit and then her tongue touched his, a quick, small nudge, but enough to let him know that she was not totally immune to this sort of love play.

He lifted his hand to her breast and held it in his palm, the weight of it overflowing, the tight crest hardening even more as he shifted his fingers and he touched the fullness surrounding it. He caught that small, hard peak between his fingers and squeezed gently, hearing her in-drawn breath, her sigh of wonder as he played gently with the bounty she had offered him.

And then he bent his head and took the tender bit of

flesh into his mouth, suckling a bit, careful not to frighten her, but wanting to give her some small bit of pleasure. Even as her breathing seemed to cease and she stiffened beneath him.

And as he suckled there, he moved his hand down her body, touched her navel briefly, felt her squirm as he did so, and he almost smiled. Indeed, had he not been so engulfed in the breast he claimed, he might have laughed aloud. The woman might be a virgin, and he had no reason to think otherwise, but she was also a flower about to open, just for him.

Elizabeth was untried, untested by any man, yet she offered him the knowledge that she was enjoying his touch, that he brought her pleasure of a sort. His hand crept lower, touched the tightly curled hair that covered her mound, and then stopped. For the woman had ceased to breathe. He lifted his head from her breast to look up at her.

"Breathe, Lizzie. You're frightening me here."

She inhaled deeply and laughed softly. "I forgot to breathe, Lucas. I'm too busy thinking of all the things you're doing to me."

"I haven't done anything yet," he told her, his hand separating the soft folds he'd discovered and his index finger exploring the length and depth of her most secret place. As he entered her with one long, wide finger, she made a sound of distress in her throat and he stopped again. "What is it? Did I hurt you?"

She shook her head, an abrupt movement, and opened her eyes as he looked closely at her face, seeking out any sign of tears and fear that might be there. "I just didn't expect you to do that, Lucas. I didn't know that a man would want to…"

Her voice trailed off and he took pity once more. "Every part of your body is important to me, Elizabeth. And some parts are more tempting than others. Your breasts are round and firm and more luscious than I expected."

"They're too big, Lucas. I feel top-heavy sometimes. My mother said it was a shame I'd never be able to wear fashionable clothes, for my shape is wrong for the current styles."

"Your mother needs her head examined, for there isn't a thing wrong with your body, Lizzie. It's shaped just right for a woman. Just right for me. I never had much luck with small women. I was always fearful of— Well, never mind that. Let's just say that you couldn't be more perfect for me if you tried. The first look I got at you, I knew you were the best deal I'd ever made. Sending for you was smart of me. I'd like to make you happy tonight."

"I don't know what to do, Lucas. Just go ahead and take what you want from me and I promise not to make any fuss."

"I know what to do, sweetheart. I'll take your virginity and be the happiest man in Missouri."

She nodded. His hand was careful, gentle as he touched her, his movements aimed at giving her pleasure. She lifted her hips to him, as though she would coax his fingers deeper within, and his hand and fingers moved to where he knew she would feel the most intense pleasure.

Her breathing quickened, her eyes closed and he heard

small sounds catch in her throat as her body writhed beneath his touch. She stiffened suddenly and he bent to her, his mouth covering hers, swallowing the sounds of pleasure from her lips as she erupted in his hands, her hips rising and falling, her body twisting against him. And then she was still, her eyes open wide, her mouth still captured by his, and he lifted himself from her and rolled to lie between her thighs.

"Here, sweetheart." He lifted her legs a bit. "Let me do this, Lizzie." He touched the opening of her body with the blunt tip of his manhood and felt the moisture drawing him within. She was warm, her legs trembling beside his hips, and he whispered soft words of encouragement as he pressed within.

"I'm trying not to hurt you, Elizabeth. Just relax as much as you can, love."

She exhaled, her legs turning limp as she opened to him and he was seated deeply within her. He felt the constriction of her maidenhood as he penetrated, and he pushed forward, knowing that if she were ever to be in pain, it was right at this moment.

But the woman beneath him was relaxed, her arms coming up to encircle him, hugging his waist, her legs stiffening to enclose him in an embrace he hadn't expected. He lost himself in that moment, deeply bedded within his wife, his body surging toward completion of this act of marriage. And then he was there, with an outpouring such as he'd never known. He lay atop her, limp, relaxed and replete.

"Now I'm your wife, aren't I?" she asked in a whisper

against his ear. "Sissy was wrong, Lucas. It wasn't painful—just a sharp twinge there for a second. And I don't care about the messy part she spoke of. I'm feeling like a wife right now."

"You ought to, sweetheart." His hands crept up to lose themselves in her hair; he tangled his fingers in the dark locks that lay spread upon her pillow. "This is what I've wanted to do all the livelong day," he whispered.

"Lie on top of me?" she asked.

He laughed aloud. "No, woman. I've needed to touch your hair in just this way, to feel it tangle around my fingers and know that no matter how you bind it up tomorrow, I'll remember how it looked tonight." And then he lifted himself a bit to look down at her. "Although lying on top of you is certainly worth a few daydreams, now that I think about it. In fact, if I weren't so doggone heavy, I'd just stay right here till morning."

"You're not too heavy, Lucas. Remember, I'm a big woman."

"You sure are, sweetheart. A fine figure of a woman, like my daddy used to say."

He rolled from her then and drew her close, covering her with the sheet, easing his hand over her hip to draw her into his long frame. She fit well, he decided. Not short and fragile as Doris had been, but a woman he didn't fear harming with his big body. And then he felt a dash of guilt for so putting Doris in the background of his mind. She'd been his wife for a long time, and he supposed she'd done her best to make him happy, but never had he felt that she fully accepted her role as his mate. She was dainty, petite and frail, and he was big, burly and strong. That said it all, he decided.

And apparently Elizabeth was satisfied with him, even if things were a little messy.

When the sun came up, Elizabeth heard the rooster crow, felt the man behind her move his hand from her belly to her breast, and recognized that she was a married woman and that her hair was in tangles and she was no doubt blushing.

"Turn over and let me look at you," Lucas said quietly.

"I can't do that." She hid her face beneath her hands and rolled to the side of the bed. "I'm going to get up, Lucas. It's time to be fixing breakfast."

"I know, but I want to see your blush. And don't try to tell me you aren't blushing, sweetheart, because I won't believe it. Not for a minute."

She grasped the sheet from him, stood and wrapped it around her body in one smooth movement. Then she turned and looked down at him. "Now are you satisfied?"

"For now, but not for long, ma'am. It's gonna be a long day, I fear."

She shook her head, her hair flying in abandon around her shoulders. "What on earth are you talking about?"

"Wait until tonight and I'll tell you. Just remember I'm planning on going to bed early tonight, love."

Chapter Three

It was different, the feeling she had this morning. As if the old Elizabeth had disappeared and in her place stood Luc's wife. The woman who had whispered and cried out her pleasure in his bed just hours past. Elizabeth smiled at the memory.

She'd like to get hold of Sissy right now, she thought. From what her sister had said, Amos was a mean man to make Sissy despise the marriage bed as she did, and Elizabeth would like to fill her head with Lucas's idea of a wedding night. And yet that would be a cruelty, to brag about her husband, knowing that Sissy was stuck with Amos, for no doubt her lot in life would not improve while she lived in his house.

Living in Lucas's house looked to suit *her* just fine, Elizabeth decided, struck once again by the fact that she could do whatever she liked in this place—fix up the garden with some care and watering, set the kitchen to rights with curtains and such, and make a marriage out of her situation with Lucas. He was a fine figure of a man, sure enough, and all hers.

She felt a blush steal over her face as she again recalled Lucas's big hands on her body, his fingers working magic where they would, and his kisses that had taken her to a place where pleasure dwelt. Pleasure Sissy might never realize with Amos.

She blushed, standing alone in the kitchen, remembering the man who had taken her body with such patience and gentle touches. Whose mouth had explored places on her body where no man had ever trespassed. Whose words had told her of his pleasure and satisfaction with her, with an air of arrogance she'd found puzzling. As if his first wife had not succeeded in granting him the pleasure due a husband.

This morning he'd come down the stairs, ready to tend to his chores, and had found her before the open oven, intent on sliding a pan of biscuits into its depths.

He'd halted beside her and waited till she stood, closing the oven door. She'd looked up at him, once more pleased to be able to look up at a man, especially her husband, and her brows rose in silent query.

"Just wanted to tell you good-morning," he said quietly, lifting his hand to touch her cheek. "I see your hair is all bundled up again, Lizzie. But I can wait till tonight, and then I'll take it down."

He eyed her with what seemed to be a degree of concern, and his voice was low, his question spoken in an undertone. "You are all right, aren't you? Did I hurt you? Last night, I mean?" He seemed a bit concerned, Elizabeth thought, as though he felt obliged to ask her such a thing, but felt uncomfortable doing so.

"No, you didn't hurt me, Lucas. Not any more than I'd have expected, anyway. I'm fine."

He nodded, bent toward her a bit and then, as if changing his mind, stood erect once more and backed away from her. "I'll be in the barn. The boys are out there already, and we'll have the chores done in about half an hour. Will breakfast be ready by then?" He peered over her shoulder to where strips of bacon lay in his biggest iron skillet.

"It'll be ready," she said agreeably, wondering if he'd thought to kiss her and then changed his mind. She watched as he turned and snatched his hat from a nail on the wall by the back door, slapped it on his head and took his leave. His long legs carried him quickly to the barn and he paused to speak to his youngest son, Toby, who was excited from the looks of him, almost dancing in place as he waved his hands and spoke loudly, pointing into the barn. He took Lucas's hand and they disappeared together beyond the barn door.

Something was going on out there, she decided. No doubt she'd find out from the boys what the excitement was all about. In the meantime, she had work to do, even as she awaited Lucas's return. For now, she knew he was in the barn and she kept a weather eye on the back door, watching for him to head for the house, doing her best to have breakfast ready when he walked in the door. The table was almost set, the bacon nearly finished and eggs awaiting the skillet. The biscuits, covered with a towel, nestled in a small crock on the table and the boys' glasses were filled with milk. She'd found thick, cream-colored china mugs in the cupboard, and now she set one of them before Lucas's place at the table. She'd say one thing for Lucas. The man had enough pots and pans and crocks in his kitchen, and she prided herself that they were all clean and ready for use.

A sound on the back porch caught her attention and she turned to see Josh, the eldest of Lucas's sons, standing on the other side of the screen door. She was drawn to the sturdy boy, already taking on the form of his father, for he was dark haired and strong featured, as was Lucas. He'd grow into his nose and ears one day, she figured, having seen numerous small boys grow year by year until they matched up to the bodies that had seemed to be changing too fast for their minds to keep up with.

No doubt Lucas had looked much as did Josh when he was but a boy. And now he was tall, stalwart and had a degree of beauty rarely seen in a man, certainly not evident in Amos, as she recalled. For Lucas possessed true beauty—not a blend of physical traits, but a sense of knowing his own strengths meshed with the arrogance of a man who'd been tried and not found wanting. Her heart beat just a little faster as she thought of the long, lean length of the man who'd made her his wife just last night, and she had to force herself to concentrate on the boy before her.

He sought her attention, bringing her gaze to the treasure he carried in his hands. And then he spoke her name. "Miss Elizabeth, want to see something mighty pretty?"

She smiled and moved closer to the door. "I'm always

eager to see beauty in any way, shape or form, Josh. What do you have there?"

He stood facing her, and nestled within his joined palms was a tiny creature, probably not more than a few hours old. He was obviously offering it for her approval.

"I didn't know you had a dog, Josh, or that she was expecting a litter."

"She had them during the night, seven of them. Pa said it was lucky that most of them were boys, 'cause the farmers hereabouts like male dogs to work their cattle."

"Will you sell them when they're old enough?"

"All but one. Pa said I could pick one to keep for a pet."

"A male? To raise for the cattle herding?"

He grinned. "Probably, 'cause Emma is a girl and she's pretty good at herding, but now she'll be busy with her pups and if she's gonna keep on having babies, Pa said we'd need a male."

"I think your pup needs to go back to the mother now, Josh. She won't like having one of them go missing. And your breakfast is ready to put on the table."

"Yeah, Pa said I couldn't take him out of Emma's box for longer than five minutes, and I think my time is up. But I'll be back in a few minutes, ma'am. I'm hungry." He turned, walking carefully down the steps, holding his prize close to his chest as he went.

Elizabeth watched as he walked to the barn, noting the arrogant stride he assumed, much like his father's she decided with a smile, wondering for a moment if it was an inherited trait or a desire to emulate the man he loved so well.

No doubt it was the arrival of the puppies that had caused Toby to be so excited, for nothing could so delight a young boy, nor please him, as could a puppy. It had been a spot of good luck when someone had dropped off a young pup at the orphanage in Boston one day, and the small creature had found himself immediately adopted by almost thirty boys, all of them eager to bestow their affection on the tiny morsel of a mongrel. She'd learned then that there was a special tie between dogs and boys, one she'd gained a great deal of satisfaction from, watching and learning about such a thing. Toby and Josh were in for a real treat, with a litter of pups to tend to. She relished the idea of their pleasure today, aware that the two boys had already managed to find a place in her affections.

She turned back to the stove, where the last slices of bacon sizzled in the big iron skillet. Automatically she picked up the wooden-handled fork to turn it. Nine slices fit neatly before her, and a crock of eggs stood at her left elbow, awaiting their turn in the bacon grease. Elizabeth lifted the bacon to a piece of brown grocer's paper to drain and set it in the warming oven atop the iron stove.

Five eggs fit neatly into the pan, the bacon grease cooking them rapidly, and she turned them over swiftly, allowing but a few seconds until she scooped them onto plates. She cast an eye toward the back porch and the yard, hoping to see signs of Lucas and his boys. And sure enough, from the barn, all three of her menfolk appeared and she smiled as she repeated the phrase aloud. "All three of my men." It was a pure delight, although she was smart enough to know that all would not always go well. There was a heap of adjusting to do on all their parts—more of it taking place on her side, no doubt. For these three were used to doing things their own way, and adapting to her notions of behavior might cause a fuss once in a while.

They halted at the horse trough and splashed water over their arms and hands, bending to douse their faces, and then with their hands they smoothed back their hair, the two boys keeping a close eye on their father as they imitated his actions. Together they trooped to the porch, and in through the back door.

"Stop right there," Elizabeth said in a stern voice, and, wonder of wonders, they obeyed. She'd used her best teacher voice, one she'd honed at the orphanage when keeping control of a herd of rambunctious boys, and these three responded as had her charges in Boston.

"Ma'am?" Lucas said, his voice carrying a query as he narrowed his eyes in her direction.

"I've just swept this floor, and unless the lot of you have stomped the dirt off outside on the porch, I'd appreciate it if you did so now. Either that or take off your boots."

"Too much trouble," Josh muttered beneath his breath, but as his father held open the screen door, he stepped onto the porch and made a big production of stamping his feet, then bending to check the bottoms of his boots for dirt. She caught the sheepish grin Lucas shot in her direction as he reentered the kitchen, and she turned to hide her own answering smile.

The man was too cocky for his own good. But he'd backed her up, made her feel her notions mattered, and for that she was grateful.

They ate her food without delay, pausing only long enough to listen as she said a few words of thanksgiving for the meal they were about to eat. Toby looked interested as she said the amen.

"Who was you talkin' to, Miss Lizzabet?" He looked puzzled, checking the corners of the room as though he'd missed a guest.

"I was praying, thanking God for our food," she said quietly, lifting her hand to her lips, desperate to hide the grin that threatened to appear as she heard the mis-pronunciation of her name.

"We never did that before," Toby said, tucking in to his scrambled eggs.

"Yeah, we did. But you were too little to remember," Josh said. "Mama always did that before we ate."

"And did she take you to church on Sundays?" Elizabeth asked.

"I dunno," Toby said, his mouth full, reaching for a biscuit.

"Mind your manners, son," Lucas said quietly, taking the biscuit from him and splitting it in half before he buttered both sides.

"We used to go, before mama died," Josh volunteered.

"But not since?" she asked, looking at Lucas.

He shook his head. "Been too busy." He lowered his head, thinking of the faith Doris had held so dear. And what good had it done her? Had the prayers of her pastor saved her life? The whole rigamarole of church seemed empty to him. But if Elizabeth was so inclined, he'd try to be agreeable about it. It was what Doris had wanted for her sons, and surely he owed her that much allegiance as the mother of his children.

Elizabeth spoke up in a firm voice. "Well, I won't be too busy, come Sunday. I'll expect an escort to church in town, or else your permission to use your mare and the buggy."

"I'll take you," Lucas said, his voice strained, as if he held back words better unspoken.

"Can we go, too, Pa?" Toby asked.

"I'll be sure to have your best shirts all ironed and ready if you'd like to go along," Elizabeth offered.

"I don't got a best shirt," Toby said, stuffing a piece of bacon into his mouth.

"Well, then, I'll check out your things and find the best of the lot."

"Making changes already, Miss Elizabeth?" Lucas asked quietly, his eyes hard. The woman was strong willed, sure enough, and he'd have to make some compromises along the way if this marriage was to succeed. Suddenly Lucas found he very much wanted things to work out with Elizabeth. She was strong and forthright, a woman to be respected.

She spoke her mind again, with a look that challenged him. "If the changes I'd like to put in place aren't agreeable to you, please feel free to let me know," she said, applying a good bit of butter to her own biscuit. They were good, he'd noted, some of the best he'd ever eaten, and that thought filled him with mixed emotions. She'd made it apparent that he would admit to one thing, at least. She was a good cook, and he was about to waste no time in telling her so.

But his younger son was a jump ahead of him. "You sure are a good cooker," Toby said, relishing his last bite of biscuit.

"Biscuits are nice and light," Lucas admitted as he caught her eye. He swept his gaze downward over her upper body, her dress buttoned up to her neck, but still outlining her generous bosom faithfully. A fact he took time to appreciate.

They ate then in silence, the boys finishing first and asking politely if they might be excused. Lucas was pleased that he'd managed to instill a few manners in them.

She faced him across the table, a fresh cup of coffee next to his plate, her own almost empty. "What are your plans for the day, Lucas?" she asked.

He looked up at her quickly. "Why, are you wanting me to do something in the house?"

She shook her head. "No, I just wanted to know when I should have your dinner ready, and if I must ring the bell to call you in, or perhaps ride out to find you."

"Ride out to find me?" He sounded disgruntled at that, and cleared his throat.

"I can ride a horse as well as most men," she said. "I thought I'd told you that already."

"Ring the bell. I'll hear it. And if I don't the boys will. By noon they'll be good and hungry. Don't forget you're cookin' for three good appetites."

"Who's been doing the cooking here before I arrived?"

He leaned back in his chair. "I've been known to open a quart jar and heat up the contents once in a while, and I know how to fry a steak and cut up potatoes. We haven't starved."

"I'm sure you've done a good job with your boys. They seem well mannered and are certainly nicely behaved. I wasn't criticizing you in any way, Lucas."

He looked away, toward the window where the swing moved a bit in the breeze. "I'm a bit touchy, I suppose, where my boys are concerned. We've had a tough row to hoe since Doris died. That's why I sent for a bride. And that's why it was you."

"How many offers did you get?"

He smiled. "More than I'd expected to. Probably over twenty or so. Some of them wanted to see a picture of me, and I dismissed them out of hand, for I've never had a picture taken, and I wouldn't have sent it if I'd had a dozen of them. My looks have nothing to do with my need for a wife and a mother for my boys. I wanted a woman who could keep house and knew how to please a man."

"I don't know if I qualify for the last stipulation you offered, but I can cook well enough to please fifty-odd children in an orphanage, and believe me, some days it was a real challenge."

"If you keep on at the rate you're going here, Elizabeth, I won't have any complaints. You're a damn good cook and I—"

"Please don't curse, Lucas. I can't imagine that it's a good thing for your sons to hear their father using such language. For their sake, if not mine, please try to watch your tongue."

"To tell the truth, Lizzie, I'd rather watch yours, especially when you're thinkin' real hard and you kinda swipe it over your top lip. Makes me want to kiss you."

Her blush was beyond pink, for she felt its heat all the way down the front of her dress. "We were talking about my cooking, Lucas, not kissing. If you have any requests for your meals, I'll do my best to fix the things you enjoy eating."

"Nah, just surprise me," he said with a grin. "I'm so sick of eating my own fixin', I'd just as soon never look at that range over there again. I even burn scrambled eggs."

"Tell me, Lucas, why did you pick me out of twenty-something other letters? I'm sure most of the ladies had the same qualifications I did."

"Maybe so, but there was something about your hand-writing, the way you took care with your letters and the things you said that let me know you were the right one for the job. I sent off the money the next day, for I figured if you could handle fifty young'uns in an orphanage, two would be a cinch for you."

She faced him boldly. "I want to tell you something. I was happy to receive your wire and the money for my fare. You took me out of a bad situation in Boston and I want you to know I appreciate it."

"Was there someone giving you a hard time?" he asked, his mouth narrowing as if he'd march to Boston and clean somebody's clock, were that to be so.

"I'd been engaged. Sort of, anyway—"

"You can't be engaged sort of, Lizzie. Either you are or you aren't."

"Well, Amos definitely liked to speak of marriage, and we talked about setting a date, so I guess you could say I was within my rights to have expectations."

"What happened?" he asked when she halted her explanations and looked down at the floor.

"My sister came on the scene. She'd been staying with my grandparents for a few years, helping out there, and Amos hadn't seen her for a long time. She'd grown up to be a lovely girl. Looks like my mama, in fact—small, blonde and about half my size. When Amos got a good look, he decided she was the better prospect and dumped me. They got married and they have a family now."

Lucas walked around the table and drew her from her chair, holding her before him, his hands on her waist, her breasts softening against his chest. "He did me a big favor, Elizabeth, and I'm not saying that to make you feel good. I mean it. And anyone who would judge a woman by her hair color or size or shape ain't much of a man, to my way of thinking."

"I wish you'd been in Boston, Lucas," she said with a chuckle. "I'd have grabbed you up and sailed off like a clipper ship."

"Well, you've got me in Missouri, sweetheart, and that's almost as good as Boston."

"You've only known me for a day or so, Lucas. How can I be your sweetheart?"

He bent low and his voice was a whisper in her ear. "You earned that name last night in my bed, Lizzie. As far as I'm concerned, you're my sweetheart, and if you want to argue about it, we can have a set-to right now."

She smiled, as if she wanted in the very worst way to lean up and kiss his cheek, but then thought better of it. "I won't argue with you over such a thing. I know enough to pick my battles."

"Is that a warning?" he asked.

She shook her head. "Nope, just a fact. And now you'd better get on out there and get busy. I've got work to do."

"If you're washing sheets this morning, I'll carry the big boiler out for you. Looks like it's steaming pretty good."

She'd put it on the stove and half filled it with water from the reservoir before breakfast, and probably planned to tote it out to the porch when Lucas left. His offer seemed to leave her without words for a moment and then she smiled, waving her hand at the steaming boiler.

"Be my guest, sir. I won't argue with a gentleman."

The sheets were washed and rinsed within an hour. She sought out a length of clothesline, searching through the pantry, and there it was, on the top shelf—a bit dusty, but looking to be a good length of rope. She doused it in the wash water she'd put aside in a bucket for washing the floor and then rinsed it in the rinse tub before she carried it out to the yard, looking for a good place to loop it. A nail on the side of the corncrib seemed a likely spot and she began there, then looked at the milk house, about thirty feet distant. Sure enough, a nail was pounded into the wall at a good height for her to reach. Surely Lucas must have used the line when he did the washing, she thought, even as she wondered how a man alone could keep up with the work in a house and barn and still bring in his crops and care for his children. He'd fought a losing battle for three years, to her way of thinking.

She looped the rope around the nail, then headed for the porch, where she wound it around one of the upright posts. It was enough line for all the sheets and pillowcases to hang, and within fifteen minutes she was finished with the job.

The rinse water went to the garden, where she wet down the rest of the green beans and the potato plants, remembering the hours spent in the garden back home, her mother at her side, picking beans and later digging potatoes. It had been a happy time and she cherished the memories.

And now she would make new ones in the garden Lucas had planted. A small family of tomato worms had set up housekeeping on the tender green leaves, so she picked them off and put them in a tin can she found in the trash. From there she took them to a bare spot in the yard, where she placed them on a piece of paper, then lit the four corners. She'd seen her mother do such a thing back home when they lived in the country, and it seemed to be suitable vengeance on the ugly worms for their destructive habits.

Toby came from the barn to see what she was doing and squatted by the funeral pyre. "Are they dead?" he asked in a dark whisper.

"If they aren't now, they will be in a minute or so," she told him, waiting till the fire consumed the paper and the worms and she could clean up the mess.

"I never saw anybody burn worms before," Toby said.

"These are tomato worms and I don't like them. They ruin the tomato plants, and if we want tomatoes in jars for the winter months, we have to take good care of the plants this summer."

"Can I watch next time you do it?" he asked, shooting her an admiring glance, as if she had somehow become a woman to respect, to his mind.

"We'll see," she said, unwilling to promise such a thing, for surely Lucas wouldn't want his son to be bloodthirsty. "Are you working out in the barn?"

"Me and Josh have been raking out the stalls, so Pa can put fresh straw in them for tonight. Pa calls it mucking out the stalls, but we do it with rakes, so I don't know where he gets that sort of word."

"It's a man thing," Elizabeth said with a smile.

"We got sheets hanging all over the yard, don't we, ma'am?" he said, seeming to note for the first time that there was a veritable fleet of sails set loose on the clothesline. "Pa never hung things so neat—just kinda draped them over the line to dry."

About as she'd suspected, Elizabeth thought briefly. "Well, these are almost dry, so I need to get the churning done before I have to bring them in and make up the beds. You go ahead and help your brother."

"Yes, ma'am," he said, turning to scamper across to the barn, where he disappeared inside the wide door.

Elizabeth went to the kitchen, dragged out the churn and poured in all the cream from the buckets of milk Lucas had brought into the house since her arrival. She sat down with the churn between her legs, and began the tedious job of churning butter. It had never been her favorite task, but it was her chore and she would gain the benefit when she sold the extra butter in town.

Impressions of Lucas began running through her mind, along with thoughts of the night just past making her blush as she recalled his words of admiration for her body. He'd admired her long hair and made much of her full breasts and she'd been glad he couldn't see the blushes she'd known were covering her body at his words. Now it seemed she was finished before she'd realized the churn was binding up. She lifted the lid and there lay the butter, in a neat circle at the bottom. She lifted the churned butter from the tall container and placed it in a lump, leaving the buttermilk to be disposed of later. She didn't know if Lucas enjoyed drinking it or not. For herself, she considered it fit for the hogs, but he might have a different preference.

She worked the butter, squeezing all the whey from it, then made four separate rounds from the mass and placed them on a large plate, covering it with a pot cover to keep it clean.

"And now for dinner. I'm a bit late starting it, but soup should be easy enough. I'll have more time to cook pork chops later on," she said quietly to herself. A large kettle from the pantry was carried to the stove, where she put a ladle of water within and then pushed it to the back of the burners.

A Mason jar with a variety of vegetables in the pantry seemed to cry for the kettle, she thought, and she opened it and dumped it in, then found an onion, peeled it, cut it up into bits and added them to the mix. It looked as if Lucas had been the beneficiary of someone's skill with a canning kettle, for he had a decent supply of jars with assorted vegetables in them and even some beef, cooked up and put aside for a night when she was in a hurry.

For now, she took a pint jar of the beef and opened it, then added a quart of tomatoes from the pantry. Altogether it made a decent-looking dinner, she thought. With a pan of corn bread, they could manage to survive until suppertime. In minutes she had corn bread in the oven and she headed to the yard to bring in the sheets. She'd make up the beds later, she decided, draping the sheets over the banister to be carried upstairs.

Before she could go to the porch to ring the dinner bell, she caught sight of Lucas and the boys heading for the horse trough, him laughing at them and swatting them as if he teased them about something, the boys laughing and scampering ahead of him. They went through the same ritual as they had in the morning before breakfast, and again she couldn't help but note the way both Toby and Josh imitated their father's actions. It warmed her heart.

She'd thought of the boys when she noticed her box of books on the bedroom floor only this morning. Straightening the bedroom, she'd considered the pair of them, wondering whether they'd listened to any of the stories she cherished as childhood memories, or whether they were ignorant of the excitement contained within the covers of a book. Especially those intended for children's pleasure.

Perhaps now was a good time to bring up the subject of reading, she decided, and proceeded to do so.

"I wondered if you boys had formed an acquaintance with books while your mother was still alive," she asked nicely. "I haven't seen you with a book in your hands yet. Do any of you read for the fun of it, or for learning?"

"You've only been here a couple of days, ma'am. You haven't seen us at our best," Lucas said. "I noticed the box of books in our room earlier and wondered if you planned on using them to educate us." His eyes sparkled as he assumed a teasing demeanor.

Josh spoke up. "You don't read anything but the newspaper, Pa. And when that gets here, you complain because it's already weeks old and all the news isn't news anymore." Josh was eloquent in his description of Lucas's ire at the newspapers from St. Louis not getting to Thomasville in a decent length of time.

"Well, that's true enough," Lucas said with a grin in Elizabeth's direction. "We're sort of out of line for the latest in news here, Miss Elizabeth."

"There are other things to read," she said primly, and then expanded on the subject.

"The books you noticed upstairs are just waiting to be put on a shelf somewhere in this house. Do any of you have any ideas as to where they can go? If we can get them out in plain sight, I wouldn't be averse to reading aloud of an evening, if any of you are interested in hearing stories from them."

Toby almost jumped from his chair, his hand high in the air as he sought her attention. "I surely would, Miss

Lizzibet. I would. I'd sit right next to you in case there were any pictures in your books to look at, and I'd listen real hard if you read stories to us. My mama used to read to us sometimes from a book with lots of pictures."

His enthusiasm tickled Elizabeth pink, and she felt a flush rise to cover her cheeks at the boy's excitement. "Well, I'm sure your mama enjoyed spending time with you that way. I could do that very thing, starting this evening, if your father would bring the box of books downstairs and place it in the parlor. I suspect I could find a table in there to stack them on, since I didn't see any shelves anywhere."

Lucas was quick to take her up on her offer, and his words were obliging. "There's an old library cabinet up in the attic, Elizabeth. I could bring it down for you. It's a piece of furniture with glassed-in doors and shelves inside. Me and Josh could figure out a way to get it into the parlor if you like."

"That sounds like a wonderful idea, Lucas. If you and Josh wouldn't mind doing that after dinner, I'd be happy to put my books in order in the parlor, and perhaps we can spend an hour this evening reading some adventure story."

"What's an adventure story, ma'am?" Toby asked, wide-eyed at the notion of such a thing.

"It's a story about people who do exciting things, or invent things that no one else has ever thought of. Sometimes it's about explorers who travel into parts of the world where no one else has gone before. Sometimes it's about animals with owners who love them."

"Were you an explorer when you came to us from Boston, ma'am?" Toby asked.

"Sort of," Elizabeth replied, casting a look at Lucas that pleaded for his help. But it seemed he was not willing to intercede for her, so she elaborated a bit as she told the story of how she had come to Thomasville.

"I got a wire from your father asking me to come here to marry all of you and make my home with you. He sent me the money for train fare and for the stagecoach from St. Louis, and I set off on my adventure. I'd never been anywhere outside a small town near Boston, and then to the city itself to live for a number of years. So seeing the countryside west of Massachusetts was an eye-opener for me. Riding the train was an adventure in itself, for I saw a number of people heading for the west, and spoke to a young man who sat next to me about his coming adventures. He was going farther west, planning to work on a ranch, and he spoke of riding horses and tending cattle. It was even exciting to see all the fields of wheat and corn growing right next to the train tracks, and we waved at folks in the towns where the train stopped.

"Then, when I arrived here and met all of you, it seemed like I'd made the right choices for my life, and I married your father and got myself a family, ready-made. I can't tell you how pleased I am to be here with all three of you. It seems to me that right here is a wonderful place to be."

"I never been anyplace but right here," Toby said sadly, as if his life were indeed bereft of all things exciting.

"But as I said, right here is a wonderful place to be,

Toby. You have a good father, a nice home and a brother. There are puppies in the barn and food in the pantry and someone to cook for you and keep your clothing clean. I'd say you have a good life here on the farm."

Elizabeth felt like a schoolteacher by the time she finished enumerating all of the things Toby should be thankful for, and it was a surprise to hear Lucas second her observations.

"Miss Elizabeth is right, Toby. You're a fortunate young man. You have food and clothing and a nice home to live in. There are folks all over the world who don't have nearly the good things we all take for granted. I'll venture to say that even in Boston Miss Elizabeth saw folks with a lot less to be thankful for than what we have right here."

Elizabeth nodded, and then recalled some of the places she'd seen and been. "There are places in Boston where four or five children live in one room with their parents, and sleep on the floor, for they have no money to buy beds or mattresses. I tend to get angry when I think of all the children in this world who have nothing, and then see rich folks who don't care about those who live in poverty."

"*You* cared, Elizabeth," Lucas said quietly.

"Yes, I did. And I still do. For I've managed to find a fine home to live in and a family to tend to and a place to call my own. I'm one of the fortunate ones."

"I thought we were the fortunate ones," Lucas said with emphasis. "What do you think, boys? Are you glad Miss Elizabeth is with us instead of in Boston, cooking for fifty orphan children?"

"Who's cookin' for them now?" Toby asked, his forehead wrinkled as he thought of fifty starving children in that far-off place, while he ate his fill here in Thomasville, Missouri.

"I'm sure there are ladies from the community who are filling in for me. It's always easy to volunteer for such a job when you know you have a nice home to return to when the day is over."

"I'm awful glad you're cooking for us, ma'am," Josh said, a smile curving his lips as he finished his soup. "I'm awful glad someone taught you how to cook such good stuff, too."

"Thank you, Josh. I enjoy cooking, and I'll admit it's easier and more fun to cook for four people than fifty."

Lucas seemed pleased with the lengthy conversation they'd shared over the dinner table, and it was with reluctance that he pushed back his chair and lifted a hand to Josh. "Let's do our duty, young'un. I promised Elizabeth we'd bring down that big cabinet for her."

Josh stood immediately and watched as his father carried his plate and silverware to the sink board, then followed suit, his father's example letting him know silently that this was the right thing to do. Toby gathered his plate up and rose, but Elizabeth reached for it quickly.

"If you'll bring the cups over to the sink, I'll take care of this, Toby."

He nodded cheerfully and did as he was bid, then followed his father and brother up the stairs. Elizabeth heard the sound of a door opening and closing and wondered at the entrance to the attic, for she'd suspected the house had such a place beneath the roof, but hadn't noticed a door.

In less than fifteen minutes she heard the voices near-ing, and noted Lucas's as he instructed his sons as to where to grasp the piece of furniture and then instructed them as to their part in toting it down the stairs. Lucas came first, bearing the weight of the load, Toby and Josh above him, each holding a corner of the top of the cabinet.

It was large, probably six feet tall, Elizabeth suspected, having seen such things back home where folks filled their parlors or libraries with cabinets such as this one. Why it had been relegated to the attic was beyond her comprehension, for she knew that if she'd owned such a thing, it would never have left the parlor for the oblivion of a dusty, dank place like an attic.

Elizabeth looked forward to telling her mother, by way of a letter, about the cabinet and the rest of the furnishings of the house she now lived in. Perhaps tomorrow would be a good time to write such a missive to her parents, for they knew only that she'd traveled west to be married, and the rest of the details were lacking.

Now, as Elizabeth watched, delighted beyond words, Lucas and his sons managed to carry the cabinet into the parlor, then Lucas looked toward Elizabeth, who had fol-lowed them and waited in the doorway.

"Well, where do you want this thing, ma'am?" he asked, setting his end on the floor and helping the boys to stand it upright. Elizabeth had been right. It was over six feet tall and probably five feet wide, with four glass shelves inside.

"Over against that wall, between the two windows. I'll move the chair first to make room." She hastened over to the designated spot and shoved an overstuffed chair from the place she'd decided on, moving it a few feet away to be tended to later.

With encouraging words, Lucas directed his sons to help him locate the thing where Elizabeth had decreed it should go, and then they all stood and looked at it, as if it were some foreign object dropped into their familiar parlor.

"If you'll bring my box of books down for me, I'll dust the cabinet and put them away in it. Tonight we can decide what we want to read." Elizabeth walked to stand before the cabinet and opened one of the doors. "It's not even as dusty as I'd thought it would be. It must be almost airtight."

"It's a good piece of furniture. Used to be here years ago, but Dor…" He paused for a moment. "We decided to put it away a few years back, since we had no real use for it. Doris wasn't much for books and such. She read a book of Bible stories to the boys once in a while, but…" He seemed to find it difficult to speak of the boys' mother, and again, as she had the night before, Elizabeth sensed an air of reticence about him.

"Well, we'll make use of it now," Elizabeth said, excitement rising in her as she thought of renewing acquaintance with her supply of books. She'd carried them across the country, unwilling to lose a single one of the volumes that had given her so much pleasure.

In her mind she began composing the letter she would write at the very first opportunity.

Chapter Four

When Lucas left for the barn a bit later, his boys in tow, he left Elizabeth with two boxes, both containing books, for he'd remembered another stash in the attic, left from his mother's things, that might be of interest to her.

She was delayed for a short while when the boy from the emporium drove a wagon up the lane from the town road. She met him at the door and helped him carry in the goods they'd purchased at his father's store, then filled the pantry shelves with the largesse that Lucas had supplied.

Lucas hailed her from the yard as the boy drove away. "I'll take care of that beef when I come in, Lizzie. Unless you're of a mind to cut it up yourself." He smiled as if he could imagine her thoughts on the subject.

She shook her head. "I'll leave the job to you. I'll just watch, thank you. Maybe next time I'll be brave enough to swing a cleaver and do the cutting up." That Luc would offer so readily to do such a task almost surprised her, and yet he'd been willing thus far to lighten her load if he could. He'd done much to please her, she realized, not least of which was his attentions to her. And now he'd offered to do a chore she had no liking for, even though it might be considered a woman's work.

With a wave of his hand he walked around the barn, and she turned back to the parlor to sort through the volumes she'd carried across the country. It was a task she relished. She filled her hands with the books from her childhood, classics and adventure stories alike. Inside the box that had belonged to Lucas's mother were volumes from the past. A preprimer from that lady's school days, volumes of history, mostly of Europe and Asia, with a few pages given over to the early years of America. Even a book devoted to cursive writing and instructions for the proper way to print the various letters of the alphabet, and write them in cursive style.

There was a big family Bible with names inscribed within, with Lucas's name on the page designated for births. An assortment of stories from the Bible, written for children and well thumbed, demonstrated his early reading material. And packed with care, wrapped in ancient newsprint, were pictures of a man and woman and their children.

These she placed on the top shelf of the cabinet—four pictures taken with a photographer's camera, from those days when men and women hired such a person to capture the present, saving it for the future in a portrait. One of the pictures was of a lovely lady with three little girls and two small boys at her knee, and the younger boy looked so like Toby, it startled Elizabeth. Surely this must be Lucas, she thought, holding it up to the window, the better to gaze upon the small boy's face.

And she found the answer then to the mystery of why Lucas had taken to her so easily. The lady in the picture, Luc's mother, was a woman of considerable size. A lovely woman, but heavy nonetheless. No wonder Luc had said he was happy with his bride. And Elizabeth almost hugged herself as she remembered just how delighted he'd been with her.

Her own books caught her attention next, begging for shelf space. She removed them from the box, wiped the covers with a cloth and sorted them out. The fiction she placed on the second shelf, leaving plenty of room for further acquisitions, should Lucas be so inclined. The next shelf held her books of history and geography, a blending of schoolbooks and things that had caught her father's eye in his regular visits to the bookstore near their home.

From behind her she heard the masculine tones now familiar to her. "Elizabeth, what are you up to over there?" Lucas asked, walking up behind her to look over her shoulder at the rapidly filling bookcase. "I used to wish..." His voice trailed off and he cleared his throat.

She turned to him, looking up into eyes that seemed to be far away from her, his thoughts perhaps dwelling on another time. Then he smiled, and she felt a thrill touch her heart, and she lifted her hand to cover that rapidly pounding organ. "What do you wish, Lucas?"

He seemed to return to her then and his smile was tender. "I used to wish that Doris would fill this bookcase of my mother's with just such a collection." He lifted his hand and his index finger touched book after book, each volume seeming to receive his attention. "This sat here when I was married the first time, and Doris said it took up a lot of room and she had nothing to put into it, so when Josh was very young, I took it to the attic."

He touched Elizabeth's cheek with that same index finger and then his full palm curved against her face, and she felt the warmth cascade the length of her body. "My mother would have approved of you, Lizzie," he said quietly. And as if that were the highest praise he could offer, he bent to her and his lips touched hers with tenderness. Not like the hot, needy caresses he'd lavished on her eager body in the night hours, but with a gentleness that made her want to cry.

He looked at the books she'd settled into place and his query surprised her. "What's next, Lizzie? Will the family Bible have a place here?" He touched it with reverence as it lay on top of the box of books she'd found.

"Indeed it will. Not on the shelf, but in a place where it can be better seen," she told him, lifting the heavy volume to settle it on the library table near the other window. She lifted the stack of storybooks and placed them on the bottom shelf, where they were easily accessible, should the boys desire to look at them.

"I had much the same assortment as a child. I think the boys will appreciate them once we read a few of the stories they hold," she said, turning pages as she spoke.

Luc's arms were around her and he held her as if he hungered for the touch of a woman. As well he might, she thought, for he'd been alone a long time. Her arms slid up to encircle his neck and she blushed at her own temerity, for she'd never been so forward with a man. But

Luc seemed to find no fault with her actions, for he held her closer, until she was pressed against his body from her knees to her breasts.

"You're quite a woman, Lizzie. Just the kind of armful I was hoping for."

"I'm surely pleased that you didn't yearn for someone small and helpless, Luc," she said with a smile. "I'd never have fit the bill."

His grin matched hers. "I'm more than satisfied with my bride, sweetheart."

And there he goes, calling me that name again. She ducked her head, her forehead touching his collarbone. "That sounds sorta nice, Luc. That sweetheart thing."

He touched her chin and lifted her face to his. "I want you to know that I mean it, Lizzie."

She brushed at his shirt, her eyes unable to meet his now, but he would not have it, for he touched her chin once more and she blinked as he lowered his head to her. His lips were not as soft, his message not as pure as before, for she caught sight of a gleam in his eyes that told her he was intent on laying claim to her, but she would not have it here.

"Oh, no, you don't, Lucas. I've got work to do and I'll wager you have any number of things you need to accomplish before suppertime. So clear out now and let me finish this and then get supper ready." She tried her best to look stern, but he laughed aloud and squeezed her tightly before he let her go.

"I can wait," he said with a grin that transformed his face. He was a handsome man, Elizabeth decided. And he was hers. *Eat your heart out, Sissy. Mine is far and away the better man. You can have Amos Rogers with my blessings.* And for the first time, she relinquished all thoughts of what might have been in favor of what she possessed.

Lucas snatched up his hat from the sofa and left the parlor, his pleasure apparent, his stride long as he covered the distance to the back door. Elizabeth covered her cheeks with both palms and closed her eyes. The man was a scamp.

By the time she'd frittered away another hour with the treasure trove in the parlor, she had to hustle to get the beds made up. The sheets lay over the banister where she'd left them and she fairly trotted up the stairs with them over her arm, then spent long minutes in all three bedrooms, remaking the beds and shaking the pillows into their cases. The quilts were tossed over the top sheets quickly and she looked outside to where the sun was rapidly falling in the western sky.

It was almost time for supper to be on the table and Elizabeth was sorely rushed to make a meal. She went to the pantry, caught sight of the pork barrel and returned to the kitchen to wash her hands thoroughly, lest she allow any bit of dirt into the lard that kept the pork fresh. Lifting the lid, she placed it on a shelf and then reached within the lard to seek out pieces of pork for their evening meal. A package, seemingly wrapped in paper, was beneath her fingertips and she grasped it and pulled it forth. Covered with a coating of lard, tied with string, it felt like chops through the wrapping.

Once in the kitchen she made short work of readying the meat for the oven, and soon seven pork chops were washed and in the iron skillet; she browned them and transferred them to a baking pan. She found a quart of tomatoes on a pantry shelf and poured them over the pork, then sliced a big onion on top before sliding it into the oven.

Potatoes were in good supply, so she peeled six of them, sliced them into a pan, added flour, milk and butter, then mixed them all together and put that pan in the oven. Satisfied that her family would not starve at suppertime, she went to the garden to see if there was any other produce she might use among the weeds that thrived there.

Sure enough, some summer squash had survived the weeds and she picked two of them to cook in one of the skillets. Peeled, sliced and awash with butter and onions, they were soon set to simmer.

"We gonna eat sometime tonight?" Lucas asked from the porch, and she spun to see him scraping his boots on the step, the two boys still washing at the horse trough.

"I was late getting started on the meal," she said apologetically. "I got busy with the books and forgot the time. I'm so sorry, Lucas. It won't happen again."

He came in the kitchen door and approached her, standing close as she turned to face him. His hands were on her shoulders, his big body just inches from hers, and she felt flustered, felt small and feminine before him. It was a good feeling, she admitted to herself, for Elizabeth was pleased to the core to be finally experiencing that sensation. Feeling small and feminine was exhilarating.

Lucas looked into her eyes. "You needn't ever apologize to me, Elizabeth. Especially since you've done nothing to be worrying over. I was teasing you, and apparently you're not used to such a thing. I'll be careful from now on to speak only the facts, and in this case, they're simple. Whenever you have supper ready, it will be fine with all three of the men in your life. We're not about to mess up the best thing that's happened to us in a number of years. Me, especially, ma'am." And again his smile won her, brought her lips to his cheek.

"Thank you," she said quietly, a bit flustered at her own actions.

He bent to her then and pressed his lips against hers, a brief touch, bearing no hint of passion, but a kiss given as a man might caress his wife in passing. He looked down at her and smiled. "Do you forgive me for upsetting you?"

She felt a strange heat sweep upward through her body, met by the warmth that flowed downward from her lips. They felt almost scorched, she decided, running her tongue over her upper lip, tasting Lucas upon its surface. Was this the thing named desire that she'd heard spoken of at times when the ladies from the church did their quilting and two or three heads would be bent over the frames, their words low, as if they did not want an audience?

For they'd spoken of their husbands, spoken of passion on rare occasions, sometimes complaining, the newlyweds among them often smiling smugly as if they knew a great secret unknown to others. *Desire.* A word unknown to her on a personal level, although she felt a hint of it—just a hint, she reminded herself—when Lucas touched her as he was now.

And all this after only two days.

They ate quickly, the boys in a hurry to be finished, for the lure of Elizabeth reading to them was one they could not resist. Even Lucas finished quickly and, as at noontime, he carried his plate and silver to the sink, Josh and Toby following his example. She was pleased, not only because they were helping her, but because it was obvious that they were attempting to mold their lives after that of the man they so admired.

She washed the dishes quickly and Lucas picked up a towel, standing beside her at the sink. She looked up at him, surprised to find him so ready to help. "You don't need to do this, Lucas. You've worked hard all day and this is your time to rest."

"How about you, ma'am? Have you been sitting on the sofa all afternoon? How did the sheets get washed, dried and then back on the beds?"

"That's different. I was late making the beds, for I dithered around with the books too long, and then was almost too late to begin supper. I lost track of time, Lucas. And don't think I don't appreciate you helping me with the dishes or for setting an example for the boys with carrying your dishes to the sink after meals today. It's how they will learn good manners and the behavior that will stay with them for their whole lives."

"I want you to know that I appreciate the way you've tried to fit in so readily, Elizabeth. My boys are fond of you already."

"Well, they're champing at the bit right now, waiting for the story I promised them," she said, drying her hands and swiping her hair back from her face. Then she walked to the parlor, Lucas on her heels.

"There sure are a bunch of books, Miss Lizziebet," Toby sang out as they neared him, standing before the big cabinet. "Look, there's red ones and blue ones and some just plain brown stuff, too."

"Sometimes the plain brown covers hold the best stories inside," she told him, opening the glass door, trying to decide on one of the books to read. Deciding that the fairy tales would not be appropriate, she went on to the adventure stories, spotting a favorite of hers, one she'd read to the children at the orphanage a year or so ago.

"This is a story about a special horse," she said, opening the book she cherished. "It is one of my favorites."

At the word *horse,* both boys perked up, for it was an animal familiar to them and they had no problem with being interested in such a creature. So Elizabeth read from the book to a rapt audience, for Lucas also sat, the three of them entranced by the cultured voice that read of the adventures of a horse and the perils it faced.

Halfway through the book, Elizabeth set it aside, amid pleas from Toby to finish the story, but she was adamant, for it was well past the boys' bedtime and she wanted them to anticipate the time to come tomorrow night when she would finish the story. With protests on their lips, the two boys climbed the stairs to their bedrooms and Elizabeth readied herself for the night. She checked over the kitchen, adding two chunks of wood to the stove lest the fire burn out before morning, then started for Lucas's bedroom, the flight of stairs assuming an enormity that was daunting, staring her in the face, Lucas beside her, keeping pace with her slowing steps.

"Are you worried about this?" he asked, and she only looked at him and nodded.

"I'd thought at first that once you had consummated our marriage, it would be enough for you, for a time, at least. But it doesn't look that way right now."

His smile was her answer, and his eyes glistened in the light of the candle he carried. "I don't see me tiring of you in a hurry, Elizabeth. I find you to be an attractive woman and an able wife, for your cooking has endeared you to the boys and myself already. Reading the book to them was the best thing you could have come up with, for you read well, and your choice of material was excellent. They're primed already for the rest of the story tomorrow evening."

"That was my aim, Lucas. I'm pleased that I was successful in involving them in a book. I find that children who read are the ones who accomplish much in school, and if they enjoy being read to, it bodes well for their own reading in the years to come."

He steered her into his bedroom, then shut the door, watching as she went behind the screen to wash and change into her nightgown. "How did you get so smart, Elizabeth? And I don't mean the education you've obviously enjoyed, but your knack with knowing how to deal with children."

"I've given you chapter and verse of my work with the

orphans, Lucas," she said from behind the screen, just as her dress was tossed to drape over the wooden barricade.

He sat on the side of the bed and tugged off his boots, then scraped his stockings off, before rising and allowing his trousers to fall to the floor. He picked them up, tossing them toward the basket of soiled clothing, and his shirt followed, leaving him in his drawers. Without hesitation he dropped them to the floor and, lowering the sheet, found his pillow and covered himself to the waist, awaiting the appearance of his bride.

She splashed water into the basin, a sound he recognized, and then he heard her humming as she washed and readied herself for bed. He narrowed his eyes, silently cursing the screen that hid her from his view, and by the time she appeared, covered totally by the white gown she wore to bed, he was impatience personified.

"You sure diddle around a lot, putting on a nightgown," he said, ruing the impatience that tinged his voice.

She lifted her chin and sniffed. "I had to wash up first and I knew you weren't going anywhere. There wasn't any hurry that I could see."

Lucas tossed back the sheet, presenting her place in his bed with a flourish. His hands itched to touch her skin, his body throbbed with the arousal he could not conceal and his eyes were filled now with the glorious abundance of the woman who lay beside him. He rolled to her and his lips found hers without hesitation. Wonder of wonders, she accepted his kiss and her arm encircled his neck, drawing him even closer.

Life just didn't get any better, Lucas decided.

* * *

They worked and sorted out their lives together for the next week, each day much like the last. But there was a sense of peace and happiness in the house he lived in, Lucas decided. Since Elizabeth had arrived, he'd found new purpose in each day, new joy in each night spent in his bed. He even enjoyed watching her at the kitchen table one evening, writing industriously—a letter to her parents, she'd said. A letter telling of Lucas and his sons and the new home she'd found in Missouri. And best of all, his sons were coming to accept Elizabeth's place in their lives, were treating her as a mother, even though they hadn't designated her as such. A fact Elizabeth didn't seem to feel was important, for she just kept on with cleaning the house, cooking for them, reading to them in the evenings and treating them as her family.

And then one morning was a different kettle of fish, for news arrived from town, a wire from the stationmaster, hand delivered by his boy. Lucas met the lad on the back porch.

"A wire from Boston for Mrs. Harrison," the boy said importantly, handing Lucas a sealed envelope. "Mr. Cunningham thought she should see it right off, so he sent me out."

Lucas drew a coin from his pocket and presented it to the lad, who lost no time in pocketing it and then turning back to his horse. Lifting a hand in farewell, the boy was gone, leaving Lucas to enter the kitchen, missive in hand.

"A wire for you from Boston, Elizabeth," he said, walking to the table where she was cutting out biscuits on the cutting board from the pantry.

Her eyes widened at his words and she dusted off her hands on her apron and stepped away from her task, taking the proffered envelope. Her fingers trembled a bit as she opened the flap and drew forth the slip of paper the stationmaster had written the message on.

She read it aloud, her voice low, her words trembling. "'Sissy died yesterday. Stop. Beware of Amos Rogers's arrival there. Stop. Your aunt Hildegarde's will read last week. Stop. You are the beneficiary. Stop. Laura.'"

"I'd say you're in for some sort of adventure of your own," Lucas said shortly. "Who is Laura? Amos Rogers is the gentleman who jilted you for your sister, right? And he's coming here to see you? If your sister indeed passed away, why didn't he send a wire himself? What purpose would he have in coming here?" Lucas seemed angered by the news.

Elizabeth could barely get her breath, so close to tears was she. The news of Sissy's death was before her, but it hadn't penetrated her mind fully. Perhaps this was a joke of sorts, she thought. But no, Laura was too serious, too devoted to her to do such a thing.

"Laura is my best friend back home." she said, confusion seeming to be engulfing her. "She would know I'd want the news as soon as possible. I wonder that my parents didn't write, too."

She read the message over again, unable to find a connection between the two deaths of her loved ones. Then the burden of grief swept over her and she dissolved, her tears falling, her hands trembling, her legs barely able to hold her erect.

Lucas moved quickly, his arms circling her. His chest a resting place, and his voice a welcome comfort as she leaned on him. Her tears soaked his shirt quickly and his hands were warm against her back. She vaguely heard him issue a command to the boys as they called from the porch and then there was silence as he led her to the parlor and allowed her to weep, offering his handkerchief as she sought to speak.

"Wipe your eyes and blow your nose, sweetheart," he said softly. Then he waited until she'd done as he'd said. Her eyes were swollen as she looked into his gaze and she could only shake her head in bewilderment.

"How could Sissy die? She's young and healthy. I can understand Aunt Hildegarde's death, for she was old. I spent much time with her when she was unable to care for herself in the past year or so, but when I left Boston she seemed to be doing well. We were close, for I knew I was her favorite. We were so much alike."

"Obviously she loved you, sweetheart. And until we know more about Sissy's death, you won't have any answers there. What I don't understand is Laura's reference to Amos coming here. I'd think he would be grieving in Boston and preparing for his wife's burial."

Elizabeth shook her head. "I can't imagine why he would come unless it was to tell me of Sissy's death, and that doesn't seem likely. As you said, I'd think he was busy with her funeral and such. And taking care of his children."

"We may find out sooner rather than later just what his intentions are," Lucas said, holding Elizabeth in a firm grip, as if he would not release her until he was sure she could stand alone. Her first spate of tears was past, but he knew there would be more to come, and he regretted deeply that she must face this double loss with her family so far away.

"I'll do what I can, Elizabeth. We'll wire Laura today and try to find out more details about your sister. Do you think you are up to a trip to town this afternoon?"

She nodded, her face against his neck, her shoulders still trembling, but seemingly she was able to speak, for she whispered his name against the side of his throat and then drew back to look up into his eyes.

"Thank you, Lucas. I don't know what I'd have done without you here with me. I'm not usually such a watering pot, but this has hit me like a ton of bricks, and I'm just beginning to take it all in."

He turned her back to the kitchen. "Come on, sweetheart. We'll get breakfast put together and afterward we'll talk."

The biscuits were ragged looking, the coffee a bit strong and the eggs a bit overcooked, but the boys didn't complain, so pleased were they that their new mother seemed to be more composed by the time they were allowed into the kitchen to eat their morning meal. Lucas spoke to them about the chores to be done, keeping the conversation to their daily tasks and relieving Elizabeth of having to speak. For she was obviously shaken by the news she'd received and merely nibbled at a biscuit half and pushed her eggs around on her plate.

Lucas took charge of the day's events, helping Elizabeth in the kitchen while the boys tended to their chores, gathering eggs and feeding the chickens and releasing the other animals into the pasture for the morning.

It was a quiet noontime meal, with a kettle of soup and thick slices of bread, but there were no complaints, for it was nourishing and hearty food and Lucas was more than satisfied with Elizabeth's efforts.

They ate quickly, then he sent Elizabeth to the bedroom to change her clothes for the trip to town. He and the boys washed up the dishes, Toby thrilled at the chance to dabble in the basin, for he'd never been given so illustrious a chore. Lucas rinsed them and Josh did the honors with a dish towel. Before fifteen minutes had passed Elizabeth appeared in a clean dress, and the kitchen was in decent shape.

They headed for town in the farm wagon, for Lucas wanted to buy some lumber from the mill as long as they were making the trip. Beside him on the wide seat, Elizabeth was busy with paper and pencil, composing a wire to her parents, and another to Laura.

"Lucas, this is going to be an expensive thing, sending two wires, and even though I've tried, it's hard to limit my messages to ten words each. I know that's the preferred length, but it's difficult to achieve in this case."

He shot her a quick look, and his smile was reassuring. "Don't worry about the expense, Elizabeth. I can afford it and it's necessary. Just write what you have to. I'll take care of it."

By the time they had reached the stationmaster, she had finished her scribbling, busily wiping tears as she went, for her grief was deep and she felt a million miles from those she loved. Lucas took over the task of sending the wires and she waited in the wagon for him to be done. Then he reappeared, a look of consternation on his face.

"It seems that a gentleman appeared this morning on the early stage. I'm wondering if it could be the man Laura warned you to expect."

"How could he get here so soon?" Elizabeth asked, confused by the turn of events.

"If he left Boston night before last and traveled without any rest, he could have taken the train to St. Louis and then caught the early stage here this morning."

"I don't want to see him," Elizabeth said quickly, bending her head lest her falling tears should shame Lucas.

"Then you don't have to, sweetheart. At least not today. He can find his own way to the farm, and I doubt if it will be before tomorrow. We'll go to the emporium and do our business and stop at the mill for my lumber."

"I don't need anything from the emporium," Elizabeth said quickly, wanting to leave for the farm before she was seen by Amos.

"Just the mill, then," he agreed, climbing up to the wagon seat and snapping his reins over the horses' backs. The amiable plow horses set off for the other end of town, where the mill sat next to the river that wound its way south from Thomasville.

Lucas picked out the lumber he wanted and between the two of them, he and the mill owner loaded the boards onto the wagon. Within a few minutes they were on their way to the farm, and Elizabeth breathed a sigh of relief that the ordeal of seeing Amos had been put off.

While Lucas and the boys unloaded the wagon, Elizabeth went into the kitchen and prepared for supper. She had plenty of time, and after she'd set preparations in order she went to the parlor, a rag in one hand and a jar of beeswax she'd found in the pantry clutched in the other. It seemed that Doris had believed in making her furniture shine with a coat of beeswax and Elizabeth had no problem in using what was left in the jar.

She worked until the wood on the library cabinet gleamed, using the vinegar to wash the glass and polishing to her heart's content on the lovely piece of furniture. Turning then to the large library table on the other side of the windows, she emptied it of the pictures and knickknacks that sat there, removed the family Bible and cleaned the whole surface.

When the wood was shining to her satisfaction, she dusted the small objects and replaced them, then turned to the rocking chair.

Within an hour, the room had taken on a new glow, and aside from the carpet, which needed to be hung outdoors and beaten, she was satisfied. Perhaps Lucas didn't own such a weapon as a carpet beater, she decided, but it was worth a look. The attic was a good starting place.

She found the doorway leading to the attic at the end of the hallway upstairs and opened it to find a steep staircase before her. How they had managed to carry that cabinet down those stairs was a conundrum, she thought, for surely it had been a job requiring more than one man. Josh was a good help, but Lucas must have used every muscle in his big body to accomplish the task. She stood with her head and shoulders above the attic floor and looked around.

There were boxes and trunks beneath the sloping eaves, and furniture in several places, chairs, a large table, a desk and various other pieces. She saw nails pounded into the wood wherever she looked and objects of all descriptions hung upon them. A set of curtain stretchers was leaning against one wall, and she filed away that information for future use, for they were familiar objects to her, having helped her mother for years with the job of stretching wet curtains on such a frame at home.

Tools of all sorts hung against the rafters, and there, back in one corner, was a familiar-looking object—the carpet beater she'd been doubtful of finding up here. With a sound of triumph she crossed the dusty floor, took the wire tool from its nail and carried it back to the stairway. She looked around, wishing she had an hour to spare to investigate some of the boxes beneath the eaves, then with a shrug, went down the stairs, bearing her carpet beater like a sword.

Only to come upon Lucas in the hallway by his bedroom door.

"Where were you, Elizabeth? I've looked all over the house and finally thought you might be sleeping. And what on earth is that thing you're carrying?"

"You obviously haven't used one of these or you'd know what it is," she said with a grin.

"Well, you're right on the spot there, for it doesn't ring a bell with me."

"It must have belonged to your mother, then, for it hasn't been in use for a long time, if the cobwebs on it are any indication."

He looked truly puzzled. "All right, I give up. What the dickens is it?"

"It's what you're going to beat the parlor rug with, Lucas. A carpet beater. And from the looks of that rug, it should have been used a couple of years ago. We'll make use of it within a week or so, for the rest of the parlor is clean but for the rug."

"It smells good in there. When I went looking for you, I noticed how everything was shining and even the window was clean. No dead flies to be seen," he said with a grin.

Elizabeth shook her head. "You take the cake, Lucas. But if you promise to use this thing when the time comes, I'll put it in the pantry and set it aside for now."

"Whatever you say, ma'am," he told her politely, bowing a bit as she passed him on her way to the stairs.

"I'll have supper ready in about an hour," she said, knowing he was right behind her as she descended.

"Can we talk while you do that?" he asked, his hand touching her shoulder.

"Certainly. I'm always open to conversation."

He was silent then, and only when they were in the kitchen and she'd tied her apron in place and found potatoes to peel did he speak again. She sat across the table from him, her paring knife busy with the potatoes, and Lucas cleared his throat.

"Why do you think Amos is here to see you?" he asked.

She looked up in surprise. "However should I know the answer to that?"

"You must have some idea of his thinking. Why would he leave Boston and his children behind, his wife not even in the ground yet, and come looking for you?"

"To tell the truth, I'm more concerned about the children than Amos. And about my aunt, for that matter. She was my father's sister, built just like him, with the same dark hair and blue eyes. My father always said she should have been a man, as tall and strong as she was."

"And do you look like her? Didn't you say your father thought you should have been a boy?"

She thought for a moment, rising to fetch a saucepan for the potatoes. She pumped water into it and added the sliced-up potatoes, settling it on the stove before she returned to the table. And then she spoke, her words firm, her eyes filled with remembrance as she thought of her family.

"Yes, I look like my aunt, the same build and coloring. As to the other, I don't know. My father taught me to do all the things a son would do, but then I suppose, he didn't have a son, only Sissy and me. I learned how to ride before I can even remember seeing my first horse, and he let me help in the barn from the time I was a small girl. He treated me as a son most of the time."

"And did you mind?" Lucas lifted a brow as she considered that notion.

She shook her head. "No, I enjoyed being with him. We were much alike, and although I had a good time with my mother, learning about cooking and baking and sewing and all the rest, the times I spent with my father were the best memories of my childhood. He…" Her hesitation was brief, and then she spoke again.

"He respected me. And it pleased me to know that I filled his expectations. Sissy was a girl, through and through. She screamed at snakes and shuddered at spiders, and mice were creatures to be feared above all else." Elizabeth grinned as she remembered. "My father said she was useless on a farm, for she couldn't even gather eggs without crying about the hens pecking her fingers, and milking a cow was far beyond her ability to comprehend."

"You were your father's favorite, weren't you?" Lucas asked.

Elizabeth nodded. "I guess I was, although I never thought of it that way. Not back then. I loved my mother dearly, but my father was the sun in my sky."

"And how did he feel about Amos? Was he pleased when you were courting? Did he think Amos would be a worthy husband?"

She frowned, pondering as she formed her thoughts. "He didn't much care for him, I suspect. He liked Amos's brother better, the one who is a doctor in Boston. But he never said I shouldn't marry him. Though I think he was pleased when Amos married Sissy instead of me. He told me that the future for me was bright, and a better man would come along one day." She looked at Lucas then, her gaze meeting his, her lips curving in a smile.

"He was right, you know. You're a better man all the way around. As I recall, Amos was never open with me about his plans for our future. In fact, he spent a lot of time trying to coax me into dark corners at the dances, and beneath the oak tree outside the Grange hall. I didn't think of it then, for I was but a girl, but he was no doubt trying to make advances and I was too dumb to know."

"No, you weren't dumb. That isn't a word I'd ever associate with you, Lizzie. You were innocent and yet smart enough to evade his advances. And smarter still to be left out of his life. I can't see that Sissy fared well in her marriage."

Elizabeth's eyes filled with tears. "She was happy with her children, but I'm not certain she was happy with Amos as a husband. But all that aside, I just can't imagine what could have happened to her. She was healthy when I left Boston, and—"

"We'll know soon enough, I think. For I don't doubt that Amos will have a fine tale to tell when he arrives. As to the other, I wonder when you'll be notified legally about your inheritance."

"I hadn't even considered that," she said, stunned as she recognized that she'd totally forgotten that Aunt Hildegarde had left her the considerable amount she'd obtained upon selling her large home. "She was married to a well-to-do gentleman, Uncle Will by name, and he left her well-off when he died. Then she sold the big house they'd lived in for years, and found a much smaller cottage in a little bit of a place outside Boston. She lived there for the past five years or so, and I spent a lot of time with her, tending to things, for she was sickly much of the time. I was there just weeks ago, cleaning her house for her and helping with her spring yard work."

"You'll no doubt hear from a lawyer soon enough," Lucas said. Then he rose and went to where she sat and lifted her from the chair, embracing her closely, her head resting against his shoulder. "Don't worry about it all for now, sweet. It'll all come out in the wash. And if you want to go back to see your parents, we'll arrange that, too. Maybe in a month or so, after things settle down. In the meantime, we'll deal with Amos Rogers."

"Thank you, Lucas. I feel…safe, here with you. I haven't had many people in my life who comforted me or made me feel at all special in any way. You've taken my part in all of this, and I appreciate it. After all, you barely know me, and yet you've set yourself up as my…my rock, perhaps. I don't know if that sounds foolish to you, but it's the way I think of you. As a solid foundation upon which I can build my marriage, a man to lean on, a man I can depend on."

"You flatter me, Elizabeth." He held her at arm's length and met her eyes. "I'm just a man. A big man, yes, but only flesh and bones nonetheless. If I can be your shelter, and stand by your side, behind you if necessary, in all of your dealings, I'll do that. You're important to me—my wife, the woman who has taken on the task of being a mother to my sons. You're right, we don't know each other well, and yet there is a bond, I think, between us. I feel that you've been meant for me all along, and our finding each other, even if it was through a newspaper ad, was meant to be. Does that sound foolish to you?"

She shook her head. "No, Lucas. It sounds like heaven to me. I'm happy thus far, here with you and the boys. I feel needed and wanted and right at home. I spent an hour in the parlor, cleaning and dusting and looking at your mother's things, and I felt that I was exactly where I was meant to be."

"She would have liked you, Lizzie. She was much the same as you, a woman not given to frippery or ruffles or such, but a woman devoted to her husband and family. You remind me of her."

"I do?"

"I saw you get off the stage and knew that you were the right woman for me."

She leaned toward him, rising on her tiptoes, and kissed his cheek briefly. It was a forward gesture, one she'd never thought to perform, but it seemed apt for the occasion, for hadn't Lucas just given her a great compliment?

"Is that the best you can do?" he asked, grinning at her.

And then he held her closer, until her breasts were imprinted on his chest, her stomach against the arousal he'd managed to produce with so little encouragement. He kissed her, his lips forming to hers with care, his arms careful not to hold her too closely, lest she feel trapped by his greater strength. It was a kiss of promise and she relished the feel of him against her body, knew the thrill of a woman who is admired and cared for.

"I'll do better another time. For now I must concentrate

on supper, Lucas. I haven't got things under control yet, and time's a-wasting."

He glanced out the window, where the sun was heading fast for the western horizon. "So it is. I'll go out and start the evening chores and lasso those boys. I suspect they're with the dog and her pups. They're scampering all over the area we closed off for them in the tack room. Josh is tickled to death with the decision of choosing a male to keep. And Toby is just pleased at the furry little bodies he's busy petting. Josh told him he must be careful and only pet carefully, lest he cause the mother to fear their being there in the tack room with her."

"Go, then, and do your chores and I'll do mine, Lucas," she said, her crying a thing of the past, her heart feeling cleansed by the salty tears that had been shed this afternoon. And as he left the kitchen, walked across the porch and then down the steps to the yard, she watched him, her eager eyes fastened on his slim-hipped stride, his long legs and the head of dark hair that gleamed in the late sunlight before he clapped his hat in place.

"Lucas Harrison, I feel I'm a most fortunate woman indeed, to be your wife," she said aloud, for even though there was no one to hear the words, she knew she must speak them for her own benefit, lest she forget for a moment how much she had gained by leaving Boston to come to this place.

The potatoes were almost boiled dry when she rescued them and took them to the table. A good scoop of butter and enough milk to almost fill the saucepan made it ready to go back on the stove. She shook flour and milk together and added it to the mixture, then seasoned it with salt and pepper. She plunged the potato masher into the pan for three or four good strokes, crushing the potatoes to edible bits, and then she put it on the back of the stove to simmer.

Potato soup was simple to make and she only had to find some peas in the garden to add to it for color and taste. The vines yielded up a double handful of peas and she shelled them amid the weeds, holding her apron up to catch the small green gems. Then back to the kitchen, where she rinsed them under the pitcher pump and dropped them into the soup.

She'd set bread to rise last night, put it into loaf pans this morning amid all the hustle and bustle that had ensued and left them atop the stove to rise again. So now she took them from the oven, the crust brown and inviting, the three loaves ready for supper.

She went to the back porch, and was spotted by Toby, who called to his father that supper must be ready for Miss Lizzibet was on the porch. He came to the barn door, turned back but for a moment, his voice loud as he gave Josh the word, then the three of them headed for the trough to wash and then to the woman who awaited them.

Lucas bent a look of promise upon her as he came in the door. "Smells good in here, Lizzie. Is that fresh bread?"

To which she nodded and reached for the bread knife, cutting thick slabs of the warm, crusty loaf she held for the hungry crew that faced her.

Washed and ready to eat, they gathered around the table, and Elizabeth sought in the pantry for a jar of jam, sliding it alongside the butter she'd churned earlier. The soup was ladled into four bowls and distributed around the table, the fragrant steam rising to tempt their noses.

Toby spoke in earnest fervor a half hour later. "You sure are a good cooker, ma'am. We sure like the way you make soup and stuff, don't we, Pa?"

And Lucas answered his son, his voice a bit gruff as he buttered his warm bread and lifted his gaze to meet that of his wife. "We surely do, Toby. We surely do."

Chapter Five

The next day a visitor arrived at the farm. He rode in a buggy driven by Ivan Iverson, the blacksmith, a man who often rented out his equipment. On this occasion his services had obviously been rented along with the horse and buggy, for his hands were on the reins, not those of the dandy who perched beside him.

"Lucas, I brung you a fella what wants to see your new wife. You want him here?" It was an open invitation to Lucas, for if Lucas shook his head, he knew Ivan would promptly turn the buggy and head back to town, and the *fella* he'd delivered with such lack of finesse would go with him.

Lucas called from the yard into the house, his voice dark and deep. "Elizabeth, there's a man here to see you. You want to come on out?" And if she didn't, the message was clear. The man could trot right on back to town.

Elizabeth came to the door and looked at the visitor. "What do you want, Mr. Rogers?"

"You used to call me Amos," he said with a laugh.

"Not anymore. Not since you jilted me for my sister, I

fear. Why aren't you back in Boston this morning?" she asked, remaining within the confines of the kitchen.

"I came to see you. I'd think that was obvious." His look at Lucas held a certain amount of apprehension, which Elizabeth noted with glee, even though her mood was far from joyous. She'd spent a half hour weeping her eyes out in the parlor, mourning the sister she would never see again. And here, as nice as you please, was the *gentleman* who had run off and left Boston and his wife behind him.

"I repeat, Mr. Rogers, what do you want?"

"I have news for you, Elizabeth. The sort of thing that's best delivered in person."

"I'm not interested," she said bitterly.

He lifted his head and his voice was solemn, as if he carried news of great importance. "I think you would be, should you be aware of certain facts."

"Anything you want to tell me you can say from right where you are, Mr. Rogers."

"You're desperately needed back home, Elizabeth. Your two nieces are without a mother and you're the only one to fill that place. Sissy is no longer with us, for she met with a dreadful accident in Boston three days since. I'm alone now, but for my two children. On top of that, there's no longer any impediment to our marriage, Elizabeth. I'm without a wife, and Sissy's children are without a mother. We need you. The children in particular."

Toby called from the barn door then, his voice piping and shrill. "Not near as much as we need Miss Lizzibet, mister."

Lucas hid a smile as he lifted one hand to cover his mouth, but Elizabeth was not smiling.

"I think you'd better come up onto the porch," she told Amos Rogers.

He leaped down from the buggy and approached the porch, his manner diffident, as if he would appeal to her good manners.

Ivan picked up his reins, but Lucas lifted a hand to halt his leaving. And Ivan, no doubt mighty curious by this time, did as Lucas had bid him. Possibly because he didn't want to miss whatever fireworks were about to ensue.

Amos Rogers approached the porch and Elizabeth came out the door, watching him closely. Josh spoke from behind Lucas, his voice carrying. "He ain't gonna take our Miss Elizabeth away, is he, Pa?"

To which Lucas only shook his head and watched the proceedings with an eagle eye.

"So what other news do you have for me, Mr. Rogers?" Elizabeth asked shortly.

Amos seemed to tremble and held one hand to his face, as if he dreaded the news he must impart. "I'm prepared to take you back with me to where your parents are waiting to see you again. To where two small children await your arrival, for they desperately need you in their lives. I knew you would want to know about the loss to all of us immediately, so I came as quickly as I could, once I spoke with your parents and discovered your whereabouts."

"And why do you think I'd come back to Boston with you?' she asked him bluntly.

"We meant the world to each other once, Elizabeth. I know I broke your heart when I was seduced by Sissy's charms, but I'm just a man and I have to admit that I was wrong to allow her to so induce me to marriage when I'd promised myself to you."

"That's a bunch of horsefeathers," she said, and watched over Amos's head as Lucas's face fell into lines of laughter. Elizabeth gained a great deal of courage from the sight.

She stood on the top step and looked down at the smug look that covered Amos's face, and he bowed his head in mock sorrow. "It's been hard for me to do this, Elizabeth, but those children need you desperately."

"And where are they now?" she asked. "Don't they desperately need their father with them?"

"Your parents are caring for them until I return," Amos said, his face contorted with a semblance of mourning.

Elizabeth lifted her chin and battled her tears as she asked the question that fought to be spoken aloud. "What sort of an accident befell my sister?"

"The house burned and she was caught in the fire and couldn't get out soon enough. A neighbor rescued the children, but no one realized Sissy was inside until it was too late. I left with the children before she was brought out, for I couldn't risk them seeing her body."

Elizabeth felt sorrow like a ton of bricks sweep over her and she faltered, one hand reaching for the upright post beside her. She looked up at Lucas and he came to her, reaching her in mere seconds with his long strides. He pushed Amos aside and stood beside her, one arm around her waist.

"I'm here, Lizzie." His words were a whisper against her ear, and she nodded.

"Won't you do as your sister would have wanted and return with me now?" Amos asked, glaring at Lucas with hatred in his eyes.

"She has no reason to go anywhere with you, Rogers," he said harshly.

"You have nothing to do with this conversation," Amos said, his manner haughty, his face contorted.

Lucas turned to face him and his hands fisted at his sides. "When you're speaking to my wife, I have every reason, sir. She's not going anywhere with you. If she wants to make a trip to Boston or New York City or any-place else in the country, she'll go with me and her new sons. I hope that's clear to you, for I won't repeat it."

"I'll go back to town and give you a day to think this over, Elizabeth," Amos said, backing from the angry man who faced him.

Without ceremony he climbed into the buggy and issued words of command to Ivan, who grinned at Lucas and turned his rig around in the yard, heading down the lane.

Lucas hugged Elizabeth close, uncaring of who might be watching, for he felt a great need to comfort her. In moments he was joined by Toby, who ran to their side and flung his own arm around Elizabeth, and then Josh, who trotted from the barn to make it a family matter. They stood together on the porch, Elizabeth holding back her tears with difficulty, but Lucas cared little for appear-ances, for he only held her tighter and patted her back.

"If you need to cry, sweetheart, go right ahead. You have every right."

She shook her head, reached into her apron pocket for

a handkerchief and wiped her eyes and nose with it. "I'm all right now. It just made me so angry to have him show up here and demand anything of me, let alone tell me I should run off with him. The dirty, no-good—"

"Never mind," Lucas said, cutting her off in midstream, lest she speak words that she would later regret. The boys were avid listeners and should she use language not proper for a lady, she would regret it immediately if the boys heard such things coming from her mouth.

Lucas led her without protest into the kitchen. He sat her down at the table and pulled the teakettle to the hottest spot on the stove, then found the flowered teapot in the kitchen dresser and put a good measure of her tea inside, to await the kettle boiling.

He found her a cup and spoon, and in between each task he stopped by her side to bend and whisper in her ear—nonsense words, but phrases interspersed that were meant for her comfort.

When the water boiled, he poured a good measure into the teapot, waited a moment till it should steep, then filled a cup with the savory drink and placed it before her, offering the sugar bowl for her use. "Do you want milk in it, sweet?" he asked, and when she shook her head, he sat down beside her.

"Don't worry about a thing. I'll take care of you," he told her, and she lifted swollen eyes to him, trying to smile through the tears that fell without ceasing. "You need to be in bed. I fear you'll be ill if you have any more upsets today."

"I won't argue with you, Lucas," she told him, leaning heavily on his arm as he led her from the kitchen.

"I'll take you upstairs and then see about carrying the milk to the milk house and skimming the cream from this morning. I haven't slopped the hogs yet, so I'll tend to that before I come back in and see how you're doing, sweet."

He led her up the stairs, and behind him he heard Toby speak softly to his brother. "I'll bet we won't hear any more about the desert island tonight, will we?"

Josh whispered a negative reply, shushing Toby quickly.

Elizabeth stood before Lucas like a child, and he sought out her nightgown from behind the screen in the corner, then gently undid her dress and petticoat, stripping her clothing from her and pulling the gown over her head. He reached beneath, taking her stockings and shoes with them. His arms encircled her again and it was difficult to release her. But with a sigh and a final kiss, he lowered her onto her pillow and pulled the sheet up over her.

"I'll be back as soon as things are settled downstairs with the boys, and the chores are done." She nodded and closed her eyes, seeming to escape into a state of being neither awake or asleep.

He watched her for a long moment before he left, going down the stairs and out to the barn. The two boys followed him silently, their faces looking troubled by the events of the evening. Lucas halted in the middle of the yard and dropped one arm across each set of youthful shoulders to speak with them. He bent low, his voice soft and his words measured as he told them the details of Elizabeth's sorrow.

The cow had never been milked so quickly, nor the animals fed with such haste, for before twenty minutes were up the animals were in their stalls and the three of them headed back to the house. The boys understood death, he knew, for they'd lived through the loss of their mother. That Sissy should have died in a fire was a harsh fact for them to handle, but Lucas told them she'd no doubt been overcome by smoke and never knew what happened before she died. And he fervently hoped that tale was true.

He assured them that Elizabeth was not leaving them, that she was happy to be here and had no intention of going away. They seemed to accept his words and nodded as he spoke. Then they went into the house together and Lucas locked the doors and sent the boys to their beds.

He went up the stairs ten minutes later, only to find both of his sons by Elizabeth's bedside, Toby sitting on the sheet next to her, Josh kneeling near her head. He went silently into the room and sent her a glance of inquiry.

She managed to smile and lifted a hand, letting him know she wanted him to draw near.

"We thought maybe Miss Elizabeth needed some company, Pa. I hope it's all right that we stopped before we went to bed, so we could say good-night to her," Josh said, his chin raised as if he felt reason to defend their choice.

"I'm sure Elizabeth appreciates your presence, Josh. She needed someone to care about her tonight, and knowing that you both do will surely make her feel better."

"That's what I thought, Pa," Toby chimed in, not willing to be left out.

Lucas sat on the other side of the bed and felt a moment

of deep pride that his sons would be so attuned to another's need. That they would know their presence beside
her would comfort Elizabeth. He spoke quietly of his own
parents' deaths and how he'd grieved over them, then
mentioned carefully how they had all felt when Doris
died. During all of that, the boys simply watched him
and nodded agreement with his words. Toby reached for
Elizabeth's hand and held it between his two small palms,
and when Lucas sought her gaze, she smiled at him, ac-
knowledging her thankfulness for Toby's gesture.

Before they left the room, just minutes later, both boys
spoke to Elizabeth, soft words that assured her they would
help her the next day with her work, that they were happy
she was going to remain with them, and then they were
excused, leaving for bed.

"I'll be in to see both of you in a few minutes," Lucas
told them as they scooted from the room.

Elizabeth looked up at him. "I'll be all right, you know.
It just hit me kind of hard, to think of Sissy being in a
burning house, unable to get out."

"I have to wonder where Amos was when all this was
happening," Lucas said, his frown dark as he considered
the man who had left just a short time ago. "It sure is odd
that he'd run off and leave things to your folks, instead of
taking care of arrangements himself. It's like he wanted
to get his hands on you, Elizabeth. I don't like it one bit.
I fear there's more to it than we know right now."

The shadows outside the bedroom windows were long,
and Elizabeth was weary. It was time for sleep, Lucas
decided. He looked deep into Elizabeth's eyes, touch-

ing her forehead with his lips in a gentle caress. "I think we'd might as well go to bed, sweetheart. Morning will no doubt bring more to-do about this whole thing. In the meantime, you need some rest."

He went to see to the boys for a few minutes, and when he returned to Elizabeth's side, he was ready to undress for bed. The door was closed and they were alone in the twilight. With little ceremony, he stripped off his clothing and slid beneath the sheet.

Without any preliminaries, he reached for Elizabeth and drew her against his big body, enclosing her in his embrace. Her back was tucked against his chest, her legs bent and enmeshed with his, and his arm circled her waist. Her body felt chilled and he pulled the sheet up to cover her shoulders, then again held her close.

She seemed to soften against him, allowing herself to soak up his warmth, perhaps gaining comfort from his nearness, and he felt her relaxing into slumber. He lifted himself a bit and dropped a kiss on her throat, just beneath her ear, whispering soft words of consolation before he brushed her hair back, uncovering more of her skin to be blessed with his lips. She murmured words he could not understand, but he only patted her shoulder and held her tightly to him.

Morning brought more news from town, for the man who handled all legal matters for the surrounding area made a visit to the farm. Horace Tennyson was a man of dignity—an educated man, a lawyer who might have made a lot more money in a large city, Lucas thought as the man's buggy pulled up to the back of the house.

"He's a good fellow. He's had his office in town for almost fifteen years or so. Knows everyone's business, but keeps everything to himself," he said to himself. And for Lucas, that was a high recommendation.

Mr. Tennyson lifted himself down from his buggy and came to the back porch, where Lucas met him with an outstretched hand. "I kinda expected you out here today," he told the visitor.

Mr. Tennyson nodded, and when Elizabeth appeared behind the screen door he doffed his hat and stepped onto the porch. "I know you've already received news of your sister's death and that of your aunt," he said quietly. Elizabeth nodded as Lucas opened the door for the gentleman to enter the kitchen.

"Would you like a cup of coffee?" she asked as Mr. Tennyson sat down at the kitchen table.

"That would suit me very well, ma'am. I left town in a hurry, once I got the message from Boston. Your parents left it up to their lawyer to contact me and in turn I was asked to locate you."

"I doubt that was difficult, for everyone in town knows that Lucas was recently married. I think my name is probably well-known in Thomasville." Elizabeth poured coffee for the visitor and brought it to the table.

"I didn't congratulate you, Lucas. I beg your pardon for neglecting such a joyous occasion. I'm sure you've found married life to be most agreeable."

"More than you know," Lucas said quickly, smiling at Elizabeth.

"Well, I bring news of an inheritance, Mrs. Harrison.

Your aunt left you her entire estate, and it consists of a considerable sum of money, not to mention the house she was living in at the time of her death. I understand this has been an especially hard time for both you and your parents, with two deaths in as many days."

He drew papers from inside his coat pocket and spread them out on the table. "This is the news I was sent this morning. The wire was lengthy and I wanted you to know all the details, so I copied everything in order. It's simple and matter-of-fact, ma'am. If you'll sign this paper, I'll mail it directly to the bank in Boston that's taking care of the inheritance. On top of that I will wire the news that it will arrive forthwith. If they find it to be a good decision, they will in turn wire the money to our local banking institution for your use. I doubt if they will wait to see your signature before they take action. It seems straightforward to me, but if you'd like Lucas to look it over, I certainly have no objections."

Lucas stepped closer and took a seat across the table. "I think both Elizabeth and I would like to read it, sir. She is no doubt as well equipped as myself to understand the documents."

He motioned Elizabeth nearer and she stood by his side. "Go ahead, Lucas. You can tend to it for me. I'll do whatever you say," she said quietly, and if Mr. Tennyson thought she was a trusting soul, he didn't seem to pay much mind to her words. Merely drank his coffee and smiled his thanks at his hostess.

"It looks pretty straightforward to me. I have no trouble

with Elizabeth signing on the dotted line, sir," he said after a few moments.

Mr. Tennyson took a pen from his pocket and unscrewed the lid, presenting it to Elizabeth with a flourish. "This is a new pen—got it from my wife for my birthday. Writes real good," he said as Elizabeth admired the utensil in her hand. She bent over the papers and wrote her legal name where Lucas held his finger to show her the place.

"Is that all there is to it?" she asked, straightening to stand by Lucas's shoulder.

"That's it, ma'am," Mr. Tennyson said, gathering up his papers and drinking the last of his coffee. "I'll be on my way back to town now and get this in the mail on the afternoon stage. And then I'll send a wire telling them it's on its way. That should provide the impetus to release the money to you. They should have this in Boston within two or maybe three days, once it's put on a train in St. Louis."

Lucas accompanied the gentleman from the house and stood by the buggy as Mr. Tennyson lifted his reins. He looked up at Elizabeth and then drew Lucas closer with an uplifted hand. "I thought it might be good to mention that there is a gentleman in town who is most interested in what's going on out here. I understand from the folks over at the hotel that he was making a lot of queries about you and Mrs. Harrison. Seemed to be awfully interested in your place out here and especially your wife. I just thought you should know, Lucas."

Lucas nodded and shook Mr. Tennyson's hand again. "I'm glad you're aware of the man, sir. He's Elizabeth's brother-in-law, and the fact that he's here is suspicious enough to warrant my doubts as to his being on the up-and-up. My thought is that he ought to be in Boston with his children. He didn't even see his wife buried before he hustled out here, trying to coax Elizabeth back to Boston."

"Well, I think you can handle him all right," the lawyer said with a smile. He lifted his reins and was gone in a few moments. Lucas came back slowly to the house, entering the kitchen to find Elizabeth at the table, her head bent, her hands clutched in her lap.

She lifted her chin and met Lucas's gaze. "I hate that Aunt Hildegarde died and I wasn't even there with her. I thought she was getting stronger before I left home. And now this," she said, her hands moving as if she could not describe her feelings.

"I suspect that Amos Rogers knew about your aunt's will before he came here. The man is a fortune hunter, if I have him pegged right," Lucas said harshly.

"If he thinks for one minute I'd go with him and leave you, he's crazy, Lucas. I don't care about the money, for I have all I need, but it angers me that he thought so little of Sissy that he couldn't even be bothered to attend to business there. My folks must have been crushed to have him just drop the two children and leave all the details of a funeral to them."

"This isn't over yet, Lizzie," he said quietly. "We haven't heard the last of the man."

Elizabeth sat down that afternoon and wrote a long letter to her parents, telling them of Amos Rogers's visit and the fuss he'd caused for her. She told them she knew of her aunt's wishes regarding her estate, and offered to pay for Sissy's funeral and the expenses involved with caring for the children if Amos didn't come back and take up his duties as a father. Having no idea how much money her aunt had left her, Elizabeth made no plans for it, for as she'd said, she had everything she needed.

She sealed the letter and laid it on the table. It would stay there until they made a trip to town, where it could be put into the mailbag at the post office and then sent via the stagecoach and the train in St. Louis, back to Boston. She could only hope that Amos Rogers would buy himself a ticket for that same train and take himself out of her life.

She went to the back porch, curious as to what Lucas and the boys were doing out in the barn, for she could hear his hammer pounding and the sound of excited voices from the pasture beyond. Deciding to find out for herself, she set off for the barn, passing by the milk house, where she peeked inside to make sure that Josh had covered the pail with a clean dish towel when he left it there this morning, and then she went on to the barn.

The sound of hammering was louder here and she heard Toby asking for the extra pieces of wood Lucas had generated with his saw. "You can have the odds and ends, Toby. What are you planning to build with them?"

"I thought about a doghouse for Emma. She always just sleeps in the tack room, and she oughta have a house of her own, don't you think, Pa?" the boy asked.

"We can do that, I suspect. But let's get this stall finished first, Toby. We'll be getting a new horse for your brother to ride right soon, and we don't have anyplace to put it when it gets here. Once I get this stall built and the manger for the horse to eat from, I'll work on a doghouse with you. Will that be all right? You'll just have to have patience, son."

Elizabeth entered the barn, her eyes adjusting to the dimmer light in but a few seconds. "I didn't know that you were getting a horse for Josh," she said.

Lucas looked up from where he was putting boards together on the floor. "It's a young animal, a mare not yet two years old, Elizabeth. Our neighbor told me I could have first dibs on it when it was born, and he's ready to let it go right soon. We'll train it ourselves to a saddle. I want Josh to begin riding a horse more suited to him. He's been up on top of the plow horses for a couple of years but he needs a mount of his own. And then in a couple of years, we'll breed her and hopefully have a mount for Toby when the time comes."

"That sounds like a splendid idea to me," she said, aware of the excitement on Josh's face as he heard his father's plans.

"I'll have a horse, too, Miss Lizzibet," Toby said. "Won't that be grand?"

Elizabeth smiled her agreement, pleased that Lucas was so in touch with his boys and their needs. Not that a horse was a necessity, but certainly they needed to know the joy of riding such an animal, and there was no better time to begin than at their young ages.

"I rode my own horse when I was a young girl," she told Josh.

"Did you really?" he asked, his interest obvious.

"Yes, and if your father doesn't mind, I'd be interested in him finding me a horse to ride so I can keep you company on your jaunts when your mare is ready."

Lucas looked up at her and his grin was wide. "We'll have to see about that right soon, ma'am. I'll warrant we can find a good gelding for you. Our neighbor has a good number of horses in his pasture and most of them are trained to bit and bridle and know what a saddle feels like on their backs. If you want a horse, we'll get you one, Elizabeth. You can work with Josh and teach him the same way your father taught you. I'll do the work of building stalls in the barn, and you can do the teaching part."

"It sounds like a long-term deal to me," she said, her gaze fastened on that of her husband. He stood then and approached her.

"This figures to be a long-term deal all the way around, Elizabeth. I didn't send for you and then marry you without thinking about it for a long time. I'm in this thing for the long haul, Lizzie. There's gonna be no looking back, or fretting about what might have been. We're married and we're gonna stay married, whether or not Amos Rogers likes it. He's not going to get his hands on you or the money your aunt left you. I'll hang him out to dry first."

"Now, that's the sort of thing I like to hear, sir," she said with a grin. "I have no intention of leaving you or the boys, and Amos Rogers missed his chance with me about six years ago. He's water under the bridge as far as I'm concerned."

Lucas hauled her closer, his arm around her waist, his

lips touching hers. "That's the answer I wanted to hear from you, lady. We'll see what sort of shenanigans that yahoo tries to pull next, but I'll tell you one thing—he'd better stay clear of me. And if he puts one finger on you, or even *looks* like he's about to, he'll have had his last chance."

Toby stood beside Lucas, one hand clutching at Elizabeth's dress. "Is that man tryin' to take our Miss Lizzibet away from us? Should me and Josh do something to help?"

"You betcha," Lucas said with a smile in the boy's direction. "You and Josh just stick right close to Miss Elizabeth and watch over her, you hear? And if that fella from the big city comes sniffin' around here again, you holler real loud for me, you understand?"

"I sure do, Pa."

It seemed that Amos Rogers was devious beyond her imagination. A few days later the president of the local bank arrived at the farm, and as her father would have said, the gentleman was hot under the collar. He drew his buggy up to the back porch and slid down from his seat, causing Toby to run from the barn, a puppy in his arms, to find out who the visitor was.

He was breathless from his quick jaunt, but he stood next to Elizabeth on the porch by the time the banker had reached the steps. Toby looked up at Elizabeth. "It's not that bad guy, ma'am. Should I go get Pa anyway?"

Elizabeth nodded at him and touched his shoulder, a silent message to do as he'd said, and Toby ran from the porch, careful not to drop his puppy, but running quickly nonetheless.

"Good morning, ma'am. I assume that you're Mrs. Harrison?"

Elizabeth nodded. "Is there a problem, sir?"

He shook his head. "Not yet, ma'am. I'm Roscoe Boyle, owner of the bank in Thomasville. I had a gentleman caller this morning and I wasn't certain as to his veracity, so I decided to check with you that he's on the up-and-up. He said his name was Amos Rogers, and that he was not only a close friend of yours, but your former fiancé. Was he correct?"

Elizabeth stood back from the door and opened it wide. "Won't you come in, sir? I think we'd better sit down and discuss this occurrence." Mr. Boyle nodded and tied his horse to the hitching rail before the porch, then walked up the steps to the back door.

As he did so, Elizabeth caught sight of Lucas coming from the barn, his steps hurried.

She ushered Mr. Boyle into the kitchen and then thought better of it. "Perhaps you'd like to go into the parlor, sir," she asked, not willing to insult the man by keeping him at the back of the house. Good manners decreed she should offer him a seat in the room where visitors were normally received.

But Mr. Boyle merely shook his head. "I'm more than comfortable at a kitchen table," he said with a smile. And then he turned his head as Lucas came in the screen door.

"Good morning, sir," Lucas said, holding out his hand politely. "I'm Lucas Harrison. Elizabeth is my wife, and if I remember right, I've had dealings with you on several occasions."

Mr. Boyle grinned. "Well, it's been a couple of years now, but I remember well when you paid off your mortgage at the bank, and then opened a savings account with us. I thought the name was familiar when I got the notice about Mrs. Harrison's money coming through."

Lucas sat down, waving at a chair across the table for the banker. "And has it come through all right? We knew it was about to happen, but haven't had a chance to come into town to find out the particulars."

"I got notice of it late yesterday, just before closing, and thought to come out here then, but put it off. Then, when the gentleman I spoke to your wife about came into the bank today inquiring about the funds, I felt it was time to come here and get things in order."

"A gentleman?" Lucas asked, shooting a quick look at Elizabeth.

"A Mr. Amos Rogers came in and inquired of me whether the money had been transferred yet, and I was a bit waylaid by him. I don't know how he had knowledge of the inheritance, and I didn't feel it was any of his business, unless Mrs. Harrison had made him her man of affairs. So the next thing was to come and see for myself. Needless to say, I put the gentleman off by telling him there were technicalities to be worked out before I would be at liberty to discuss Mrs. Harrison's funds with anyone."

Lucas grinned. "You're a smart man, sir, for Amos Rogers is a man to be feared. He knew my wife in Boston, and the only reason he's here now is to try talking her into returning to the city with him."

"And is there a chance of that happening?" Mr. Boyle asked, glancing at Elizabeth as if he would have her input.

Lucas shook his head. "Not a chance, sir. He was married to my wife's sister, and she died in a fire, we were told, a few days ago. Instead of staying there to tend to business, the funeral and the disposition of their children, that scalawag arrived here with the express purpose of taking my wife back with him. I suspect it had a whole lot to do with the inheritance money she was in line for, since her aunt passed away at the same time as her sister. My considered opinion is that Amos Rogers is a man to be avoided at all costs, for he is unworthy of trust. In fact, he even told my wife that since her sister was deceased, there was no impediment to her marrying him."

Mr. Boyle looked aghast at that news and turned to speak to Elizabeth. "I want to offer you my sincere condolences on the death of your sister and that of your aunt, and I want you to know that I will let the sheriff know of Amos Rogers and the stunts he's tried to pull here in town. He was intent on knowing whether or not you had been told of your aunt's death and the money you had coming to you. I was surprised to find that the estate had been settled so quickly, but it is my understanding from the wire I received from her lawyer that everything was cut-and-dried and she knew how serious her illness was and made arrangements that you be made aware of the money and it be available to you immediately upon her death. The only thing you must do is to sell her home outside Boston. Do you have family back there who might handle such a thing for you? Someone you can trust?"

Elizabeth nodded. "My parents are there. At the moment I'm sure they have their hands full, for they were left with my sister's two children to care for and the funeral arrangements for my sister. Mr. Rogers is a man I would consider dangerous, sir. For I don't know the details yet about my sister's death, only that she perished in a house fire. Mr. Tennyson came out here and told me of the inheritance and that was when I signed the papers instructing the money be sent to your bank, sir."

Mr. Boyle nodded, then drew forth papers from his pocket. "Well, this is the receipt for the money I received at the bank. Mr. Tennyson has been with me and gone over everything and we find all the details to be in order, ma'am."

That evening as Elizabeth readied for bed, Lucas spoke from his perch on the side of the mattress. "I hate to add any more to the plateful you're facing right now, Lizzie, but there's a day coming up this week you'll need to know about in advance. You'd be angry did I not inform you of the birthday of our youngest son. Toby will be eight years old on Friday. Josh's birthday is next month and he'll be ten. I'd thought to find something kinda special for Toby, for Josh's gift will be his new horse. What do you think?"

"I'm in agreement, Lucas. And don't worry about me having too much to be thinking about. Those two boys are the most important things in our lives, and their birthdays are very special times. We'll celebrate with a meal of Toby's favorites and somehow I'll come up with an idea for a gift that will be suitable. Perhaps I'll take him to town and we can look at the mercantile for something he'd like to have."

"I'm not sure I want you trotting around town without me, Lizzie. So long as Amos is in these parts, you're vulnerable to him."

"I'll take your gun. I know how to shoot a gun, Lucas. I promise to hold it across my lap in the buggy and carry it with me into the store. Should he approach me, I'll give him one warning and then shoot. Besides, I'll have Toby with me and he knows how to shout out loudly for help, I'm sure. If necessary I'll send him for the sheriff."

Lucas grinned widely. "You've got it all figured out, haven't you, lady? I didn't know I was married to a sharpshooter. I'll get my shotgun ready for you, and when you leave here, you can take it with you. Just don't fear pulling the trigger. Amos Rogers is a dangerous man."

She nodded, pleased that Lucas trusted her abilities

The next day passed in its usual rhythm, with meals eaten and chores done and a session of reading in the parlor ending the day to the boys' satisfaction. Lucas and Elizabeth looked in on both of the children before they went to their own room, and then they retired for the night.

The morning was a measure of what their days had been and likely would be in the future. Breakfast was eaten, the chores done and Elizabeth churned butter while the bread she'd mixed rose atop the warming oven. The eggs and butter were packed, nestled in her big basket. She was ready for her trip to town with Toby.

She'd prepared well for dinner—a ham from the smokehouse had been baking all morning, providing a big meal for Lucas. He could survive on sandwiches from it later on today, she decided. Her meal was ready and she called the three of them into the house.

All of them ate well, then Elizabeth lowered the boom. "I'd like to take that trip into town, Lucas, that we spoke of yesterday. I'll take Toby with me, and I'd thought you might go to the neighbors while I'm gone to tend to business there."

Lucas looked up, lifted a brow and then seemed to consider her words. "I'll take care of the business we spoke of—that's no problem. I don't know if I feel secure about you going to town without me, Lizzie."

"I have a letter to mail to my folks and I really want it sent out as soon as possible, and the other thing we spoke of should be handled right away. I'll take all caution possible and Toby will be aware of what's expected of him."

Lucas leaned back in his chair, obviously considering her words and thinking of the pros and cons of her plan. "The spoke in the wheel may not even be in the picture any longer," he said finally. And then as if he would make the decision hers, he looked at her and shrugged.

"Give me a half-hour head start, and I'll go to the neighbor's and take care of business there. I'll have the buggy ready for you and tied out back to the hitching rail.

But at least let me get my business handled so I'll be free if needed."

She smiled. "I can do all of that. I'll have to pack the eggs and butter into the buggy first, and my bread is ready for the oven. I'll do that right now and wait for it to be done, probably about an hour. Will that be all right?"

He nodded and rose. "Get your hat, Josh. We're going for a visit to the neighbor's place. I'll need you with me."

Josh looked puzzled. "You *need* me along, Pa? Whatever for?" But without hesitation he rose, ready to accompany his father. Lucas put his arm over the lad's shoulders and led him to the back door.

And then, as if recognizing he'd forgotten something of value, he turned back and approached Elizabeth. She had risen and was putting the bread pans into the oven.

"Lizzie, look here, will you?" he asked.

She shut the oven door and looked up at him, her cheeks rosy, her eyes sparkling. "What is it, Lucas? What did you forget?"

His arms went around her and he bent his head to her, whispering in her ear. "The most important thing about my trip. I forgot to kiss you goodbye, sweetheart. Didn't you notice?" And then he whisked his mouth across hers, lifting his head to taste her on his lips before he lowered it again. This time the kiss was longer, more detailed and certainly contained more enthusiasm. "I just wanted to take along a memory of how good you taste."

She laughed, licking her bottom lip before she swatted at his shoulder. "You're a mischief maker is what you are, Lucas Harrison. Behaving in such a way in front of your sons."

"We don't care if Pa kisses you, ma'am," Josh said quickly from where he stood near the back door.

"Nah, he can kiss you all he wants to," Toby added, laughing behind his hand.

"Well, now that's settled, I'll take Josh and be off," Lucas said, snatching his hat from the hook by the door and leaving the house, Josh at his side.

"Are we really going to town, ma'am?" Toby asked her.

"Yes, in less than an hour, like your father said, or at least as soon as the bread is done baking. I'll clear up this mess first and you can take out a pan of milk to the puppies, please."

The boy was eager to perform the chore, for it gave him a chance to spend time with the animals both boys had come to love. Elizabeth wasted no time in pouring out the milk for him, then turned to the dishes that awaited her. She cleaned up the kitchen and welcomed Toby back from the barn, noting that the hour was about up. A clean housedress completed her preparations and she was ready.

Within another fifteen minutes she and Toby had climbed into the buggy, Luc's shotgun across her lap. She lifted the reins, turning the horse from the rail to the long drive that led to the town road. Beside her, Toby wiggled and squirmed, excited about the unexpected trip and all agog as he wondered why he'd been especially included as her escort.

Elizabeth turned onto the road and then allowed the horse to settle into a trot before she turned to Toby. "I want to tell you something, Toby. We're going to town for a very special reason. A couple of them, in fact. I have a letter I want to mail, and I'd like it to go out today on the afternoon train to St. Louis. Another reason is that your birthday is coming up in a couple of days, and your father and I want to have a special celebration for you. I'd thought to cook your favorite meal perhaps, and then we both want you to have a gift from the two of us. It should be something that you've decided on for yourself. You can be thinking about it on our way to town."

"That's something we never did before, ma'am," Toby said, his eyes gleaming as he considered the day to be devoted to his pleasure. "And I'll have to think of my favorite meal for a little while, for there's lots of things I really like eating, specially since you came to live with us, for you're ever so much better at cooking than Pa is. He did his best, and me and Josh ate whatever he fixed, but now we can't hardly wait till mealtime, with you here."

Elizabeth blushed at his praise, appreciative of her three menfolk. "Well, you be thinking of a special gift you'd like, Toby. And another thing, when we get to town, if I tell you to get help, you run as fast as you can to the sheriff's office and tell him I need him. Do you understand what I'm saying?"

"I sure do, ma'am. It's that bad man that came out to the farm and wanted you go with him, ain't it? He's still in town and you're worried he'll be after you again. Is that why you brought Pa's shotgun with you?" he asked, eyeing the weapon as it lay across Elizabeth's lap.

"That's exactly why," she said, looking about the fields

and trees as they traveled, checking the horizon and paying special mind to the roadside they passed. For should Amos be hiding somewhere, she didn't want to be unprepared. Although he would have no way of knowing she was en route to town today.

The buildings of Thomasville came into sight, and when they'd passed the first establishment, the church and parsonage beside it, she slowed the mare to a walk, preparing to stop at the small post office to send her letter. Then she decided to send Toby in with it, leaving her in the buggy with the gun.

He agreed to do as she asked and within a few minutes they were once more on their way, rolling up in front of the general store. Toby jumped down and tied the horse and buggy. Then he held out his hand for her to grasp, as he'd seen his father do numerous times before. She thanked him nicely and handed him the basket full of butter and eggs to carry. With her shotgun in one hand she approached the door.

Toby opened it for her and together they went inside. Harvey Klein greeted her with an uplifted hand and reached for the basket Toby carried. "Can I lend a hand, boy?" he asked, and Toby relinquished the basket into his care, watching as he took it to the counter. "How many dozen do you have today, Mrs. Harrison?"

"I counted eight," she said. "And there's four rounds of butter in the basket with them. I'd thought to do a bit of shopping today, with Toby as the subject under consideration."

Harvey nodded, transferring the eggs to his crock on

the counter, where they would soon be purchased by the town ladies who didn't have chickens of their own. He removed the rounds of wrapped butter and put them on a wide plate next to the egg crock.

"These will be gone within the hour, I'll warrant, for the ladies are always asking after fresh butter, and this looks nice and yellow, even through the cheesecloth. Your cow must be producing a goodly amount of cream for you."

"It's a Jersey, and she's a good milker, sure enough," Elizabeth said, pride in her voice as she spoke of the cow she held in high esteem.

"I'll put down the amount in my book for you, ma'am, and you just go on ahead and look at whatever it is you have in mind. Is there a special occasion we're celebrating?"

"Yes, Toby's birthday is coming up and we need to find something very special for his gift." She took the boy across the store and they stood before the counter where shoes and boots were lined up in boxes, trousers and shirts in glass cases on the wall behind the long countertop.

"Ma'am? I'd surely like a pair of boots for my birthday. Do you think they'd cost too much money?" Toby's eyes were fastened on the larger boxes, where boots were kept in a variety of sizes.

"If that's what you want, Toby, I don't see any reason to look any further. Although I'd like to buy you a new shirt to wear to church on Sunday. Do you remember that we spoke about going and you said you didn't have a best shirt to wear?"

He grinned up at her. "I don't, ma'am. Have a good

shirt, I mean. And yes, I'd like to have one, if you want to pick one out for me."

She turned to Harvey Klein, calling him by name, and when he approached, she mentioned the shirt issue to him. He laughed and took down two different glass cases, both of them containing neatly folded shirts in sizes to fit young boys. He drew one forth and held it up.

"I think that's a bit small," Elizabeth said, looking from the shirt to Toby and back, at which Mr. Klein refolded the garment and found another a bit larger.

"Let me see that one," Elizabeth said, and held it up to Toby's shoulders and back, brushing it down to see if it would be the right length. "Do you like this blue one, Toby? Or would you rather have one of a different color? Perhaps white, or brown?"

Toby jittered around a bit, obviously excited about the choices available to him. "I kinda like the white one, ma'am. Would that be all right? Pa's good shirt is white, I know."

And it was important to look as much like his father as possible. Elizabeth nodded, and Harvey set aside the white shirt in the proper size. "And now for boots," Elizabeth said, looking at the pile of boxes.

"Perhaps I'd better tend to that part," Harvey offered, coming around the counter to usher Toby to a bench obviously provided for just this purpose. He sorted through the boxes and opened several, showing boots to the boy, waiting for an opinion and then opening another box.

"I think these will fit," he said, slipping Toby's shoe off and kneeling before him. The boot in question slid onto the boy's foot readily and Toby stood and looked down at his heart's desire, his grin so wide, Elizabeth wondered if his face would ever be the same again.

Mr. Klein felt the toes of the boot, his long fingers moving then to the sides where he pressed inward to see how the boot fit. He sat back on his heels. "How does that feel, son?" he asked.

"Could I try them both on, sir?" Toby asked, his voice almost a whisper. At which the storekeeper slid the other boot into place and stood.

Mr. Klein waved a hand at the boy. "Walk across the floor, son, and see if they stay where they belong. We don't want them sliding up and down on your heel."

The door of the store opened then and Elizabeth heard Toby's indrawn breath. She looked past him to where Amos Rogers was sauntering slowly in her direction. "I thought I saw you coming into town, ma'am," he said politely, his eyes gleaming with purpose.

Mr. Klein had gone back to his business at the counter and was writing in his account book as Amos spoke. Elizabeth looked to one side, where she'd laid her gun on the front counter near Mr. Klein, and was angered at her lack of caution. Fortunately it was only a matter of three steps or so and her hands were on the weapon. She lifted it, trembling slightly, and pointed it as steadily as she could in Amos's direction.

"I'm not a terrific shot, Amos, but I'm sure I can hardly miss from here. I'd suggest you hightail it out of here right now."

He laughed, a cruel sound as he eyed her from where

he stood. "I doubt you'd shoot me, Elizabeth. You don't have enough nerve."

"You might be surprised, sir." Her words were clipped, her tone angry as she lifted the shotgun to aim directly at his chest. As if he thought better of it, Amos turned and left the store.

"Figure my purchases, please," she said to Mr. Klein, the weapon tucked against her body. "I'll have Toby carry them to the wagon for me. He can wear the boots. Just put his shoes in the box."

"Will you be all right, ma'am?" the storekeeper asked, peering past the front door as if seeking out the presence of Amos.

"I'll be fine. I know how to shoot the gun, and I'm not afraid to do it," she said firmly.

Toby grasped the packages by the string Mr. Klein had tied them with and headed for the door, Elizabeth at his heels.

They climbed into the buggy and Elizabeth turned the vehicle toward the road leading back to the farm. She didn't spare the horse any, but urged the animal on quickly. When they arrived at the farm, she looked in all directions, then helped Toby carry in his birthday gifts.

"Run out and find your father," she told him, feeling apprehensive about Lucas being out beyond the barn.

Toby was gone in a flash. His small body disappeared around the side of the barn, and then she caught sight of him running through the meadow where the horses grazed. Apparently Lucas was farther from the house than she'd thought, but no matter, she decided. He'd be here in no time. She went into the pantry, reaching to place the birthday gifts on the top shelf, and turned back to the kitchen.

There in the doorway, a grim look on his face, was Amos Rogers.

"I followed you, Elizabeth, on the other side of the trees where you couldn't see me. And now we're going to take a little trip. Just the two of us."

Her gun was in the buggy, and she cursed silently as she realized she'd left herself unprotected.

He stood before her now and his hands were harsh as he tugged her against him. "Come on, Elizabeth. Out the door with you." He was stronger than she'd thought, for she could not escape his hold, and he wrestled her onto the porch. One hand dipped into his coat pocket and in seconds he'd brought forth a hypodermic needle. With no hesitation he plunged the tip into her arm, through her sleeve and deep into her flesh.

She felt a hot flush envelope her, and then a weakness such as she'd never known came over her. When Amos lifted her from the porch onto his horse's back, she fell face-first over the saddle. "Don't go wigglin' around, Elizabeth, or you'll fall off and get hurt," he warned her, and then she knew no more as a cloud of darkness fell upon her.

Toby ran across the pasture as quickly as his short legs would take him, shouting hoarsely for his father as he went. He'd looked back just as Amos rode away, and he was scared. In the distance he caught sight of Lucas and

Josh, stretching fencing across the back of the meadow, and even though his chest hurt from the physical strain, he ran on.

"Pa! Pa!" His voice was that of a small child and it was long minutes before Lucas heard him call.

He dropped his hammer and headed quickly toward the child, recognizing that Toby was out of breath and could barely speak. "What is it, son? What's happened?"

"Miss Lizzabet—I saw that man take her away."

Lucas felt his heart twist within his chest. He'd not looked for her so soon, or he'd have been back closer to the house. Now he searched the horizon, finally spotting a horse crossing the town road and into the field beyond. It carried a full load, for it looked as if the man sat behind the saddle, and a figure was lying atop the leather. He saw a skirt flying in the wind and knew beyond a shadow of a doubt that it was Elizabeth.

"You boys go in the house. I'm going to saddle my gelding and find Elizabeth. Understand me?" The two boys nodded quickly and Josh ran ahead, into the barn, where he located Lucas's saddle and had it on end when his father came in, leading his mount. It took but seconds to saddle the horse and slip his bridle in place, and Lucas was atop his back and shouted at Josh.

"Find me my rifle, Josh. Quickly."

"It's in the pantry," Josh hollered back, even as he sped toward the house.

"Pa, Miss Lizzibet forgot to take the shotgun in the house when we got home," Toby cried, tears running down his cheeks.

"That's all right, son. The rifle is what I need right now."

And even as the words were spoken, Josh came out the door, rifle in hand. The gun was loaded, for Lucas kept it ever ready in case of emergency. Josh lifted the rifle high, handing it up to Lucas without a word. Then he put his arm around his brother's shoulders and led him into the house.

"Lock the door," Lucas shouted as he turned his gelding toward the town road.

The man he followed seemed to be heading across country, in the general direction of town, but obviously not using the road so often traveled. Lucas urged his gelding into a gallop and leaned forward, his eyes fixed on the target he sought.

Firing at Amos Rogers from this distance was too dangerous to be considered, for it would be too easy for a bullet to go astray, perhaps hitting Elizabeth. He knew he stood a good chance of catching them, for his horse was fresh, and obviously the mount Amos rode had already been driven hard for at least five miles today.

His quarry disappeared behind a grove of trees and Lucas kept his eyes peeled for the man to reappear, for the trees thinned out just ahead. If he had the chance, he'd fire once he got a hundred yards or so closer, he decided. Then Amos appeared again and looked over his shoulder, catching sight of the man following him. He pulled his horse up sharply and dropped to the ground, lifting his own weapon to his shoulder.

He'd never have a better chance, Lucas decided, pulling on the reins and leaping to the ground, rifle in his hand.

He lifted it, held it steady and his finger eased against the trigger. His heart was pounding in his chest and he took a deep breath as he saw Amos stagger when the bullet hit him. Amos spun sharply and flew backward, hitting the ground. The gun he'd held landed eight or ten feet away, and Lucas watched carefully as he remounted his gelding, lest the man should crawl toward the weapon. But by the time he'd traveled fifty feet or so, he realized that Amos was unconscious. Blood stained his shirt, a crimson patch readily visible even from where Lucas traveled, his horse almost upon the man now.

He rode next to the horse upon which Elizabeth lay, jumped to the ground and drew her carefully from across the saddle. Lowering her to the ground, he felt her throat for a pulse. It beat strongly—a bit slow, but she was alive and that was all that mattered.

His horse would hold two with no problem and he lifted her to the saddle, holding her there as he put his foot in the stirrup and swung into place behind her. Her body was totally limp and he held her across his lap, one arm beneath her head, the other on the reins. It took only a few minutes to gain the back porch and he shouted loudly for Josh to open the door.

The boy did as he was told and then stepped out onto the porch. "Oh, Pa," he cried, jumping to the ground and standing beside his father's gelding, "is she hurt? Is Miss Elizabeth alive?"

Lucas nodded, an abrupt movement of his head as he slid from his saddle, holding on to the woman in his arms as best he could. He lifted her then and carried her through the door, past the kitchen and into the parlor. The sofa held her nicely, and he knelt beside her.

"What can I do, Pa?" Josh said.

"Get me a clean washcloth and rinse it in cool water. Wring it out good and bring it here."

Without speaking, the boy ran to the kitchen and returned in moments with a cloth, his hands trembling as he handed it to his father. "Now get on my horse and go to town, quick as you can, Josh. Get the doctor and tell him it's an emergency. Hurry, now."

In mere moments Lucas heard the horse's hooves hitting the earth as Josh galloped past the parlor and down the long lane to the road. Toby stood anxiously by his side, his hand reaching for Elizabeth's hair, his fingers tangling in the dark locks as tears ran down his cheeks.

"She'll be all right, Toby. Do you know what happened? Did you see Amos Rogers in town?"

"He came in the store while we were there and Miss Lizzibet aimed the shotgun at him and told him she'd shoot him if he didn't get out of the way. He kinda laughed at her, but I think she really would'a shot him, Pa, if he hadn't gone out of the store."

"She probably would have," Luc agreed, hardly able to contain the grin that begged to curl his lips. His Elizabeth was a corker, that was for sure.

As he wiped her forehead and then her hands, soiled from being dragged about, she opened her eyes a bit—not fully, for she seemed to be in a fog of sorts.

"He used a hypoder…a needle on me," she said, her words tangled as she spoke.

Lucas cursed aloud. "Damn him to hell," he said, his voice filled with hatred for the man for what he'd put Elizabeth through.

"Did you shoot him?" she asked, her tongue fumbling with the words. Her eyes kept closing as she spoke and he took pity on her, brushing her hair back from her face.

"Close your eyes, sweetheart. You're safe and sound. He apparently drugged you with something in that needle he used. The doctor will know what to do when he gets here. Just sleep, Lizzie. I'm here and I won't leave you alone again."

"Me neither, Pa," Toby said in a frail voice, his eyes still red from the tears that would not cease.

Lucas tugged the boy closer and held him tightly. "You're a good boy, Toby. I'm proud of you, running all the way across the pasture to get me."

"I was so scared, Pa," the boy cried, his words fractured by the sobs he could not withhold.

"She's safe now, Toby. You did well, son." And together they waited by the sofa, their eyes on the precious woman who had so nearly been taken captive by Amos Rogers.

The doctor showed up before too long, his buggy wheeling up to the porch, the man himself leaping from the high seat to run through the back door, black bag in hand.

He came into the parlor and his eyes tangled with those of the man who rose to meet him. "Is she all right? Your boy said to come quick, and Harvey Klein ran out from the store when he saw all the commotion in the street. He said the stranger in town had accosted your wife in the emporium, and she threatened him with her shotgun, chasing him out the door. What did he do? Follow her home? And then grab her?"

Even as he spoke the doctor approached the sofa and knelt beside Lucas, his hands reaching for gauze in his bag, then he poured a good measure of alcohol on the pad and wiped his fingers and hands with it. "This oughta do for now," he said, his fingers on Elizabeth's pulse, his eyes meeting Lucas's as he nodded.

"He didn't hurt her?" he asked, even as his hands ran swiftly over her arms and hands, then down her legs beneath the skirt she wore.

"I don't think he had a chance, Doc. But she said he put something in her with a hypodermic needle."

"Where is he?" the doctor asked quietly, aware of Toby listening as they spoke.

"About a quarter of a mile from here, in the field across the way, past the grove of maple trees. His horse is there, too. Although I suspect it belongs to the livery stable. He must have rented it when he set out to chase down Elizabeth and Toby."

"You want to leave her here for the night? Or can you carry her upstairs?"

"I could carry her for miles if need be," Luc told the medical man. "I'll take care of her. But tell me first, what did he shoot into her arm? She was awake long enough to tell me he used a needle on her."

"From the way she's sleeping, I'd say laudanum. But if she's already roused enough to speak to you, I wouldn't worry about her. She'll get a good night's sleep, that's for sure."

"Thanks, Doc," Luc said, reaching to take the other man's palm in his own. "I appreciate you coming out here. Maybe you'd better take my wagon and haul Amos Rogers back to town with you. I'll go with you to pick him up if you like."

"Naw. I'll just sling him across the back of my horse and deliver him to the sheriff."

In moments he'd closed his bag and taken his leave. Toby and Josh sat on kitchen chairs and waited until their father came out to speak with them.

"I'm gonna carry Elizabeth upstairs to bed," he told them. "I want you both to run out and feed the chickens and gather up the eggs. I'll milk after I finish in here."

Both boys nodded vigorously, more than willing to help in any way they could. "Pa? Is she gonna be all right?" Josh asked, his voice trembling. "I wouldn't want anything to happen to our new mama."

Lucas nodded and touched the boy on his shoulder. "She'll be fine. Just needs a good night's sleep, the doctor said."

And as his sons went to the chicken coop to do their chores, he lifted his wife in strong arms and carried her up the stairs. The love in his heart added strength to his muscular arms and he could only be thankful for each breath she took as they traveled up the stairs and into their bedroom.

He stripped her quickly and tucked her beneath the sheet and quilt, aware that she'd be upset to find herself in the altogether in the morning. But no matter, he'd keep her warm and comfortable tonight, and explain matters as best he could when the sun rose in the east. And in an hour or so, he crawled into the bed beside her and lifted her into his embrace, his mouth finding her cheeks, her forehead and lips and the place on her throat where her soap had left a sweet scent for his pleasure.

His heart was thankful, his hands careful against her flesh as he held her, and she obligingly curved her lush body against him, much to his delight, her soft murmurs making no sense as she whispered to him, but his name seeming to be on her lips frequently.

He loved her, this woman who had filled his heart and life with her presence in so short a time. And his mouth spoke words of thanksgiving as he offered his mind and body, his very being, into her keeping

Epilogue

The farm had never known such a joyous time, with such an enormous amount of company in the house. The bedrooms upstairs overflowed, with the arrival of Elizabeth's parents and the two little girls from Boston. The parents were buzzing with news of Amos Rogers's trial for murder. His wife was found to have been shot before the house was set afire. He had left her there while he carried off his children to the elder Collinses' household, there to leave them while he went westward, chasing down Elizabeth.

His brother, Dr. Evan Rogers, had appeared at his trial, and testified that Amos had invaded his office, which was in one wing of his Boston home, and made away with several doses of laudanum, complete with syringes, one of which he'd used to dose Elizabeth. With the murder charge and kidnapping and assault charges due to his encounter with Elizabeth, he was sentenced to life in prison with no opportunity for parole, probably wishing Lucas's bullet had killed him.

Now the house was simply wreathed with joy, for the

boys were thrilled at having acquired new grandparents and Elizabeth was overjoyed to have her parents so close. She took her father on a grand tour of the barn and the animals in the pastures. Josh proudly showed his new horse to his new grandpa and was given an immediate lesson on training the animal.

Elizabeth carried her nieces around the house, with happiness almost causing her heart to burst, for her mother had confided that they were willing to leave the young girls with their aunt, should she so desire. And she indeed did so desire, for they were small bundles of joy, and she was delighted to accept the responsibility.

Lucas was all for the idea, saying that it was an ideal way to increase his family, and announcing that he'd always wanted a houseful of girls. He took to them in great style, carrying them hither and yon, Josh and Toby showing them the puppies and announcing the arrival within a week or so of a new pair of kittens from the neighboring farm where a litter was too much for the farmer there to contain in his barn.

Elizabeth was happy beyond words to have her parents for a long visit, even with the overshadowing events of Sissy's death casting a pall on them when it was least expected, for their hearts ached with the loss they felt.

Luckily the two small girls were not feeling that particular strain, for they both were delighted to be at the farm, happy to be with their auntie and new uncle, who paid them so much attention. It was a joy to watch them, to see the happiness they exuded and the relief on the elder

Collinses' faces when they recognized that they would not be called upon to be parents to two children so small.

As for Lucas, he was overjoyed by the series of events. He could not grieve for Sissy's death, for he hadn't known her, but supporting Elizabeth in her own grieving was a task he took on without hesitation, for his love for her had grown by leaps and bounds over the weeks.

And so when it was finally time for the grandparents to take their leave, having endeared themselves to the two boys and having to leave behind two little girls who promised to bring joy to everyone they encountered, it was a difficult few moments. They'd all gone to town aboard the wagon. The afternoon stagecoach arrived in good order, and when the bags and baggage had been loaded aboard, and the grandparents had taken their seats, it was a bittersweet occasion, for four children waved farewell, urging the travelers to hurry back.

Lucas and Elizabeth each held one of the small girls, heads of golden curls bobbing beneath the afternoon sunshine as the toddlers waved and then were held closely to the new parents, who had vowed their love to them without hesitation. And so although Elizabeth shed a few tears as the stage pulled away, the joy of the small bundle she held in her arms overshadowed the loss of her parents in her home.

They drove in the wagon back to the farm, Lucas silent as he handled the reins, Elizabeth holding two small girls on her lap—one of them already asleep, the other not far behind—and two boys rattling on about their grandpa's knowledge of horses and riding.

In no time at all they'd put away the wagon and team of horses, carried the girls into the house and then sat around the kitchen table together, the space filled to capacity, with two new chairs added. Lucas said he would build a higher chair for the youngest girl, Adelaine, for the eldest, three-year-old Alice, could kneel on a full-sized chair and thus eat more readily.

Their lives were full, as Lucas said later that night when the small girls had been settled in the fourth bedroom upstairs, pillows beside the big bed, lest one or the other of them fall to the floor in their sleep.

Elizabeth crawled beneath the top sheet, thinking of the day to come, of the week ahead, for she would be busy with sewing dresses for her nieces, the wardrobe her mother had brought along not sufficient for their needs. But for now, Lucas bent over her and bid her to put all her thoughts aside, and to concentrate for just a while on her husband. An order she was happy to obey, for hadn't Lucas given her every wish she could have asked for?

Not only did she have a home and family, but now she had two more children to love and care for, and a husband who in turn bestowed upon her the love in his heart he'd been saving just for such a time.

"I'm so happy it was you, Lizzie," he said softly, his kisses abundant across her face, his hands busy with the curves beneath the sheet. "I needed a wife, but more than that, I needed a woman to love who would answer my needs, and just look what I got." He leaned back a bit and smiled at her in the candle glow, his face a picture of happiness.

"I was worried, Lucas. For I'd been the big one, the heavy sister, the tall girl in the family for all my life. And I doubted I'd ever find a man to love me as I am."

"Well, here I am, pleased as punch to hold you in my arms. You're just the right size for me, Lizzie. Just the right shape and just the right woman to answer all my needs and make me the happiest man in the world."

And with that he kissed her soundly and Lizzie was silent, for she knew in her heart of hearts that Lucas Harrison was about to spend on her ample curves the benefit of all his loving tenderness, and there was nothing else she could possibly ask for. Not in this life, anyway.

* * * * *

HER
ALASKAN GROOM

Kate Bridges

Dear Reader

Have you ever wondered what kind of woman would be motivated to be a mail-order bride? It must have taken a lot of courage for her to pack her belongings, say goodbye to family and friends—if she had any— and board a train or ship to an unfamiliar destination and the arms of an unknown man.

John and Sophie's love story starts with a problem in their paperwork. In their time communication abilities were limited, since there were no computers or telephones, and so I wondered what would happen if a man sent for one mail-order bride but mistakenly got two.

The humour of the situation is soon lost on both John and Sophie, as neither is what the other expected. Poor Sophie has to learn the hard way—perhaps the better way—about what this man is made of and what he stands for.

HER ALASKAN GROOM adds to my collection of several stories I've set in Alaska and the Klondike. I hope you enjoy the adventure as it unfolds, with Sophie stepping off the ship onto the beautiful banks of Skagway, and the sun warming your cheeks…

Bon Voyage!

Kate

Dedication:

This story is dedicated to my mother,
who was never a mail-order bride.
However, like many women of her generation in
post-WWII Europe, she dreamed of a better life
for her future children. So she packed one suitcase,
sewed a hundred dollars into the hem of her skirt, and
boarded a ship for North America. Thanks, Mom.

Chapter One

Skagway, District of Alaska
May 1899

"**Y**our bride has changed her mind, sir." Sophie Mead Grant practiced saying it aloud, but the words still choked in her throat. How would he accept the news? With an anxious look at the crowds ahead, she hopped off the platform of the swaying ship onto the busy banks of Skagway, Alaska.

Sophie set down her bags in the hot May sun. Clutching the torn advertisement for Seattle Mail-Order Brides, she peered at the scrawled name she'd stared at for the past twenty-two days at sea.

John Colburne.

Swarms of passengers bumped her shoulders as they passed her on the docks. When she looked up again, a man the size of a statue was staring at her from twenty yards away. Fringed suede jacket, cowboy hat, shoulders the breadth of a doorway.

It was *him*. Heat seeped up her neck.

"I've got shocking news," she whispered under her breath. "Sorry, Mr. Colburne." Her lips moved incoherently as his eyes held hers.

How disheartened would he be? Or...maybe this course of events would turn out in his best interests.

And hers. At one time, Sophie had let her father make her decisions for her. But no longer. Stepping onto Alaskan soil was her new breath of freedom. She'd be living her life for herself from now on.

Your weakness is— The harsh words of her father rushed through her ears. *You're much too sympathetic. You must pull up your spine and do what needs to be done. Clearly you're not suited to being a midwife.*

Yes, she was. She straightened her posture in the blazing sunshine. She'd prove it to her father. She'd prove it to all the doubters. That she was stronger and braver than he ever gave her credit for.

She had to muster her nerve and simply tell John Colburne the truth. With a fresh wave of resolve, Sophie picked up her satchel in one hand, her obstetrical bag in the other, and pressed toward him through the sea of bodies.

Her long skirts swirled about her ankles. The sun's rays singed her face. The ocean mist lashed at her tucked-up hair. Flies no bigger than flecks darted up her nose. With a yelp, she tossed her bags to the ground and shooed the bugs.

"First thing," he said, stepping to her side, "we've got to get you a proper hat. Bonnets aren't enough to shield you from the flies and sun."

Sophie lifted her face to get a good look at him. Sand-colored blond hair, blue eyes and the rippling of muscles beneath his white shirt. My, he was a lot of man to handle. She flushed just thinking about a night alone with him.

Surprising her, he lowered his face, pressed his warm lips to her cheek, pulled away, then kissed her other cheek.

The lump in her throat solidified. Paulette Trundle didn't know what she was missing.

"Pleased to meet you, Paulette," he said incorrectly. "I'm John." The fringes on his jacket swayed as he moved forward and crushed Sophie in a hug. When he stepped back again, he gave her a handsome smile. "Aren't you going to say anything?"

He believed her to be his bride, Paulette, but she was an impostor. She fought for something coherent to say. "You're much taller than I expected."

He let out a soft laugh, and she rolled her eyes at her silly comment about his physical traits. Taller? Why not say more powerful and primal and brawny?

He had an easy way about him, a rhythm of speaking. She averted her gaze, pretended to swat at the flies and opened her lips to confess.

"Colburne," shouted a deckhand from a lower gangplank. He was leading a horse from the bow of the ship. "John Colburne!"

Mr. Colburne wheeled around, like a tornado gathering thunder, and whistled in pleasure. "My mare!"

Hoisting both of Sophie's bags with one hand, he leaped down the docks and motioned for her to follow. The deckhand with the horse nabbed him, while she was stopped on the docks by other disembarking passengers.

"So wonderful to have traveled with you, my dear." Mrs. Rutledge, a woman Sophie had gotten to know on the ship, patted her face. Her husband nodded. Carrying a small barrel of rum, he eagerly looked over to his other kegs to ensure they were being properly unloaded, next to the livestock.

Behind them, an old sailor also waited to say goodbye to her, followed by the two middle-aged sisters who were here as seamstresses. Then the bearded Captain Waycott himself.

"Skagway Arms Hotel." The captain pointed to her right, reminding her of the hotel he'd recommended earlier, which she'd asked about in case her secret plans with Mr. Colburne didn't turn out. "Straight down the main street."

"Thank you, sir," she said, then hustled to catch up to Mr. Colburne, who was admiring his new mare by the lower banks.

She gulped a breath of fresh air, unable to get enough. She was finally here. The icy mountains and the power of the ocean were much more magical than she'd anticipated.

The high peaks bore ice halfway down their slopes. Ocean waters swirled in a dozen hues of blue and green. The town itself looked charming—docks lined with sailors, fishermen, rich gold miners, shacks, shops and arriving throngs of European immigrants who spoke languages she didn't understand.

She hadn't told anyone on board the ship the private

message she had to deliver to Mr. Colburne. Or why she had come to Alaska. Some things were confidential. Some things were easier to bear alone. Her whole life so far had been a testament to that philosophy.

Two more paces and she reached his side. Thankfully, they had a bit of privacy, with the ship behind them and the horse in front that blocked the view of passersby.

"Isn't she a beaut?" He patted the mare's flanks as the deckhand spoke with a passenger on the other side of the animal. The mare was a little lean from the rough voyage, but her coat was a glossy reddish-brown.

"A Thoroughbred," he announced with pride.

"For your line of work?"

He frowned. "Well, yes…I mentioned it in my letter."

Perhaps he'd mentioned it in his letters to Paulette, but not to her. Sophie crossed her arms over her jacket front and opened her mouth to finally, finally spill all.

"You're more lovely than I expected." He stepped closer, surprising the sweet Moses out of her. She swallowed hard at the daring look in his eyes. Her stomach contracted. Before she could resist, he swooped down and kissed her.

His kiss was magic. She hadn't been kissed like this in…she'd never been kissed like this. The kind of kiss where a man didn't give a damn who was watching, just rolled her up in his arms and kissed her with all the longing he'd been building for months. Untamed. Wild. Free. Like Alaska itself.

Lord, it had been so long since she'd been kissed at all. But this kiss wasn't meant for her. Her conscience flared. When they parted, she had a feeling her eyes had been closed longer than his had. When she opened them, he was looking at her with the side of his lips turned up in good humor, and his head tilted as if trying to read what was going through her mind.

The brim of his hat put his eyes in shadow. "Now, what've you got to say for yourself?"

"I'm not Paulette." Her lips were dry. "My name is Sophie Grant."

His smile receded as her stomach turned inside out and sideways.

"Damn. I am sorry for that kiss." Stunned by the news, John swung around to scour the docks, looking for the right woman. "Where's Paulette?"

He peered down into Miss Grant's enticing green eyes, over the sprinkling of blond hair scattered about her forehead and a damp residue of ocean mist on her cheeks. Her lips were rosy from the sun, tinted from the voyage.

His embarrassment mingled with a sense of confusion. This was not Paulette, and Paulette Trundle was the young woman he'd promised to marry.

"I do apologize," he repeated.

"No need. I won't tell anyone." Miss Grant blinked up at him. She was dressed in a pretty blue wool suit that molded to her shapely curves. He cleared his throat and stepped behind the mare to get a closer look at the faces in the crowd. Lots of men in all shapes, sizes and financial status, but no single women.

"When I saw you step off the ship, I assumed..." He looked down at her gloved fingers and saw that she was clutching an ad for Mail-Order Brides. "I don't under-stand. Do you know Paulette?"

"A little. We stayed in the same hotel three days before the ship left Seattle."

"Please. If you'd be so kind, point her out to me."

Miss Grant touched his sleeve. "She's not coming."

His full attention riveted to the smooth curves of her face. "What's that?"

"It's weighed heavily on my heart the entire voyage."

He watched her lashes fall, her mouth struggle for words as his heart thudded. "What has?"

The young woman yanked at her bonnet, then surged ahead with her words. "Paulette never boarded the ship. She decided she couldn't go through with it, I'm afraid. Marry you."

John blinked. He looked away and rubbed his jaw. What? He peered down again at Miss Grant, but there was no smile to belie her comment, no mistaking what she'd said. The news rippled up his spine and made his mouth go dry.

Alone again.

Seeking a moment to gather his thoughts and hide his embarrassment, he spun away from her and the mare. He found a spot next to the gangplank, where it overlooked the docks and the swarm of workers.

The gold rush and influx of settlers had brought him to a place he loved, Alaska, but he didn't wish to spend the rest of his days surrounded by nothing but men.

He took a good look around. Men who worked the sea were pulling on ropes and nets and unloading crates.

Farther out on the docks, old fishermen snoozed in chairs, adolescent boys raced along the pier, men in their thirties and forties bartered with each other for incoming supplies. John spotted only five or six bonnets in roughly a hundred cowboy hats and sailor's caps.

Miss Grant spoke quietly beside his shoulder. "The chief officer has a letter for you from the agency. And one from Paulette. Explaining everything."

"I see."

"And there he is," she said, pointing to the officer. "Sir, over here!" Sophie flagged him down. The young man in uniform dodged past two crates filled with chickens, confirmed John's name, handed him two envelopes sealed with wax, then darted back to the ship.

John said nothing. His pride prevented him from explaining his sense of loss and loneliness to Miss Grant.

The few decent women who did arrive here were snatched up faster than the hot strike of a match. He'd been so focused on his livery stables the past year, rising with the birds in the early morning, going to bed with the late call of wolves, there'd been no extra time to pursue the fairer sex. No time to dine a woman, take her dancing, or any other such extravagance. He'd finally vowed to make time, and then a neighbor had recommended the mail-order-bride catalog. He'd gotten to know Paulette from a few letters they'd exchanged, and her character seemed strong and understanding.

He lowered his head, chafed with hurt pride and disillusion.

Silence grew between him and Miss Grant. It muted the

calls of the sailors working around them, and the stomping of hooves as his mare was led away.

His mare. John waved his arm at the deckhand. "See to it she gets to my main livery by the hour!"

"Yes, sir!"

John turned back to the young woman. His skin bristled, knowing she was witness to his intimate humiliation. He wasn't the type of man who normally went about ordering a wife, and he'd had his doubts at first, too. He should have followed his gut from the beginning. This would be the last time he jumped into such a hasty arrangement. Seeing the pity in Miss Grant's eyes made his stupidity all the harder to bear.

"Thank you for the news," he said gruffly. "Good day."

He turned to walk away, but she called out. "There's more to tell you!"

Good grief. What more? He stopped in his tracks, swung around and frowned.

She'd gone pale. "There's no obligation required on your part. I believe the agency spells it all out in the letter." She hauled her bags up to her waist, as if ready to turn and run at any moment. She peered up at him and hesitated.

"What is it?"

"If you agree…if the circumstance pleases you…the agency sent me as replacement."

Chapter Two

For the next few moments John was so stunned at Miss Grant's declaration, he couldn't speak. He weighed the idea in his mind, trying not to let his churning sentiments interfere with his logic. But he couldn't help it.

"Everything's explained in the letter." She fumbled with her two bags. Disembarking passengers streamed behind her, headed for the boardwalk and center of town. "The agency thought we might be a good match."

"Just to make sure I understand this. You've agreed to be my bride?"

Her bonnet shielded half her face from the sun, but the rays lit up the soft curves of her other side. "Well…I…I wanted to meet you first, and then…"

Was he supposed to take this lightly? The agency thought they could just send a replacement without consulting him first? Obviously they cared only about collecting their fee. "I don't think I'm ready for this."

"Sir?"

His temples were beginning to pound. He tried to control his mounting storm of emotion, but it seeped out in the cold spurts of his voice. "It's too much to take in. Up until ten minutes ago, I thought I was marrying Paulette Trundle. Now I'm supposed to turn my head around and take another woman?"

She colored fiercely and pulled at her bonnet with a gloved hand. "I've had more than twenty-two days to think about it, and you've only had a minute."

"Exactly." His voice rumbled louder. Passersby turned their heads to stare, but he didn't give a damn. "I'm still trying to sort through the blow. The woman I've been corresponding with for ten months decided she didn't want to marry me. I have to ask myself why."

She lowered her voice, darting glances toward the gawking strangers. "I don't think it was you. I think it was the thought of living so far away in Alaska that got to her. But if you'll read her letter…" she urged him again.

Maybe it was his anger at Paulette or his frustration at the agency that made him speak without thinking. He lashed out recklessly. "What about you? You think it's perfectly fine for me to switch the juicy roast beef sandwich I was about to bite into for a slice of ham? One woman's as good as the next? Where's the dignity?"

"Uh." Her mouth dropped open in horror. "How dare you!"

Tension sucked the oxygen out of the air. Then with a snap of her skirts, she whirled around, clenched a bag in each hand and stomped toward the boardwalk.

He groaned. Had those words come from his mouth?

"I'm sorry." He chased after her, ducking under store signs and twisting his broad shoulders through the crowd to get closer. Now they were truly creating a commotion. People were openly staring. "I'm sorry."

"Stay away from me!"

"I didn't mean it."

"You meant every word!"

He had. He truly had. And he was unable to muster the necessary facial expression to lie about it.

"It's nothing personal about you. I meant it in a general sense. Here, let me help you." He tried to grab one of her bags, but she smacked his chest with it instead. "Ow!" Recovering quickly, he hastened to explain. "I meant my dignity! Not yours!"

"Liar! Don't come near me! Help! Anyone! Help!"

He planted his hands in the air in a gesture of surrender. "Hey, don't do this. Don't do this."

Those green eyes he'd initially thought were so attractive now stabbed him with defiance. "Help!"

Three or four men took a step toward him. Heads pivoted on the boardwalk. A crowd formed around them. Just what he needed. More witnesses to his stupidity.

Miss Grant pulled back her shoulders and pressed up against the storefront sign of the ice cream parlor that read Salesclerk Needed. "This man won't leave me alone."

"Better get out of here, Colburne," said the boot maker. "She doesn't seem to like you."

"It's not what you think," John told them. "I'm trying to help her with her bags."

"She doesn't seem to want your help, John," said a miner.

She lifted her chin and snapped, "I'm perfectly capable

of crossing the street, *on my own,* to the hotel. Where I'm sure I can buy myself a *nice ham sandwich!*"

He winced.

Just then, one of his stable hands came around the corner, spotted John and Miss Grant glaring at each other, and shouted, "Congratulations, John. This must be the lovely Miss Trundle."

With a loud scoff of disgust, Miss Grant spun toward the stairs of the boardwalk and flounced toward the hotel and its bright red canopy. She already had a following of two or three men eager to help. Eager to court her was more likely.

What the hell was John supposed to do now? Did she have enough money to pay for a room? How long could she support herself in Alaska? Was he supposed to marry her out of pity?

How in blazes had this orderly situation gotten out of control?

That damn agency. And his damn meddling neighbors. He never should have listened to anyone for advice on how to find himself a wife.

After he'd finally calmed down and left the crowds for a quiet corner near the grassy slopes overlooking the harbor, John pulled out the letters. With a queasiness rolling up his throat, he read Paulette's first.

DEAR MR. COLBURNE,
I'M AWFULLY SORRY TO DISAPPOINT YOU, BUT I SIMPLY CAN'T GO THROUGH WITH THIS MARRIAGE. IT'S NOT LIKE

ME TO UP AND LEAVE EVERYTHING AND EVERYONE I
KNOW. MY TWO BELOVED SISTERS LIVE ONLY TWO CITY
BLOCKS AWAY. IT SEEMS LIKE SUCH A DIFFICULT VOYAGE
TO ALASKA, AND I THINK YOU'RE BEST SUITED WITH
ANOTHER CHOICE THE AGENCY MAY SEND.

REGARDS,
PAULETTE TRUNDLE

The P and T in her name were signed with a flourish.
She'd underlined her signature with three swirls. Regards.
That was all. Her three previous letters had been signed
with loving regards.

He read it a second time. Then a third. It still said the
same thing. She didn't want him.

Was there a pattern here in his private life? His last
engagement, years ago, hadn't worked out either. Through
no fault of his own.

He sighed and looked out to the docks, where the crew
of Miss Grant's steamship was still unloading trunks,
baggage and livestock.

He pulled out the second envelope, this one from the
agency, unsealed the wax and read.

Dear Mr. Colburne,

Unfortunately, your first choice for a bride is unavail-
able. Miss Trundle sends her apologies and we must
respect her decision.

On a brighter note, we do have several other suitable young American women, hardworking and interested in raising families. In her interviews, Miss Grant displayed a wonderful charm and sensibility to the harsher conditions of Alaska. She is widowed with no children. She comes from a remarkable family of physicians, and she herself wishes to practice midwifery.

In strictest confidence, I must tell you she parted ways with her father over his refusal to allow her to work. However, knowing the higher acceptance of working women in Alaska, I thought you might appreciate her skills in midwifery, and in regard to possibly raising your own future children.

If you find her unsuitable, please send word immediately and I shall seek a replacement. As we initially agreed, your fee is not refundable.

With very best wishes,
Mrs. Diana Shankford
Chairwoman, Seattle Mail-Order Brides

There was a lot to absorb in this letter. John stared at it for a long time, then tucked it back inside his jacket and headed for the Skagway Arms Hotel.

Still fuming at John Colburne's insults, Sophie checked in to the smallest and least expensive room they had. She removed her bonnet and suit jacket, washed up, then barreled down the stairs again to speak to the desk clerk. A handwritten sign on the pine desk read Kitchen Maid

Needed. It was gratifying to know there was work in this town.

"Could you please notify the ship's crew where I'm staying? They said they would deliver my trunk."

"We'll look after it, miss." The round-faced clerk pushed his drifting spectacles up the bridge of his nose.

"And where might I get a bite to eat?"

She had to be careful with her money, but her stomach pangs were turning into cramps.

"Straight down the hall to your right. The hotel diner. I believe the two gentlemen are waiting for you inside."

"They didn't leave?"

"No, miss. Insisted they'd like to buy you a meal."

With trepidation, Sophie nodded. Several other passengers from the ship, seeking rooms, nudged past her to the front desk. Three men of various ages and sizes stepped back to take a second look at her face, openly interested. She wasn't used to such attention and stepped away to the carpeted hall.

Her situation had changed so drastically from what she'd been expecting. John Colburne was not the man she hoped he'd be. She was looking for someone with a gentle side to him, but he was outspoken and rude.

She was officially "unengaged" again. A deep disappointment took root. After twenty-two days at sea, wondering and hoping for the best, trying to make herself as friendly and pleasing to the eye as she could, she'd been rejected. The sting of failure crept up her cheeks. Wasn't there anyone out there for her?

Would her six years with Miles be the only marriage she'd ever know?

Not that she was complaining. She had at first, when her father had insisted that women didn't belong in medical school but in the home of a good man, and had arranged for his forty-six-year-old accountant to marry her at sixteen. She'd fought her father and two brothers with every argument she could think of. She was too young; it wasn't right she had no choice; she wanted an education like her brothers; her mother, in her grave, certainly wouldn't approve of her only daughter not having a say in her own marriage. Nothing had worked.

So she'd married Miles. He'd turned out to be remarkably generous. But he continued to work his long hours, and, a year later, suffered from a brain inflammation that left the entire right side of his body permanently paralyzed. Fortunately she still had five more lovely years with him. And she'd gotten to know his loving sister, Belinda, a trained nurse and midwife who'd helped Sophie care for Miles. Belinda had been a godsend and had secretly trained Sophie in midwifery.

Oh, how her father had disapproved when he'd discovered it.

Sophie sighed. Her eyes still watered at the memory. Trying to gather her composure before she entered the dining hall, she stopped to look at a wall hanging. It was a landscape of Alaska, a watercolor painting of the midnight sun, blazing over ocean colors in striking depths of clarity. A pack of beautiful wolves roamed the slopes.

Whatever was meant to be, would be.

Lots of women in Skagway worked, she'd been told in Seattle by Mrs. Shankford. Laundresses, shop owners, even gold miners.

Back home, her two brothers, both surgeons like her father and equally demanding that women shouldn't become doctors, were just as stuffy as he was. "I'm pleased," she whispered to the big wolf in the painting, "to be out of the house in Portland." Trying to cheer herself, she found the humor in her situation. "It got very confusing with Dr. Mead, Dr. Mead and Dr. Mead."

The wolf's lonesome eyes stared back at her.

She couldn't support herself yet as a midwife. Miles had left her with very little money, since he'd been unemployed for the last five years of his life. She had hoped that a marriage to a successful businessman in Alaska would work to her advantage. As a widow, she was often overlooked by Portland's eligible men, other than the much older ones, and this time she was hoping for adventure with someone closer to her own age.

Mr. Colburne's insinuation that she had no dignity still blistered her pride. She had plenty of dignity. Enough to send him packing.

She was also aware of something unexpected about this town. The looks and admiration of the men around her had been disconcerting at first, but made her realize there were many eligible men in the vicinity.

Skagway wasn't such a big frightening place. True, it *was* a crude town with simple buildings and many rough-looking characters, but it was also thriving. The possibility of meeting another suitable husband was quite high. If she found work in the meantime, she needn't hasten into a marriage with *anyone*.

Perhaps she had more freedom here than she'd initially thought. It did worry her that she had only enough money to stay in the hotel for roughly two weeks, but she'd find work—of any kind, be it as a salesclerk in the ice cream parlor or a kitchen maid—until midwifery could support her.

Still, her heart bruised with thoughts of Mr. Colburne's harsh words. If she ever laid eyes on him again, she'd slap his face is what she'd do—

"Hello."

She wheeled around and her chest prickled with a thousand barbs. It was *him.* Cradling his hat at his chest, his blond hair rippling in the sunshine pouring from the front windowpanes, he towered over her.

"You again," she muttered.

"I'd like to speak with you, Miss Grant."

"I don't have anything more to say."

She took a step toward the diner, but he blocked her path. His bulk nearly filled the hallway.

His firm and serious profile was such a change in demeanor from the man who'd passionately kissed her on the docks.

But that kiss wasn't meant for her. It was meant for another woman he didn't truly know, Paulette Trundle.

Brushing aside the intimate memory, she glared at him.

He shifted his weight. "You have every right to be angry. Give me a chance to explain. There's something we need to—"

"Hold on a minute," she interrupted. "I know why you're here." When the thought came to her, she was even more discouraged and heartsick at this man's character.

Chapter Three

With mounting annoyance, Sophie tried to skirt around John Colburne, but he stretched his arm across her path, touching the wall. "And why's that?" he asked.

"You'll have to write to Mrs. Shankford for a refund."

He sputtered, speechless, and dropped his hand. It gave her some satisfaction to know she was getting to him as much as he was getting to her.

"I have no need for a refund. I'd like to pay for your voyage home."

She clenched her jaw. "Impossible. This is home now."

"Then allow me…" He opened his fringed suede jacket and removed his billfold, taking out a generous sum of thirty dollars. Back home, an average month's pay for a man.

Half of her was riveted at the sight—being paid off by a stranger in a hotel as though she were a painted woman. The other half was acutely aware of why he was doing it.

He held out the money, but she didn't go near it. He huffed in frustration and stuffed the money into her satchel.

"All right. I accept your money. Thank you. You're hereby absolved of any further duty toward me."

"I'm not trying to pay you off."

"Oh, no?"

What was it about this man? Why was her pulse leaping from her wrists? Why couldn't she order herself not to react to him?

Because in the course of less than an hour this man had pulled her into his arms with a wild kiss, abandoned her, and was now trying to pay her to keep her distance.

Her direct stare was enough, apparently, to make him squirm. He shuffled and fingered the brim of his hat. "Maybe when you calm down you might see things from my perspective. You brought word that my intended bride jilted me. I was looking forward to her company for months. It wasn't you I was angry at, but you happened to be the one who got it. I apologize. But I can't jump into another marriage as though I'm some thoughtless adolescent boy, craving the attention of any female. You don't deserve that."

She hated that he made sense. Hated that he had a point and she couldn't fault him for it.

"It seems to me we both got trapped into a difficult situation." He rotated his hat in his fingers. "I read the letters, and understand you're looking for work. There's a nurse's clinic on the east side of town you might want to visit. Three nurses. They'll be friendly to a midwife."

She focused with keen interest. "And the doctors? Someone on the ship told me you have two."

"Recently left for the Klondike. Seeking gold like every-one else."

"The nurses handle all the medical problems in town?"

"And beyond."

Good grief. This place was more uncivilized than she'd imagined. Was there no one here to do surgery? To advise her in her duties, should she need it?

The nerves in her stomach tightened. If she had known in Seattle that she would've been practicing alone, like this, she likely wouldn't have come. But she *was* here, thrown into the situation, and she *would* cope.

"Miss Grant?" One of the men who was waiting for her stepped out of the diner, a fine gentleman dressed in a wool suit. He was a banker, he'd told her, who'd worked for Wells Fargo in Texas, come to Skagway to start his own bank.

Everyone was calling her Miss Grant. Since they didn't know her circumstances of widowhood and she wasn't eager to spell it out for them, she let the Miss stand.

Mr. Colburne twisted up his nose at the sight of the banker.

She lifted her skirts and sailed past him. "Good day, Mr. Colburne."

The banker gloated and tipped two fingers goodbye, in mock salute. "John."

Whatever more John Colburne had to say to her was sadly irrelevant.

An hour later as Sophie ate dinner with her gentlemen friends, she was still bruised about her encounter with the livery owner. Dinner with the other gentlemen, one a banker, one a sailor, was interesting enough. They entertained her with conversations about the town, the best shops, the dangerous places to avoid, but her thoughts were focused on how she was to survive on her own.

She raced through dinner in order to stop by the nurse's clinic. Unfortunately the clinic doors were closed. A sign attached said the women had gone out of town to check on patients along the coast, returning Tuesday. In three days.

Deeply disappointed, Sophie slowly made her way back to the hotel, had the maids fill her tub with hot water and scrubbed herself clean from twenty-two days at sea.

She leaned back in the tub, enjoying the steam, and wiggled her toes on the other end of the porcelain.

Her breasts tipped in and out of the bathwater, nipples pert, skin round and smooth. Water lapped gently at her hips, along the muscles of her thighs and shadow of curls visible beneath the soapy surface.

As she looked at her naked body, she thought of one man. Her plans for a wedding—and her wedding eve— had been so different from how things had turned out.

Alone in his house, John scrubbed his back in the tub harder than necessary. Two days had passed and he still couldn't get her face out of his head.

Sophie Grant was not his responsibility. She was an adult with a mind of her own. He hadn't asked her to come to Alaska. It was a scheme cooked up by an agency and had nothing to do with mushy feelings or duty. Then why the hell did he feel so damn inadequate when he thought of her?

He leaned back in the tub, trying to savor the heat of the water. Rivulets of moisture trickled down his temples, down his neck, along his ribs and farther down the lightly matted hair of his muscled stomach.

Resisting thoughts of Sophie, he opened his eyes, lunged for the cake of soap and lathered up his arms. Canceling the wedding ceremony with the minister hadn't been easy. The man was understanding enough, but John hadn't felt like going into the details of Paulette's letter.

Letting friends know they were no longer invited to a large reception in the back garden of his house this coming Saturday had sparked even more difficult questions.

He answered them as they came. No, the wedding hadn't been postponed—it was canceled. No, Paulette was no longer coming to Alaska. No, he was no longer getting married.

Tuesday finally came, and Sophie introduced herself to one of the nurses inside the clinic.

Victoria Windhaven—a vibrant and cheerful young woman—was in charge. The other two nurses were making calls. Victoria seemed appreciative that Sophie was a midwife, because she smiled and gave advice on all kinds of things as Sophie helped her boil and sanitize her instruments.

A huge brown braid rippled down Victoria's shoulder as she stood over the crackling stove. "I can recommend a good boarding room. You'll have to put your name in for Mrs. Scranton's, but you'll get one of the cleanest and biggest rooms in town."

"Are there any ladies in need of midwife services?"

"Only one I'm aware of. Why don't you meet me at Callie Thornton's home Thursday at ten? She's due in a month and a half."

"Sounds lovely. Where does she live?"

"Right across the street from Colburne Stables."

Sophie's pulse leaped with the name. Victoria wouldn't know anything about Sophie's connection to John Colburne because she hadn't mentioned her humiliation. She had, however, disclosed the circumstances of her widowhood, although she disliked the pity it always provoked, including Victoria's. Sophie didn't want pity. All she wanted was friendship.

Acting as though she didn't care about the mention of Colburne Stables, Sophie extracted a set of bullet forceps from the boiling water and laid them next to the others.

"Go straight down the main street toward the mountains. Turn right at the hardware store, left at the willows. Stables are right there. He's got two others on the outskirts of town, but that's his main one."

"All right."

"Poor John Colburne. Heard he just lost a bride. Paulette somebody. It's all over town."

Thankfully, he seemed to be keeping to himself the news that Sophie was the replacement. She removed a pair of medical scissors from the steamy water and changed the subject. "How on earth do you manage with no doctors? What happens to the folks who might need surgery?"

"Well, Trish does some of it. Minor things like a finger amputation. She's been a nurse for thirty years and seen just about everything. For the bigger things we recommend a person return to the lower States if they can."

"And if they can't?"

"Afraid there's not much we can do for them."

It was shocking to hear the nurse actually say it. They truly were in the middle of nowhere.

"We're expecting a few medical students any day, so that's a blessing. From Philadelphia. We've been promised by the dean."

Victoria was a lovely person, confiding in Sophie like an old friend, telling her exactly who had what ailments in town, and who had just gotten married and might be needing midwife services in the near future. The word *marriage* always seemed to come up, no matter how much Sophie tried to avoid it.

"And then there's Callie Thornton and her new husband. Lord, they're as young as schoolkids themselves, but are truly devoted to each other."

Sophie looked down at her task, nodding where it was appropriate to nod, and smiling where appropriate to smile. She shoved all thoughts of John Colburne firmly from her mind.

On Thursday morning Sophie's nerves fluttered along with the hotel-room curtains as she prepared for her first appointment with a patient. Dressed only in a corset and thigh-high stockings, she strode to her beaten leather trunk. Her pearl necklace swayed on her breasts as she decided on a dress—the rose-colored suit with the princess seams and pleated skirt.

She'd do well today, she told herself, despite her father's insistence that she was too timid. He'd never seen her with a patient, had he?

She wiggled into her clothes and was out the door and down the boardwalk fifteen minutes before the appointed hour.

Inhaling the scent of salty air, she passed through the haze of shoppers. Some men's heads swiveled as she passed, but she ignored their admiring stares. She was pleased to see more women this morning than she'd seen all week. One was working in the window of the jewelry store, another taking loaves out of the baker's outdoor ovens.

The horn of a newly arriving ship blasted the air. Sophie jumped at the sound.

She found Callie Thornton's home with no problem, walking past the large clapboard building that was marked by a wood-burned sign, Colburne Stables. The stables also doubled as a travel depot for stagecoach services. Victoria prayed the livery owner himself wasn't around as she knocked on the Thornton door.

"Over here!" Victoria popped out of the front door of Colburne Stables. "Come join us! Callie's here!"

Sophie groaned. She squirmed uncomfortably in her suit. How could she leave? This was potentially her first new patient. Taking a deep breath, she made her way to

Victoria's side. They entered the livery, engulfed by the scent of straw and horses.

Two men in overalls looked up from cleaning the stalls. A gray-haired man walking a goat tipped his hat.

Callie was standing by a Jersey cow. The animal was pregnant, and Callie was patting its nose. She was freckle faced, gracious and beautifully plump. "Nice to meet you."

Sophie smiled. "Congratulations on your first."

Victoria set her medical bag on the straw.

"I bumped into Victoria yesterday," Callie said with bubbling excitement. "She told me all about you, Sophie. I'd like to hire you."

"Oh," said Sophie. "I'd like that, too."

"Then you'll come for coffee next door? I've got the laundry on the line, if you'll give me ten minutes or so." With a nod goodbye, Callie shuffled out.

Victoria, her long dark braid coiling around her pretty lace blouse, turned to Sophie. "I'll let you and Callie get acquainted. I've got to call on another patient."

"Couldn't you stay…"

Victoria's skirts were already whirling past the stalls. "When you're done, drop by the clinic." She disappeared out the back door while Sophie headed for the front, panicking that she might accidentally bump into *him*.

"Good morning." John Colburne's deep voice rumbled through the air behind her.

Her stomach contracted. She wheeled around, obstetrical bag knocking against her thighs. "Morning, Mr. Colburne."

"Please call me John."

The word needed extra time to leave her lips. "John."

Carrying a bucket of feed, he was dressed in a blue shirt and faded denims. Tall, muscled and powerful.

John's wide shoulders tightened beneath his shirt. "Where you headed to, Sophie?"

Her name sounded exotic rolling off his tongue. Something special and wonderful. Not so wonderful that he'd wanted to marry her. Ham sandwich indeed.

"Callie Thornton is my patient."

John tilted his dark head. "Things are working out, then."

She nodded awkwardly. The cow chomped on the feed he'd dropped into her stall. They watched for a moment. John stroked the animal's shoulder, then lowered his large hand to pat her pregnant belly. It was unexpectedly tender. "Morning, Abbie." He turned to look back at Sophie.

She blurted, "Thanks for sending me in the direction of the nurses." Her shoulders heaved up and down with a big breath. Today she'd let her long blond hair hang over her shoulders, the front strands tied loosely in the back.

"You look too young to be a widow."

She searched his face. "Mrs. Shankford must've mentioned it in the letter."

He nodded. "Sorry to hear it."

Losing Miles two years ago was something she was coping with, but there wasn't much anyone could do to ease the loneliness when it came.

John unhooked a cowboy hat from the boards and tossed it to her. "Present for you. It'll work better than a bonnet."

She twirled it in her hand. Black felt.

"Since you're not throwing it back at me," he said with amusement, "I'll take that as a good sign."

She was debating whether to give it back, but softened at his words. The cow's munching echoed off the boards. When Sophie turned her face slightly in John's direction, his expression turned solemn, as though caught by some unexpected emotion.

"We could start again." His eyes pulsed with hope. "Pretend we just met."

What was he saying? He'd like to court her?

"Would you like to join me for dinner tonight?"

There went her pulse again. "I don't know...there's a lot of hurt feelings on both sides."

He stared down at her. His blue eyes flickered with bits of gray. When he reached out and touched her cheek, the nerves inside her stomach squeezed.

"Hello!" A female voice interrupted them, jolting Sophie. "Anyone here? I'm looking for John Colburne."

Sophie twisted to the front doors, nearly knocking his hand from her face, not fully believing she recognized the voice.

"Sophie," the young woman called. "I didn't expect to see you here."

It was her. The white-hot heat of embarrassment raced up Sophie's face. She adjusted her buttoned jacket, fumbling as though she'd been caught at something improper.

John stepped out to greet the visitor. "I'm John."

Dressed in a brown suit and plumed hat, the young lady with brown ringlets of curls pressed forward. She looked around the vast stables, nodding her head as though pleased. "How do you do? I'm here a few days late, but I hope…I mean I dearly hope you can forgive me. I'm here to live up to my end of the bargain."

John turned to Sophie for an explanation, but Sophie's mouth couldn't move. The young woman gave him a broad smile. His face paled, her identity perhaps suddenly dawning on him.

The woman held out a gloved hand. "It's very nice to finally meet you after our wonderful exchange of letters, John. I'm Paulette Trundle."

Chapter Four

John's mouth went dry as he looked from Paulette's cheerful expression to Sophie's dampened one. He was just getting to know Sophie. He'd just asked her out for dinner. How on God's green earth had he managed this—standing between two lovely ladies, both promised to be his mail-order bride?

He extended his hand to Paulette. "So you came."

She shook it weakly and her cheeks colored.

Sophie shuffled in the straw next to him and extended her hand to Paulette, as well. "Welcome to Alaska, Paulette. I should be going. I know you have a lot to talk about."

"Please stay," John called after her, but she already had her bag in hand and was rushing toward the door.

"Bye, Sophie," said Paulette.

Sophie didn't turn around, so he wasn't able to read her expression.

"You must excuse me," Sophie called over her shoulder. "I have an appointment with Callie. Good luck to you both."

Paulette turned and watched Sophie leave, and when

her pretty silhouette passed through the door, Paulette turned back to John.

Her dark lashes flickered and cast shadows on her cheeks. "I'm terribly sorry for what I must've put you through. Did…did Sophie give you the letters?"

"Yes. Listen, we can talk about that later. You must be exhausted. I heard the blast of a ship earlier. Did you just arrive?"

She nodded, and he noted the circles beneath her eyes. She wore a hint of rouge, but it seemed only to accentuate the paleness of her skin. The voyage obviously hadn't been easy for her. And now here they stood, awkward as hell, he rubbing his mouth with the back of his hand, trying to figure out what to say. She was running a hand over her waist and fluttering her lashes as if they would pick up precisely where they'd left off in her previous letters.

What was he supposed to do?

So help him, he'd never recommend that blasted mail-order catalog to any of his friends.

He picked up her satchel, motioned to the door and escorted her out of the stables. Sunshine heated his shoulders through the fabric of his blue shirt. "I'll walk you to your hotel. Where'd you leave the rest of your bags?"

"The small hotel close to the docks. Everything else is booked up."

"You're lucky you got that."

"Luck seems to be with me today." She offered another of her smiles, and he realized she was a pretty woman. Any man would be delighted to have her.

Should he be?

He searched inside himself, struggling to recognize the dozens of emotions churning through him. Confusion at her arrival, optimism he'd felt with Sophie, anger at being put in this position. His pulse was throbbing beneath the surface.

They strolled along the boardwalk.

"Lovely town," she said.

He murmured in reply, trying to force himself to tell her exactly what he felt. Could he be that open with her?

But she'd come all this way, he argued to himself. Perhaps he should calm down before saying anything.

They neared the quaint plank building across from the loading docks and he felt as though he was approaching a gallows with the hangman waiting.

She'd only just arrived, he thought, and needed a day or two of rest before he said anything. Besides, he needed to think about things before blurting out anything he might regret later. Look how he'd reacted to Sophie at their first meeting.

"Do you think the minister would still be available, should we need him?" Paulette stopped outside the shade of the covered boardwalk and leaned into the alcove of the building.

"You're not even interested in how I felt when I got your letter, Paulette?"

She stammered. "W-well—well, of course, John. You must've been devastated that you couldn't marry me."

He shook his head at her wording. She was nervous, he told himself, and not choosing her words wisely.

"We corresponded for months. I thought I knew you. Somewhat."

"It was a silly impulse on my part to call it off. Terribly sorry. That time of the month, I'm afraid. When my mind goes fluttery." She smiled too readily, and the excuse was lame.

"Actually, Paulette, I think you did me a favor."

"A favor?" She brought her gloved hand to her throat and laughed with nervousness. The curls stacked upon her hair jiggled. "Ah, I see. It made you realize just how much you'd lost."

He shook his head. She needed to be told in a forthright manner, for he had no inclination for games. "How much I'd gained."

"Gained? You need a wife, John. A man with three livery stables and still expanding. Who will run your household? Organize your servants?"

"I never told you I had three livery stables. How did you learn of it?"

"Wasn't it you?" Her forehead creased in feigned surprise. "Who else—"

"You found out in Seattle." That was why she'd come back.

"No, no, I believe you were the one."

He set down her bag beside his big cowboy boot, crossed his arms and looked across the street at the pedestrians, who were oblivious to the delicate situation he was in. "Paulette, I trusted you once, and quite frankly, you did nothing to honor that trust. It was your choice to marry or not marry me. I don't hold your change of mind against you. In fact, perhaps I respected that more than…more than this."

"More than what?"

He groaned, wishing she'd drop the stage act.

A man's deep raspy voice called out from behind the hotel. "Paulette, have you come back, my sweet?"

When the gent appeared, sporting a cane, dapper gray suit, top hat and bejeweled fingers, he balked at seeing John. By his fresh attire, the man was obviously a newcomer, too. Perhaps someone she'd met on the ship? His eyes traveled over John's work clothes, which were rugged and casual.

The gent pointed the gold tip of his cane at John but spoke to Paulette. "I see you've got one of the stable hands to help you with your satchel. Did you speak to the Colburne fellow? My offer still stands."

John winced. Paulette's neck turned a shade of pepper-red. How many offers did she have? It didn't take a sharp-shooter to see what her priorities were.

The gent frowned and looked from Paulette to John. Her mouth wobbled with unspoken words, searching perhaps for something to say to keep all her options open.

"Sir," said John, picking up her satchel and putting it next to the gent's polished high black boots, "John Colburne wishes to let you know that she is free to take you up on any offer she pleases."

Paulette gasped. Her friend grinned.

John tipped his Stetson to her. "Good day."

Several hours after her embarrassing encounter in Colburne Stables, stuck between Paulette and John as they introduced themselves as future bride and groom, Sophie took another step down the stairs of her hotel and sighed.

Kerosene lanterns lit the hall. Fading sunlight streamed in through the front windows, but it was too weak to reach the inner rooms. Carpeting beneath her feet deadened the sound of her footsteps as she reached the landing of the main floor and twirled to the front exit. Her hair swung around her shoulders as she planted her new cowboy hat on her head.

"Evenin', miss," said the man at the front desk.

She nodded and smiled politely, masking the rush of sadness she'd been feeling most of the afternoon.

How could Paulette come now?

Well, it was her right.

But she'd said she no longer wanted John.

So she changed her mind.

They had an agreement long before you planted your boots on this soil.

Yet the feelings of abandonment lingered. John had asked her out for dinner this evening. Not Paulette.

With another sigh, Sophie pushed through the door and turned right to find the café down the street where she might pick up a sandwich or a crock of soup to take back to her room and eat in solitude. The way she'd eaten her meals for months. Years, in fact.

Alone.

Oh, what did it matter if John and Paulette decided to marry? Sophie had known her chances were not 100 per-cent before she'd taken her assignment from the agency.

She'd known there was a risk she'd lose out on befriending and marrying John Colburne.

Either way, it was a pleasure to know him, and she wished him all the luck in the world in his new life.

Inhaling a lungful of fresh air and feeling somewhat brighter, she adjusted the brim of her hat against the descending ball of sunshine and searched the signs above her for the right one.

Mercantile. Jessie's Boots. Laundry and Mending.

She bounced down the stairs of the boardwalk and nearly crashed into the arms of a stranger.

"Sorry," she said with a chipper lilt to her voice. She looked up with a smile, saw his face and froze. "John."

"I saw you from across the street. I'd like to talk to you, please."

"The hat?" Embarrassed, she snatched it off her head, smoothing the strands of blond hair that rose with it. "You're right. It wouldn't be proper to accept such a personal gift. Now that Paulette is here. She wouldn't like it. I mean…I mean I wouldn't like it, if I were her."

Inwardly she winced at her stupidity. How awkward this was, and would she ever be able to look up into these glistening blue eyes and not think of how she'd once imagined herself with John—the two of them in bed together?

"Please keep the hat."

She let it fall to her side, its woolen felt brushing against the fabric of her long linen skirt.

"Paulette must be busy, getting ready for a wedding." Sophie gulped and looked down at the hat, toying with the thin leather strap that knotted beneath it. There. She'd said it.

"I imagine she is. She is getting married." John pressed his warm fingers to Sophie's chin and lifted her gaze to meet his. "But not to me."

Sophie's heart thundered. First at his touch, then at his words. "How do you mean?"

"I walked her to her hotel and discovered there's another man she traveled with. Someone with a lot of money who's apparently made her an offer."

"Oh." Sophie's sympathies went out to John. Yet her heart continued to boom. Why wasn't he dropping his hand? How could she think clearly if he continued to touch her? "You must be devastated. Rejected by her twice. I know how much you enjoyed her letters."

"You are a sincere and honest person, aren't you?" But it wasn't a question—it was more of a statement.

He lowered his hand and she felt a surge of separation.

"I'm not devastated, Sophie."

"You're not?"

He shook his head. Dark blond hair whispered along his blue collar. "On the contrary. I'm grateful she declined my offer the first time around, so that I was able to meet you."

Her pulse soared. Her breathing tripled. "You really believe that?"

"Absolutely. Our first meeting wasn't the best impression I could've made, Sophie, and I hope you'll forgive me for that. Now that we're getting to know each other, I do believe we're compatible."

"Yes," she said slowly, carefully, taking in every beat of his words. "We are."

"Then if you'll have me, I would very much like to marry you."

Chapter Five

The wedding was scheduled for two days later.

For superstitious reasons, Sophie didn't wish to enter John's splendid-looking house—beyond the grounds of the livery stables—until she became his bride, so she stayed at the hotel until the afternoon when she was to meet him at the chapel.

The chapel was only a few steps away, across the street and around the corner, so she walked. John had offered to send a carriage, but she'd insisted it was unnecessary.

He had been busy at the livery stables all morning, practical man that he was. And she'd worked right up until last night, when she'd gone out on a medical call with Victoria to tend to a man with gall bladder problems. How similar she and John were in that regard, their hardworking and logical natures.

Curious heads turned in Sophie's direction as she crossed from the boardwalk to the grassy hill of the chapel in her simple wedding dress.

"Good afternoon," she responded.

"Nice day for a weddin'," said a man in overalls.

"Certainly is."

May had turned to June just yesterday, and the warm gentle wind, a reminder that summer was on its way, ruffled her hem.

She had no friends with her, unfortunately, because Victoria and the two other nurses had had to leave town at the crack of dawn this morning when they'd gotten word of a near drowning in a fishing camp.

The other people Sophie knew in Skagway were patients, strangers really, and she couldn't very well ask any of them to attend her wedding.

The minister's wife was to be her witness.

Sophie urged herself to get over her bout of nerves, gripped her small bouquet of wild roses, picked up the skirts of her satin ivory wedding gown and walked up the stairs of the chapel. She wore no veil. A simple wild orchid adorned her long blond hair, which fell over the shoulders of her lacy bodice. A high collar circled her throat, embroidered with shiny buttons and pearls. It was a secondhand gown, bought yesterday with a precious ten dollars, and very practical.

Was everything about this moment a matter of practicality?

We're compatible, John had told her. That's what he was looking for in a wife. Friendship. Camaraderie. Someone to share his days with. All the things she'd wanted, too, when she'd first agreed to be a mail-order bride.

A niggling doubt rose inside her. Shouldn't there be something more to marriage? Like illogical feelings. Crazy emotions. Daring excitement that had nothing to do with reasoned compatibility. She'd never felt any of those things with Miles, and she'd been desperately hoping for something more with John.

She knew she felt it—a throbbing rush of sentiment and desire whenever she laid her eyes on his handsome face—but apparently he didn't.

Her palms grew damp. She got to the landing of the stairs, dropped her skirt to the ground and stared at the closed wooden door.

John was waiting for her inside.

The thought gave her hope for a wonderful future together, where he'd perhaps grow to want her passionately and wildly. She smiled at the private notion. It was a delicious fantasy. Putting on her most cheerful expression, she tugged open the door with shaky hands and walked in.

It was cold and empty.

John hurried to tie his gray silk cravat while looking into the hallway mirror of his home. His best man, red-haired and dashing Hugh Westwood, called orders to the other young men who were scrambling to get things done.

"Get her luggage from the hotel and carry it over here!"

"Has Mrs. Norton got the meal prepared?"

"His boots, his boots! Toss 'em over!"

With great laughter, the shiny new cowboy boots, tan-colored with silver tips, hit the floor at John's feet. He shoved his arm into the sleeve of his black suit jacket being held up by another friend while Hugh leaned over and held one boot up for John.

"We're late." John grabbed the boot and shoved his foot inside. "I hope she's not there already."

"Brides are always behind schedule." Hugh checked John's hair and gave him a nod of approval. "Don't worry. We'll be there in ten minutes. Well before she is."

"But what if—"

"The minister and his wife will take care of her."

"But she doesn't know anyone—"

"Let's move," Hugh shouted to the roomful of neighbors and friends.

And suddenly John was out the door and bolting toward the chapel, on foot.

"Aren't you riding in the carriage?" Hugh hollered behind him from the vicinity of the stables.

Not without Sophie, thought John, and only after the ceremony. If only to bring them from the chapel to his home. He should have insisted the carriage swing by her hotel and take her to the church. He shouldn't have bowed to her wishes.

He turned onto the boardwalk and picked up his pace. Customers coming out of stores stopped to stare. He heard twittering and murmurs when he broke into a run.

Late for his own wedding.

He leaped off the boardwalk and sped up the grassy slope of the chapel's hill.

He had the gut feeling that twenty minutes could seem like a lifetime if one were standing at the altar alone.

Panting, he reached the front door of the church, whipped the door open and burst inside.

He groaned at the sight.

Sophie was sitting alone in the front pew, facing the altar where Reverend Peters was preparing his Bible and broad Mrs. Peters was murmuring in her husband's ear.

Sophie had her head lowered, silent and lost in her own thoughts, when his footsteps on the wooden planks of the aisle made her head jar.

At the sight of him, Mrs. Peters let out a big sigh of relief.

Sophie didn't turn around, though.

His muscles tensed as he neared her side. A pretty flower was pinned into the golden streams of her hair. Her bouquet of flowers sat nestled in the lap of her ivory gown, and she twirled her fingers nervously at the ribbon.

He bent to one knee in the aisle. "I'm sorry," he whispered.

She looked over, and then smiled gently. Her lips were a little shaky.

"You must've wondered if…I'm sorry," he repeated.

"You're here now. And it's lovely to see you."

"Abbie delivered."

"She had her calf?"

"Yeah."

"Is she all right?"

"Both fine. There was a complication. The cord was tied around the calf's neck and I had to stay to help."

Sophie's face turned radiant. "Of course. Of course you had to stay. I'm glad you did. Are you sure they're all right?"

"Absolutely."

Her resulting smile lit up the chapel and he was suddenly aware, it seemed for the first time since he'd met her, that she was about to become his bride.

They were about to promise their days to one another, about to share their nights.

She stood up beside him. The folds of her gown fell to the floor. She was breathtaking in the creamy color, with the light from the stained glass windows reflecting off the beads at her collar and neckline. It was a modest dress, buttoned to the top of her chin, yet the elegance and the sway of the fabric against her hips was more enticing than if the neckline were scooped low to reveal her cleavage.

John swallowed hard. He was about to have her in every sense of the word, and perhaps they weren't quite ready.

He had no more time to think about it, for his friends bustled through the doors.

Hugh led the pack, then John's neighbors who owned the jewelry stores in town, then the owner of the biggest casino, followed by the man and wife who ran the café, even the boot maker and the local laundress.

Dozens and dozens of neighbors, coworkers and businessmen.

He was proud to have such a group with him, amazed that they'd heard about the wedding and insisted on coming. But when they all sat on one side of the church— the groom's side—he felt a wave of trepidation.

There was no one on Sophie's side.

"This way, please." The minister hailed them, white hair slicked back in a razor-sharp fold. "John and Sophie."

Perhaps Reverend Peters would ask the congregation to spread out.

John held his breath with hope.

The reverend didn't ask anyone to move.

John stretched his neck beneath his cravat, which felt suddenly hot and constrictive.

Perhaps the minister's wife would ask them to even things out.

She didn't.

She withdrew a hankie from her thick sleeve and stepped in beside Sophie. Hugh ran a hand through his auburn curls, adjusted his bow tie and took his place beside John to face the minister.

Perhaps Sophie hadn't noticed the lopsided numbers, thought John. He hadn't meant to make her uncomfortable. He wanted her to feel welcome.

"Dearly beloved," Reverend Peters began.

John discreetly stole a glance down at Sophie. Her eyes skimmed the empty pews, her mouth fell open slightly, her lips trembled, then she turned to the bespectacled preacher.

Had John imagined it, or were her eyes glistening with an emotion he couldn't quite read?

Was she upset at the way the wedding was turning out, or touched by the spiritual moment?

It made no difference, for he was unable to speak up to reassure her, nor to question how she felt.

Reverend Peters was speaking and John wanted to listen to every word.

Forty-five minutes later, after the scriptures were read and the promises made, Reverend Peters beamed at John. "You may now kiss the bride."

Mrs. Peters, her smile stretching from one freckled cheek to the other, dabbed at her tears and blew her nose into her hankie.

A hum of approval rippled through the congregation, then an interested silence fell when John leaned over Sophie and kissed her lightly on the lips.

Her mouth was soft and gentle and pliable beneath his. He hadn't kissed her since she'd first stepped off the ship, when he'd thought she was Paulette.

He'd made the right choice, he told himself as he studied the warm curves of her cheeks. But he wondered what his new wife was thinking, so quiet and withdrawn.

Chapter Six

The wedding ceremony was over and Sophie's thoughts shifted to the next hurdle. How would their night together in the bedroom go?

Sophie couldn't shake the nervousness from her mind an hour later as they sat in John's house at the dinner reception, surrounded by folks, mostly men, she'd never met before.

While they passed along the trays of food to the dozen or so tables squeezed into every part of his home, Sophie sat stiffly beside her new husband. Feeling like the newcomer she was, wishing to fit in with these people, wishing she felt a thread of love from John.

Callie waved to her from across the room, and Sophie smiled back. Callie was seated next to her tall husband, Edward, who worked with John at the stables. The woman placed her cheek against the lapel of her husband's jacket and he touched her chin. Both young, in their early twenties. Edward drew back stiffly from his wife's attention, though, appearing uncomfortable at his wife being so affectionate in public.

Sophie wished John would be affectionate with her.

"Here, Sophie, try the venison." One of John's friends stabbed a couple of pieces onto her plate.

"Thank you."

The din of chatter and laughter was loud enough to reach the livery stables a hundred yards away, she was sure.

The house itself was much more opulent than she had expected when she'd passed it on the street.

Tucked onto the edge of the block, near the far side of town away from the harbor, the two-story plank building had been built only last year. Wood sawn and cut at the brand-new sawmill. Victorian furniture ordered and shipped directly from London. Plush rugs from the Orient. A kitchen filled with fragrant spices from Italy and Europe.

She'd had no idea John was this wealthy.

Of course, she'd had an inkling, seeing that he owned a livery stable—in fact, three—but she'd had no clue about the pride he took in creating a home for himself here in Alaska.

She had been accustomed to the wealth of her father's home, although she'd never felt tied to it, seeing as she'd done nothing to earn any part of it herself. Later, when she lived with Miles—he without an income for five years and dependent on her father—her stature had dropped considerably in their modest two-room home.

So much so that she felt uncomfortable in this wealth.

Taking a deep breath, Sophie vowed she would do her best to earn her place at John's side, contributing to the town in her midwifery practice and seeing to it that she never had idle hands.

The guests were gracious to her, smiled whenever Sophie glanced their way, commented on how pretty her dress was and how tasty the food—prepared by a wonderful neighbor, thin and frail Mrs. Norton, who was still fussing over John's platter of venison and potatoes. However, there didn't seem to be much more the men could think of saying to Sophie as she watched them pour champagne into her crystal flute.

John, however, didn't have that problem with his friends. She admired how everyone wanted to talk to him.

"A toast," said his best man, Hugh, rising to his feet. His red hair fell over his shoulders. "To a man we've all come to admire and respect, since the day you first put a shovel into this soil and bothered your neighbor—me—for an hour of my time. Little did I know you'd come knocking on my door every day for the next month."

The gathering laughed, including John.

"And a toast to your new bride," Hugh continued as the chuckling subsided. "I hope Sophie won't be as troubled by your calls as I was."

Sophie smiled at the good-natured ribbing. Hugh sat down. Another couple of men stood up and spoke.

"Here's to a long and happy life." An old gent in a weathered blue suit toasted them.

He was followed by a younger man in gold spectacles. "To a dozen kids!"

Sophie's cheeks blistered with heat as John cleared his throat. What was his opinion on that?

To her right, two other men were discussing something even more embarrassing.

"Word is Paulette Trundle got married two days ago. Same day she landed."

"You don't say? She was his first choice, I heard tell."

"Shh. Best not to speak of it here," the first man said.

A quiver shot up her throat. Sophie lowered her head and tried not to dwell on the gossip.

She sipped champagne and rolled the sweet bubbly liquid on her tongue. John touched her elbow, the brush of contact against her sleeve and skin causing her stomach to expand and dip like a block of ice bobbing and melting in water.

"Are you enjoying yourself?" He lowered his face next to hers.

His soft voice whispered against her cheek and she blushed at the thought of the night ahead.

"Yes, thank you. It's a lovely wedding and you have very interesting friends."

John chuckled when she said the word *interesting.* Whatever more he had to say was interrupted.

"John, when do you expect your Thoroughbred will be ready to breed?"

Another called, "Can I bring my buggy in Monday for oiling?"

And yet another. "Won't you come look at my mare and tell me what you think of her injured hoof?"

They ate in this noisy manner and John never had another opportunity to speak privately to her as they finished the meal, rose and shook hands with the guests.

There was no music. No dancing, either. No time, she supposed, to prepare for any of it.

She was a good dancer. She missed it. Hadn't really had the opportunity to dance for the past few years, since her late husband had suffered from his fever and illness.

Two hours later the guests began to leave and Sophie's stomach went tight again with the question rolling through her mind.

How would their night in the bedroom go?

Sophie looked scared.

Finally alone with her, John extinguished the lanterns downstairs and carried one up the stairs as he studied her. She glanced at him as they turned at the top of the landing.

He hooked the lantern just inside the bedroom door and whirled around to face her. "I never got a chance to do this outside, since there were so many people about. But I can do it now."

With a cry of delight, he scooped her up and carried her over the threshold of the bedroom. She was light and soft in his arms, squirming to catch her balance. She smelled nice and he liked the feel of her.

When he lowered her to her feet, however, right in front of the wide-berth bed, she stepped away and hastily smoothed her skirts.

"You do want this, don't you?" He frowned in the moonlight cascading from the windows.

"Yes. Of course. It's all very natural. Yes." She spun to

the four-poster bed and grabbed the bottom post, gripping it as if she were hanging on for dear life.

He couldn't see the full color of her face due to the dim lighting, but sure to God, that red stain flushed through her cheeks again.

"Then why do you look like a cornered badger?" He was trying to make her laugh, let her see the amusement in the situation.

Her spine stiffened to a rod. "Whatever do you mean?"

"You look like you're trapped in the wilds, and I'm about to swoop in."

"Well…that comment certainly does nothing to put me in the mood."

"I'm trying to help you relax. We'll get through this together, Sophie." Although he didn't need any help with this night, for he knew exactly what he wanted to do, maybe if she thought he was a bit nervous, too, it might ease her mind.

"Yes, of course." Her voice reached a higher pitch. "Let's get through this business."

"Business?" Now her choice of words was getting to him. "This night isn't a business deal."

"If you're going to jump on every word I say—"

"I'm your husband, not your enemy—"

"Why don't you just order me to get onto the bed—"

"If you weren't so uptight—"

"Uptight?" She stepped away from the bed, fists at her sides, eyes widened in disbelief. She strode into the adjoining bathing room, closed the door and turned the latch with a loud click.

Oh, great. This was just great.

With a loud sigh at the closed door, he waited for her to come back out again. Waited and waited. When he heard the soft thud of her shoes being removed, he realized she had no intention of coming out anytime soon.

With resignation, he removed his jacket and pants, hung them in the armoire and slipped into his side of the bed, stone-cold naked. Not that she'd ever discover the fact.

Not tonight, anyway.

He listened to the sounds coming through the closed door—water sloshing in the basin, her luggage being slid across the Oriental carpet where he'd ordered it delivered, and the thudding of her bare feet.

With a sigh, he punched the center of his pillow and adjusted his awkward frame on the mattress.

When he was younger, he'd had his share of women. On the trails in Texas, flitting from town to town, easy women who'd made themselves available. But no one like Sophie.

Earlier this evening he'd had visions of undressing her himself. Of having the pleasure of slipping that pretty gown off her shoulders, or perhaps unlacing her corset and rolling down her silk stockings.

Fat luck.

All right, he admitted, so she was nervous. That was understandable. They barely knew each other. For her it was a new land, new town and new people. A new husband, to boot. But hell, it wasn't easy for him either.

He waited and waited and waited for her to come out and join him on their wedding night, but his lids couldn't carry the weight any longer. He'd just rest them a moment, for surely he'd awaken when she finally slid in on the spring mattress beside him. Surely then, the two of them…

In the blackness of the night John's eyes bolted open. Who the hell was in his room?

With a start, he turned his head and saw Sophie's feminine shape outlined by quilted covers tucked up to her waist. Sleeping soundly.

No need to panic, he thought with a soft groan. He was married now.

And she'd finally come to bed.

He wondered what time it was and twisted toward the night table, about to look at his pocket watch, but couldn't seem to move his eyes away from the picture she made.

He settled back onto his shoulder and watched her breathing, her breasts moving up and down in the frilly white nightgown she wore.

Sophie was his wife. His to protect. He had an urge to tell her things would work out, that he understood her difficulties here, but that she'd grow accustomed to the town, the folks who were her neighbors and to him.

When she stirred, moonlight skimmed her soft features, accentuating her high cheekbones, straight nose and the lushness of her lips. She had a gorgeous mouth—an unusual one, with a distinct curve to her Cupid's bow at the top and full bottom lip that always looked ready to be kissed.

Her lashes flickered in the soft glow. Still sleeping, she

turned toward him, tucked her covers beneath her chin and settled her warm body mere inches away from his.

His muscles tightened in response. His hard body came to full alert. He inhaled the scent of his wife, the sounds of her soft breathing, the delectable vision she made.

This was too much torture, he thought. He leaned over and ran his fingertips along the warm muscles of her slender neck.

Chapter Seven

Was she dreaming? Sophie felt the warm touch of his fingers and leaned into him. Her pulse began to throb and her body flushed.

He felt so real…she struggled to open her eyes. Had to lift the lids… She strained and strained until they finally opened.

John was staring at her from his pillow.

"Ah," she mumbled, startled at his proximity.

"Hey, don't be scared," he murmured in the moonlight.

"I'm not scared," she said. "I'm…surprised."

Her eyes traveled over his open lips, the flared nostrils and the shimmer of his blue eyes.

But maybe she was scared, just a little. The way her heart was hammering, he might as well be a total stranger lying in bed with her.

He leaned forward and kissed her neck and she lurched backward, suddenly panicked.

He chuckled into the base of her throat, kissing the private spot before working his way down her opened neckline and making every inch of her skin tingle.

"You want this as much as I do," he proclaimed with no shame at all. As if *she* had as little control as he did over his physical needs.

She could control herself.

He brought a hand up from between the sheets unexpectedly, ran it over the fabric along her rib cage, and she jumped with alarm.

She got another chuckle in response.

"It's not a matter of you giving in to me," he said in a low rumble. "It's a matter of wanting it for yourself."

"That's ridiculous. I do *not*…it's not as if I'm a man who's gone without for so…so long…."

His daring hand worked its way up her ribs and the side of her bosom. The heat of his touch and tantalizing strokes as he cupped her heavy breast, while working his mouth down her breastbone and parting her neckline with his lips, moving ever so closer to her nipple, made her objections melt away.

And when his hand suddenly left her side to lift the low hem of her gown and slide its way to her naked thigh, she audibly gasped.

He continued to laugh softly, irking all sensibility from her thoughts.

His fingers on her thigh made her turn to mush, unable to fight him, unable to turn her body away. It felt so good to be caressed by John.

Expertly he slipped his hand up to her belly, and her muscles contracted involuntarily. His soft smile told her he was noticing and enjoying his effect on her.

She had many insecurities coming into this night, and she wondered if he knew them all.

How could he?

How could he know that she worried about being enough for him in bed?

He was very much younger than her late husband, physically more robust and demanding, had more stamina and expectations of her. Of making love.

On many levels she felt as inexperienced as a virgin. Certainly since her late husband's stroke she hadn't had sex a single time.

And now this…this… John's fingers were drawing from her an exhilaration she hadn't known existed…or perhaps had buried deep in her heart, figuring that passion in bed would never come to her again.

As John drove his hand upward and cupped her breast, she gave in to the temptation and turned her body willingly toward him, pleasuring in the contact, the way his fingertip circled her nipple and made her womanly parts throb. Blood rushed to her center, wet and pounding, as he lowered his face to her breast and sucked.

An instant pang of heat and desire flew through her. He positioned himself closer, between her legs, and she readily splayed her thighs, urging him inside.

His shaft bobbed on her stomach, so large and hard she nearly gasped. He worked his fingers downward and parted her wetness, rubbing the sensual button till it drove her wild with want.

When she was near the brink, he moved his fingers away and guided himself into her, firm and tight.

The pleasure…the feeling of being filled from top to bottom with John, the ecstasy of allowing him to thrust in and out as he bore into her with an urgent need of his own.

With his hands on either side of her hips, her nightgown scrunched up above her breasts, he moved with an intensity that pulled the muscles of his face into handsome planes and angles.

She ran her hands up the muscles of his chest, broad and angular, and watched him, mesmerized by his beautiful strong body in the moonlight as he rocked into her, caught in the splendor of her own mounting climax.

She neared the brink. The contractions came, a wonderful spasm of release that thundered through her limbs and throbbed in the womanly part of her that came alive with John.

With his eyes half-hooded, he watched her move beneath him and suddenly he clenched his own muscles, closed his eyes and came inside her with the power and glory Mother Nature intended.

He was incredible to watch, the glow of light from the window cascading upon his tight muscles, the tan lines of his chest ending near his flattened stomach, the sheer power of his force spinning her heart with awe.

When they were finished, he rolled off her and patted her thigh affectionately.

She lay there, shocked at how much she'd taken pleasure from this, shocked at how much he'd been able to make her respond.

"I enjoyed that, Sophie," he whispered up to the ceiling.

"Mmm. It was a lovely surprise." She wanted to tell him all the things she felt, the insecurities she had, the desire to make this union right in every regard.

But he spoke first. "You see…it was a matter of wanting it for yourself."

"There's much more here than the physical act alone."

"Of course. But even so, physical desire is not a bad place to start. And I appreciate you coming back to bed to—"

"I did not come back to seduce you. It was you who—"

"No sense fighting it. What this proves is that your appetite is as big as—"

"What this proves is that you're good in bed and terribly conceited for knowing it."

When he laughed softly again, she rose to go to the bathing room, tossed a pillow at him and watched him duck.

John let her rest the following day, Sunday, thinking she might not take too kindly to his advances so soon again.

Not that he didn't want her. After the exhilarating time they'd shared last night, it was all he could think about as they ate breakfast, served by his housekeeper, Mrs. Dickson.

"Let me get that, ma'am." Mrs. Dickson wiped her wrinkled hands on her apron and reached for the coffeepot Sophie was also reaching for on the stove.

"Thank you." Sophie dropped her hands, nervously tucked in the back of her skirts and sat across from him.

"Nice morning." John stirred his coffee while the house-keeper served them fried bacon and eggs.

"Um-hmm." Sophie reached for her napkin and tucked it onto her lap. Her lacy blouse, frilly from the top down, clung to the swell of her bosom, and he was reminded of how beautiful she'd looked, naked in the moonlight.

He swallowed hard and bit into his bacon.

"Will you be needing me anymore before church, ma'am?"

Sophie's forkful of eggs froze in midair. "Huh? No... no. Please do go about your tasks the way you normally would. I'll be able to look after myself, thank you."

The older woman tapped the back of her coiled white hair and frowned. "Thank you, ma'am." She swooshed out of the room in her heavy skirts.

"She doesn't want you to squeeze her out of a job." John smeared marmalade on his slab of rye bread.

Sophie looked up at him directly. "I see. Is that—is that what she thinks?"

"I pay well and she lives conveniently nearby."

Sophie fingered her cup and saucer. "Then I'll try hard to pretend that nothing's changed around here."

"Plenty's changed." He looked at her with great amusement. "After last night."

"I think you need to go to church." Matching his heated gaze with a steady one of her own, she bit into her toast as if challenging him to reply.

He chuckled under his breath. "Better be careful. That's the dangerous way you looked at me when I was locked between your—"

She uttered a gasp of shock and stopped him from finishing. It only made him smile more. After a pause she dabbed her lips with her napkin and sashayed out of the room as if she knew he was watching her hips sway with every enticing step.

An hour later, as they sat side by side in the front pew of the congregation, John had a quiet opportunity to think more carefully about things. Obviously they were matched well in the bedroom. No problems there, on a physical level. He couldn't ever foresee getting enough of her. Even the scent of her skin as she leaned over to reach for the hymnal made him want her.

But…something deeper still nagged at him. He realized it wasn't easy for her to walk into a strange town and marry someone she'd met only days before, but was it any easier for him?

There was an awkwardness between them, despite the intimacy they'd shared last night.

Part of it had to do with him. The only other time he'd come close to marriage was in Kansas when he was a love-smitten boy, engaged to Sally Ann Beuford next door. Unfortunately she hadn't thought so highly of her promissory vows, because he'd caught her half-naked in the cornfield with one of his best friends.

No amount of pleading on Sally's part had been able to erase the vision from his mind. And as for his best friend, well, the punch to the jaw that John had delivered had said it all.

Quietly and completely John had withdrawn. Within two weeks he'd left to seek his fortune in Texas. Working on the cattle ranches for years had honed his muscles and his resolve that he'd make something of himself one day. When the opportunity to join the gold rush in the Klondike had come, he'd left with all his savings, determined to open his own livery stables.

Hard work and perseverance had gotten him through the painful reminders of his doomed love affair.

Was that what was required here, too? Hard work and perseverance to prove to his new wife that he was worthy of her love and respect?

The minister stopped speaking, the sermon over, and the congregation filed past John and Sophie to the outdoors, where they congratulated them on their new vows.

John ran his hand down her spine, guiding her through the crowd, allowing his hand to linger longer than necessary at the warm curve of her back.

The simple touch was enough to arouse him. When they returned to their home, he followed her into the kitchen.

"I suppose Mrs. Dickson won't mind if I prepare a snack of biscuits and stew?" Sophie walked to the kitchen counter and pulled out a wooden chopping block.

John reached for Sophie's hand on the butcher knife. "She gets Sunday afternoons off."

Sophie let the knife go and patted the counter. "I see."

Standing behind her, John pressed his torso along her back, enjoying the lovely feel of her behind pushed up against his front. He dipped his head and kissed her neck. Heavenly warm skin met his lips. He inhaled the downy softness, bringing his hands up along her hips, at her waist, and upward along her ribs to the front of her blouse, over her breasts.

She moaned softly in approval, cupping his hands with her own as he undid the buttons of her blouse.

Still behind her, he felt the rise of his blood pressure, the pounding through his arteries, the heat that flushed his skin, the rip of muscles that came to life.

When her blouse was undone, he searched for the top of her corset that could barely contain the size of her breasts, rewarded as they spilled into his hands.

With one hand he caressed her nipples, heard the pleasing sounds of her increased breathing, and with the other he pulled up the back of her skirts.

"That's quite a bit of fabric," he murmured into her ear.

He was met with soft laughter. And judging by the way she pushed out her hips, an invitation to go farther.

Running his hand over her pantaloons, he pulled them down and reached bare, splendid thighs.

He could hardly restrain himself as he gently slid his hand between her thighs, groaned at the wetness he found, then pulled back to slide off his own pants.

When he was naked, his erection so hard that he felt he'd explode before he could even please her, he slid inside her.

She leaned over the counter, while he still held her breasts between his hands, loving the feel of her, the way she arched her back and urged him to go deeper.

"Are you all right?"

"Yes," she murmured softly, pressing her hands over

his on her nipples and digging back against his shaft as if she couldn't get enough. "Faster, please."

"Well, I must abide my new wife."

Sophie giggled at his comment, in between her moans, then they got so caught up in the love act that they spoke no more. For the second time in twenty-four hours they climaxed together, and when it was over, he wished they had more to say to each other. She quietly cleaned up in the bathing room of their bedroom, then said she was going to visit the nurses who were due back from their medical trip this afternoon.

The next time John spoke at any length with Sophie was the following morning in the livery stables, as he and his stable hand, Edward, were checking over a stagecoach just delivered by ship and due to go out on the trail next week.

John was tightening the nuts and bolts underneath the carriage, lying on his back, when Sophie's pointed black boots appeared beside his head.

"Can I speak with you for a moment, John?" Her shoes tapped on the pounded dirt floor, and he knew in a flash what she had to say wouldn't be good.

Chapter Eight

Sophie was beside herself with worry as she waited for John to slide out from under the painted red stagecoach. Not even the pleasant sight of the newborn calf, walking outside the huge opened doors of the stables with its mother, could calm her.

Sophie shifted in the stale air. Dry straw bit at her nostrils. She lifted her heavy obstetrical bag and set it on the stall boards.

John's torso appeared, then his face. He jumped to his feet, towering over her, while she tried to forget about the intimacies they'd shared over the past two days to focus on solving the very big problem she had on her hands.

Dressed in blue denim from head to toe, he brushed straw off the sleeves of his massive shoulders and indicated they walk toward the open back doors where no one else was within earshot.

She bobbed her head around his chest, looking for Edward. The man was oiling the wheels of the stagecoach and not paying any heed to her arrival. His long dark hair brushed his shoulders. His youthful face was skewed in concentration.

John followed her gaze. "What is it?"

"A problem with one of your staff."

"Who?"

"Edward."

"What in tarnation has he done?"

"It's not what he's done. It's what he's not done. By coming to you, I'm hoping you can arrange for him to take time off work to be with his wife."

"Callie's in trouble?"

Sophie nodded. "She's…she's got dark circles under her eyes and has no energy. Yet she insists on doing the wash and cleaning the house and baking when she should be resting."

John stared at her intently. The curves of his cheeks hardened. Sunlight streamed in around them, lighting the left side of his profile. "What else, Sophie? What else are you worried about?"

She looked down at her boots, her skirts rustling around the straw. "She's not listening to my concerns about her need to rest. Neither of them are. Callie nods and says the right things, but as soon as she sees something that needs to be done around the house, she goes ahead and does it."

"Shouldn't you be having this discussion with him?"

Sophie rubbed the back of her neck and appealed to his sense of reasoning. "I tried this morning. Right after breakfast. He gave me some noncommittal replies, then promptly came to work. Callie's at home right now scrubbing Mason jars and making beds."

John's blue eyes softened. "Some women are active right till the end. You sure she's just not the normal kind of tired?"

"I'm sure."

His lips tightened with resolve. "Then come with me."

John led her quietly to Edward's side. They came in behind him. The young man held an oilcan in one hand, a rag in the other as he wiped down the stagecoach wheel. He glanced up at John. "I'll repaint her this afternoon. Same shade of red, like you said. I'll go to the mercantile and see if they can come close to matchin' the color."

"Maybe that's not such a good idea. I've got other men who can do the painting. Maybe you should spend the day with Callie."

Edward lowered his oilcan to the ground and got up very slowly. He gazed at Sophie with distrust. "How am I supposed to earn a livin' for my new wife and child if I take time off?"

Sophie took a step closer. "All that comes secondary to her health."

"None of the nurses seem to be worryin' too much about Callie. We dropped by the clinic yesterday and had them check her out."

Sophie drew in a big breath. They'd wanted a second opinion, she gathered, and she tried not to take it personally. But for some reason she thought of her father and his parting words that she'd never be strong enough to deal with what was necessary in medicine. The potential heartache and pain. "I value the opinions of those nurses, but I'm an expert in the field of maternity."

"In what? A year's time? How long have you been at this?"

"I've been studying for over eight." Her late husband's sister had given Sophie notes and textbooks and told her real-life accounts of problematic pregnancies. Sophie had gone out with Belinda, secretly, for the past two years and helped her with actual deliveries. "I have to tell you, Edward, if your baby delivers at seven and a half months, he or she will likely be too small to survive."

John stood beside her and didn't budge. He crossed his arms and looked point-blank at Edward.

With a mumbled exclamation, Edward tossed his rag beside the wheel of the stagecoach and walked out.

"I'm alienating everyone in town," Sophie murmured.

John cupped her shoulder. "When you know in your heart you're doing the right thing, stick to your guns."

It was a kind thing to say. She tried to remember it over the course of the next week as Callie stayed in bed and Edward did the housework. He grumbled a lot when Sophie came over to check on Callie, but Sophie tried to ignore his complaints.

"I'll take care of his paycheck," John told her the following Monday, a week to the day she'd ordered Callie to rest. "Don't worry about that."

"Thank you." But it wasn't easy to bear Edward's disgruntled looks the following morning as Sophie did her check on Callie.

Callie sat up on the mattress in their bedroom in the

back of the house. Her disheveled hair lay in swirls around the shoulders of her nightgown. Edward sat in the rocking chair at the foot of the bed, big boots tapping the wooden floor.

Sophie put her stethoscope away. Heartbeats of both mom and the unborn baby sounded strong and steady. "Those dark circles aren't fading. Are you eating enough?"

"I try, but it doesn't go down easy. Edward has been such a godsend, cooking and fussing over me."

"That's wonderful," said Sophie, trying to remain cheerful, trying to ignore Edward's frustrated glance in her direction. His first child, yet he had no patience to set aside the time that needed setting aside. She understood he was much like the new Thoroughbred John had bought—strong and muscular and built for moving.

For the following days, in her quiet evenings with John, Sophie came to life after dinner. She enjoyed the time they spent together making love, wondering if she should bother him with tales of her working day and wishing he'd open up to her more about the minute details of his daily workings at the stables.

"Hard day at work?"

He nodded as he stirred his coffee one morning.

"Did you get the stagecoach painted?"

"Pretty much."

"How about the new calf? How is she doing?"

"Feeding like an elephant."

He confided more in his men, it seemed to Sophie. Two days later she had a couple of hours off from helping Victoria at the clinic, so she rushed home for lunch.

Eager to invite John to join her, she stepped into the livery stables to locate him. He was sitting in the office behind his desk, talking with Hugh, his best man from the wedding. Hugh had his arm wrapped around a pretty young woman with a sharp blue hat.

"You'll warm up to each other," said Hugh. "It hasn't been that long."

"How can you compare a mail-order bride to a normal one?" asked the woman. "There are shortcuts to marriage, but no shortcuts to love."

"Yeah," said John, opening up a ledger and running a pencil down the columns.

He was talking about her. In the most private of terms. What else had he confided to people she didn't even know? Sophie's heart rippled with hurt. She blinked and swallowed past the lump in her throat as she made her way back to the house alone.

There are shortcuts to marriage, but no shortcuts to love.

What did that mean? John didn't love her. He hadn't actually said the words, but he had agreed with that woman. A woman who didn't even *know* Sophie.

Sophie stared up at the ceiling of their bedroom. The rays of the sun shone past the hanging chandelier, candles unlit, casting sharp shadows on the wall.

"You getting up, Sophie?" John called from the stairs.

"Coming!" She scooted out of bed, feeling guilty for lingering when she had so much work to do, and with John already leaving. The thud of the door thumped up the stairwell, reminding her she was alone with Mrs. Dickson, who was likely heating porridge for Sophie and brewing a fresh cup of coffee.

Sophie didn't have time to languish over breakfast, as she rushed out to check on Callie. A quick exam, likely finding nothing unusual, then possibly a visit to a new patient, a young woman who'd apparently arrived yesterday off the ships, several months along with a new husband and new dreams for a better life.

Sophie sighed as she knocked on Callie's door. Dreams for a better life. How easy that was to mentally conjure, yet so difficult to actually create.

No one answered the door. Sophie knocked again.

Still no answer.

"Edward!"

Things were as quiet as a field of corn.

Sophie whirled around. The livery stables were quiet, too, at least from the outside. No one walking on the boardwalk. Could Callie be outside at the laundry line?

Before she went to look, Sophie tried the handle of the door. It opened. Her obstetrical bag banged against her knees as she peeked her head inside. "Callie?"

A moaning coming from the bedroom made Sophie's breath leap. She ran through the foyer to the bedroom.

Callie lay on the floor, nightgown bloodied at hip level, completely still.

Sophie dropped to her knees. "Callie?"

No response. Lips pale. Eyes closed. Breathing, thank God, but in a strange panting sort of way. Was she pushing?

With a quick examination, Sophie noted the obvious.

No limbs broken. No outward signs of distress. The bedsheets were rumpled, and it appeared that Callie might have slipped as she'd tried to get out of bed.

"Edward," Sophie called, hoping he might be in the house. "Edward!"

No one came running.

Sophie didn't want to move Callie until she figured out exactly what was wrong, in case she caused more distress.

But with a groan of fear, Sophie looked at the bloodstain on the flannel nightgown and knew, in her gut, that the baby was in trouble.

Whipping out her stethoscope, Sophie checked for a fetal heartbeat and timed it to her pocket watch. *Yes,* thought Sophie with a moment of triumph, still there and steady. But a touch on the fast side at 198, above the usual range of a baby's resting heartbeat. Which meant the baby was in distress. But it might be a normal type of distress, as in possibly on its way down the birth canal.

Sophie reached for Callie's wrist. Her heartbeat was fast, too. Thready and weak.

There was a pool of sticky liquid on the floor, indicating Callie's water had broken. It should be clear, though, with no streaks of blood. Blood loss would explain a weak pulse.

What exactly did it all mean? Hemorrhage of the mother, the baby, or the placenta?

With dexterous fingers Sophie palpated Callie's abdomen. Praise heaven, not firm, but soft and pliable. Which meant the problem was not a placenta that had started to detach before the baby was born. A fatal catastrophe for the child—and mother—if it had.

"Callie, honey, can you hear me?" Sophie patted her hand. She lowered her mouth to Callie's ear. "Honey? I think the baby's coming."

A loss of blood was not good, no matter what was happening.

Sophie ran her hands over Callie's head, gently feeling for anything unusual. Ah, there it was. A lump at the back of the occipital bone. She'd fallen and bumped her head. That might explain the unconsciousness.

"Ahh!" Callie moaned, making Sophie jump with surprise.

Sophie placed her hand on Callie's stomach. A tight contraction followed. Callie was moaning because she was in heavy labor. But the moaning indicated she wasn't totally unconscious. Only a mild concussion, perhaps. More blood gushed out, and Sophie grabbed a towel off the nightstand and soaked it up.

She had vital decisions to make. Leave Callie for a few minutes as she ran for help to the livery stables? Or simply run to the door and scream her lungs off?

The truth was, Sophie couldn't leave a woman and baby in mortal jeopardy. She couldn't take her eyes off Callie for a moment. If the umbilical cord were suddenly to appear between Callie's legs, who would be here to ease the pressure off it? To ensure the safest delivery possible of the healthiest baby possible? Even if that baby was premature, even if that baby might be too small to survive.

Seconds mattered. Besides, what could Edward or John or any of the men nearby do, in practical terms, to help?

Nothing that Sophie couldn't do on her own.

She wasn't physically strong enough to lift Callie off the floor to set her on the bed, so this position would have to do. It was safer for Callie anyway, not to disturb her physically or cause more stress.

However, the one thing Sophie was unprepared to do, wanted to avoid at all cost, was to deliver this baby by cesarean section. She'd assisted with two while in Oregon. One woman had survived, one had not. Sophie had the instruments with her. But how would she accomplish that alone?

Please God, don't make Callie need one.

Sophie jumped up to the bed, reached for a pillow and blanket, brought it down to Callie's level. She washed her hands in the basin, dipped a washcloth and applied it to the young woman's tender face.

"Callie, honey, wake up. Please wake up." Sophie gently patted her face.

Where in the world was Edward?

Callie sputtered.

Another groan. Another contraction. And another.

"Callie," Sophie nearly shouted. "Callie, the baby's coming."

More sputtering. Another contraction. And dear Mary in heaven, more fresh blood.

Chapter Nine

John's thoughts flickered to Sophie as he sat in his office and printed out a new schedule for stagecoach services. She was supposed to meet him at nine o'clock to pick up some banking papers, make a deposit at the bank, then go on to buy medical supplies she'd heard were coming in on this morning's ship from Seattle. Also to check out a potential new patient.

What could be keeping her? She was half an hour late and John had to head into the valley in twenty minutes to pick up a couple of horses.

He rose from his desk, put the schedules in the drawer, picked up his Stetson and headed out the stable doors. He nodded to one of the stable hands, a young cowhand from Nebraska. "If my wife comes by, tell her I'll be back by ten."

The cowhand looked up from filling the water troughs. "Sure thing, boss."

John hustled out of the stables into the blast of sunshine. He squinted as he looked to his two-story house. It sat undisturbed beneath a ring of trees.

Right next door, though, he spotted Edward coming out of his barn with a pail full of milk.

"Hold on," John shouted. "Have you seen Sophie?" He rushed toward Edward's front door.

Edward lowered his pail to the porch and shook his head. He smiled with pride. "I was down at the docks buying a brand-new cradle for the baby, along with some other things. They'll arrive this afternoon. Callie's gonna love 'em."

"You left her alone?"

"Just for an hour. She was sleeping."

"Did you see Sophie at the docks?"

Edward shook his head. "Nope."

"Here, let me get the door for you."

John leaped up on the porch and opened the door to allow Edward to pass inside.

"Much obliged."

"See you later." John, standing on the porch, was about to turn away when they heard a cat's meow coming from inside. "You get a new kitten for the baby, too?"

Edward turned pale. "No." With a panicked expression, he stumbled through the door. "Callie?"

"In here," Sophie hollered unexpectedly. "Help!"

Edward should've put down his pail, but the poor man was so distraught he tripped over the rug, the pail went flying and milk sloshed over the floor. "Callie!"

Another soft wail cut through the air, and John realized with a bolt to his heart that it wasn't a kitten's whimpering, but a baby's.

Edward ran. John jumped over the whirlpool of milk to follow.

They rushed into the bedroom.

There on the floor, Callie was lying with a pillow tucked under her head. Sweat plastered her hair to her forehead. Her face was red and she was panting. She'd just delivered a baby. She looked up at Edward, then over at the tiny face and body that Sophie, kneeling beside her, was toweling off. The newborn little girl couldn't have weighed more than four and a half pounds, but she was thrashing her limbs and complaining with a whimper as Sophie rubbed the towel over her wet body.

"We have to keep her dry and warm." Sophie, her temples also moist with perspiration, was totally focused on the newborn. "Congratulations." She smiled briefly at the new parents, then frowned gently with concern. "It's a girl. She looks to be about a month early, like we calculated."

"Will she make it?" Edward asked.

"I'm not sure. Her lungs are working, but she's weak. Appears to be perfectly formed. That's very good news."

Edward crumbled to his knees beside his wife. "Callie. Forgive me. Are you all right?"

She wiped her drenched hair off her forehead. "I think so."

Sophie interjected. "You may have a concussion, Callie, from the fall."

"What happened?" Edward asked his wife.

"Felt a contraction and tried to get up. Must've fallen."

"Sophie was right all along. I should've listened."

"Shh," Callie said to him. "Help her with the baby. Please just help her."

"I wish she'd cry more," Sophie whispered to John as he got down on the floor next to her. She removed a bulb syringe from her bag and suctioned mucous from the baby's mouth. "I wish she'd scream at the top of her lungs."

Edward's voice shook with fear as he looked at the stained blankets. "Why was Callie bleeding so much?"

Sophie shrugged gently at the couple. "We might never know why. She's stopped, though. The placenta's out and the extra bleeding has stopped."

John grappled with all he was observing. Sophie, bless her heart, had been here alone to handle the trauma.

He wouldn't have known what to do. He would have been scared to his boots.

Sophie had shown strength and intelligence to help Callie deliver the baby. But there'd been a lot of bleeding beforehand, judging by the saturated towels, and it seemed to him the moment was still rife with impending doom.

Half an hour passed. Sophie ensured Callie was resting comfortably in bed and took the baby to the warmth of the kitchen. Concern for the newborn had Sophie's pulse throbbing in her ears, and her heart still bursting at full speed, but she barely noticed her own reactions as she tried to remain outwardly calm.

She spoke to Edward as John mopped the spilled milk from the hallway into a wooden bucket, listening to her words from the open door between them.

"The baby's not as vigorous as I'd like to see."

Edward rubbed his jaw. "What does that mean?"

"Here, won't you hold her?"

He waved his hands. Such a tall young man, so young himself he likely couldn't grow a full beard yet. "I'll break her."

"What I meant was the baby's too quiet. She needs to scream and empty out her lungs of all this mucous. Needs to work up a big appetite. If she were hungrier, maybe she would have fed when Callie brought her to the bosom." The baby seemed to have a sucking reflex, but not the strength to pull out any milk.

Edward studied his daughter. "She can't survive without eating."

Exactly. "We need goat's milk."

"I can get some." Edward turned toward the door, but was interrupted by John.

"You stay here with Callie. I can be back with goat's milk in thirty minutes."

"Yes, please," Sophie called to her husband at the door. "And please send word to Victoria that I need her here!"

John was as good as his word. While Callie slept in the other room, checked every fifteen minutes by Sophie to ensure she wasn't hemorrhaging, Edward sat on the rocker watching her. Sophie stoked the stove with fresh wood. The baby lay safely bundled into the crux of an armchair when John returned with a large jar of warm milk.

"The lady two doors down keeps goats." John hooked his Stetson on a peg in the kitchen. "She'll be happy to supply you with all you need."

Sophie took out an eyedropper and fed the baby in short squirts. Nestled in Sophie's arms, she was the most incredible beauty. Faint brown eyelashes, pink face, cheeks as supple and warm as a little chipmunk's.

John sat down on a chair opposite them. "Sophie? How are you doing? That was quite a scare you must've had."

"Not nearly as bad as the one Callie must've had. Or Edward when he came in and saw his wife."

They were interrupted by a knock on the door. The knob turned and Victoria peeked around the pine slab. "Anyone home?"

With relief, Sophie shared the next hour with her dear friend, recounting the steps of delivery and explaining every detail to her colleague. John sat quietly in the corner, listening and watching the baby's face as she slept.

"You did everything you could have," Victoria told Sophie. "It's up to the baby to pick up enough energy to eat."

"That's what I'm worried about."

Victoria's assurances were a comfort that Sophie had done all she could have in the circumstances, but unfortunately only confirmed that they had to wait it out and see if and how the baby pulled through.

Sophie sat in vigil for three days and nights, never leaving the Thornton home. She took turns with Edward checking on Callie, keeping the fire warm, heating the goat's milk during the night and feeding the baby every two hours. Even though Edward preferred to do it only if Sophie held the newborn.

"Come home, Sophie," John whispered the first night.

"We can get some other women to sit with the baby at night. You can't do it around the clock."

"I've got to be here."

"You can't do much if you're exhausted."

"I'm responsible, don't you understand?" Sophie snapped at him more quickly than she'd intended. Perhaps he saw that in the way he looked at her.

"Mother Nature will run its course, darling. It's not something you can be responsible for."

Ouch. Such a harsh blow.

Couldn't he see?

Didn't he see this was what her father had warned her about? That she wouldn't be able to handle this. The toughness of practicing on her own without the guidance of doctors nearby. That she wouldn't be able to support these two new parents, this tiny babe who needed help to survive.

That Sophie would never be enough, just the way she was, no matter how hard she tried.

She wouldn't budge to go home.

After the first two nights John stopped asking and let his wife be.

Sophie let her thoughts run freely, especially when she was awake and alone in the kitchen at night.

Why had she come to Alaska? Whom had she helped? What had she accomplished?

Her feelings of misery multiplied. The babe was losing weight—albeit most full-term babies lost a few ounces in the first few days, too, till their systems adjusted, but in this case, the newborn didn't have enough in reserve.

Sophie was losing the baby as well as any intimate connection with her new husband.

Somewhere into the middle of the fourth night, Sophie fed the baby with the eyedropper, then fell asleep on the armchair. The new cradle had been delivered and the baby was sleeping soundly beside her.

And that's when it all came tumbling down for Sophie. She was pushing John away.

If this tiny babe were lost, if the Lord did take her, would that make Sophie any less of a midwife?

It made her sick to think of it.

But would it prove her father right?

Sophie bolted out of her chair. She ensured the babe was warm and safe, signaled to Edward in the bedroom that she was leaving for a few minutes, then grabbed her shawl and raced out to find her husband in the purple twilight in the land of the midnight sun.

Chapter Ten

John couldn't sleep. He checked on the animals in the livery stables, then stepped outside to the corral and leaned against the railing, thinking of how far he'd come with Sophie, only to see it slipping away night by night. How much longer could she do this, physically? Was this how she was going to handle every emergency that came her way?

When he heard racing footsteps crackling on the pathway to his right, he whirled around in alarm.

She was running toward him, loose blond hair flying, skirts lifted by the wind. The bluish tinge of the sun, still hanging over the ocean despite it being the middle of the night, outlined her figure.

"Don't tell me things turned bad."

"No," she panted, reaching his side. "The baby's fine. Callie's sleeping. Edward's keeping an eye on them both."

John recovered his equilibrium and glanced down into her face. He lifted his hand and stroked the softness of her jawline. "I miss you."

Sophie turned her lips to his hand and kissed it. He caught his breath at the unexpected gesture.

"We've come a long way, haven't we, Sophie?"

She nodded, eyes riveted to his, mouth parting with a tremor of sentiment.

"When you first stepped off that ship, I have to tell you I was disappointed."

She took a step back, shoulders taut in the shadows, as though she was unsure of his meaning.

He hastened to explain. "Disappointed when you told me you weren't Paulette."

Her shoulders fell in relief.

"Of course I tried to hide it. Then when you told me you were her replacement, I was angry at being put in that position. Angry that it wasn't going to be as simple as I thought, selecting a wife."

"I thought you were upset with *me,* personally."

"I was upset with myself. Thinking I could pick and choose from different women as I pleased, and being ashamed at what I was putting you through. Took me a while to figure that out."

He leaned across the top of the railing. The sleeves of his white shirt took on the bluish light of the sun. "You know what I'd like most of all? You've been shortchanged in marrying me so quickly. I'd like to have a true court-ship with you. Take you out for dinner. Dancing. Buy you things."

Sophie, as gentle as the wind that ruffled through his hair, hiked herself up on the rung beside him. Her long skirts and petticoat shuffled around her high-heeled brown boots. "That would be nice."

She looked over to the mountains, the icy caps and the treetops thrashing in the wind. Night birds called in the distance. "Your time with me hasn't been easy."

He leaned over and clasped her warm hand in his, ignited by the contact, as if his heart was skipping over the ocean. "I imagine we'll have times that are easier than others. I want to help you in times like these, Sophie. What can I do?"

"I thought you were bothered by the days and nights I've been working."

He drew closer. "You've been amazing in there, Sophie, the way you've handled Callie and the baby."

"They're afraid to name her." Sophie's voice caught on the words. "In case they lose her. I've been trying to convince them otherwise, but Edward says he's not going to pick out a name until Callie's fully recovered."

John took her face in his hands. "Whatever it is that your father told you, he was wrong, Sophie. You were meant to be a midwife."

Her dark lashes fluttered with the compliment. The tender lines of her cheeks and lips moved upward in surprised fascination at him.

"Is it so hard to understand how I feel about you?" he asked.

She let out a sob, half laughter, half wrought with other deeper emotions. It had been a long four days for Sophie without proper sleep and rest, and perhaps it was catching up to her.

His hands moved downward and cupped her supple shoulders. "Do you believe in love at first sight?"

"Love?"

"Yes. Do you believe it?"

Her eyes glistened. She stood speechless.

"I didn't till I met you," he murmured. "Sophie." He took her in his arms and kissed her.

Standing in the glimmering light, they wove their bodies together, thigh to thigh and chest to chest. Her breasts pressed against him, and he was lost to the world. His arms traveled downward along her spine. He loved the feel of her backside in his palms.

She responded by sliding her arms up his rib cage, farther to his shoulders, and fingering the tendrils of hair at the back of his neck. He shuddered at her touch, marveling at her ability to instantly arouse him.

"Darling, you better get back to the Thorntons. But know that I'd rather scoop you up and carry you to our bedroom."

Breaking her lips from his, she laughed into the side of his cheek, kissing his jaw and throat and whispering the words he'd thought might never come.

"I love you, too, John."

Sophie pushed the door and came out of the mercantile with John, giggling as she slid her hand into the crux of his elbow. More than three months had passed since she'd first stepped onto the banks of Alaska and met her husband. Bubbling with joy, she carried the parcel he'd just bought her, wrapped in brown paper and tied with a big red ribbon.

The August sun streamed down over the roof of the boardwalk and spilled out onto the street. Pedestrians and carts pulled by horses went every which way in the noon sunshine.

"Here," said John, "allow me."

He took the package from her—he was a mountain of muscle and brawn in a black shirt, denim pants and silver-tipped cowboy boots. He thumbed the brim of his Stetson while she admired the handsome cut of his jaw.

The sleeves of her lacy white blouse danced at her wrists. She kicked at the hem of her long blue skirt with each step.

"I don't know why I get the new dress," she remarked, "when it's a christening party for Rosemary."

"That little girl's got enough dresses to last a year. I've never seen a mother sew so fast as Callie. Besides, you're the godmother. You've got to look good for all the dancing we're going to do."

Sophie giggled again. Callie and Edward had finally named their new little girl. She weighed over ten pounds now that her mother was nursing her, and had been since Callie had fully recovered from her concussion.

"Maybe this time next year," said John with a wink, "we'll have one of our own."

Sophie smiled with gentle approval. They'd been trying hard—nearly every night.

"Maybe you should be coming home for lunch every

day." She raised her eyebrow at him. She wasn't against trying harder.

His lips rose with amused approval, and there went her pulse, rippling like a tide.

They strode down the stairs of the boardwalk and were still caught up in each other when another couple approached.

"Sorry." Sophie took a step sideways to avoid the woman, then looked up to her face and stopped.

"Paulette."

"Hello, Sophie." Paulette, with shiny brown ringlets pinned on top of her head, made up with pale cosmetics and wearing a pretty satin green dress, looked from Sophie to John. "John."

"Nice to see you," John told her.

Her husband, a fellow twenty years her senior and sporting a gold-tipped cane, was dressed in a white suit. An unusual color for the wilds of Alaska. He nodded in greeting. His dark hair had a streak of gray at each temple.

"Please, meet my husband, Mick Kodiak."

"Afternoon, Mick." John extended his hand and spoke without the slightest hesitation. "Congratulations on your marriage."

"Thank you." The man tipped his bowler hat.

"Congratulations to you, too, Sophie." Paulette's eyes shimmered with sincerity. "On the wonderful work you've been doing in town."

Sophie, trapped for words, couldn't think fast enough to speak. She had thought of Paulette on and off for the past three months, wondering how different their lives might have been if they'd taken a different turn, and had hoped the two of them would someday meet when they were both ready.

"I'm proud of my wife." John tapped Sophie's hand, still tucked into his elbow, silently reminding her he was near.

"Very kind of you to say," Sophie told her.

"The whole town speaks highly of you," Paulette continued, sliding her own hand around her husband's arm. The gent, in turn, smiled broadly at his wife, and in that one moment of clarity, Sophie realized he was smitten by Paulette. She'd found love and friendship with her new husband.

"I'm expecting." Paulette beamed, her eyes shiny with moisture. "I was hoping perhaps…I could…we could… at the clinic or wherever you think…"

Sophie understood. She stepped forward and touched Paulette's arm. "I'd love that. Please do come by. I'll be at the clinic all day Monday. And Tuesday. Or I could drop by your house. I see it on the hill every time I walk to the bank."

Sophie was rambling, perhaps a bit too fast due to nervousness, but Paulette smiled in such a wonderfully uplifting way, Sophie didn't feel at all silly.

"Monday, then."

Paulette stepped out of their path, the group nodded their goodbyes and John moved on with Sophie at his side once more. Their boots clacked on the weathered planks of the boardwalk, the sun sliced through the air and near the far end of the street, gulls circled high over the blue waters of the ocean. Sophie's spirit soared with the gulls.

"It's going to be a great day," John whispered in her ear.

"Ready for lunch?" She pretended she had nothing more than food on her mind, but laughed softly as John let out an exclamation of delight and increased his pace toward home.

* * * * *

Mills & Boon® Online

Discover more romance at
www.millsandboon.co.uk

- **FREE** online reads

- **Books** up to one
  month before shops

- **Browse our books**
  before you buy

...and much more!

For exclusive competitions and instant updates:

 Like us on **facebook.com/romancehq**

 Follow us on **twitter.com/millsandboonuk**

 Join us on **community.millsandboon.co.uk**

Visit us Online | Sign up for our FREE eNewsletter at
www.millsandboon.co.uk

WEB/M&B/RTL4/LP

BoPP.